"You saved me."

Sara pressed her mouth to his.

Perhaps in some part of her mind, she had intended it to be a reassuring kiss. Or maybe a simple thank-you.

But as soon as Jack's lips touched hers, the moment turned frantic.

As he held her in his arms, the realization slammed into her that she might have died.

She started to tremble. He was trembling, too, as he ran his hands over her back, her shoulders, gathering her closer, so that she melted against him.

In this reality they had known each other only a few days. But for Sara it was so much longer.

Maybe in some way he knew that, too.

HER BABY'S FATHER

BY
REBECCA YORK

First published in Great Britain 2013
by Mills & Boon, an imprint of Harlequin (UK) Limited,
Eton House, 18-24 Paradise Road, Richmond, Surrey TW9 1SR

© Ruth Glick 2012

ISBN: 978 0 263 90632 5
ebook ISBN: 978 1 472 01195 4

46-0613

Harlequin (UK) policy is to use papers that are natural, renewable and recyclable products and made from wood grown in sustainable forests. The logging and manufacturing processes conform to the legal environmental regulations of the country of origin.

Printed and bound in Spain
by Blackprint CPI, Barcelona

To Norman,
who is always there for me.

Chapter One

A sharp, stabbing pain grabbed Sara Carter's middle, and she gripped the steering wheel tightly, struggling to maintain control of her car.

The contractions were getting more intense and closer together. She'd had a nagging backache since early morning, but hadn't even realized she was in labor until a gush of water between her legs sent her running to the bathroom.

Even now liquid continued to trickle out of her.

Amniotic fluid, she realized.

The hospital had told her to come in right away, and she thought she had time to get there. It wasn't even snowing when she left the house. Now it looked like she was inside a giant, freshly shaken snow globe.

"Dear God," she prayed. "Let me get to the hospital in time. Because nobody's going to find me out here if I get stuck."

Doubtless the hospital staff assumed she'd be with her husband. But she didn't have one. She probably never would. Unless she met a guy who could live up to her memories of Jack Morgan, the father of her child.

At least there were only a few cars on the road. Other motorists had wisely turned back or found shelter. But her only choice was to plow ahead.

She certainly wouldn't find help at home. The little rented

house in the rural end of Howard County, Maryland, was the only thing she could afford at the moment because her savings were dwindling. And she was going to be out of commission for at least a few weeks after she delivered. Hopefully, sooner rather than later, she could get back to work staging houses—making them look their best for potential buyers—on a limited basis. But she was bound to lose a lot of her customers to competitors by turning down jobs.

Life as a new mother would be tough.

Jack's wealthy family could have helped ease her financial burden, but they'd turned their collective backs on her after his death.

She snorted as she remembered the conversation with Jack's father when she'd given him the news. If she wanted child support, she'd have to prove paternity with DNA testing. And sue them.

She shuddered. If she did prove the baby was Jack's, they might try to take him away.

"Never," she whispered, to the child she carried.

A boy. Named Daniel. He was all she had left of the man she loved, and she would raise him in a way that would have made his father proud.

She didn't want to think about how hard that was going to be. Instead she let memories of Jack Morgan comfort her. He was the wounded war hero who'd come back from the Naval Medical Center to try to pick up his life.

She'd met him at an expensive house her friend Pam Reynolds was showing. Tara in Howard County, she'd jokingly called it.

His brother had dragged him along to look at the property, and Jack had obviously been annoyed to be there. Maybe she'd seen him as a challenge at first. But the relationship had quickly become important to both of them.

"Oh, Jack," she whispered as she leaned forward, trying

to see through the blinding whiteness ahead of her. "It should have worked out differently. If only you were still here."

But he wasn't. And there was no use wishing that her life hadn't gone careening off the rails in such spectacular fashion. All she could do was make the best of her future.

A future without the man she loved.

Sometimes she wondered how warm, caring Jack Morgan could have come from such a cold, money-obsessed family. But that wasn't her immediate problem.

Another contraction made her gasp. Pulling to the shoulder, she waited for the clutching pain to diminish. As soon as the contraction subsided enough for her to concentrate, she nosed back onto the road.

Only fifteen minutes to Howard County General Hospital now. Well, maybe under better conditions. Should she stop and call for help? No, she might end up having the baby in the car if she risked waiting here.

"You're going to make it," she told herself. Or that was what she thought. Until she came around a curve on Route 108 and saw the pickup truck stalled at the bottom of a hill.

As her car began the long slide toward the disabled vehicle, she frantically turned the wheel, trying to avoid a collision. But the wheels failed to catch on the slick surface, and she felt the car gaining momentum—hurtling her toward disaster.

The bone-rattling impact of the car slamming into the truck stunned her.

Air bag? Where was the air bag?

The moment her forehead smashed against the windshield and glass shattered, she knew she and the baby were going to die.

Sara couldn't feel her body, but her mind floated somewhere in darkness. Ahead of her, she could see a beautiful golden light. The warmth drew her, but something held her from going there.

A presence hovered around her. No, two of them. They

had come to guide her to the light. Where she'd be warm and safe. And all her problems would be gone.

But something was wrong.

She could hear them talking. Arguing.

"It's not her time."

"Of course it is. Look at her."

"I mean, her life wasn't supposed to work out this way."

"She shouldn't have been driving in a snowstorm."

"She was on her own. It wouldn't have happened if he'd been with her."

"He's long gone."

"Maybe it doesn't have to be that way."

The one who objected made a dismissive sound. "What are you talking about? We're not authorized to change history."

"We can rectify mistakes."

"Not on our own."

"She's got strength and determination. She doesn't deserve to end this way."

"Not everybody gets what they deserve."

"Give her an opportunity to change fate."

There was a long pause. "We could be making a terrible mistake. We could be punished."

"It won't be noticed."

"You want to take that risk?"

"Look at it this way. Either everything turns out the same again, or she has a chance to change her destiny."

Chapter Two

In the moment between sleep and waking, Sara remembered hearing voices. Talking about her.

What was it they'd been saying?

She scrabbled to get a sense of the conversation. They'd come to take her to a place that was warm and safe. Where all her troubles would vanish like mist evaporating in the heat of the sun.

Then they'd changed their minds. Or one of them had. When the other had objected, the first one had persuaded him to go along.

Him? Were they men? They had sounded both gentle and commanding. If that was possible.

Before she could decide, she jerked awake. She was in her car. On her way to the hospital?

Could that be right?

Hazy memories swam through her mind, and she struggled to make them come clear.

The last thing she recalled was the car skidding down a long hill on a snow-slick road and crashing into a truck, but that couldn't be true.

She looked around at tall trees with new green leaves, filtering bright sunlight. Below them were blooming azaleas and carefully planted beds of bright annuals—impatiens and begonias.

Not winter. Spring.

But the snowstorm had seemed so real. Obviously she'd dreamed it.

Disoriented, she struggled to remember why she was here and what she was doing.

Recollections surfaced as she focused on a huge white house with a circular brick drive and Doric columns holding up the two-story front porch. Tara in Howard County, Maryland, she'd called it. Conveniently situated between Washington, D.C., and Baltimore.

She knew the inside layout of the mansion. Six bedrooms. Six bathrooms. A great room and a kitchen as big as the modest home where she'd grown up. This house was too big for any one family, as far as she was concerned. It was the kind of ostentatious property people bought when they wanted you to know how well they were doing.

It was also way out of her price range, but she wasn't planning to buy it. She'd been hired to stage the place for an important client, a rush job that had kept her here from early in the morning until early afternoon. Real-estate agent Pam Reynolds was paying extra because she had a live one on the hook.

Sara had worked feverishly to get the property ready, using two of the college students who helped her out part-time when she needed to move big pieces of furniture.

After they'd left, she'd climbed into her car to catch a few minutes of sleep before Pam arrived.

She blinked, still feeling like her brain wasn't quite engaging with reality. The images and emotions from the vivid dream simply wouldn't go away. It wasn't just that she'd been driving through a snowstorm. She'd been on the way to the hospital—because she was having a baby.

A baby! Oh, please. She wasn't even dating anyone. And she wasn't the type for one-night stands.

Somehow her unconscious mind must have conjured up that scenario from an old movie or TV show.

But now it was time to get back to the real world.

She pulled down the sun visor and looked at her face in the mirror, fluffing her shoulder-length blond hair a little. Then she stroked on a little lip gloss. She had just slipped the tube back into her purse when a silver Mercedes pulled up in the circular driveway, and Pam got out.

She was tall and fit, with a halo of ash-blond hair, and was wearing a tailored pantsuit today.

Smiling, she came over to Sara's car. "Are we all set?"

"I think so," Sara answered, hoping it was true.

"Thanks for the rush job. I appreciate it."

Sara climbed out and shut the door, then, as she stood beside the car, she looked down at her body, expecting to see the swollen belly and big breasts that had been the hallmarks of her advanced pregnancy. Instead she was lithe and slim in jeans, a yellow T-shirt and tennis shoes. Her work clothes.

She should get out of here before Pam's high-priced client arrived.

Her breath caught. No. She needed to stay because this was the day...

The thought trailed off in confusion again as she tried to remember what was so important.

"Let's take a look," Pam was saying. "I always love to see your work. Did you use that antique armoire that I admired so much?"

"I think so."

Pam peered at her. "You look a little...pale. Are you feeling okay?"

"A little sleep deprived, I guess."

"Sorry I got you up so early."

"It's okay."

Pam wiped her palm on a pants leg in an uncharacteristic show of nerves. "I'm glad you're here. Since that murder last week, I've felt kind of spooked, staying in a vacant house by myself."

Murder? Sara scrambled to dredge up what Pam was referring to, then remembered that a woman real-estate agent had been raped and murdered in an empty house where she'd been waiting to meet a client. The man had showed up and taken advantage of the isolated location. So far the cops had no leads, and it seemed all of the women in the local real-estate business were on edge.

Sara had thought about that when she'd been working at this three-acre property early in the morning. But Peter and Brad had been here most of the time. They'd only left a little while ago—and taken her truck back to the warehouse space where she stored the furniture and knickknacks she used in her work.

The real-estate agent hurried up the front steps and stepped into the house.

Sara followed more slowly, marveling at how much easier it was to walk without all the extra weight of advanced pregnancy. She'd forgotten how it felt not to be dragging around the equivalent of a couple of gallon jugs of water.

No, wait. Had she really been pregnant? She was still having trouble sorting reality from…what?

Not a dream. More like a different reality.

When Pam glanced back, Sara hurried to catch up. Inside, her gaze swept over the work that she'd completed this morning, starting with the antique side table that she'd centered along one wall of the large foyer. On the polished surface sat a whimsical elephant lamp and one of the orchids that she kept in the greenhouse in the back of a friend's garage. They were easy to grow, bloomed for months and always added a touch of elegance.

On the wall was an ornate mirror that she'd patched up with spackling compound and refinished herself.

Finding and fixing up pieces that would work as part of the rooms she furnished was both her skill and her pleasure.

"The elephant's a nice touch," Pam remarked. "Garage sale or auction?"

"Garage sale. The base was coming off, but I superglued it back together. Love that stuff."

Pam headed for the kitchen where Sara had used Dansk Kobenstyle casseroles, tall glass jars of preserved herbs and red-and-white-checkered dish towel accents. The round table was set with more garage-sale plates and goblets. The centerpiece was a bowl of mixed citrus fruit.

Pam eyed the display. "Aren't those old casseroles expensive? Where did you find them?"

She was glad Pam had asked. The questions about her work were tying her more firmly to the present. And she was relieved to discover that the answer came more easily than she might have expected. "On eBay. I get ones that have hard use and fix them up."

Pam made a dismissive sound. "How can you fix up a metal casserole?"

"With spray paint."

"Clever."

"Of course, you can't put them in the oven," she added, anxious to make a full disclosure.

"Nobody's going to cook in them. And they're a lot more interesting than the plastic food you see in so many model houses."

As Sara showed Pam the property, the scene became increasingly real to her.

She remembered carefully draping the colorful Peruvian shawl on the tan sofa and arranging candles in the fireplace.

She and the boys had done only one bedroom, but it was a masterpiece of sophistication, using earth tones with touches of bright color.

"If this doesn't hook Ted Morgan, nothing will," Pam murmured.

Ted Morgan? Not the right Morgan. "I'm sorry. I forgot who he is," she stammered.

Pam took in her perplexed look. "Come on. Morgan Enterprises. They're into everything from construction projects to oil exploration."

"Uh-huh," she murmured.

Pam put a hand on Sara's arm. "Stay here with me after he arrives, okay?"

Sara's heart started to pound. She remembered this conversation from the first time.

"You're nervous?" she managed to ask.

"A little. Ted's a big deal around here. He's getting married, and he wants a family home."

"This is the kind of house where the kids and the parents would never have to see each other."

Pam laughed. "If that's what he wants, fine with me. He's a very rich man who can get me a six percent commission on two million dollars."

"Well, that does put him into perspective."

Sara knew Pam was doing well as a real-estate agent and living a high-flying lifestyle she wanted to maintain. Sara, on the other hand, wasn't into "lifestyle." Instead she was willing to live modestly to build her business. Money had never been that important to her. Well, it had become more important when she'd discovered she'd need to support a baby on her own. And the Morgans were doing their best to make her want to move away. But that was getting way ahead of herself.

There was no baby. Not yet.

She shook her head, grappling with the continuing confusion of what was then and what was now. But she suddenly knew what day this was. The day she had met Jack Morgan. The father of her child.

Because she couldn't simply stand there, she turned and

headed back to the kitchen to stow her purse in one of the lower cabinets. Straightening, she gripped the kitchen counter, the hard surface helping to anchor her.

Outside, the sound of a car pulling up made her heart begin to pound inside her chest with a mixture of excitement and dread.

She understood the excitement and struggled to banish the dread.

Pam rushed to the window and peered out. "He's here."

She kept staring, and Sara waited to hear what she was going to say.

What if this was the wrong day? What if Sara was totally crazy?

Pam's next words settled the question. "I guess Ted doesn't trust his own judgment. Or he wants outside approval. He's got someone with him. I think it's his older brother, Jack Morgan."

Jack Morgan!

Oh, Lord. The reality of hearing Pam speak his name was like a kick to the solar plexus. This really was the day everything turned golden—and at the same time started to unravel.

Thank goodness the other woman was already out the door and starting down the steps, because Sara knew her face must reflect the jumble of emotions surging through her.

Anticipation. Shock. Relief. Fear. Sadness.

All of those.

"Jack," she whispered. "Oh, Lord, Jack."

She felt numb. Jack was dead. He'd been murdered ten months ago. Or ten months in the future if you granted the outrageous idea that Sara had been sent back to her own past by forces she would never understand.

But one thing she knew for sure. Jack's death was in the future of this current reality because he was alive now. Through the open door she could see Pam hurrying down the steps to meet him and his brother.

"I'm so glad you could make it," she said to the other man—Ted Morgan. The one who cared about having a grand house he could show off to visitors.

Which was so different from Jack's attitude about his home. She knew he didn't give a fig about appearances. He'd never been into flaunting his wealth. And his stint in the army had helped solidify his values.

He trailed behind his brother, looking like this was the last place on earth he wanted to be. Feeling light-headed, she steadied herself with a hand against the side table in the hall, trying to arrange her features and her understanding of what was happening.

A few minutes ago she'd been driving alone in a snowstorm, on her way to the hospital to deliver Jack's baby. The baby who would never know his father. Now she was going meet him for the first time.

That couldn't be a coincidence. It must mean something important.

Or was this all a cruel joke? A reminder of how much she'd lost? Maybe there was another explanation for what she thought she was experiencing now. Just the opposite of what she'd been thinking. She'd been in an auto accident. Was she lying in the hospital in a coma, hovering between life and death, dreaming all this?

She pressed her hand against the surface of the table. It didn't feel like a dream. It felt as real as the first time she'd lived through this day, only every moment was overlaid with what she knew about the future.

She wanted to scream a warning to Jack. And to pledge to whoever had put her here that she wouldn't waste this opportunity.

Dimly she remembered the conversation that had swirled around her after the car crash. She hadn't seen who was talking, but she'd heard two voices arguing about her fate. And now here she was being given a second chance to make everything come out differently.

But how? Last time she and Jack had been relentlessly swept along by events they couldn't control.

She straightened her spine. This time, since she knew what was going to happen, she could change everything. Well, she knew the end result. But that wasn't enough. Could she figure out who wanted Jack dead and why? Then stop the killer from murdering him?

She clenched her fist, digging her nails into the tender flesh of her palm.

If she wanted it badly enough, maybe she could change history. Well, nothing so grand as the history of the world. Just Jack's history—and her own.

Her pulse was pounding as she watched the two men come up the walk with Pam. The real-estate agent was engaged in an animated conversation with Ted. Jack followed a little behind, walking with the slightly awkward gait of a man who'd almost lost his leg, then spent months getting the muscles and ligaments to work properly.

The injury was the result of a roadside bomb in Afghanistan. It wasn't the only consequence of the explosion. He'd been thrown forward in the vehicle, dislocating his shoulder. Shrapnel had peppered his chest and midsection, and a few shards had dug into the skin of his face.

He'd spent weeks in the Naval Medical Center, which had taken over army cases from Walter Reed, then weeks in rehab. But he'd been lucky. And he'd worked like a fiend to get back in shape and prove to himself that he wasn't impaired for life.

He'd been going to reenlist. Instead his family had persuaded him that he'd done enough to serve his country. He'd come home, not sure who he was.

His war wounds had done a number on his self-image. Which had made him quiet and withdrawn. Yet the two of them had clicked almost immediately.

As Jack walked toward her, she struggled not to turn her total focus on him. He wouldn't like that. Not when they were just about to meet. He'd think she was staring at him because of his limp—and the scars on his face.

She struggled to assume a casual aspect, struggled not to look like a woman taking the first view of the man she loved, after they'd been separated for months. After she'd believed he was dead.

Still, her chest tightened as she waited for her first contact with Jack in an eternity.

No, her first meeting with him at all, she reminded herself. At least as far as he was concerned.

For a wild moment she thought about taking him aside and trying to explain everything to him. But he'd only think she was crazy. Anybody would think she was crazy if she started talking about events that hadn't happened yet. Which was one of the problems of this whole situation.

Right now, all she could do was experience the joy of seeing him alive and well.

Still, there was a dreamlike quality to watching him come toward her. Eagerly, she drank in his appearance, taking in everything in one sweep. His height of six feet. His dark eyes and hair. His strong jaw. The scars on one cheek that showed through the dark stubble. His lips that looked so hard but could be so incredibly soft against hers.

He was dressed in a dark knit shirt, jeans and running shoes because his doctor had advised him to stick with footwear that gave him good traction. He took that advice, partly because it suited his casual manner and partly because he wanted to give himself every physical advantage.

As he came toward her, she stifled the impulse to pat her hair into place.

"Ted Morgan. Jack Morgan. Sara Carter," Pam said.

"Nice to meet you," they answered.

"Are you working with Pam?" Ted asked.

"I have my own business, staging properties for sale."

"Staging?"

"Getting them ready to show," she answered without explaining exactly what that meant.

She remembered the first time this scene had taken place. She'd wanted to get home and go to sleep, but she'd stayed because Pam had asked. As the tour had proceeded, she'd been glad because she wanted to get to know Ted's brother better.

Pam had mentioned the Morgan fortune, but Sara really hadn't known much about the family. Now she did. Unfortunately, that made her anxious about the impression she was giving. Jack's mom and dad were very particular about who their sons hung out with. Could she present herself differently? Probably not.

Don't get started down that road, she warned herself. *Not now. He's not going to be interested in you if you come across as a phony.*

Which might be a moot point, she realized. What if he walked away from her without connecting the way they had before?

Lord, that was something else to worry about. One of too many things that were competing to make goose bumps pepper her arms.

"Why don't we look at the house?" Pam said. "Isn't it marvelous? Notice the spacious foyer. It makes a good first impression for your guests." She opened a door to the left. "And the closet right here has ample room for coats."

Ted nodded.

Sara and Jack trailed into the kitchen as Pam continued to point out the features of the house.

"Don't you just love the top-of-the-line stainless-steel appliances? The refrigerator's huge and the gas stove has six burners," Pam was saying. "The Mexican tile on the floor makes a statement."

Sara looked at Jack, and they exchanged what might have been conspiratorial glances.

She remembered that he hated tile in a kitchen because it was slippery, and he needed all the traction he could get.

Pam ushered Ted into the living room. "There's lots of space for entertaining," she said. "Notice the easy flow into the family room. And the large windows let in plenty of natural light."

Ted took a quick look at the rooms before proceeding to another that could be a first-floor office. Turning, he said, "I'd like to see the upstairs."

"Of course."

She led the way up, but Sara and Jack stayed on the first floor, watching the other two disappear around a corner.

"Are you responsible for all the homey touches?" he asked.

"Uh-huh."

"They're charming."

"Thank you."

"Do you own a furniture store or something?"

"No. Just a warehouse where I keep furnishings and knick-knacks. If the house is already furnished, I advise the home owner about what to keep and what to put in storage. And which things to replace. It takes away from the salability of a house if the sofa arms have been scratched by a cat." She struggled to act casual when she ached to reach out and pull Jack into her arms.

She longed to feel his body against hers. Feel his strength and the wonderful way he had of wrapping her close like she was the most precious thing in the world. At the same time, she ached to keep him safe, if that was in her power.

The emotions swirling inside her made it difficult to focus on his words.

But she realized he was saying, "You've obviously got an eye for design."

"Making houses look their best is as much fun for me as it is a job."

He was giving her a critical inspection, and she stood with her hands at her sides.

"Are you all right?"

"Why do you ask?"

"You have a strange look on your face."

She laughed, struggling to make light of a moment that was so important to her that she could barely breathe. "I guess it's from working eight hours straight getting this place ready."

"All by yourself? Wasn't a real-estate agent killed recently in an empty house?"

"Yes. I wasn't alone. Several big, strapping college students help me move furniture. Two of them were here with me today."

"Good protection."

"And since I'm on a budget, using them cuts down on costs. The recession set me back for a while. I had to take some temp work to afford the rent."

"That must have been frustrating."

"Yes. But the real-estate market is picking up again. When I get more clients, maybe I can afford to hire some permanent help."

"But right now you're running yourself ragged," he said.

"Do I look that wrung out?"

His expression turned rueful. "Sorry. That came out wrong. It's not what I meant."

JACK DRAGGED IN A BREATH and let it out, thinking he was out of practice when it came to women. He'd told himself he didn't care what they thought about it. At the moment, he cared—a lot.

"I'm making a mess of this."

"No."

He shifted his weight from one foot to the other. "Actually, I'm trying to get you to do me a favor."

"Like what?"

"My brother dragged me here because he wanted me to see this expensive house that's too big for one family, but he's probably going to buy it anyway. You can see he doesn't need my approval, but I came in his car, so I can't leave on my own."

"Inconvenient."

Going for broke, he said, "If you get me out of here, I'll buy you dinner."

"That's a very tempting offer."

"Good."

He strode to the steps, and called up. "Sara and I are leaving. See you later."

"What?" Ted called down.

"We'll talk later," Jack answered, then turned back to Sara. "Come on, before Ted puts up an argument."

"Are you sure it's okay?"

"Yes," he answered, knowing it wasn't true. Ted was going to be pissed off. He liked things to work out the way he planned, but Jack was going to accommodate him only so far. He'd come along in an attempt to be brotherly. Now there was something else he'd much rather do.

"I've got to get my purse."

He watched Sara head for the kitchen, noting the feminine sway of her hips. She was a very pretty blonde with blue eyes and a trim figure. His type. Well, that had been his type, when he'd felt better about himself.

Sara hadn't stared at the scars on his face. What would she think about his mangled leg? He stopped himself from going down that road. At least he *had* two legs and the important parts between them. A lot of guys had come back in much worse shape.

Besides, he was getting way ahead of himself with Sara.

He'd just met her. Yet he couldn't banish the tempting picture of the two of them in bed together.

He strove for a neutral expression as she came back with a leather bag slung over one shoulder.

They walked outside together, and he looked at the two cars that had been parked at the property when he and Ted had driven up. A Mercedes and a Honda.

"I'm guessing you picked good gas mileage over luxury."

"And also utility. I sent the truck back to my warehouse with the boys." She gave him a direct look. "Actually, I'm living there for the time being. It's a good way to save money."

"Is that legal? Living in a storage facility?"

She shrugged. "The management didn't ask. And there wasn't anything about it in the lease. It came with a bathroom. And a little kitchen area, actually, so I can function there very well."

"Okay." He held out his hand. "Why don't you let me drive?"

HAD SHE DRIVEN LAST TIME this scene had played itself out? Or had he? She honestly couldn't remember. Back then, she was focused on getting to know Jack. Now everything had more than one meaning. And one of her jobs was to keep from saying anything that would put him off.

"Sure," Sara answered, fishing her keys out of her purse and handing them over. When he unlocked the door, she climbed into the passenger seat, and he slid behind the wheel, then adjusted the seat to give himself enough legroom. She was glad the car was neat. Sometimes the back was full of items she hadn't needed for a staging.

"Where do you want to eat?" he asked.

She thought for a moment. He'd asked her last time, and she'd suggested a place called the Pasta Station in Lisbon. Could she start changing their history by changing the venue? "There's a little restaurant and bakery in Ellicott City. Genevieve's," she said, naming a place that was miles from the one where they'd eaten last time.

Ellicott City was an old mill town with a commercial area that hadn't changed much in two hundred years because there was nowhere to expand. The antique buildings on either side of Main Street hugged the sides of a rocky ravine. Capitalizing on that disadvantage, the town had long ago transformed itself into a quaint shopping and restaurant area.

"I've passed it and wanted to go in."

"The food is good, and the prices aren't high."

She leaned back, ordering herself to relax as she slid her eyes toward Jack, watching him put the car into gear and head down the driveway.

It was amazing to be sitting so close to him again. Amazing that they had this time together. In fact, she felt like every second was a gift from God.

The interior of the car was filled with his scent, so dear and familiar to her. She watched his strong hands as they clasped the wheel, somehow keeping herself from covering the closer one with her palm. She ached to touch him. Kiss him. Do all the things that she'd thought she'd never do again. Now he was tantalizingly within reach.

Of course, he wasn't aware of any of her longings. For him, this was their first meeting.

He turned right, out of the development where the lots were supersized and the custom-built houses vied with each other for presence.

They were at the far edge of the county, and she hadn't thought about the route to Ellicott City until Jack turned onto a major cross-county road.

Route 108.

Familiar scenery sped past. She tried to place it, then drew in a quick breath.

"Sorry, I guess I'm going too fast," Jack said, completely misinterpreting her reaction.

"You're fine," she managed to say, but her mind was racing and her chest felt like it was being constricted by heavy bands.

She knew exactly where she was. This was the stretch of highway where she'd slid down the long hill in the snow. Where she'd hit the pickup truck and...what?

She couldn't say for sure what had really happened. Would it happen again? Now?

Was this what fate had in store for her? A cruel joke? A few minutes with the man she loved—then blackness.

"No," she whispered.

Reacting to the alarm in her voice, Jack looked toward her, just as a car rounded the curve ahead, passing another vehicle illegally and coming straight at them.

Chapter Three

Sara grabbed the handhold above the door.

"Watch out."

Jack swore under his breath, his attention snapping back to the road as he yanked the wheel, moving them to the right so that he hugged the edge of their lane. When the car remained on their side of the road, he honked the horn and muttered, "What is that fool doing?"

Slowing their speed, he bumped onto the shoulder. Sara wanted to close her eyes. Instead she couldn't take her gaze from the other car. Leaping back to its own side of the road, it passed them with inches to spare, but Jack was already too close to the edge of the shoulder.

The right-hand wheels were skimming the margin of the gravel now, and he was having trouble steering.

Looking to the right, Sara saw a steep hill with a creek at the bottom.

Her heart was in her throat as she braced for the long slide down. Like last time, but different. Beside her, Jack was still fighting to avoid disaster, slowing their speed and struggling to stay off the hill. Somehow he managed to keep the vehicle mostly on the shoulder. When he had enough traction, he swung back onto the center of the shoulder and stopped the car.

She gave him a grateful look. "Thank goodness. You're a heck of a driver."

"You mean good or bad?"

She felt a nervous laugh bubbling inside her. "Good, of course."

Swiveling around, she looked behind her. *If I'd been driving, we'd be down there in the creek.*

He was the only thing that had saved them this time. Last time she'd been here, she'd been alone.

"I'm sorry," she whispered, as he pulled back onto the road.

"How was that your fault?"

"I distracted you," she said, thinking that one of the questions circling in her mind had just been answered. Everything wasn't happening exactly as it had the last time. The first time around, there had been no near accident on the way to dinner.

Was that a bad sign? Or was it actually good? What if nobody was after Jack now?

She wanted that to be true, so much, but she couldn't count on it. Not when whoever was trying to kill him before had been so totally relentless.

Tempting as it was to relax her guard and just enjoy being with Jack, that wasn't a smart idea.

She glanced at him and saw his brow wrinkle. "That's right. You gasped. Just before that guy rounded the corner. But you couldn't see him coming, could you?"

"No." She scrambled for an explanation and came up with something plausible. "A woman I knew had an accident here. She was killed." Saying it out loud sent a shiver through her. But it was the truth. Well, not the friend part. Sara Carter had been killed here. Or would be killed, unless she could change her fate—and Jack's.

"That's rough. When did it happen?"

"Last winter." She swallowed. "I knew her pretty well."

"And seeing the spot where she died brought it back."

"Apparently. But I don't really want to talk about it."

"I understand."

"Because guys you knew in Afghanistan were killed?"

He stiffened. "How do you know I was in Afghanistan?"

"You're a war hero."

"I'm no hero," he said in a hard voice.

She wanted to tell him that she knew otherwise. Before getting wounded, he'd saved the lives of two men on patrol by pulling them back to safety, while under enemy fire. His act of bravery had earned him a Bronze Star. But telling him things about himself wasn't a good idea. She'd have to wait until they came up when he got to know her better.

They were both silent for several minutes. The accident hadn't happened before. Neither had this conversation. Or driving past the very hill where she'd been killed. Or would be killed. It was still hard to sort out the references to past and future.

She shook her head.

"What?" Jack asked.

It seemed so natural then to reach out and cover his large hand with her smaller one, to press her palm against his knuckles.

"I get nervous every time I pass this place," she murmured. "Unfortunately, I wasn't thinking about the route we were going to take."

"I get nervous in thunderstorms," he answered. "The thunder is like being in battle."

"Sorry."

"I have to deal with it."

Reluctantly she took her hand away.

Switching to a different subject, he asked, "How did you get into the business of…staging houses?"

"My mom had an antiques shop in Ellicott City."

"Which shop?"

"Well, antiques and…weird stuff. She called it Past Is Prologue."

"I remember it. I used to wonder what was in there. But it's closed now?"

"Yes. She died a couple of years ago."

"I'm sorry," he said, and she realized they'd said that twice now.

"I miss her."

"You have brothers and sisters?"

"No. My dad…" She should tell him what had happened to her father, but she simply couldn't make herself do it. Not yet. "He left us on our own."

"Rough."

"We managed, but we didn't have a lot of extra cash. At least it taught me to be frugal. I was making a lot of my own clothes by the time I was in middle school."

He was probably thinking about how different her life had been from his, even though they'd grown up in the same Maryland county. It was one of the wealthiest in the country. She just hadn't gotten much advantage from that.

"How come you didn't want to run the store?" he asked.

"I saw what kind of hours she kept, and I didn't want to be tied to a shop all the time. But I loved arranging the merchandise. And picking up items at estate sales and auctions. Then when I was home from college on summer vacation, a real-estate agent I knew asked if I could stage a house for her with some of the merchandise from Mom's shop. I agreed. She liked what I'd done and recommended me to her friends. I haven't done any advertising. My business comes from word of mouth in the real-estate community."

"Which means you're good at what you do."

"I hope so."

He took the scenic way into town, the long hill that wound down through restored houses, even a couple of log cabins, to the commercial area where Main Street was confined by the sides of the river gorge.

"Did your mom's shop get caught in any floods?" Jack asked.

"A couple of times. Everybody did in the old days. Until

we had some serious flood control on the river." She pointed down the hill. "Genevieve's is near the train station."

He continued down the narrow street toward the stone building that had been the first terminus of the Baltimore and Ohio Railroad and was now a museum.

Parking in the old mill town was always at a premium, but Jack found a space not far from the restaurant.

It was getting dark. Darker down here in the river valley, and Sara told herself not to be nervous as she got out of the car. Still, she was remembering that something bad had happened when they'd come out of the restaurant the first time around.

But this wasn't even the same town.

Still, she was on the alert as they strolled along the sidewalk. And she breathed out a little sigh as they stepped into Genevieve's.

It was owned by a husband and wife team, Patrick and Laura Walsh, both in their early forties. Laura was the chef, and Pat manned the front. They had owned a restaurant in New York City and had come to central Maryland to find a less hectic way of life.

"Haven't seen you in a while," Pat said when he spotted Sara. He was a slightly overweight man who obviously enjoyed his wife's cooking.

"I've been busy. But I'm happy to be here now. What's good tonight?"

"Laura has a yen for spring cuisine. She's got a killer asparagus soup. A spinach salad to die for. Lamb kebabs. But you should sit down and look at the menu."

He led them to a quiet table in the back where Jack winced as he sat down.

"What's wrong?"

He looked like he wished she hadn't asked, but he said, "I was wounded in Afghanistan. The leg gives me some trouble. And don't say you're sorry."

She laughed. "Yeah, let's not make that the word of the day."

He grinned at her. "Wine would help. One glass, and I'll still be okay to drive."

They had already exchanged a good deal of information in the car. At dinner they each ordered different dishes and had a taste of the other's selection. Sara got the asparagus soup and lasagna, and Jack ordered the spinach salad and the shish kebab, all of which were excellent.

They kept the conversation light, discussing music they liked. She already knew his tastes, but it was fun talking to him about the Eagles, Bob Seger, Bruce Springsteen, Fleetwood Mac.

Still, she felt tension gathering inside her as the meal drew to a close. She was waiting for two things—one of them good and one of them bad.

They were finishing a shared piece of key lime pie when Jack looked at his watch. "It's after ten. You probably need to get some sleep."

"I guess dinner woke me up. And the conversation. I was enjoying myself."

"Me, too. But I'd better get you home. Especially since you have to drop me off first."

"Right. I wasn't thinking about that," she lied. Of course she was thinking about it.

"Or I could call Ted."

"Don't bother him. Well, unless you live in the next county."

"No. My address is actually Ellicott City. But not the old part."

After he'd paid the bill, she felt a stab of disappointment. Last time...

Instead of standing up, he leaned toward her.

"I was thinking about your job."

Her pulse started to pound.

"It's not so different from an interior decorator," he continued.

"Not exactly," she felt duty bound to say.

"But close enough." He cleared his throat. "Morgan Enterprises is planning to move to a new building. I was wondering if you might be interested in doing some of the decorating for us."

She dragged in a breath, then let it out. "I'm overwhelmed. That's a dream job for me. But are you sure the company would go along with it?"

"It's my decision." He laughed. "They're trying to get me more involved. I'll tell them what I saw that's unique in your work, and why I think you're the right person to hire."

"Okay. Then yes."

"You haven't even asked what we're paying."

Because she already knew. She laughed. "Oh, right. What?"

He named a figure that would have made her blink if she hadn't heard it before.

"That's fantastic."

"If you don't have to work tomorrow, I can show you what we need done."

"As far as I know, I'm free tomorrow," she answered, feeling light-headed. She'd been afraid it wasn't going to happen, but he'd asked her to work with him—which meant that they would be seeing a lot of each other.

"I'm glad that's settled." He stood, and she did, too.

He glanced around. "It looks like we're closing up the restaurant."

As they walked through the almost-empty establishment, she was thinking that the other test was coming up.

Patrick said goodbye and held the door open for them. Then they were on the street.

Sara kept her eyes open and her ears peeled for trouble. As they approached the car, she breathed out a little sigh.

It wasn't the same.

She stole a glance at Jack as he reached to open the car door. She knew his expressions, and the look on his face told her that he was thinking about kissing her.

Which was fine with her. She'd been hoping for something like that all evening.

Then everything changed in an instant as a man stepped out from behind a parked car. A man holding a gun.

Chapter Four

Jack had spent the most enjoyable evening in recent memory, and he was thinking that it was only going to get better.

Then, in one of those terrifying moments that could change everything, a man with a gun stepped toward him. A guy about average height, with thinning dark hair.

Caught off guard, Jack grappled with the seismic shift, but Sara was already moving. From beside him, she leaped forward, swinging her purse like a bolo, using the strap that had held it on her shoulder. The heavy leather bag hit the man square in his pockmarked face, wringing a shocked exclamation from his lips.

As the purse dropped, he whirled toward Sara, his eyes fierce, his mouth bloody, and the gun pivoting in her direction. But Jack was already springing forward, plowing into the guy and knocking him backward against the fender of the car.

The man straightened and tried to retaliate with a head butt. But Jack dodged aside, making the guy lose his footing. Taking advantage of that, Jack stomped on the man's gun hand. He screamed as the automatic went flying across the sidewalk.

A gun had made the guy brave. With the deadly weapon suddenly yards away on the sidewalk, his face became suffused with panic. In a desperate move, he reared at Jack, throwing him backward so that he landed against the exterior wall of the restaurant. With the breath knocked out of him, he struggled to stay on his feet, but his bad leg gave out from under him, and he toppled onto his butt, hitting the sidewalk with a teeth-rattling impact.

As the man dived for the gun again, Sara thrust out a foot and kicked the automatic off the curb and under a car.

"Bitch." The man's face was a study in anger, his hands curled into claws. Jack's fear leaped into his throat, but as he struggled up, the man apparently decided to cut his losses. After one more angry look, he whirled away and ran, disappearing around a corner.

His own anger boiling over, Jack started after him, but Sara darted forward, grabbing his arm and holding him back.

"Don't."

He tried to wrench away, but she held fast.

"Let him go."

Rage had fueled his aggressive instincts, but he knew that he had little chance of catching the guy. Not when his running speed had been cut substantially by his injury. Plus the attacker probably had mapped out an emergency escape route before the attack.

Still, he was torn between imperatives.

The door of the restaurant burst open, and Patrick stepped out, his gaze landing on them. "I heard a scuffle. What happened?"

"A guy tried to rob us," Jack answered.

"I don't know," Sara mused.

Jack turned toward her, seeing the indecision on her face. "You don't think it was a robbery? I mean, what else could it have been?"

She looked torn. "He didn't ask for our money, did he?"

Jack laughed. "I guess he didn't get a chance to. You hit him in the face with your purse."

"Yeah, I guess that's right," she conceded.

"Fast thinking."

"I took a self-defense course."

"Don't they advise you that it's better to give up your wallet than get shot?"

"Yes. But I just...you know..." She raised one shoulder in a helpless gesture.

"I'm going to call the police," the restaurant owner said, pulling out his cell phone and dialing 911.

Sara looked shaken.

Jack reached for her, pulling her into his arms, feeling her tremble.

She whispered his name in a way that made it sound like they'd had a whole lot more shared experiences than just what had happened today.

"Are you okay?" he asked.

"I am now. I was so scared."

"But you didn't lose your cool."

She nodded against his shoulder, clinging to him, wrapping her arms around his back and pressing close.

Holding her in his embrace was wonderful. And he had the odd feeling that it wasn't for the first time. There was a familiarity about her that sent a wave of contentment—and longing—through him. He wanted her, even when he knew that letting her get close to him could lead to disappointment.

He stopped worrying about that as he hugged her to him. He'd wanted to feel her body against his all evening. He hadn't thought he'd get an excuse so quickly, although this wasn't the kind of reason he'd have elected, if he'd had a choice.

He slid his hands up and down her back, wishing he could do more. He wanted to kiss her. More than kiss. He wanted her in a bed. Which astonished him. She'd see the scars on his body. The scars that reminded him of the worst day of his life. The scars that had shocked another woman.

But he couldn't do the things he craved now. Not out here on the street. Not with the restaurant owner looking at them and the cops on the way.

She must have understood that, too, because she eased away from him, her gaze going to his.

"I'm glad you're okay," she said.

"Same here."

"The gun was pointed at you."

"You put yourself in danger."

"I was terrified for you. I just acted instinctively."

Patrick cleared his throat. "Both of you just had a pretty nasty experience. Come inside and sit down."

"Yes. Thanks," Sara answered.

She followed the restaurant owner into the building, where chairs were now upside down on the tabletops. Quickly Patrick reached for the closest group and pulled four of them down.

His wife came out of the kitchen, looking concerned when she saw two of their diners had returned, both appearing somewhat the worse for wear.

"What happened?"

"Attempted robbery," her husband said.

"You poor things," she sympathized. "I'm Laura Walsh," she said to Jack.

"Jack Morgan." He looked from her to her husband. "Has there been a lot of crime down here?"

"Not a lot. But it happens from time to time. I'm so sorry you got into trouble right outside the restaurant."

"Not your fault," Jack answered.

"Can I get you some brandy?" Patrick asked.

"Yes. Thanks," Jack answered.

Patrick stepped behind the bar and poured two glasses of Azteca de Oro and brought them over.

Jack took a sip. "Good stuff."

"My best."

Sara also took a small swallow. "Yes, this is good."

"How are you doing?" Jack asked.

"Better. Thanks."

The casual conversation stopped when the door opened and a uniformed officer stepped inside. He was young and fit, and had that confidence a uniform gave you until something bad happened. Jack knew all about that from his time in Afghanistan. He'd gone over there thinking the U.S. Army could whip the asses of the Taliban. He'd found out they didn't give in easily. And they had no problems with fighting dirty.

"You called in an attempted robbery?" asked the officer, whose name tag said Robards.

"Yes," the restaurant owner answered.

"We were the ones he assaulted," Jack said, gesturing toward Sara and himself. "We'd just finished dinner and stepped outside."

Robards looked at Sara. "You're the woman who stages the houses, right?"

"How do you know?"

"My wife has taken me to a couple of showings. I saw you at one of them."

Sara nodded. "I was working on a job all day. Jack and I came down here for some dinner—and to unwind."

Jack laughed. "It didn't turn out quite the way we expected."

"It did until a few minutes ago," she answered, her gaze searching his.

"Yes."

Again, he forgot that they weren't alone, until the police officer said, "Let me get some basic information."

He took their names, phone numbers, addresses and email addresses. "Can you tell me what happened?"

Jack gave an account of the incident.

When he finished, Robards looked at Sara. "You were taking a chance with that purse stunt. He could have shot you."

"I guess that's right." She shifted in her seat. "I just reacted when I saw the gun pointed at Jack." Even though she told the cop the same thing she'd told Jack earlier, there was something about her expression that gave him an odd feeling, as though she were holding information back.

"What did the man look like?" the cop asked.

Jack raised one shoulder. "There wasn't anything remarkable about him. He was medium height. His hair was thinning. But mostly I saw the gun."

"What kind of gun?"

"An automatic." Jack looked at Sara. "You kicked it under the car. Maybe it's still there."

"Show me where," Robards said.

They all got up and went outside. Sara pointed to the spot where the weapon had disappeared. It was lying against the curb, and the officer was able to retrieve it and put it into an evidence bag.

"Good," he said. "Anything else you can add to his description?"

She nodded. "Like Jack said, he was medium height. Thinning hair. A high forehead. A wide mouth. One of his front teeth was a little crooked."

"You noticed that?" Jack asked.

"I was thinking he ought to get it fixed."

"Anything else?" Robards asked.

"Bad skin. Well, you know, teenage acne scars."

"Yeah," Jack chimed in. "I forgot to mention that."

Sara spoke again. "He was wearing dark slacks. A dark, long-sleeved knit shirt. His shoes were dark. I guess he was hoping to make himself inconspicuous."

"Did you see his eye color?" the cop asked.

"They were light," Sara said. "I don't know exactly what color." She thought for a moment. "Except for the scars, his skin was very pale. I don't think he goes out much. And, uh, he didn't sound like he was from around here. More like a New York accent."

"He didn't say much," Jack answered.

"I know. Just an impression I had."

"Had either of you seen him before?" Robards asked.

"No," Jack answered.

Sara said the same thing, but she was a beat behind him.

"Are you willing to come in and look at some mug shots?" Robards asked.

"Yes," they both said at the same time.

"Can you come in tomorrow morning?"

They both agreed.

By the end of the interview, Sara was looking wiped out.

"I'll drive," Jack said when they returned to her car.

She flopped into the passenger seat, leaned back and closed her eyes, but he saw her hands were clasped in her lap.

He started the car, pulled out of the parking space and headed toward home.

"Your quick thinking made a difference," he said.

"Don't give me too much credit," she murmured. "You beat him up, and he ran away."

"I think he'd have shot me if you hadn't reacted."

She nodded.

"Then you came up with a lot of details I didn't notice."

Her eyes snapped open. "I've trained myself to think about details. That's part of my job."

"Yeah. When the cop asked if you'd seen the guy before, you hesitated."

She turned her head toward him. "I was trying to think if I *had* seen him."

"And I assumed I hadn't."

"I guess it's just the way we think about things."

"Right," he answered, still mulling that over. He hadn't thought about his powers of observation until tonight.

Sara closed her eyes again, and he wondered if she wanted to sleep—or to avoid talking about their answers to the cop.

It was only a short ride to his house, which was a fifty-year-old rancher on a couple of acres off Route 144. The property had appealed to him because he hated the way the county was being built up with houses crammed onto tiny lots.

He shared a long driveway with several other home owners who also wanted some privacy. When he pulled up in front of the house, Sara opened her eyes and looked around. A security light had gone on, illuminating the low, rectangular front of the house, and he saw her looking at it.

"Not very impressive," he said.

"I'm guessing you didn't buy it to impress anyone."

He laughed. "That's for sure. I just wanted a place to live where I could be by myself."

She nodded, and he wondered if he had given too much away with that answer. No use explaining that his parents had invited him to move back in to their mansion, and he hadn't wanted the obligation of making conversation. Or having anyone comment on his physical-therapy schedule.

Jack knew that Mom and Dad were being protective of him. They hadn't liked him joining the army. They'd been sick with worry when he'd gone off to Afghanistan. And they were still worried about his physical and mental shape.

He understood all that. Maybe he was making a dramatic improvement tonight. At least mentally.

He'd intended to tell Sara that he knew she was tired. Instead he heard himself say, "Do you want to come in?"

"Yes," she murmured. "But I think I shouldn't."

"Because you decided this isn't going anywhere?" he asked, wanting to get the disappointment over with in one fell swoop.

"Because I *know* it is. And if I come inside, there's no telling what will happen. Then you'll think I'm the kind of woman who..." She stopped and laughed. "I'd better not make suggestions, but I'm thinking we're safe out here."

As she spoke she reached for him across the narrow console, pulling him into her arms. "Oh, Jack," she sighed, as she clung tightly to him.

"We both had a frightening experience," he answered.

"It's not just that, and you know it." She pulled back so that her eyes could meet his.

"Yes." He held her gaze for a long moment, then moved in closer again, lowering his head to cover her lips with his.

He was out of practice kissing. Out of practice with any kind of intimacy. But as soon as their mouths touched, he knew exactly what he was doing.

She made a small sound as his lips moved over hers, the friction setting up a vibration through his body.

He hadn't wanted to admit it, but he knew that the two of them could have died on the street outside the restaurant. Or he could have, if she hadn't been with him.

Would he just have handed over his wallet if he'd been alone?

Probably not.

Since he'd come home, his mood had been reckless. He hadn't cared much about what happened to him. That had changed as they'd sat over dinner. Changed even more when the man had come at them with the gun.

"Something could have happened to you back there," he whispered against her mouth.

"Or to you," she answered, turning her head so that her lips rubbed against his, then settling down with a more steady pressure.

He didn't have to ask her to open for him. She simply did it, giving him access to her sweetness.

He liked the faint taste of brandy in her mouth. He liked the way she kissed. Loved the way she was doing exactly what he wanted. Like she was reading his mind. She couldn't be, but they'd clicked in a way that was almost magical.

He stopped trying to analyze the attraction or his reactions or anything else. He simply wanted to enjoy this moment with her—to enjoy this woman.

He loved the soft skin of her arms when he stroked them,

the feel of her breasts pressed against his chest. Her scent, which wasn't anything he could define but was unique to her.

She kissed him as though they were two lovers at the end of the world who had thought they were doomed to live out their days alone. Then they'd found each other, and everything had changed.

"Jack," she murmured against his mouth, her tongue finding the inside of his lips, the line of his teeth, stroking him with a maddening sensuality.

They had met only today. He had to keep reminding himself of that when he wanted to pick her up in his arms and carry her into the house. Straight to his bed.

And she would have come with him. She'd as much as said she would. Or she wanted to.

He ached to slip his hand between them and cup her breast, and it took all his restraint to stop himself from doing it.

He warned himself not to go too fast. Not to do anything that would ruin things before they really got started.

Forcing himself to go slowly, he pulled away. His breath was coming hard and fast. So was hers.

She looked into his eyes for a long moment, then lowered her head to his shoulder, gripping his arms.

He could have sat here all night holding her, if she would let him. "You should go before I take this too far."

"I know." The broken sound of her voice tore at him.

She didn't raise her head or let go of him, but stayed where she was.

"Jack," she said again, his name easing out of her like a long sigh. "I never thought this would ever happen again."

The words jolted him. "What do you mean 'again'?"

Chapter Five

Sara pulled away and kept her head down, because looking at him might make her reveal what she knew about their past and their future. "I didn't mean to say that," she said. "It just slipped out."

"I don't have any right to pry," he answered in a gruff voice, and she knew he was wondering about what she could possibly have meant.

She dragged in a breath and let it out, fighting panic. What was she going to say now? It had to be something that made sense, but her mind stayed blank until she heard words coming out of her mouth.

"I was in love with someone. It was a very intense relationship. We were going to get married. Then he died."

"I'm sorry."

"It was very difficult for me to deal with."

"I understand," he said, and she knew he must be trying to imagine what that must have been like for her.

She went on quickly. "I've been kind of closed off since it happened. I guess you can say I threw myself into my work."

"I understand," he said again.

"When that gunman came at you, all I could think of was protecting you," she admitted.

He reached for her again, holding her close, and she was overwhelmed by how much she was feeling—hope, turmoil, confusion, overlayed with panic that the past would repeat itself, after all. The urge to explain it all to him was like steam pressure building up inside her. But she knew she couldn't do it. He wouldn't believe her. She had hardly believed it herself when she'd woken up in the car outside the mansion. But it had gone on too long for her to doubt the truth.

If she couldn't speak, she could allow herself the joy of holding on to him for a little while longer. Her hands crept around his back, and they clung together.

Finally, she knew that if she stayed any longer, she was going to end up in his bed.

"I should leave."

"I don't want you to."

"We'll see each other soon. You wanted me to look at that new building." She made a snorting sound. "And we're forgetting that we agreed to a romantic meeting at police headquarters to look at mug shots."

"Funny how that slipped my mind."

"It's not exactly a fun expedition."

"Yeah. But I can pick you up, and we can kill two birds with one stone. If that's okay?"

"That's fine. I don't have any urgent jobs. I'll be at the warehouse."

"Okay."

She fished one of her cards out of her purse and gave it to him. Then they both exited the car. He walked toward his front door and stayed there as she climbed behind the wheel, closed the door and backed up, before turning to wave at him.

Then she left, wondering if she had made a mess of everything.

Since the attack by the gunman, her mind had been spinning as she tried to weigh every word before speaking. Which wasn't a good idea because that was going to make her sound like she was hiding something. Which she was.

She had told him that she'd loved someone, and he had died. That was Jack, of course.

And she couldn't tell him that.

So what if he asked about her dead lover? Was she going to make up a name for him? Or was she going to say it was just too painful to talk about?

Hopefully the latter, if she could get away with it, because she hated lying. And she'd done it over and over all evening. Starting with her story about the hill on 108. When she'd realized where she was, she'd been terrified. She'd distracted Jack, and a car had almost plowed into them. The past meeting the present. Or the future meeting the present.

Her mind was half in tonight's reality and half in the former one as she reached Route 144, where she waited for a truck to rumble past.

Her head was pounding from the details of the evening.

The man who had come at Jack was the same guy who had tried to kill him last time. Only in a different restaurant in a different town.

How had he even known where to find Jack? Or had he followed them from the house? Which would mean he'd known where Jack would be.

And then there was the big difference. Last time she hadn't hit the man with her purse. Last time someone had come out of the parking lot and shouted at the gunman. The distraction had been enough for Jack to leap on the guy, like he did tonight. And after that, the outcome had been the same. The man had pushed Jack down and run away.

But tonight she'd been prepared with the pocketbook because it was later and she'd assumed nobody would be on the street.

She'd go to the police station with Jack, but they weren't going to see the guy's picture. At least she didn't think so because she couldn't be certain how things were going to work out this time.

Like, for example, Patrick hadn't been there to make the call last time. A different police officer had shown up. And she certainly hadn't ended up telling Jack that she'd had a lover who'd died.

That could turn out to blow up in her face. But it had seemed like the only way to keep from looking like a nut.

She took her bottom lip between her teeth, wondering what she should have said and done.

It was useless to keep second-guessing herself. She was just going to have to act as normal as possible. Normal for a woman who'd just met a man who interested her. Not normal for a woman who was meeting the father of her child. A man she thought was dead.

Only there was no baby. Not yet. That was in the future.

Could she keep from getting pregnant? That was a leading question.

Did she want to keep from getting pregnant?

In the darkness of the car, she shook her head. If Jack got killed again, she wanted to have his child.

"Stop it," she almost shouted, then spoke more calmly. "He's not going to get killed. That's why you're here. To stop it from happening."

She wished she could be sure of that.

The problem wasn't the guy with the gun. It was whoever had sent him.

At least she was pretty sure they wouldn't try the same method again. Because they wanted Jack's death to look like an accident or a random act of violence where he was just at the wrong place at the wrong time. Which meant two different robbery attempts wouldn't seem like chance.

Or would they?

She gripped the wheel, wishing she could stop her mind from going in circles like a hamster running on an exercise wheel.

She turned into the industrial park where she lived. Not

one of the country's upscale areas, but the low rent was a big inducement for the tenants.

There were no cars in the lot, only a few trucks, and she was suddenly aware of how isolated the location was. Hers was one of a long row of warehouses with varying purposes. Most were rented by businesses that didn't feel the need for showy premises. The man who owned the space next to hers sold garden furniture there, although his primary job was insurance agent. A few doors down was a carpet company. Next to that was a dealer in pinball machines and other old arcade games. Beyond him was a co-op artists' studio with stained glass and pottery.

The industrial park was busy during the day. But she was the only tenant who lived here, and usually she was the only person around at night.

She pulled around so that her car was facing outward, toward the strip of trees that bordered the other side of the parking lot. She'd always liked the way it gave a woodsy feel to an area that was otherwise devoid of charm. Tonight she peered into the darkness under the trees and shivered. As she imagined someone standing in the shadows, watching her.

The attack in Ellicott City had been aimed at Jack, but that didn't necessarily mean she was safe.

She'd played a part in saving Jack tonight. Would the man with the gun report her involvement to the person who had hired him? Or would he want to skip over the news that a woman had slammed a pocketbook into his face?

Maybe she'd just directed the killer's attention toward herself by getting personally involved, and maybe that meant she was in danger. Perhaps it would be a good idea to get a gun—and learn how to use it.

Lord, what if this time around she was the one who got killed and Jack survived?

As that new idea took hold, she shuddered. Quickly she got out of the car and crossed to the steps that led up to the loading dock. At one side was the door she used when she wasn't emptying or loading the truck.

The security light didn't go on, and she remembered that she needed to change the bulb. Better not put that off, she told herself, as she unlocked the door and stepped inside.

In the warehouse, another wave of unfamiliarity hit her. She'd been living here when she met Jack, but after he'd died and she'd found out she was pregnant, she'd started looking for another place to live, because she couldn't raise a child in a warehouse.

Tonight she was back here. And Jack was going to pick her up here tomorrow. She switched on a light, trying to see the place from his point of view. This part of the building was filled with furniture that she used as needed at display houses. The sideboards, desks, armoires and tables tended to be older pieces that she'd found at garage sales and auctions, and refinished or refurbished. The chairs and sofas were mostly modern, since she wanted them to be comfortable. Along one wall were shelves of knickknacks and other small items that she used to create a homey feel at each property.

At the moment, there was something she needed to check.

She'd told Jack that she could go with him tomorrow to see the new Morgan offices because that was what had happened last time.

Was it still true that she had the day free?

She hurried to the back of the building and stepped through the door that separated her living quarters from the furniture storage.

Inside she'd made herself a cozy little efficiency apartment, if one ignored the industrial cinder-block walls and the high ceiling with the ductwork overhead. Her bed was on one wall, with an Indian spread and pillows that made it look like a couch. Several easy chairs came from her warehouse stock. Her computer was on an old library table. And she'd kept several cabinet pieces that she loved, a Victorian dresser and a chest of drawers. The clothing she needed to hang up was in a vintage armoire. At the end of the bed were open shelves where she stored her decorating books and some of the small items that might go out to various model houses.

The kitchen was along the wall opposite the bed. It had a small sink, an under-counter refrigerator, a two-burner stove and a microwave. The small bathroom was next to it. There was no tub, but a previous tenant had put in a shower.

After booting her computer, she quickly checked her calendar and was relieved to find she actually was free for tomorrow.

She was just checking her email when her cell phone rang. There was no landline in the warehouse, which had worked okay because she did a lot of her business through email.

She tensed, until she saw the caller ID. Jack.

How could she have forgotten that he'd called that evening to make sure she was okay?

Pressing the Receive icon, she raised the phone to her ear.

"Hi," she said, thinking that she probably sounded a little breathy.

"I wanted to make sure you got home okay. And—you didn't get my number."

"Right. I was kind of scattered."

"Understandable."

He gave her his home and cell numbers, and she wrote them down, although she already knew them by heart.

"You're okay?" he asked.

"Still a little spooked."

"Likewise." He waited a beat before asking, "What time should I pick you up tomorrow?"

"What's convenient for you?"

"How about ten? We can do the police station bit, then look at the office spaces, then have some lunch."

"That sounds good."

There wasn't much more to add to the conversation. Well,

there was a whole lot more she wanted to say, but she knew none of it was appropriate at this stage in their relationship.

"Do you own a gun?" he suddenly asked.

She drew in a quick breath. She'd been thinking about that. "No."

"You should probably get one."

"I've thought about it. Actually, my mom had one at the shop. And when I was a teenager, I took shooting lessons. So I know how to handle one."

"But you don't have one now?"

"No."

"Maybe we should visit a gun shop."

"Not a bad idea," she said, thinking it wasn't a very romantic line of conversation.

"It's a date." He laughed. "Well, a weird kind of date."

"Practical."

"I should let you go. You need to get some sleep."

"You, too."

"See you tomorrow."

He hung up, and she sat with the phone in her hand, smiling to herself. How many guys would offer to take a woman gun shopping? They were falling quickly into a comfortable relationship. Which gave her a warm feeling, until she thought about the job she had ahead of her. The job of saving his life. And maybe her own.

JACK REPLACED THE RECEIVER in the cradle and leaned back in the easy chair in his bedroom. He was feeling elated, and at the same time doubts crept into his mind.

It was a long time since he'd been so attracted to a woman, yet he couldn't shake the feeling that there was something odd about her. She seemed to be open and, at the same time, on guard. And sometimes he had the feeling that she knew what he was going to say before he opened his mouth.

He wished he didn't want to second-guess everything that

was happening between them. He wished he could just relax and enjoy himself with her.

And maybe he should.

Enjoy himself how far?

He'd had a girlfriend before he'd left for Afghanistan. Bonnie Worthington. He'd met her at one of his parents' parties, and they'd hit it off. Mom and Dad had approved of his seeing her because she was from the right social class. But he hadn't been sure he wanted to settle down with her for the rest of his life. Which was one of the reasons he'd enlisted and gone to officer-candidate school.

They'd corresponded while he was overseas. And she'd come to see him in the hospital when he'd come home. But he'd realized right away that his injuries spooked her.

Because he knew she wasn't going to be comfortable with a disfigured man, he'd broken it off.

But her rejection had hurt, even when he'd known he wasn't totally committed to her.

Ever since then, he'd been cautious about relationships. In fact, he hadn't met anyone he wanted to spend a lot of time with—until Sara.

And what would she think when she saw his body?

Hating himself for caring about his looks, he pulled off his shoes and socks, then stood up, unbuttoned his shirt and draped it on the back of the chair. Finally he pulled off his jeans and underwear and turned to the full-length mirror on the back of the closet door.

His gaze went to his mangled leg, covered with scars. They'd saved it, and he could walk on the damn thing, but it was never going to look pretty.

There were more scars on his chest and belly. And, of course, his face.

She hadn't been turned off by those, as far as he could tell. What about the rest?

As he thought about making love with her, his body reacted. With a snort, he turned away from the mirror. No problem with his male equipment.

Of course, she didn't necessarily have to see him naked for him to make love with her. Yeah, or they could do it in the dark. But he didn't want to go down that road.

He had just pulled on gym shorts and a T-shirt in preparation for his nightly session in the gym when the phone rang.

His heart leaped inside his chest when he thought it might be Sara calling back. When he saw the caller ID, he pressed his lips together, then answered.

"Are you all right?"

The voice on the other end of the line was his brother, Ted.

"I'm fine. Why do you ask?"

"Because somebody tried to rob you tonight."

"How do you know that?"

"I have my sources."

"One of your friends in the police department. Well, tell him I'm fine."

"You were with that woman, Sara something or other."

"Sara Carter."

"The two of you ducked out before you got much of a look at the house."

"I figure you'll buy it if you want."

"If I can get the price down a hundred thousand dollars."

"Good luck with that."

"The real-estate agent thinks the buyer might go for it."

"Okay." He considered telling Ted that he was hiring Sara to do the office-building job but decided against it. It might lead to an argument, and he wasn't up for that tonight.

"Take care of yourself," Ted said.

"I do."

"I don't like to think about you getting shot."

"It came out okay."

"Sara hit the guy with her purse?"

"Yes."

Ted laughed. "You've got a live one on your hands."

"I guess so," he answered, then said, "I'm kind of worn out. I'll talk to you tomorrow."

"Just making sure everything's okay."

Jack hung up, thinking that he didn't need a babysitter. But his family had been hovering around him ever since he'd come home. He could understand why they were being protective, but he didn't have to like it.

Of course, he wasn't sure exactly why Ted was being so solicitous. Maybe he wanted to report to Mom and Dad that he'd called. Or maybe he had his own reasons for checking up on his brother.

Sometimes he thought that Ted resented his coming back to the company. He'd had the future of Morgan Enterprises all to himself until Jack had stepped back into the picture with a leg that was never going to work quite right.

He headed for the basement recreation room he'd turned into a gym for the physical therapy that he rarely skipped. As he strapped on ankle weights and sat down on the edge of the padded table, he was still thinking about Ted.

He and his brother had never gotten along as kids. They were too close in age, and the rivalry between them had never subsided.

Jack was eighteen months older, which had given him somewhat of an advantage.

They'd both been on the high-school football team, but Jack had been the captain. They'd both gotten into top colleges, Jack to Harvard and Ted to Yale.

He did his leg curls, two sets of fifteen reps, rested for a few minutes and did them again. As always, he felt the strain in his left leg, but he knew he was getting stronger.

At least physically. But what about mental strength? Was he using Morgan Enterprises as a shelter? So that he didn't have to make any big decisions about his future?

Ironically, one of the reasons he had gone into the army

was to get away from Ted and the family. The Morgan brothers had both been expected to join the family business. Ted had liked the idea. Jack had wanted to strike off on his own. He'd been an excellent officer, and he'd seen himself rising through the ranks to maybe general. Ambitious, but the goal had been achievable until that roadside bomb had ended his chances.

There were wounded guys who stayed in the service. Jack had always felt sorry for them. They had a limited future, and he wasn't interested in being promoted because the brass felt sorry for him.

Finished with the leg curls, he took off the weights and slipped a black band around his ankles. This was one of the exercises he hated most, but he did it anyway. Starting at one end of the recreation room, he began walking sideways, stretching out the band and bringing it back to the almost-slack position as he walked. He made himself do three laps back and forth, then lay down for some leg raises.

He switched his thoughts to Sara as he sat down at the leg press. Things just might be looking up. If the woman he'd met today turned out to be what she seemed.

And if he had the guts to let her see his mangled body.

Chapter Six

Jack Morgan's nemesis paced the room, anger flaring even three hours after news of failure had come and gone.

War hero Jack Morgan should have died in a robbery on the street outside a restaurant in Ellicott City. Instead he was at home, probably tucked into bed.

Or down in the basement gym where he was trying to get his mangled body into a semblance of normality. And worked off his frustrations. Undoubtedly he had plenty of those. He hadn't had a woman since he'd gotten home. And God knew how long before that, considering that little prude he'd been dating, Bonnie Worthington.

The war hero had reason to be worried about his body image, but he could always go down to Baltimore and find a hooker who wouldn't say a word about his deformities, if he paid her enough.

Now there was a new wrinkle. A blonde named Sara Carter whom Jack had met by chance a few hours earlier.

Since they'd been together in Ellicott City, he must have asked her to dinner with him. Which was a serious break in Jack's pattern of eating alone and sleeping alone.

So who was this Sara Carter person? If she kept seeing Jack, she needed to be investigated.

Apparently she'd saved the bastard's life by slamming her purse into the head of the attacker.

Too bad she'd reacted so quickly. Maybe she had to be eliminated before she caused any more trouble.

Meanwhile the plan to eradicate Jack had to get back on track, because time was of the essence.

SARA WOKE UP WITH A START. She was in her little apartment at the back of the warehouse. For a moment she lay very still with her heart pounding, looking around.

She was still here.

The night before she'd lain awake for a long time, wondering if everything would disappear if she went to sleep. Finally, fatigue took over, and she closed her eyes, dreaming of being in a car sliding down an endless hill in the snow.

But she was awake now, and she was still at the warehouse.

It must be real. And she'd better hustle because she had an appointment with Jack this morning.

Eyeing the jar of instant coffee on the counter, she told herself it was okay to have some. She wasn't pregnant, and she didn't have to worry about what would be good for the baby.

Anxious to look her best, she took a quick shower and dressed carefully in a subdued paisley dress and dark heels. It was different from the outfit she'd worn the last time she'd lived through this particular day.

But that was then. This was now.

Was Jack really going to show up? And what would happen when he did? Last time he'd complimented her on the cozy living area she'd fixed up in the warehouse. Maybe this time he'd hate it.

When the buzzer at the front door of the warehouse sounded, she took one more look at herself in the full-length mirror propped against the wall beside the bathroom door. Her outfit was dressier than what she usually wore to work. Last time she'd worn her usual jeans and a knit top. This time she knew Jack wasn't the only Morgan she was going to see today. At least, that was her assumption.

And she had no time to change now, she thought as she hurried through the storage area to the door.

Jack was standing on the landing looking through the pane of glass reinforced with wire mesh.

She looked back at him, her heart pounding. It was still hard for her to realize that she was with him again—after all the sorrow she'd endured.

Schooling her face, she unlocked the door. "Come in."

He followed her inside and closed the door behind him. "You've got a security system, right?"

"Yes."

"Good." He looked around with interest at the furnishings she'd stored. Walking over to a rolltop desk, he tested the mechanism.

"You have some charming pieces here. This looks like a big investment."

"I work hard at picking up things at low prices. The desk came from an old broom-making company in Baltimore."

He laughed. "I didn't even know they made brooms in Baltimore."

"It's down in Camden. The building's been converted to offices—and some retail businesses on the lower level."

"Besides old broom companies, where are the best deals in vintage furniture?"

"Often at garage sales. People are getting rid of things they don't want, and they're usually willing to bargain." She pointed to a low shelf. "I got that whole box of china for nineteen dollars."

He kept walking toward the rear of the warehouse, and she followed with her heart pounding.

"This where you live?" he asked, stopping at the door to her apartment.

"Uh-huh."

"Can I look inside?"

"Well, I straightened it up," she answered, "in case you asked."

He stepped into her private space, again taking everything in.

"You know how to accomplish a lot on a budget," he said.

"I try."

"It's a real skill."

They were standing so close together. Standing by the bed. They could end up there together, she thought in a kind of daze. All she'd have to do was reach out and pull him into her arms. Lift her face and bring his lips to hers.

She ached to do that, and a lot more. He didn't know her well yet. But she knew him, all the way to the depths of his soul. He was the same man she'd loved before. And she had a second chance to have everything she'd dreamed of last time. Being with him again was a miracle, and she knew how wonderful it would be to make love with him. But she also knew that rushing the physical part of the relationship would be a mistake. What if she spooked him? Sent him running in the other direction?

He swallowed, and she watched his Adam's apple bob. He must be thinking about the bed, too. But she knew he wasn't ready for intimacy.

He took a step back, still looking around. "Is there a back way out of here?"

"Yes."

"Good. I'd hate to think of your getting trapped in here— if something happens."

He walked out of the apartment and into the warehouse proper. "Show me the back exit."

She led him to a back corner where the door was located.

"Where does it lead?"

"To an alley. There's another row of warehouses in back of this one." She turned her head toward him. "You're spending a lot of time thinking about escape routes."

"Better safe than sorry."

She thought about that, thought about what had happened to him. There'd been no escape for him last time. Was it because he hadn't been thinking about his own safety? Or because someone else had made him forget about it?

That was one of the many things she would never know. Instead she asked, "What's the project you want me to look at?"

"We've bought an older office building that we're renovating. We're going to have tenants and also use the space for the offices of one arm of Morgan Enterprises."

"The company's that big?"

He lifted one shoulder. "Yeah. Sometimes I wonder if the right arm knows what the left arm is doing."

"That doesn't sound good."

"There's a certain amount of infighting going on right now." He stopped abruptly. "I shouldn't be complaining about it to you."

"I realize it's…proprietary information," she said, using one of the phrases she'd learned from him.

"Not just that. You don't have to be concerned about it."

She nodded, knowing that it wasn't true. The disputes in the company were going to affect her. But she couldn't let on that she knew any of that.

She grabbed a loose-leaf binder that she'd left on the table near the door.

"What's that?"

"Some examples of my work."

"You don't have to convince me."

"But you're the only one who's seen anything I've done."

"And Ted."

"Right."

After locking the door, she followed Jack down the steps to the new Lexus parked at the loading dock.

"Nice car."

"I figured I could indulge myself," he answered.

She knew he'd used money from his trust fund to buy the car. His salary in the army had been relatively small, but he and his brother each had access to family money.

"I wish we didn't have to go to the police station," she said, as he pulled out of the parking space and the industrial-park exit.

"We have to do our civic duty."

She wanted to tell him it would be a wasted morning, but maybe she'd be wrong.

The police headquarters was in a modern redbrick structure located up the hill from the restaurant where they'd been attacked. It was also near the courthouse, because Ellicott City was the county seat.

"Ever done this before?" Jack asked, as they headed for the station.

Another trick question, although he didn't know it.

"I've never been a victim before."

"Victim. I don't like putting it that way."

"It's reality," she answered, casting around for another topic.

Since the county office buildings were on the hill above them, she settled on, "Do you remember the old courthouse?"

"Yeah. Built of the same stone as the stores down along Main Street."

"I thought it was a really beautiful building. Then they enlarged it and added that new granite facade. And ruined it."

He laughed. "You think so because you have an acute sense of style." He gestured toward the redbrick police headquarters. "What do you think of that?"

"It's fine. They weren't trying for grandeur. Just utility."

They pulled into a visitors' space, entered the building and explained to the desk sergeant why they were there.

A uniformed officer showed them to a room where she and Jack sat down at a battered metal table. Robards brought in a stack of large loose-leaf binders with plastic sleeves. Each page held several mug shots.

"I've made up some six-packs for you to go through."

"Six-packs?" Jack asked.

"Six guys to a page. Most of these are men who were arrested for armed robbery," he explained. "Some are robbery arrests without weapons involved. Maybe we'll get lucky and find the guy."

Sara nodded, wishing she could just get up and leave.

Instead, she and Jack began dutifully looking through the books. She tried to turn the pages slowly so it would look like she was serious about this, even though she knew it was a total waste of time. The guy wasn't going to show up.

Although she tried to focus on the faces, she was thinking about a job she had coming up and what furniture would work best.

She was halfway through her third book when an image registered on her consciousness.

A man with thinning hair. A high forehead. A wide mouth. A crooked front tooth. Teenage acne scars.

When she caught her breath, Jack looked up. "What?"

"It's him," she managed to say, pointing to one of the pictures as she shoved the book toward Jack.

He stared at the photo. "You're right. I'll get Robards."

As he left the room, Sara sat with her heart pounding. The guy was in the book. And last time, he hadn't been.

What did it mean?

Another case where the reality she'd experienced last time had shifted out from under her.

The two men came back, and Jack peered at her.

"Are you all right?"

"Yes."

"You look like you had a bad shock."

"I was thinking this was going to be an exercise in futility. But I guess I was wrong." She pointed to the picture. "Who is he?"

Robards pulled out the photo and turned it over. "Tucker Swinton."

"Never heard of him," Jack said.

"He was released from jail a few months ago."

"I guess he didn't know any other way to make a living," Jack said. "You have any idea where to find him?"

"No. But now we have a name and a face. Thanks for helping us out."

"What's the chance of catching him?" Sara asked.

"Better than before you identified him."

"Glad to do it," Jack answered, then added, "You'll tell us if you pick him up."

"Of course."

"And you'd want us to testify, right?"

"Yes."

"I'd like to send him back to prison where he belongs," Jack said, and led Sara out of the police station and to his car. Once inside he said to her, "So we were just at the wrong place at the wrong time."

Sara wanted to tell him that probably wasn't so. Probably someone had been looking for a convicted felon to do a job. They'd found out about Swinton's record and gotten in touch with him. But she couldn't say that. And maybe she was wrong. Maybe this was all different. Unknowable.

No. She couldn't allow herself to slip into that mode. She had to focus on figuring out what was going on. Without acting like she knew any more than Jack did.

Chapter Seven

Two people had planned a midmorning meeting at a vacant farm for sale in the rural part of the county. One was Jack's nemesis and the other was a petty thug named Tucker Swinton, whom Nemesis had hired for a simple job: rob Jack Morgan and kill him in the process.

Only it apparently hadn't turned out the way they'd planned it.

Nemesis arrived well before the appointed time and pulled the car around the back of an old barn that was in danger of falling down.

After twenty minutes, Tucker Swinton arrived in a battered Ford that he'd bought with money advanced by Nemesis.

"Anybody home?" Swinton called, as he got out and looked around the property.

Nemesis waved an arm from the shadows inside the barn. "Over here."

Swinton came ambling in, confident that the transaction would be completed quickly. And it would be.

"You got the money you promised me?"

"I hired you to do a job you said you could pull off. It didn't turn out the way you said it would. Obviously, Jack Morgan is still walking around."

"How did I know that stupid broad was gonna swing her purse at me?"

"It was a robbery. You should have been prepared for trouble."

"I was, but not from her."

"I want you out of the county."

The felon pulled an outraged face. "I grew up here. I got family here. Where am I supposed to go?"

"I can take care of that." In one smooth motion, Nemesis brought out an automatic pistol and shot the guy in the heart. He crumpled to the ground with a look of shock on his face.

Nemesis prodded the body with a foot. Yeah, probably the guy had thought that a high-class employer would be gentler with the hired help.

That had been another of his mistakes.

Now the question was, what to do with the dead guy? Taking him somewhere else could be messy—and a hassle. It could leave evidence in a car trunk. Probably it was better just to leave him here.

And what if the cops found him? There was no reason to suspect who the guy had been meeting. Really, he might not have been meeting anyone. He could have been hiding out here after the failed robbery attempt.

Nemesis checked the battered Ford to make sure the guy hadn't brought anything that could connect his employer with his murder.

Satisfied to be in the clear, the killer drove away, in a hurry to make another appointment on time.

"SO WHERE'S THE OFFICE BUILDING?" Sara asked Jack, not wanting to discuss the robbery anymore.

"Off Oakland Mills Road. In Columbia."

"How did they choose it?"

"Dad picked it up cheap when the owner went bankrupt."

Jack pulled out of the parking space, and they made their way through the parking lot, heading for Columbia.

Although it was adjacent to Ellicott City, the two were

nothing alike. One traded on eighteenth-century charm while the other represented state-of-the-art late-twentieth-century city planning.

Forty years ago Columbia had been built on former Howard County farmland, the brainchild of mall developer James Rouse, who put together a think tank of experts charged with creating a new model for urban living.

Some of the concepts, like preserving open space and connecting neighborhoods with bike paths, had proven their worth. Others not so much. Rouse had wanted all the businesses "hidden," with no prominent signs on major streets, which had made it difficult to find them. And the old downtown had been focused around what proved to be an outmoded mall concept. Recently, shops, a movie theater and restaurants had been built outside the mall, opening up the commercial area.

As they reached the entrance to the police parking lot, Sara noticed a car at the curb. In the side mirror, she saw it pull out and follow them.

When her gaze remained fixed on the vehicle, Jack swung his head toward her.

"What?" he asked.

"I think that car is following us."

He glanced in the rearview mirror, then sped up. The car kept pace with them.

A housing development was coming up. Jack turned in, and the car took the same turn.

"I think you may be right," he muttered. When he stopped at a house with a For Sale sign on the front lawn and pulled into the driveway, the other car went past, and Sara saw the driver was a man with a baseball cap pulled low over his face. The killer? Or someone else he'd hired?

"He's gone past," Jack said.

"Maybe he doesn't want us to think he's interested in us."

"Why would he be interested in us?"

She shook her head. "I don't know. What if he's a friend of Tucker Swinton?"

"Also a robber?"

"I wish I knew." She gave him a direct look. "And I'm not the only one who's jumpy. You quizzed me on escape routes from the warehouse and told me you'd take me to a gun shop."

He laughed. "Yeah. I guess getting assaulted will make you start to think."

"Yes." Last time, it had taken longer for her to notice that someone was tailing Jack. This time she was watching for it, which didn't help her relationship with him.

In fact, she was getting more and more worried that she was going to screw this whole thing up by making him think she was crazy.

Try to relax. Act normal, she told herself, as he drove past downtown Columbia and on to the office park where the building was located.

Of course, what was your definition of normal when you'd come back from ten months in the future?

They pulled up in front of a two-story building made of light brick. Through the large window in front, she could see workmen moving around. One was a painter. Another was an electrician.

"Are you using it yet?" she asked.

"Just on a minimal basis. Almost everything is still being run from the old offices."

Sara grabbed the loose-leaf binder before exiting the car, then followed Jack into the building. They stepped into a large open space.

The only furnishing was an empty desk several yards from the door. As Sara and Jack stood in the middle of the room, a young woman with light brown hair and dark eyes rushed in.

"Oh, I didn't expect to see you here," she said as she sat down, unlocked a drawer and pulled out a laptop computer.

"I didn't expect to find you here, either," Jack said.

"There were some contractors coming in, and I'm here to oversee."

"Where were you?"

"I had to run out to the bank."

Jack nodded and Sara tried not to gnash her teeth. Barbara Bateman was one of the executive secretaries. One who had never liked Sara. She tried not to take it personally. Maybe Barbara had wanted Jack for herself and had been dismayed to find him giving a prize assignment to an attractive young woman. At least that was one way to think about it. Another was that Barbara had a reason to be working with whoever was trying to kill Jack. Or did she have some secret, personal reason to dislike him?

All of that flashed through Sara's mind, but she hoped it didn't show on her face.

"Barb, this is Sara Carter. Sara, this is Barbara Bateman. She's our top administrator."

Barbara flushed with pleasure at the compliment.

"Nice to meet you," Sara said, although she knew it wasn't going to be a pleasant experience.

Barbara was here on temporary assignment and probably reporting directly to Morgan management. Jack thought he was giving Sara free rein to decorate the offices. Instead Barbara was going to get various Morgan executives to come in and inspect the work—and ask for changes. Was it because they didn't like her style—or because they wanted to give her a hard time?

"What can I do for you?" Barbara asked.

"Sara's going to be decorating the lobby area and some of the offices," Jack said.

Barbara looked surprised. "Is this cleared through Bill and Ted?"

Bill was Jack's father.

"No. I thought I'd take care of it on my own."

"She has the qualifications?"

"Most of my experience has been in staging homes that are for sale." Sara held out the binder of photos that she'd brought along. "This is some of my work."

Barbara thumbed through the pictures. "None of these is office space."

"Her touches will make the office more homey. More inviting for clients. Like she does with houses. And I think she can make the lunchroom a much friendlier place."

"Um."

Jack turned back to Sara. "Let me show you around."

As she followed him toward the back of the building, she did something she hadn't thought of the first time. She glanced back to look at Barbara and saw the woman hunched over, punching in a phone number. Sara had a pretty good idea whom she was calling.

Beyond the lobby, the interior was more broken up. As Jack showed her the various spaces, she kept wondering about the phone call, then focused on the reason for their visit. Getting out a tape measure, she found the length of several of the walls. She also got out her cell phone and snapped pictures of the various areas.

"You didn't take any pictures or measurements out front," he said.

"I didn't want to disturb Barbara."

"You're not going to be any more disturbing than the workmen. She's used to functioning in the middle of chaos."

"A good skill to have."

"Let's look at the lunchroom."

He led her to the back of the building to a space that might have been part of a deli.

"Pretty uninviting," she murmured.

"What would you suggest?"

"Making it look more like an inexpensive but charming restaurant. Wood-grained tables. Comfortable chairs. Nice posters on the walls. Plants." She looked at him. "Does

Morgan Enterprises have a service that tends the plants and changes them out when they get straggly?"

"I don't know."

"We should find out."

"I like your restaurant idea."

"It's always good to have a nice environment where people can relax."

She slowed down as they returned to the front of the building. An older man now stood beside Barbara's desk. Dressed in a navy sports coat with brass buttons, gray slacks and a crisp white shirt, he appeared to be in his late sixties, although he was actually a little older. His salt-and-pepper hair was thinning on top but carefully cut to minimize the effect of the loss.

His eyes were dark, and there was a strong family resemblance to Jack.

Her heart began to pound inside her chest as his gaze fixed on them. Today he was wearing his pleasant public face. And not just for her benefit.

"Dad," Jack said, as they approached. "I didn't know you were going to be here."

"I stopped by to check on the work," he said.

Sure. Sara was almost certain Barbara had called him as soon as they had left the reception area.

"Dad, this is Sara Carter. Sara, this is my dad, Bill Morgan. He's the heart and soul of Morgan Enterprises."

"Well, chairman of the board, now," he said modestly. "I'm turning the heavy lifting over to my boys."

They shook hands.

Her encounters with him after Jack's death had been far from pleasant, leaving sharp memories. But today he hadn't yet developed a strong dislike for her. Now she tried to give him the benefit of the doubt. He was a man who had used the money he'd inherited to build up a formidable company and who wanted to keep the rewards of his labor in the family. He was also a man who was used to wielding power—until recently. Now that he was getting older, he was trying to let go of the reins, although the process wasn't exactly graceful.

And perhaps his son's death had been a blow that had knocked the stuffing out of him. Perhaps he hadn't been exactly rational. He'd acted like he thought Sara had something to do with Jack's murder, although that could simply have been an elaborate act.

One thing she'd known for sure. He was determined that she wouldn't get her hands on any of the Morgan money.

"You've hired Sara to decorate the offices?" Bill Morgan asked carefully.

"Yes. She's excellent."

"Are you an interior decorator by training?" Bill asked.

"I'm self-taught."

"Have you ever taken on a project this big?"

"Actually, no."

"Probably we shouldn't make a hasty decision," Bill said.

"I've brought some pictures of my work," Sara answered.

She handed the loose-leaf binder to Bill, who flipped through it.

"See what I mean," Jack said to his dad.

"Um," the older Morgan answered.

Sara would bet that one way or the other, she wouldn't actually be getting very far into the assignment. Either her association with the Morgan family would end the way it had the first time, or Bill would find a way to obstruct her. For now, she thought it was best to give him an easy out. "We could start on a limited basis. I could do a couple of offices and see if you like my work."

Jack shot her an annoyed look, but Bill smiled like a man who had won a minor victory.

"I appreciate that," the elder Morgan said.

"I'll work up some concepts," Sara said.

When they'd left the building, Jack turned to her. "Why did you suggest starting small?"

"Because he was worried enough about my taking the job to rush over here."

"He said—"

"You don't think Barbara called him, and he dropped everything to meet us?"

Jack was silent, and she wished she hadn't been so direct.

"I don't want to start off on the wrong foot with the company," she said.

"You're not."

"Let's see how he likes my concepts."

"It's not enough that I like your work?"

"He's turning over a lot of control of the company, but the image of Morgan Enterprises is important to him. He wouldn't want anyone to think he decorated the new offices on the cheap. Or that Morgan couldn't afford the best."

Jack nodded. "Perceptive of you."

"I'm trying to see it from his point of view. Actually, I always try to do that with clients."

"You'll give him some drawings that will knock his socks off."

"I'll try." She could have added that Bill Morgan might not like anything she gave him, but she kept the observation to herself.

Jack waited a beat before asking, "Where do you want to eat?"

"I picked last night, and look how it came out. Maybe you should choose."

He laughed, then thought for a minute. "What about Partridge Farm?"

"Sounds good," she agreed. It was a restaurant located in a rural area of the county, in an old house, the same place they'd eaten the last time around. And it was only a ten-minute drive from the office complex.

The car she'd spotted earlier followed at a discreet distance, then drove on past as though the driver hadn't been interested in them at all. Jack didn't seem to notice it, but she suspected he was preoccupied by the run-in with his father. And maybe by her comments, which she wished she'd kept to herself.

They were able to get a table on the patio, shaded by tall oaks and poplars.

"How's the cream of crab soup?" Jack asked the waiter.

"Excellent. And we're having a special on penne pasta with a puttanesca sauce."

They both ordered the soup. Jack got the pasta, and she got chicken and fruit salad for her main dish, then looked at Jack. "I see they have onion rings. I love them, but I don't think I can eat a whole order. Want to share?"

"Great idea."

She wanted to relax and simply enjoy his company after the morning's stress.

But as they ate their soup, he said, "I guess you can see there are some tensions in Morgan Enterprises."

"Yes."

"Dad used to have control of every aspect of the business. He's having trouble delegating responsibilities to Ted—and me."

"Your brother wanted to stay here learning the ropes, and you left to join the army."

He sighed. "Right. So to Dad's way of thinking, I defected."

"Hard on you."

"But I feel like I owe it to the family to give it a try."

"What would you do if you could pick anything you wanted?"

He answered immediately, "Run programs for kids who have physical handicaps."

"You didn't have to think about that very long."

"It's been in the back of my mind."

"Why?"

"It would be something important. And I have some idea of how the kids feel."

"Why don't you do it?"

"I think I have to give Morgan Enterprises a fair shot, first."

"Even if it's not what you want to do?"

He shrugged. "I don't have enough money to finance the program myself. I'd want to build a facility where the kids would be comfortable—and hire a staff. I'd have to do some fundraising for all of that."

"You'd be good at it."

"Fundraising? I'm not sure. I don't love public speaking. Which is what I'd have to do to get donors."

"Or do it in small groups or one-on-one with people who might be interested."

"Who?"

"Local sports figures who want to give back to the community—or attach their names to a worthwhile project. People who had some handicap as children that they overcame."

"Those are interesting ideas." His gaze focused in the distance as his mind worked. "There's a property Morgan Enterprises owns that would be perfect."

"Around here?"

"On Willow Lane. It's got an old house on it now, but the parcel is about fifteen acres. It goes back to the Little Patuxent River."

Willow Lane. She hadn't remembered he'd mentioned it during this conversation. Then it hadn't meant anything to her. Now a little shiver went through her as she recalled the location. That property was where someone had lured Jack—and made it look like he'd fallen off the roof and broken his neck.

It was suddenly hard for her to breathe. She wanted to scream, "Stay away from Willow Lane!" but she couldn't do that. All she could do was try to calm the pounding of her pulse.

Chapter Eight

"Have you talked to your family about your plans?" she managed to say.

"I did ask about maybe using the property, but I made it sound like I wanted to build a house there," he said, his eyes on her. "What's wrong?"

"I just got a piece of crab shell in my soup." She lifted the napkin to her mouth, pretending to remove the shell.

"It's easier to talk to you than it is to them," Jack was saying.

"I'm flattered," she answered, and she was. What she really wanted to say was that if he got away from the environment of Morgan Enterprises, maybe he'd be safe. But she couldn't suggest that. And she certainly hadn't known him long enough to get heavily involved in his decisions.

When the onion rings came, they both reached for one, and their hands met. They both went very still, staring at each other, until they pulled away and he said, "Go ahead and take one."

After they received their main dishes, he took a few bites then said, "The Morgans are having a reception tomorrow night. Would you come with me?"

"What kind of reception?"

"At Mom and Dad's house. They like to give a couple of big parties a year. This is the spring extravaganza."

"It's okay to bring me?"

"I can bring any date I want."

She nodded, knowing that he might have skipped the party if he'd had to be there on his own.

"I'd love to go with you." The part about being with him was true, even when she knew she wasn't going to love the party. But it gave her an opportunity she hadn't considered before.

Last time she'd been intimidated by the grandeur of the Morgan estate and by the high-society guests. This time she could focus on everyone's interactions with Jack.

"Is it very dressy?"

"What passes for casual with the Morgans."

"What time tomorrow?"

"I can pick you up at seven."

"I have to look over a house where I have an upcoming job. But I'll be back home by then."

"Good."

When he drove back to the warehouse, she looked for the car that had ridden their tail. This time it wasn't with them.

What was the purpose of the surveillance? And who had ordered it?

"Thanks for a fun afternoon," she said when he pulled up in front of her door. "Well, it didn't start off as fun."

"I like being with you. Even looking at mug shots."

"I guess the feeling's mutual."

He reached for her, and they kissed. She could feel the passion rising between them.

"I'm not used to moving this fast," she murmured when the kiss finally broke.

"Yes. But I like where we're going," he answered.

"Agreed." She reached for his hand and leaned back in her seat, closing her eyes.

With his free hand, he stroked her lips, the line of her jaw, the column of her neck, his hand coming to rest just above her breasts. Her nipples tightened in response.

"Are you trying to convince me to invite you in?" she asked.

"Maybe. Or maybe I just can't keep my hands off you."

"Don't tempt me too far."

"Then you'd better escape inside."

Reluctantly, she took his advice.

Inside, she stood breathing hard with her back against the door. This was going fast. Even faster than last time. She craved him. And she knew he felt the same. Soon she was going to make love with him, and the thought made her almost giddy.

Ordering herself to cool down, she checked her email. But she kept thinking about Jack. About how to play their encounters.

The thought process made her stomach knot. She shouldn't be "playing" anything. She should just be letting the relationship build naturally. Only that was impossible when there was so much she knew and so much riding on every encounter.

Was there anything she could do to make a better impression on the Morgans?

Maybe a preemptive strike.

Last time good old Bill Morgan had dug up some information on her and presented it to Jack like she'd been hiding something. If she got it out in the open first, maybe that would prevent the blowup they were going to have.

She sighed, hating the way she was second-guessing everything.

For the rest of the day, she focused on inventorying her stock of items on hand—and also noting which were out at various houses.

JACK MORGAN'S NEMESIS SMILED in satisfaction. Jack was going to the party at his parents' house tomorrow. But he'd be able to stand the well-dressed people and the idle chitchat for only so long. There were places he liked to visit when he was at the old homestead. Which presented another opportunity for an accident. Maybe it wouldn't work out. But maybe it would, and then everything would be over. Jack Morgan would be dead, and the world could go on the way it was supposed to.

Nemesis's hands clenched in anger.

Jack had been stupid enough to join the army. Then he'd been sent to Afghanistan. It could have ended there. But the older son had come home to screw everything up.

Now it was time to set things back on their proper course, before everything went wrong.

THE NEXT DAY, SARA WENT to a property she was going to be staging. This was a different kind of assignment. A homeowner was hiring her to help sell the house they were still living in. Which meant her job was to persuade them to put two-thirds of their possessions in storage to show off the sizes of the rooms to the best advantage.

It was a tug-of-war between people who loved every piece of furniture and knickknack they'd accumulated over the past thirty years and Sara's judgment about what needed to be cleared out. By the time she left, they had reached a satisfactory understanding.

She was home in time to lie down for twenty minutes before she had to start getting ready for the party.

Last time she had felt out of place because she'd taken Jack's word for "casual." This time she was going to wear a sophisticated black-and-white sundress and strappy black high-heeled sandals that would be as stylish as anything the other women were wearing.

She showered and washed her hair, then applied a bit more makeup than usual. But not too much, because she didn't want the Morgans to think she was doing anything extra special to impress them.

Jack was right on time, looking good enough to eat in a crisp white shirt and dark slacks.

And he was gazing at her as though he thought the same thing.

"You look fantastic," he said.

"Thanks."

"How did the work go today?" he asked, as he pulled out of the parking lot.

"Fine. I even got a little time to relax." She leaned back in her seat. "Where do your parents live?"

"Glenwood."

"The high-rent district."

"Of course."

She and Jack had grown up in the same county, but they'd been worlds apart. She'd gone to public high school. He'd gone to private schools, first locally, then in Baltimore. She'd gotten a scholarship to the University of Maryland. He'd gone off to Harvard. Which he hadn't told her yet.

Again, she'd have to make sure she didn't trip up and mention something they hadn't talked about.

Fifteen minutes later, they turned in through stone gates and took a winding drive to a huge stone mansion. She peered at the house in the fading light, thinking it would have been at home in the English countryside.

Parking attendants were directing visitors to temporary rows of parking spaces on the lawn, but Jack pulled up in front of the garage next to a caterer's truck and cut the engine.

Turning to Sara, he studied her face. "You look tense."

"I'm fine," she lied. She was thinking that probably one of the people here was planning to kill Jack. Last time she hadn't even realized what was going on until too late. This time she had to figure out who wanted him out of the way.

Of course, it could be someone else. But she was pretty sure that the people with the most likely motives were right here at the mansion.

"Tell me whom I'll be meeting," she said.

"Don't worry about it."

"Indulge me with some hints."

He laughed. "Okay, you already met my father. And my brother, Ted. His fiancée, Janet, will be here. My mom. I'm sure Barbara from the office will also be here. Some other people from the firm. Gary Lambert, our lawyer. Dick Mac-Donald, Dad's broker." He stopped abruptly and looked back at the cars that were already pulled up on the lawn. "Too many to enumerate."

"Right. Sorry. I'm not that good at a million names all at once."

When she climbed out, he came around to her side of the car and took her hand.

His hand was warm and strong, helping to reassure her as they headed for the house.

Inside she heard music and laughter, the tinkle of glasses and classical music playing softly in the background.

The house was furnished in a traditional, fairly formal style. Not what Sara would have picked, but it was very taste-fully done. Doubtless with the help of a decorator.

While Sara usually looked for old furniture she could fix up and use in houses she was staging, many of the pieces she saw in the Morgan mansion were genuine antiques. And the art on the walls was also impressive. There were a number of paintings that could have been hanging in galleries, like the Picasso print over the stone fireplace.

A passing waiter offered them champagne, and they each took a flute. She stayed close to Jack as they strolled through the parlor into a huge sunroom that ran across the back of the house. It was less formal than the rest of the house with comfortable wicker chairs and love seats and a lot of tropi-cal plants. A parrot wouldn't have been out of place among the greenery.

Ted spotted them and came over with a surprised look on his face—before he rearranged his features.

"Sara Carter," he said. "I didn't expect to see you here."

"She's with me. Obviously."

"Obviously. Glad you could make it." He looked over his shoulder as a tall, blonde woman in a black sheath and three-inch heels approached. Her makeup was flawless, and her hair was swept up into a French twist.

"Sara, this is Janet Harrison, Ted's fiancée," Jack said.

"Nice to meet you. I haven't seen you here before."

"Jack and I met a few days ago."

"She's the woman I was telling you about," Ted said. "Who staged the house I showed you yesterday."

Janet's expression brightened. "Your work certainly added to the appeal of the house."

"Are you going to buy it?" Jack asked.

Janet glanced at Ted, looking eager.

"I think so, but I'm still negotiating the price. In this market, I think they're asking a bit too much," he answered.

Jack nodded.

"Dad said something about Sara working on the new office project," Ted said.

"Word gets around fast."

"We should discuss that."

"Did you mean now?" Jack asked.

Ted waved a dismissive hand. "No. This is a party." He turned to Sara. "Please. Enjoy yourself."

"I will," she murmured, thinking that she'd enjoy herself a lot more after they got through the next month—and Jack was all right. No, it was more than that. She wouldn't rest easy until the killer was behind bars.

As the engaged couple stepped away, Jack reached for Sara's hand. "Sorry about that."

"Let's take his advice and enjoy ourselves," she answered, trying to sound like she meant it.

He squeezed her fingers, and she tried to relax. It was easier to meet these people the second time around, not that she enjoyed it any more. But armed with knowledge about them she could evaluate them better.

Like Carolyn Morgan, who was talking to a group of people across the room. She was a woman in her early sixties who dressed well and made up her face carefully. Her gray hair was professionally dyed blond. Probably she'd also had plastic surgery because her skin was firm and smooth.

Sara knew that she was an avid bridge player and also a devotee of recreational shopping.

On the surface, she was gracious and thoughtful. But Sara knew that she thought more about herself and her family than anyone else.

Bill was at her side, the perfect host to her perfect hostess. Yet Sara was sure that he'd told his wife about meeting her at the new offices. Jack might have hired her to decorate the spaces, but they were thinking it was a ploy to keep seeing her, because he didn't want to come right out and date her. And they were already worried that Jack was getting involved with someone who didn't meet the Morgan family's standards.

Or were they really worried he was getting involved with someone who would look askance at their family values? Which were pretty skewed, Sara thought. They had pots of money, which they enjoyed spending. They were also people who looked out for themselves first, and the hell with the rest of the world—unless it fell in with their plans.

If they gave to charities, it was a calculated move to show themselves in a good light. Those assessments might be cynical for people she'd just met. But it wasn't really for the first time. She'd had plenty of opportunity to observe the Morgans and think about their tactics.

When she saw her older son, Carolyn signaled to her husband, and they detached themselves from their group and came over.

"You've already met Dad," Jack said. "This is my mother, Carolyn Morgan."

"Nice to meet you."

"Where are you from?" Carolyn asked.

"I grew up right here in Howard County. I went to Howard High School."

While they were talking to the elder Morgans, Dick Mac-Donald, the broker, joined the conversation. Sara thought of him as a salesman type, always trying to make the most of his social contacts.

He was in his mid-fifties and looked like he'd lost his hair early, then had transplants. His complexion was ruddy, and Sara suspected that he drank a bit too much, not a great trait for someone who handled other people's money.

"So you're self-employed," he said when she told him what she did.

"Yes."

"Have you thought about preparing for your retirement?"

"I've thought about it, but right now I'm plowing money back into my business."

"If you do have some cash to spare, I'd be glad to advise you on investments with excellent returns."

"I thought you were supposed to be wary of any investment that was advertised to pay too much."

He gave her a pained look. "That's only with...unscrupulous brokers."

"Well, then maybe we should talk," she answered. He was one of the Morgans' friends that she hadn't gotten a handle on. She instinctively didn't like him, but that didn't mean he had anything against Jack.

MacDonald had started scanning the crowd, probably looking for more likely prospects. As he headed toward an older man wearing a light summer suit, Sara heard a voice call her name and turned. It was Pam Reynolds.

"I didn't expect to see you here," the real-estate agent said in a surprised voice.

"Jack and I got to know each other when you were showing Ted the property."

"And you skipped out on me," Pam said with a laugh.

"It seemed like the thing to do," Jack answered.

Pam nodded, looking like she wished she'd snared the attention of Jack Morgan.

"Got to talk to Ted about that property," she said and went off to find the brother, leaving them alone until Gary Lambert, the family's lawyer, also came up to them. He was a man about Bill's age, and Sara knew that the two of them had gone to college at the University of Virginia together.

"Good to see you, Jack. Glad you're looking so well," he said in a hearty voice.

"Thanks."

He turned to Sara. "And who is this stunning young lady?"

She flushed as Jack introduced them.

Last time around Sara had had some business with him, on a far less friendly basis. When she'd told the family she was pregnant with Jack's child, Lambert had come at her with some unpleasant legal maneuvers. He might be friendly now, but she knew his affability covered a core of steel—and a stunning ruthlessness. She was praying that she wasn't going to come up against him the way she had last time.

They chatted for a while, before Jack asked her if she wanted something to eat.

The buffet was in the dining room, set up on an antique sideboard and the long Chippendale table. A catering company had been hired for the evening, and uniformed attendants were busy keeping the serving dishes full and taking away used plates and cutlery.

The food was sumptuous. Poached salmon with a dill sauce, roast beef sliced to order, chicken Marsala. One salad included marinated artichokes, olives and hearts of palm and another with sliced tomatoes, basil and fresh mozzarella. There was also asparagus with Parmesan and green beans amandine. Something for everyone.

They made their selections then took their plates out to the patio, where candlelit tables with crisp white cloths had been set up.

"This is quite some party," Sara murmured.

"Mom likes to put on the dog."

"'Put on the dog.' That's a nice way to describe it," she said before taking a bite of the salmon. "Excellent."

"Nothing but the best."

JACK WAS GLAD THAT HE'D INVITED Sara to the party. She was so different from most of the people here, which reminded him how isolated he was. He took all this for granted. The food. The big house. The people. He knew them all, but he didn't exactly fit in. Maybe he never had, which was why he'd joined the army—to make his mark in a completely different world.

He flashed back to his last post—in Afghanistan. He'd been eating cafeteria food in a mess hall and living in a plywood room with a bunch of other guys. And if he wanted to go to the bathroom in the middle of the night, he had to pull on his boots and his coat. That was the hardship part. The danger part was just as pervasive. Finally he'd taken a hit. And been shipped home.

Unfortunately, now he was remembering everything he hated about living here. Or had hated until he'd met Sara. She was a breath of fresh air in his life. And she also made him realize he was letting himself drift. He had to make a decision about his life. Did he really want to spend the next decades working for Morgan Enterprises? Or should he start organizing that program for handicapped kids?

He was certain Sara would approve. His parents would be disappointed. Probably Ted would breathe a sigh of relief.

He'd taken over a lot of the management of the company from Dad, and he didn't love sharing it with his brother.

What if Jack asked Ted to buy him out? How would that work? Or would he be met with resistance? He had the feeling that Ted was hiding something from him about the company. Maybe he should find out what it was before he tried to negotiate any kind of deal.

He glanced at Sara and found her watching him.

"What are you thinking?" she asked.

"Deep thoughts about my life."

"Are you going to share them?"

"This isn't a good time—or place."

Sara nodded, knowing it was a mistake to press Jack. They were at a party, where he was surrounded by people he knew. And she didn't.

As they ate, some of the Morgan family friends and business associates stopped by to talk. This time around, she wasn't scrambling to keep the names and faces straight, so she had the luxury of studying them—while pretending she was only interested in social conversation.

But she could tell that Jack was getting tired of all the people and small talk.

"Why don't I show you around?" he said when they'd finished some of the small pastries and coffee from the dessert table.

After they put their plates and cups on one of the trays stationed around the terrace, Jack led her onto the lawn. It wasn't quite dark yet, but the shadows were lengthening.

This was new. Jack hadn't taken her onto the grounds last time around, and she was interested to see where they were going.

"Did you like living here when you were a kid?" she asked.

"Yes."

"What did you like best?"

"This is a big estate. It backs onto a pretty big creek. There are lots of animals. Squirrels, raccoons, foxes. Sometimes I'd come back here and sit really still, and they'd walk right by me. Ted and I had a tree house near the water. A few times we even spent the night."

"Your mom allowed that?"

"She wasn't happy, but Dad persuaded her it was safe. I wonder if it's still there."

He started off downhill, and she followed. It was dark in the shade of the trees, and she stumbled a few times.

"Maybe we should go back," Jack said.

She glanced up at the dim light still filtering through the trees. "No. That's okay. I'd like to see where you played as a boy."

"It's hard to tell which tree," he muttered as he looked up at the branches.

She tried to help, also looking up, but she was also thinking that being out here alone with Jack might give her a good opportunity to tell him about her father. Get it out in the open before his dad sat him down for a chat about her.

He walked farther into the wooded area, and she followed.

"Found it!" he called out.

She was focused on how to introduce the topic and keeping her eyes on Jack's shoulders. When her foot hit a small concrete ledge in the ground, the obstruction was totally unexpected.

With a scream, she pitched forward, feeling the world rush away beneath her as she dropped below the level of the ground into a dark shaft. One of her shoes fell off, hitting with a splash far below her, and it flashed through her mind that this time she was the one who was going to die.

Chapter Nine

Tree roots broke Sara's fall, slowing her downward tumble. She scrambled to catch one and anchor herself. Finally she hit one large enough to grab on to and came to rest, panting, her evening bag swinging against her side.

She was in a dark shaft. As she tried to get a better grip on the root, a piece broke off and splashed into water far below.

Above her, Jack was shouting her name, his voice frantic.

"Sara. Oh Lord, Sara. Answer me. Sara."

He sounded beyond terrified. For her. But she couldn't speak until breath returned to her lungs.

Gulping in air, she clutched tightly to her perch. Nothing like this had happened before.

"I'm here," she called, hearing her voice echo up the dark shaft.

"Sara?" He was coming closer.

"Yes."

His curse rang out above her.

"Where am I?"

"You're in the old well. It's supposed to be covered. I'd like to know why it's not."

She had a good idea of the answer. Someone had thought Jack might come out here, and they'd set a trap.

Someone who knew he would be at the party.

The light shifted above her, and she knew he must be peering down at her.

"How far did you fall?"

"I'm not sure. There are tree roots. They slowed me. Then I grabbed on to a big one."

"Thank God."

"I don't know how long it will hold."

"I'm going to see if I can get you." She heard scuffling noises as he lay on the ground and reached into the well, then cursed.

"You're too far down. I'm going for help."

Panic shot through her as she felt the root begin to bend under her weight. "No! I mean, I could fall before you got back."

Again he cursed.

"I don't suppose you have a rope."

"No. Wait…maybe I do. Hang on."

She had no choice about that. Grimly she clung to the root, praying that she was going to get out of here.

Or maybe she wouldn't. Maybe she'd been living on borrowed time since she arrived back at the property Pam was showing Ted.

She didn't want to think that was true. But she had no idea what this fall meant.

She struggled to remember the last time she'd been to this party and recalled that Jack had said something about taking her out here.

But he hadn't done it. A woman had come to him. Her brother was in Afghanistan. She'd been worried about his safety, and Jack had talked to her about conditions there.

By the time the conversation was over, it was dark, and he'd decided it wasn't a good idea to go beyond where the grounds were lit.

All of that ran through her mind as she clung to the root, shifting to press her feet against the side of the well to ease the pressure on her arms. She'd lost one of her shoes in the fall, and she carefully slipped the other one off so that her feet would balance against the rough surface of the well's interior. Miraculously, her purse was still dangling from her shoulder.

She had thought Jack would be right back, but as the seconds ticked by she began to fear something had happened to him. Maybe the person who had taken the cover off the well had ambushed Jack out here.

She bit her lip to keep from calling out. If someone else was out there, she didn't want to give herself away.

Could she get out of here herself? She didn't think so.

After an eternity, Jack finally called down to her. "Sara?"

"I'm still here," she answered, unable to repress a hysterical laugh.

"Sorry I took so long. There was a rope hanging from the tree house, but I couldn't get it down."

Panic bubbled inside her. "Then what?"

"I mean I finally did. Sorry. I'm not thinking too clearly. I'm going to lower the rope to you. Tell me when you've got it."

He did, and after a few moments, she felt it bump against her face, then come down lower.

"I felt it."

"Can you tie it around your waist?"

With one cautious hand, she fumbled for the end. It was at her shoulder level, with no length to spare.

"It's not long enough."

She heard him curse softly.

"How long is it?"

"Fifteen feet, I think."

That must be how far she'd fallen.

"Grab the end, and I'll pull you up."

Cautiously, she transferred one hand to the rope, grasping it firmly before she let go of the root with the other hand. When the rope swayed, she gritted her teeth.

"Okay?" Jack called down, and she knew that he'd taken her weight on the upper end of the line.

"Yes, but I'm going to keep my feet braced against one side and my back against the other," she called up.

"Good." As he began to pull on the rope, she walked her feet up the side of the well, feeling the rough brick scrape against her back.

It was agonizingly slow going.

Jack kept reeling in the rope, and she did as much as she could from below.

Perhaps she was three feet from the top when the line lurched and dropped a few inches. She gasped, picturing herself tumbling all the way to the bottom. But she didn't drop any farther.

"Sorry. My hand caught on something sharp."

She sucked in a breath.

He waited a beat before pulling her upward again, this time more slowly.

There wasn't far to go. She could feel the air growing warmer as he pulled her toward the surface. Finally, when she dared to look up, she could see the rim above her.

"Hang on." With one more mighty heave, Jack pulled her over the edge, and she saw him kneeling over her as she flopped out onto the ground.

They were both breathing hard.

"Thank God," he cried out, gathering her close. "Are you all right?"

"Just scared. And maybe a little bruised."

He hugged her to him, and she clung just as tightly.

"I'm sorry," he whispered.

"For what?"

"Taking you out here. It was a dumb idea."

"You didn't know the well was open."

"But—"

"You saved me."

She pressed her mouth to his.

Perhaps in some part of her mind, she had intended it to be a reassuring kiss. Or maybe a simple thank-you.

But as soon as his lips touched hers, the moment turned frantic.

As he held her in his arms, the realization slammed into her that she might have died.

She started to tremble. He was trembling, too, as he ran his hands over her back, her shoulders, gathering her closer, so that she melted against him.

In this reality they had known each other only a few days. But for Sara it was so much longer.

Maybe in some way he knew that, too.

No. That wasn't possible.

Still, he kissed her as though she were precious to him.

When he angled his head first one way and then the other, she made a small, needy sound.

Lying back on the grass, he pulled her on top of himself so that her body sprawled along the length of his.

One of his hands slid down her body, holding her tightly. She felt his erection and moved against him, making her craving for him worse.

She was all raw nerves and desperate feelings that the fall into the well had unleashed.

Needing more, she clasped her arms around his shoulders, pressing her breasts against his chest.

The fall might have ended in disaster. Now she needed to affirm her escape. In Jack Morgan's arms.

As they clung to each other, it was only a small leap to the next step. *He must feel it, too.* The need to claim her for his own.

Somewhere along the line, she had forgotten where they were. Forgotten everything but the man who held her in his arms.

His hands stroked over her back, then down to her hips while he kissed her like a starving man offered a feast.

He worked his hand between them and cupped her breast, then glided his thumb across the beaded nipple.

It felt so good.

How long had it been since he'd touched her like that?

Too long. An eternity.

She might have worked her skirt up and reached for his belt buckle, but a burst of music from the mansion made them both go still. It must be the sound system. Somebody had turned it up for a moment, then quickly adjusted the volume again, but that was enough to inject reality into the moment.

"Sara," he murmured, holding on to her for seconds before he sat up, bringing her with him. "I'm sorry."

"For what?"

"For going too far."

"Did it seem like I was objecting?"

"No." He looked around at the darkened woods. "But this isn't a good place for…" He didn't finish the sentence.

She moved off his lap, running a hand through her hair, removing a twig.

"I must look like a mess," she whispered. "I can't go back to the party."

"Right."

He helped her up. But as he stood, he winced.

"You're hurt."

"I'm fine," he snapped, and she knew he didn't want her to know his injured leg had taken a beating as he'd struggled to get her out of the well.

He swiveled around, staring into the darkness. "I know you want to go home, but do you mind if I take a look around first?"

"Of course not."

"I'd like to see if I can figure out what the hell happened out here, before we arrived."

"Somebody was careless."

"Hard to believe." He dragged in a breath and let it out.

"I need a flashlight. There's one in the garage. We should be able to get in there and out without the guests seeing us."

She wasn't so sure, but she wasn't going to object. It sounded like he thought someone had deliberately taken the cover off the well, which might mean he was starting to think in the right direction.

"My shoes," she whispered.

"What about them?"

"They're in the water down there."

"I'll get you another pair."

"Please, there's no need."

"It's the least I can do."

She could think of a lot more he could do. In fact, she was going to make sure he did it, when they got back to the warehouse. But she wasn't going to share those plans.

Instead, she walked silently with him back toward the house, looking at the blazing lights shining from the huge mansion. The idea of getting anywhere near the party made her stomach churn, but so did staying out here by herself.

They skirted the lit area, as he led her to a side door, which was unlocked.

It led directly to the garage.

Inside, he switched on a light, then walked to the utility shelves along one wall. Tools and other equipment were neatly arranged by somebody who valued order in his life.

"Is this your father's stuff?" she asked.

He laughed. "You don't think he fixes anything by himself, do you?"

"Some executives enjoy hands-on work."

"Not Dad. This is where Bruce, our handyman, keeps his tools."

"Could he have taken the cover off the well?"

"Why would he?"

"I don't know."

Jack took a flashlight off the shelf and led her back the way they'd come.

They had just stepped back out of the garage when a figure blocked their path.

A woman gasped, and Sara realized that they had run into Carolyn Morgan, of all the bad luck.

Chapter Ten

Beside Sara, Jack cleared his throat. "Mom? What are you doing out here?"

"Going out to see if the caterers have more dessert in the truck. They're running out of it in the kitchen." She gave them a careful inspection, and Sara had to keep from finger-combing her hair or smoothing out her dress.

But she couldn't stop from moving her arm, which brought Carolyn's attention to her.

"What have you been doing?" she asked, taking a better look at Sara's disheveled appearance.

"I was showing Sara the property, and she fell down," Jack answered.

Mrs. Morgan's expression looked a shade less hostile until her gaze dropped to Sara's feet. "What happened to your shoes?"

"Lost them in the fall," Jack said.

"This is sounding very odd."

"We're going out to have a look for them," Jack said, holding up the flashlight.

Which probably didn't help, Sara thought. Probably his mother assumed they'd been rolling around on the ground and misplaced her shoes. Maybe Carolyn even assumed she and Jack were high on drugs.

She wanted to say, "It's not what you think." But she knew the protest would only make it worse.

"You'd better get those desserts," Jack said. With his free hand, he knit his fingers with Sara's, and they started back down the hill. But she could feel Mrs. Morgan's gaze burning into her back.

"You know what she thinks we were doing," she whispered.

"Do you care?"

"Actually, yes. With you, it doesn't matter so much, but for me it doesn't make a good impression, and I want your parents to like me."

"Don't worry about it."

She did worry, but she didn't keep arguing. He'd been secure in his place in the family for years, and he wasn't going to understand her point of view.

They were more cautious as they walked back to the shade of the trees. Jack played the light around the grass.

"Footprints," he said, pointing.

"They could be yours."

"Yeah." He searched for a little while longer. "But they lead off this way." He followed the trail and found the wooden top that should have covered the well. It was several yards away, half-hidden in a raspberry thicket.

"I don't think a fox dragged it," he said.

"I guess not. What do you think it means?"

He shrugged. "Nobody knew we were coming out here. I mean, it was a spur-of-the-moment thing."

"Uh-huh." She racked her brain for a way to make something more specific of it but couldn't think of anything that would sound plausible.

They returned to the garage, where he replaced the flashlight. And she was thankful that they didn't run into any other guests.

As they drove away, she breathed out a little sigh. But the closer they got to the warehouse, the more she felt her nerves jumping.

Maybe Jack's were, too, because the moment was ripe with possibilities.

When he pulled up at the loading dock, she said, "Come in."

"Yes."

She got out, glad that she hadn't lost her evening bag. There wasn't much inside because she hadn't been driving herself to the party, but she did need her key to get back into the warehouse.

They stepped into the shadowy storage area, and she led him down the central aisle to her apartment where she'd left one lamp burning.

She'd been thinking about inviting him in before she'd left. The room was straightened up. And the lamp cast a warm, inviting glow on her eclectic furnishings.

He stood looking around a little uncertainly. Likely he would chicken out if she didn't press the issue.

"All during the party, I was thinking about being alone with you." Reaching for him, she wrapped him in her arms, holding tight. For a moment he held himself stiffly, and she knew why. He was worried about what she would think when she saw his body.

It was going to make her think of everything he had endured, but she couldn't tell him that.

"Jack, don't fight what's between us."

"We haven't known each other very long."

That might be true for him. Not for her. Again she couldn't explain that. Instead, she said, "It feels to me like I've known you for ages."

Her heart was pounding so hard that she thought it might break through the wall of her chest as she waited to hear what he would say.

It was only one word. "Yes." Spoken in a voice rough with emotion.

"Because this is so right," she answered.

His resistance crumbled. With a sound low in his throat, he slanted his mouth over hers. His lips touched down, settled. And then he was devouring her the way he had after he'd rescued her.

His response thrilled her to the marrow of her bones. Finally, after all this time, he was in her arms, kissing her with uncensored emotions. She had been longing for this moment since she'd realized where she was. And when.

Or had she been waiting for centuries?

Was this the wrong thing to do? So early in their relationship? She didn't think so. And it didn't matter because she couldn't stop now. Not when she knew how much the two of them had meant to each other.

No, what they would mean to each other. This was only the start of something extraordinary.

With her eyes closed, she held on to him as they swayed together, neither of them steady on their feet.

Needing more of him, she reached around him, tugging at the bottom of his dress shirt, pulling it from his slacks so that she could slip her hands under the shirt and flatten her palms against the heated flesh of his back.

He drew in a sharp breath when she moved her fingers against him.

It had been like this before. With her taking the lead because she'd sensed his reserve. Now that she understood better where it came from, she had no intention of letting it stop her from getting what she craved. What they both craved.

She wanted him naked, but she also wanted him so hot that it would be impossible for him to refuse her. And she knew she was halfway there because she could feel his erection pressing against her middle.

She wanted to unbuckle his belt, lower his zipper and reach inside to clasp him. But she knew that was much too bold. Instead she swayed in his arms, moving her body against his, tantalizing both of them with the friction of it.

"I don't want to stop," he whispered.

"Neither do I."

"I need to tell you…"

She raised her face, her gaze meeting his.

He swallowed. "I've got some scars that aren't very pretty."

"Do you think I care about that?"

"You haven't seen them."

She was so drunk with arousal that she almost told him that she had.

Instead, she reached for the buttons at the front of his shirt, undoing them, until the sides of the shirt hung open. Pushing the fabric aside, she touched his chest, tracing the line of a scar, then bending to follow her finger with her lips.

"Medals of honor."

He made a snorting sound.

"And you worked hard to get yourself back into shape."

"Reasonable shape."

"You're a hero. In so many ways."

"I don't think of myself that way."

He stopped protesting as she found his nipples, tracing circles around them, then replacing one of her fingers with her tongue, tasting him, reveling in the puckered texture of the nubs and the shiver that went through him.

She stepped away so that she could toss throw pillows onto the floor, then turn back the coverlet.

"Can you unzip my dress?" she asked, her voice barely under her control.

"Yes."

When she turned around, he lowered the zipper. Baring her back.

The sundress was the kind that made a bra unnecessary. She tugged down the front, exposing her breasts. Then she pulled the dress the rest of the way down so that she was wearing nothing but her sheer panties.

Still standing behind her, Jack made a strangled sound,

reaching around her, his hands cupping her breasts, taking their weight in his hands.

She leaned against him, arching her back as he stroked his thumbs over her nipples, wringing a little sob from her.

"That's so good," she managed to say.

"Oh, yes."

She remained against him as he played with her breasts, before stroking one hand farther down her body, into her panties, then into the slick, wet folds of her most intimate secrets.

He pressed her back against himself, one hand at her breasts, the other at her sex, giving her pleasure beyond imagining.

Maybe he wanted to push her over the edge, to give himself an excuse to stop there. Before he could tease her any further, she turned in his arms, undoing his belt buckle, then lowering his fly so that she could reach into his pants and clasp her hand around him.

He dragged in a ragged breath as she stroked him, pushing him past the point where he was going to object to her looking at his mangled leg, or anything else.

She brushed his shirt off of his shoulders, then dragged his pants and underwear down, clasping his naked body to hers.

They clung together for a breathless moment before she eased them both onto the bed.

He came down on top of her, kissing her, stroking her, saying her name.

Opening her legs, she guided him to her, and they both cried out as he claimed her.

He looked down at her in wonder, and she was sure he only half believed that they were doing this.

She thrust against him, and he answered her, the intensity building between them into an explosion of pleasure and satisfaction she had never imagined.

Not last time and not now.

He followed her into ecstasy, clinging to her, his breath

ragged, and she stroked the damp skin of his back, so grateful for this time together.

He rolled off of her, flopping to his back, turning his head toward her.

She reached for his hand, linking her fingers with his and holding tight, and he answered the pressure. Having him in her bed again was a miracle. She wanted to weep with the joy of it, but she held back the tears as she lay beside him.

"I'm glad you…trusted me enough for that," she murmured.

"I've been alone for a while."

She nodded against his shoulder.

"I didn't take you to the party expecting to end up in your bed," he said.

"Of course not. You don't do things because you make calculations."

"How do you know?"

"I know you better than you think."

"I'm transparent?"

"You're honorable. A man with integrity. Smart. And nice. That's important, too."

"That's how you see me?"

"How do you see yourself?"

He hesitated for a moment, then said, "Damaged."

"No. You have a lot going for you. And I'll bet you worked like a demon getting yourself back into shape. You don't even walk with a limp."

She held his hand more tightly, wondering how much she dared say to him. "Do you believe in reincarnation?" she asked.

"I don't know."

"I can't stop thinking that we've known each other intimately…in another life. Do you sense it?"

"I think so," he answered, and she let out the breath she'd been holding. "It seemed like fate that we met. I mean, I might

not have gone to that trophy house with Ted. I didn't want to
see the damn thing, but I had the feeling there was a reason
I should go. And there you were."

She raised up, sitting beside him, tracing the line of the
jagged scar that snaked down his leg.

He winced.

"Am I hurting you?"

"No."

She looked down at his body. "You don't have to hide
from me."

"It's hard to...realize that."

She swallowed. "We're good for each other, but your parents aren't going to think so."

"You're sure of that?"

"They have high standards for the Morgan family."

"How do you know?"

"It's an educated guess." She swallowed hard before saying, "I'll bet your father started having me investigated as
soon as you introduced us."

His expression darkened. "Oh, come on."

"Do you want to make a bet?" she heard herself say. "He's
going to dig up something about my family that doesn't sound
real good."

"What?"

She hadn't wanted to tell him like this, but now she felt
compelled to say, "That my father was in jail."

"Was he?"

"Yes."

"For what?"

Her mouth was so dry she could hardly speak, but she
managed to say, "Grand larceny."

"Uh-huh."

"Jack, I'm sorry. I guess you didn't want to hear that. I
mean that your father's going to tell you about it."

"I don't like the conviction in your voice."

She winced. Making love with him had been wonderful. Now they'd gotten off on the wrong foot. Or the wrong tone. Which was her fault.

She'd been going to talk about her family background, tell him what his father was going to find out. And somehow it had seemed like an attack on the Morgans.

"I should go," he said.

"Jack…"

She pressed her lips together, silently damning herself for saying anything about his family. She'd named some of his attributes. She should have remembered "loyalty."

She watched him get up and pull on his clothes.

Moments ago she'd been so happy to have him in her bed. Now he was leaving because she'd made a stupid mistake.

It couldn't be over, could it?

Icy fear clutched at her as he walked out of her apartment and through the warehouse.

Chapter Eleven

On shaky legs Sara got up and pulled on the T-shirt and yoga pants that she'd hung in the armoire before she'd gotten dressed for the party.

She tried to hold in the tears burning the backs of her eyes, but she lost the battle as she made her way across the warehouse and looked out the door. The spot where Jack's car had sat was empty.

Of course. What did she think, that he'd changed his mind and was only sitting out there preparing to come back in?

Her hand trembled as she locked the door, then leaned back against it, struggling to stop her tears and catch her breath.

"What a mess," she whispered, as she swiped a hand across her face.

Nothing like this had happened last time. Which meant that the story she was telling herself was completely off the rails.

Maybe she *was* crazy, and she'd had a dream about meeting Jack Morgan. About being pregnant with his baby. Trying to drive herself to the hospital.

No. She shook her head. She couldn't explain it away. She knew too much—considering she hadn't even known Jack Morgan until she'd met him at that house Pam was trying to sell to Ted.

She went back over the past twenty minutes, trying to see where she had gone wrong.

It wasn't difficult to realize that if she'd just kept her mouth shut about the Morgans, Jack would still be lying on her bed, warm and comfortable. But she'd taken a fateful step down the wrong path, then another and another because she'd wanted to beat Bill Morgan to the punch with the damaging information about her father.

And now Jack was gone.

Was he coming back? She had no way of knowing. Maybe she'd ruined everything.

She clenched her fists as all sorts of scenarios went through her mind. What if he was safe now? What if the only reason somebody was going to kill him was that he was with her?

If she was out of the picture, he'd be all right. If that were true, she'd give him up, she thought with a terrible pang. Only she couldn't make herself believe that.

But then what?

She dug her nails into her palms. He'd walked out the door, and what could she do about it?

She couldn't call him up and beg him to come back. That would certainly turn him off. Pursuing him would only confirm his family's conviction that she was out for the Morgan money.

A laugh bubbled in her throat.

Nothing was the same, except that she'd met Jack and knew she loved him. Once again everything was turning into a horrible mess. Maybe this time it only applied to her—not to Jack.

She tottered back to her apartment and lay down on the bed, reaching for the pillow that Jack had used. And as she hugged it to herself and breathed in his scent, the tears returned.

Their relationship had been so new. But not for her. She'd presumed too much, because she knew too much.

Maybe she'd get a chance to rectify that, and maybe she wouldn't.

JACK LEFT THE WAREHOUSE with a hollow feeling in his chest. Since he'd first met Sara, he'd sensed something between them he couldn't put into words. She'd made him feel more alive than he had felt any time since coming home from Afghanistan. That had been enough to let him trust her.

Or maybe it was easier to explain. Maybe his physical needs had finally overwhelmed him, and he'd given in to the desire to make love with her.

And it had been magic. More than he ever could have imagined. Then she'd started talking about his family like she knew them better than he did, and he'd felt a sudden chill.

He hadn't known what to say, exactly. So here he was in his car, driving away and wondering if he was ever going to see her again.

He'd asked her to decorate the new offices. But they hadn't signed any kind of contract. Really, they'd just talked about it. The only fleshed-out idea they'd discussed was the lunchroom. Did he have to go ahead with that?

He made a snorting sound. It would be pretty shabby of him if he changed his mind without a good reason.

Was her opinion of his family a good enough reason to cancel the offer?

Maybe. But it wouldn't make him feel very good.

JACK'S NEMESIS HAD REASON to be angry. The trick with the well cover had taken some effort and netted nothing. Jack was still walking around, instead of lying in a broken heap at the bottom of the well.

That little home decorator, Sara Carter, had been with him. And they'd come back to the party looking disheveled. Had he fallen in the well and she'd gotten him out? Or maybe it was the other way around.

Too bad there was no way of knowing what had happened out there.

But maybe there was better news on another front. Jack

had been really thick with the Carter woman. But he'd left her place pretty quickly after driving her home from the party.

Maybe that little affair was over and the woman was no longer a factor. Jack would have to rely on his own resources to save his life. And if he had no idea what was going on, he wouldn't be prepared for trouble.

Nemesis grimaced.

Too bad for Jack that he'd gotten injured in Afghanistan and gotten shipped home. If he hadn't been in the wrong place at the wrong time, he might have stayed in the army where his talents were appreciated.

Because he certainly had no talent for business.

He didn't belong here, and he would have to be eliminated, one way or the other.

WORK HAD ALWAYS BEEN a refuge for Sara. The next morning she was going through her filing cabinet looking for the sketches she'd made for a house she was scheduled to stage.

As she riffled through the folders, the tab of one caught her eye and she went stone still. It said "Morgan Office Project."

She hadn't done any work on the project, not since she'd made the mistake of talking to Jack about his family. But here was a folder she'd set up.

With a trembling hand, she pulled it out and opened it. As soon as she saw the sketches, her breath caught.

These were the pictures she'd come right home and drawn after the first time Jack had taken her to the office. Before his father had said that it was too big an undertaking for an amateur like her.

It was spooky to thumb through the sketches now and remember how excited she'd been about working with Jack on the Morgan building.

For the lobby, she'd used a Maryland theme. With a huge statue of a crab, fishnets, a lighthouse, seascapes and mallard ducks from the Eastern Shore.

Jack had loved them. His father had hated them and suggested she try something else.

Her eyes misted at her long-ago enthusiasm. And the way her hopes had been dashed. In so many ways.

When a tear splattered onto one of the sheets, she wiped it away and shoved the pictures back into the folder.

For a moment she thought about taking them to the sink and burning them. But she stopped herself and put them back where she'd found them.

JACK SPENT THE NEXT TWO DAYS trying to convince himself that he'd done the right thing by walking away from Sara's accusations. That theory started to fall apart when he'd gotten a call from his father.

"I'm glad I caught you," Dad had said in that fake hearty voice that Jack remembered from his childhood. It hadn't fooled him then, and it didn't fool him now. "Can you come over?"

"Why?"

"We want to talk to you about something."

"Can we do it over the phone?"

"We'd prefer that you come over," his father had said, his tone becoming firmer.

"Sure," Jack had answered, hating himself for caving in, yet interested to find out what his parents wanted.

Now here he was stepping into the front hall of the Morgan mansion. Once this place had been his home. It didn't feel like it anymore.

His father came striding down the hall from the back of the house. "Thanks for coming over."

"You wanted to talk to me about something?"

"Let's sit down."

Dad turned and disappeared down the hall again. When they arrived in the sunroom, he expected to see his mother waiting. But the room was empty.

She appeared moments later, with Ted's fiancée, Janet, at her side.

Jack stared at her in surprise, and she looked like he was the last person she wanted to meet up with. "Are you part of the discussion?" he asked.

"What?"

"Did you come here to talk with me, Mom and Dad?"

She shook her head. "No. I didn't expect to see you this morning. I came here to talk to your mother about the wedding plans."

Jack stared at her, wondering if she was telling the truth. What were the odds that they'd both been summoned this morning?

Janet turned and hugged his mom. "I'll look over those menus, and we'll talk soon."

"Thank you, dear," Carolyn answered, and Jack wondered if they'd really been talking about him, but nobody was going to admit it.

He brought himself up short, attempting to cancel the paranoid thoughts. The world didn't revolve around him, after all.

Or maybe this morning it did.

He settled into one of the wicker chairs, waiting to find out what his parents wanted to discuss.

"You're looking well," his mother said. "How is your leg doing?"

"All right. Did you ask me over to question me about my health?"

"No," his father answered.

When he and Carolyn Morgan exchanged glances, Jack tensed.

"It's about that woman you've been seeing. Sara Carter."

Struggling to keep his voice even, he asked, "What about her?"

"She's not exactly qualified to decorate the new Morgan

Enterprises offices. That's not her job. She only sets up rooms in model homes."

"If you saw the work she's done, you might change your mind."

"You shouldn't have hired her without consulting your father or your brother," Carolyn said.

Jack looked at his father. "You wanted me to take more interest in the firm."

"Yes, but you've been away a long time," his father said. "You can't just come back and make big decisions."

"Hiring a decorator is a big decision?"

"The offices make an impression on business associates."

Sara had told him that would be his father's attitude.

"So you're asking me to fire her?" he asked in a tight voice.

"There's something else you need to know."

Jack clasped his hand over the arm of the chair, waiting, afraid he knew what he was going to hear.

"Her background is questionable," his mother said.

"In what way?"

"Her father died in prison."

Jack sucked in a breath and let it out. "Are you saying you had her investigated?"

His father shifted in his seat. "We did a background check on her."

"Did you do that when Ted started dating Janet?"

"Of course not." His mother's voice had taken on an outraged tone.

"Why not?"

"Do we have to get into that?"

"You're the one who started the conversation."

Carolyn sighed. "Because we've known Janet since she was a little girl. We know her family. They go to our church. There wasn't any question that she's suitable for Ted."

"Did you share that insight with him?"

"Jack, stop questioning us about our motives. We only want the best for both of our sons."

"Sure."

"There's no need to get sarcastic," his father snapped.

His mother was more conciliatory. "I know the information about Sara must be a shock," his mother said.

"As a matter of fact, it's not."

Both parents gave him a questioning look.

"She told me."

That got wide-eyed, jaw-dropping reactions from both of them.

"Why would she do that?" his father finally asked.

"Probably because she thought you'd investigate her background," Jack said in a clipped voice. "And she wanted to tell me first. Is that the worst thing you could find about her?"

"Her mother was a shopkeeper."

"I guess she had to support her daughter after her husband went to jail. That's a strike against her?"

"She's just not of our social class," his mother blurted.

"You think that makes a difference to me?"

"It should," she answered. "And what were the two of you doing at the party, rolling around on the lawn?"

"We weren't rolling around on the lawn."

"Then what were you doing?"

Jack stood up. "I think this discussion is over."

His father also stood. "Son, we're only trying to keep you informed. You're interested in this woman, right? Are you sure she's totally honest?"

"Yes, I'm interested in her. And yes, I think she's totally honest," he bit out before turning and walking toward the door.

"Jack, come back here," his mother called.

He kept walking.

He'd always had a certain image of his parents. They were a little bit stiff. Proud of their position in the community.

Sure that they were right. But he hadn't thought of them as underhanded.

Well, he guessed that from their point of view, they were trying to make sure their son didn't date an unsuitable woman.

But Sara had anticipated their reaction to her. He'd been outraged when she'd said they were going to dig into her life. Now he needed to apologize to her, if she was willing to speak to him again.

He could have called her. But he wanted to see her. After leaving the mansion, he drove to the warehouse. At the top of the steps, he pressed the buzzer and stood with his heart pounding. When there was no answer, his heart began to pound even harder. Had something happened to her? Or was Sara refusing to see him?

He wouldn't blame her for that.

He called her name.

Still no answer.

It was then he noticed a plastic envelope hanging on a hook next to the door. Inside was a notice that Sara was out staging a house. The sheet gave an address off Old Montgomery Road.

Jack copied down the information, then climbed back into his car and drove to the house, which turned out to be a standard developer model that was now on the resale market.

As he rounded a bend in the street, he saw her truck in the driveway and also her car. A sigh of relief trickled out of him.

She was here. He could apologize.

After pulling up at the curb, he got out and took a deep breath before starting up the walk.

The front door and storm door were propped open, probably so Sara could carry things in and out.

When he stepped inside, his gaze went to her. She was wearing jeans and a Ravens T-shirt.

Her hair was mussed, and she wore no makeup, but she was the most beautiful sight he had ever seen.

He started toward her, then realized she wasn't alone. She was working with two well-built young men, directing the placement of a sofa between two windows.

Sara looked up at him, and the expression on her face wasn't exactly welcoming.

Chapter Twelve

Sara's heart started to pound.

Jack. She searched his face, seeing his wary expression. Which meant what, exactly?

The last time they'd been together, he'd accused her of bad-mouthing his family.

Her throat had turned so dry that it was difficult to speak without first clearing it. "Jack. What are you doing here?"

"I need to talk to you."

"About what?" she asked, noting that her two helpers were following the exchange with interest.

Jack glanced at their audience, then back to her. "Can we speak in private?"

She nodded, then turned to Pete and Brad.

"I'll be right back. When you get the sofa placed, bring in the Hepplewhite end tables and the Eastlake marble-topped chest."

Then she turned toward the back of the house, leading Jack through the kitchen and out onto a back deck.

When she faced him, she saw the tension in his features.

"I'm sorry," he said, reaching for her.

She could have stepped away. Instead she came into his arms, clinging to him.

"Jack," she murmured, closing her eyes and hanging on to him. "Oh, Jack."

She lifted her head, and he lowered his. Their lips met in a kiss that was full of emotion. Relief. Gratitude. Apology. They were all there. All mixed together.

She wasn't sure what would have happened if they'd been at the warehouse. But they were in the backyard of a house she was staging. And her helpers could walk back here at any moment. For that matter, neighbors might be looking out the window.

When he lifted his head, she took a half step back.

He found her hands, holding tight.

"You were right," he said. "I got an earful from my parents about you."

"How did that make you feel?"

"Angry at them. And mad at myself for not trusting you."

"I could have been way off base."

"You weren't. How did you figure it out?"

She swallowed. "I've been on edge since I met you."

"I noticed."

"I mean, I've felt like meeting you was the best thing that ever happened to me. And at the same time I was worried."

He nodded.

"This is going to sound weird."

"Try me."

She hadn't been sure what was going to come out of her mouth, but she needed a plausible story, and the only thing that made any sense was something close to the truth. Well, a lie, but maybe a plausible lie.

"I went into D.C. last year for a museum show. To get some ideas for rooms. There was a street fair, and on a whim, I stopped at a fortune-teller's booth." She raised her face and looked at him.

"She started talking about my future, and at first I thought it was a bunch of, you know, bologna. I rolled my eyes when she said I was going to meet a man who would be very important to me. We were perfect for each other. I mean, isn't that the kind of thing they usually say? Stuff they think you'll want to hear."

She gripped his arms. "But she didn't keep on in that vein. She said you were in danger. That someone would be trying to kill you, and I had to help you find out who it was and stop them."

He stared down at her, obviously shocked. "She said all that?"

"Yes. And of course I didn't want to believe the bad part."

"Who was she, exactly?" he asked.

"I don't know. I mean, I saw a fortune-teller tent, and I went in. On a whim. Which isn't like me. I don't do things impulsively," she added, feeling like she was digging herself into a deeper hole.

The truth trembled on the edge of her tongue, but if she told him the truth, then he'd really think she was crazy. And this was the best she could do.

"And she also talked about my family?"

"Some. She said they wouldn't think I was suitable for you. Which set me up to worry about that."

"Yeah."

She waited a beat before going on.

"I'm not the kind of person who runs my life by what I heard from a fortune-teller. But what she said stuck with me. And when we met—it was like fate bringing us together. Or what she'd predicted was coming true. But then I started getting nervous. And when we left the restaurant, that guy came at you with a gun."

"That was a robbery. We found him in the book of mug shots."

"You think that we just happened into a felon who needed money?"

"What else?"

"Suppose someone sent him."

"Why?"

"I wish I knew. But that wasn't the only bad thing that happened. There was the well at your parents' house."

"An accident."

"How did the cover end up being taken off?"

When he didn't answer, she continued, "What if you were the one who was supposed to fall in?"

"That's a lot of assumptions."

"I know. Which is why I didn't say anything."

A sound from the doorway made her jump, and she looked up to see Brad staring at them.

"I'm sorry," he said. "We're finished with the big pieces in the living room. What did you want us to do next?"

"Take the bed to the master bedroom, and set it up."

Jack watched her helper leave. "This isn't a good time for a discussion."

"Unfortunately."

"When will you be finished?"

She looked at her watch. "Probably around three."

"I can come back here."

"Come to the warehouse. I can fix you dinner."

"In that little kitchen?"

"You'd be surprised what I can do. What about five?"

"Is there anything I can bring?"

"We could probably use a bottle of wine."

"White or red?"

"Do you like chicken?"

"Yes."

"Then white."

"I'll see you later."

When he left, she breathed out a little sigh. He hadn't rejected her story out of hand. But she'd have to be careful not to come across as too crazy when she tried to get Jack to take a proactive role in saving his own life.

She walked to the front of the house, watching him drive

away, wishing she wasn't reduced to telling lies. But she couldn't come up with any alternative.

JACK DROVE SLOWLY AWAY FROM the house that Sara was staging. Of all the things he'd expected to hear, it wasn't her story about the fortune-teller.

But, taken at face value, it did explain her somewhat strange behavior. And yeah, there were people who put a lot of stock in that kind of thing. She'd said she wasn't one of them. She'd also said this instance was different.

He made a rough sound. The kind of people who believed in mumbo jumbo weren't the ones he usually hung out with.

Then he thought about the time he and Sara had spent together. Like when they'd made love. It had been fantastic. But what if she wanted him to think so? What if she was making calculated moves?

Clenching his hands on the wheel, he ordered himself to cut off his paranoid thoughts.

He sensed that Sara liked him a lot. More than liked. And she seemed genuinely concerned about him. Unless she had some ulterior motive.

He guessed he'd have to listen to what she had to say and see how it came across.

Well, it was more than that. She wanted him to think about who might have it in for him. He wanted to answer "nobody," but maybe he'd better try to wrap his head around the concept.

The nearest liquor store was a couple of miles away. Truth be told, he didn't know much about wine. But he was sure the clerk could give him some decent advice.

He let his eyes flick to the rearview mirror. A car followed close behind, and it stuck with him as he headed down Old Montgomery Road.

Waiting until a light was about to turn red, he zipped through on the yellow, then made a right into a development, where he wound his way through several residential streets before coming out on the highway again.

Satisfied that no one was behind him, he made the run to the liquor store, then headed for home.

The same car picked him up on Route 144 again, which meant that whoever it was knew where he lived.

Not exactly reassuring.

The car didn't follow him up his driveway, however.

Once inside the house, he locked the door and went to the locked drawer where he kept a SIG Sauer automatic pistol. He checked the gun. Then, feeling a little weird, he took it into the bathroom with him while he showered and got dressed.

Interesting how quickly his view of his own safety had changed.

SARA WAS SURE OF ONLY ONE THING. Jack was going to like her chicken cacciatore. It was the first meal she'd made for him last time, and he'd loved it.

The first time around, he'd asked her to go to a movie, and she'd asked him over to dinner first.

They'd never made it to the movie. Instead they'd ended up in her bed, where they'd spent a very memorable evening.

This time, she had vital business to discuss with him.

Her nerves were jumping as she shopped for the ingredients she didn't have on hand—chicken, green pepper, onions and mushrooms. There was a lot riding on this meal, and not just whether Jack Morgan liked her cooking.

Back in her little kitchen, she began chopping vegetables. The simple work helped calm her. As she sautéed onions, green peppers and mushrooms, she thought about what she was going to tell Jack. And what she hoped to accomplish.

After getting the chicken, tomato sauce and vegetables simmering in the skillet, she took a quick shower, then made a salad, using a bag of prepared greens, plus tomatoes, cucumber and a fresh, simple dressing.

As she worked, she kept glancing at the clock. Jack was late, and she started to worry that he'd changed his mind. Or—

She stopped herself from going there. The killer hadn't pounced. This was weeks before he'd been killed. They still had time.

Or did they?

She was fighting down panic when the door buzzer sounded around ten after five, and she rushed through the warehouse to let him in.

"I was starting to worry," she blurted before she could stop herself.

"Sorry. There was an accident on Route 144. And people were slowing down to gawk." Switching the subject, he said, "Something smells good."

"My chicken cacciatore. It's ready."

He followed her into the apartment, where she'd set the small table at the edge of the kitchen area.

"The table's small, so we can take our food from the stove and the counter," she told Jack.

They each took helpings of the salad and the main dish, which she served over penne pasta. At the table, Jack opened the wine and poured it into antique stemware she'd gotten at an auction.

"This *is* good," he said after taking a bite.

"I love cooking. If I had a bigger kitchen, I'd do it more."

"How did you learn?"

"My mom taught me some things. I learned others by looking through cookbooks and following the recipes."

He ate appreciatively before asking, "What else do you like to make?"

"Chili, spaghetti sauce. A lot of different soups. There are people who aren't inspired to cook for one. But I hate eating prepared food. And cooking helps me unwind. I like fixing things that I can eat for several days." She took a bite and swallowed. "We're stalling."

"Yeah."

"Can you tell me who might want to kill you?"

"That's pretty blunt."

"I feel like I don't have a choice."

"Then make some suggestions."

She caught the hostility in his tone. He didn't like this exercise.

Neither did she, really. She knew all the players. She'd tried to analyze their relationships to Jack and what they stood to gain from his death. In fact, she could offer plenty of suggestions, but they wouldn't really make sense for the amount of time she'd known him. And she remembered what had happened when she'd said anything negative about his parents. "You know the people. I don't."

"You met them at my parents' house," he shot back.

She wanted to scream at him that she wasn't doing this to make him feel uncomfortable—or disloyal. And she wasn't doing it to herself because it was some kind of game. This was deadly serious. And his life was on the line.

With a grimace, she scraped back her chair and stood up, paced to the apartment door and stood there for long moments before she felt composed enough to speak.

When she came back, she stood beside him and laid a hand on his shoulder, thinking how much she loved touching him, and wondering how long that would be possible. "I guess you don't want to do this."

His voice was strained as he said, "I don't want to think that somebody wants to kill me."

The words and his tone squeezed her heart. "Nobody would, and I hate making you do it. But I think you have to." She pulled her chair around so that she was sitting close to him, then laid her hand over his. "Jack, please. Make yourself consider what could be going on."

He gave her a dark look. "Okay. How about this. Nobody expected me to come home and join the company. It could be anyone who finds that inconvenient. And that's a lot of people. So you have to think about who would be ruthless enough to want me out of the way."

"Or desperate enough," she added.

Names ran through her head. She couldn't discount his brother, Ted. Or what about Janet, Ted's fiancée? Before Jack had come home, she'd thought her husband was going to control Morgan Enterprises. And suddenly there was his brother back in the picture, taking half the money. Sara thought the woman had an enormous sense of entitlement, but was she ruthless enough to get the brother out of the way?

And what about Jack's parents? She hated to put them on her personal suspect list, but did they resent his coming back? It was hard to believe they'd want to eliminate their own son. But they did favor Ted. Maybe one of them had been relieved when Jack had chosen another career. Now he was back and changing the dynamics of the family—and the company. Did one of them want Jack out of the way?

She shuddered.

"What?"

"I can't speculate without something concrete. What if we went to Morgan Enterprises and poked around in the computer system? Do you think we'd find anything?"

"Maybe. I don't know." He scraped back his chair. "If we're going to do it, we should go over there before I change my mind."

"Oh, Jack." She stood, then reached for him and pulled him into her arms, holding tight to him. She ached to give up her wild plan and take him to her bed instead. But that would get her only temporary reassurance and pleasure.

And in truth, she had the feeling that if she led him toward the bed, he would resist. Since she'd suggested that someone might want to do him harm, she'd felt a subtle wall between them. Probably he still wasn't sure of her motivation. It wasn't like they had a long-standing relationship. He'd known her less than a week, and she'd started making accusations.

The best thing would be if she could back them up.

Still, she clung to him for heartbeats before she eased away. "Just let me put the food into the refrigerator."

"I'll do the plates."

They worked together well, with her covering the serving bowls and putting them away while Jack rinsed the dishes and stacked them in the sink.

"Do you have a gun at home that you could bring?" she asked.

"I do have a gun. In the bedside table. But I'm not taking it. If someone saw us there, I don't want them to find out I'm armed."

She wanted to argue, but she knew that when Jack was sure of something, he wasn't likely to change his mind.

Instead she asked, "Isn't there a surveillance system in the building? And what about guards?"

"There are no guards that work exclusively for Morgan Enterprises. My dad's too cheap to hire them."

"Isn't he afraid of—" she flapped her arm "—I don't know, corporate theft?"

"He does have a surveillance system. But we can turn it off."

"Okay."

She thought for a moment. "If you leave fingerprints in the building, it won't matter, because you go there frequently. But it's different with me."

She crossed to her dresser and took out a pair of leather gloves. Also a small LED flashlight.

"Good idea," he said, as they exited the warehouse.

The old Morgan Enterprises building was also in Ellicott City, in an office park that had once been fashionable but had now fallen into disfavor. Which was why the company was moving to the Columbia location.

As Jack drove, Sara kept an eye on the view behind them.

"You're thinking we're being followed?" Jack asked, as he turned off the highway into the office-complex area.

"I hope not." She cleared her throat. "But maybe we shouldn't pull up in the parking lot."

"Where did you get your spy training?" Jack asked.

"Television." She swallowed. "I wish I knew more about… covert operations."

He laughed. "You've got the jargon, anyway."

He kept driving, past the building and around to the next block, where he parked in the dimly lit far corner of another office building's lot. As they pulled into a space, a car passed on the road, and she tensed, but it kept going.

Someone else out late in this office complex?

They walked back through the darkness to the two-story Morgan building. As they crossed a stretch of open ground where trees were planted, Sara shivered. What if they had to leave in a hurry? Would the trees give them cover?

The moon was almost full, providing enough light to walk. Still, Sara stumbled on an uneven patch of ground, and Jack grabbed her hand.

"Okay?"

"Yes," she answered, thinking that twisting her ankle would screw up their escape if they had to make a quick getaway.

As they kept walking, she tested her footing more carefully and was glad when they reached a paved surface again.

They circled around to the front of the Morgan facility, where Jack used his key to let them in. Then he walked to the keypad and turned off the alarm. At the same time, he disabled the surveillance system and erased images from the past ten minutes.

"We're in the clear," he said in a low voice.

"What are they going to think when there's no footage from this time period?" she whispered, as she pulled on the gloves she'd brought.

"That the system went down. It needs updating, and we talked about doing it. But we decided it wasn't worth it, given the amount of time we were going to spend in this building."

"Convenient for us." She looked around the darkened area. "I guess we shouldn't turn on any lights."

"Right."

She switched on the flashlight she'd brought and handed it to him, wishing it gave more light. She'd never been here, and she looked around with interest. The building might be in the wrong location, but the interior was designed to impress, with expensive-looking paintings and modern free-form statues occupying an open area with comfortable seating.

"You really think the company would like my decorating style?" she blurted.

"I like it a lot better than this place. It's cold and pretentious."

She nodded, then pointed to the computer on the front desk. "Can we use that workstation?"

"I don't think it has full access. We have to go upstairs."

When she started toward the elevator, he held her back. "The stairs are probably better."

"Right."

He led her to the back of the building and opened the door into a space that was a lot less grand than the lobby. It was strictly utilitarian, with painted cinder-block walls and concrete risers over a metal framework.

They climbed to the second floor, both of them making an effort to muffle their footsteps. It was strange that they were sneaking around through a building where Jack should have complete access. But apparently neither of them felt good about getting caught here.

Sara followed him to the second level, where their footsteps rang on the tile floor as he lit their way to a workstation in the secretarial area. Along the front was a row of desks with computers. Behind them were cubicles with privacy screens.

The whole room was surrounded by large windows, giving them enough light to see.

"This should be as good as anything else," Jack said, looking around.

He sat down at one of the desks in the front row, and Sara stood behind him, watching the screen flare to life as he booted the computer.

"Enter password" appeared on the screen.

Jack typed in a sequence of letters and numbers.

"Incorrect password."

He muttered something under his breath and tried again.

"Incorrect password. Warning. If another incorrect password is typed in, the system will notify Beltland Security."

"What the hell?" he muttered.

"What's going on?" Sara asked, fighting a sick feeling.

"I thought I could get into the system. It seems that somebody locked me out."

"Who?"

"I'd like to know. Maybe my father."

"Why would he shut you out?"

"I don't think it's deliberate. And I don't come in here every day. He probably just forgot to tell me he changed the code," he said in a voice that told her he wondered if he was fooling himself.

She also had her doubts. Was the elder Morgan starting to forget things? That was an interesting theory, but she wasn't sure how it fit into the picture.

"What's Beltland Security?"

"I don't know."

"Can you get around the computer?"

"I don't know. If I get it wrong again, an alarm bell might start ringing."

He was flexing his fingers when she heard a noise far below them.

Jack's hands stilled.

"Did you hear that?" she whispered.

"Yes."

"I think someone came in."

"Who would be here?" he asked.

"Maybe someone from that security company that you never heard of."

"Why?"

She shrugged. "Do I know?"

He lifted his face and she could see the anger in his eyes. "I have every right to be in this building. Morgan Enterprises is my family's company."

"But do you want to get caught trying to access the computers in the middle of the night? I mean, what's your explanation?"

"I guess there isn't a good one."

"What are we going to do?" she asked, switching to their more immediate problem.

"Take the back way out."

Jack had just shut off the computer when a door opened at the stairwell where they'd come in.

Sara froze in place.

Jack might have opted to tough it out. Instead he took her arm and pulled her into the shadows behind a set of storage cabinets. Her heart was pounding as they stood in the darkness, huddled together behind the cabinet, listening to footsteps approaching. At first they could see nothing, and she felt Jack tense beside her. What was he going to do if they were discovered?

Whoever was out there kept walking past them. With the intruder's back to them, Sara dared a look around the side of the cabinet. It took her a moment to understand what she was seeing. The figure's head seemed to be a blob. Then she realized that their stalker was wearing a ski mask. He also had on dark clothing. With the mask, it wasn't even possible to tell for sure if it was a man.

But the object in his hand was very distinct.

It was a gun.

Chapter Thirteen

Sara struggled not to make a sound as the gunman walked quietly along the line of desks, then disappeared down one of the corridors into the darkness.

When he was out of sight, she moved her mouth to Jack's ear. "Did you see him?"

"Yeah. I guess I should have taken your advice and gone in armed."

"And shoot it out when we don't even know who it is?" she murmured.

He made a rough sound. "I guess not."

"What kind of security guard wears a ski mask?"

"Nobody who has the right to be here," Jack replied in a barely audible voice.

She was glad that Jack had given the right answer. As far as she was concerned, this situation was proof enough that something weird was going on at Morgan Enterprises. Unless someone had come to rob the place—on the exact same night that Jack and Sara had snuck in.

Yeah, like a thug had showed up to rob her and Jack outside that restaurant.

"We'd better get out of here," he mouthed, his lips still close to her ear.

She nodded, sorry that she'd suggested the expedition. Yet she couldn't help feeling vindicated. Jack had thought she was paranoid because she'd argued that someone might be after him. Or maybe he thought she was making up the idea that he was being threatened—for her own reasons. Now they would have a lot more to talk about, if they got out of this alive.

They ducked low, hurrying down a corridor between a row of cubicles. She watched him moving awkwardly and knew that his leg was hurting, but he kept going because that was their best alternative.

They turned a corner leading to the executive offices and stopped to listen. The intruder was still somewhere on the second level, and he must have bumped into a trash can or something, because it clattered across the floor, and she heard a curse.

"Stay here," Jack ordered.

"What are you going to do?"

"He gave me an idea. I can make him think we went the other way."

She wanted to grab his arm and hold him beside her, but she thought maybe that wasn't the best way to get out of this trap.

As Jack moved away, she sat down on the floor, pressed her back against the wall and hugged her knees, straining her ears as seconds ticked by.

She heard nothing until a great clattering filled the empty offices. It was followed by the sound of gunshots.

Her heart was in her throat as she waited. Where was Jack? Was he all right?

Jack came back, his expression grim.

"What did you do?"

"Threw a trash can down the front steps."

"And he shot at it?"

"Yeah. I guess he's jumpy. We'd better get out of here before he discovers it's not us down there."

Jack led her to another exit, but when he turned the door handle, it was locked.

Now he was the one who cursed under his breath.

"It's supposed to be open?" she asked.

"Yeah."

He stopped, listening. It sounded like the shooter was moving their way.

Jack motioned for her to follow him into one of the executive offices. She grabbed his arm. "Aren't we trapped here?" she whispered.

He shook his head and gestured more urgently. Hoping he knew what he was doing, she followed him inside.

It was a large office. A wide, uncluttered desk and a separate, smaller desk with a computer on top were arranged to form an L shape. The space also had two guest chairs, carpeting instead of tile and a seating area with more chairs and a sofa. Obviously the province of someone high up in the company. Maybe even Jack's father.

Jack stood with his back against the wall, moving his leg, probably trying to get the kinks out of it. She saw the pain on his face and ached to do something for him. But there was nothing she could do besides give him the space he needed.

After a few seconds, he pushed away from the wall and crossed to the other side of the office where floor-to-ceiling drapes covered the window. Using a hand to hold one panel open, he fumbled inside. She followed him and held the drape. Behind it she could see a sliding glass door, which he carefully slid open to reveal a narrow balcony.

They both stepped out, and she closed the door behind them.

"I didn't know there was a balcony out here," she whispered as they moved along the wall.

"Dad had it custom-built," Jack answered. "The question is, does the guy out there know, and if he does, will he think of it?"

AS THEY STOOD TOGETHER, backs pressed to the wall, Jack slipped his arm around Sara. He felt her shiver and held her more tightly. If anything happened to her, he'd never forgive himself. Well, there wouldn't be an opportunity for that, because he'd be dead, too.

He turned, looking through a crack at the edge of the curtains, and wondered if the gunman would figure out where his quarry had gone.

He'd come here only half-convinced by Sara's theory that someone was trying to kill him. Now he knew she was right.

He picked up sounds from inside. The intruder was coming toward them along the hall, moving faster now. The guy must know the stairway door was locked. Had he arranged that with someone in the office? But who?

Jack clenched his teeth. He was starting to think like Sara now.

As he peered through the small slit at the edge of the curtains, a figure dressed in black stepped into the office. Jack couldn't tell who it was. Just someone up to no good, with his face covered by a ski mask.

The man—if it was a man—still held his gun in firing position, ready to shoot.

Shoot whom? Jack and Sara? Or was he looking for someone else?

Even as that thought surfaced, Jack dismissed it.

On the way over, he knew Sara had been worried about someone following them. She hadn't spotted anyone, but what if someone had been driving behind them with the lights off? He'd asked himself why someone was tailing him. Maybe they'd been looking for an opportunity to attack.

His breath frozen in his lungs, he waited to find out if the man on the other side of the curtains would open the balcony door.

And start shooting. Could Jack grab the gun when it poked through the door? He might have to.

And maybe it wouldn't work.

How would Dad feel about his son getting killed? At this

point, Jack didn't honestly know. The whole family had been upset when he'd announced he was joining the army. He'd been welcomed home with joy—and a kind of "I told you so" attitude.

Then he'd been in D.C. for much of his long rehabilitation, cut off from them again. When he'd gotten back here, they'd made a place for him in the company, but he couldn't be sure if they really wanted him or if they felt obligated.

Really, he thought, if he stayed around here, he should get a master's in business administration or something useful so that he could make a real contribution. But was that what he really wanted to do?

He wasn't sure why these thoughts were running through his mind. Maybe because he didn't want to think about the person with the gun.

The guy stayed in the office for long moments, looking behind the desk and under the sofa. Finally, with a muttered curse, he turned and exited into the hallway.

Jack could hear Sara letting the air trickle slowly out of her lungs. He tightened his arm around her, pulling her toward him.

She clung to him, her head against his shoulder and her arms tightly around him. They held each other for several heartbeats. He wanted to keep cradling her in his embrace, but he knew that they couldn't stay here. They had to get away before the shooter doubled back to have a second look.

"He's probably still in the building," she whispered.

"We don't know for sure that it's a man."

"True. But it's easier to give him a gender."

"Yes," Jack agreed. "Let's hope we've got some time."

"For what?"

He walked to the edge of the balcony and looked over. It was on the second floor of a building with high ceilings. Too far to jump without the risk of breaking an ankle.

They needed a rope if they were getting down this way. Which they didn't have, of course.

Then he remembered the office parties he'd attended here over the years. The food was brought in, but Dad liked to keep supplies from year to year.

There were long tablecloths that were stored in the closet down the hall.

"Stay here," he told Sara.

"What about you?"

"I'm going to get some table linens we can use as a rope. If you hear any shooting, you'll have to take a chance and jump."

"No."

He ignored the protest. "Lower yourself by your arms first."

He saw the panic in her eyes but also the strength. How many women would still be standing here having a rational conversation instead of going to pieces?

"I'll be okay," he whispered, hoping it was true.

Before he changed his mind, he stepped back into the office, leaving the sliding glass door ajar. As silently as possible, he crossed to the office door and peeked into the hall. When he saw no one, he hurried to the storage closet several doors down.

The contents were arranged on shelves. Still it took precious moments before he located the cardboard box.

After scooping up a banquet cloth, he closed the closet door.

Far away, he thought he heard someone moving around and waited with his heart thumping inside his chest. When the gunman didn't appear, he brought the cloth back to the office where he'd left Sara.

She hadn't followed directions. Instead of staying on the balcony, she was in the office, looking anxiously toward the door.

"What are you doing in here?" he whispered.

"I was too worried about you to stay out there."

He gave her a direct look. "If I'd gotten shot, you'd need to tell them what happened."

She made a low sound. "You're sure they would believe me?"

"What's that supposed to mean?"

"Sorry. I'm just being cynical. Why should they believe my wild story?"

"Because it's true," he snapped.

"That's not always enough reason."

Once he would have disputed that. Now he knew better. He'd resisted the idea that someone was trying to kill him. Even when they'd broken into Morgan Enterprises, he'd still been skeptical. Then he'd been locked out of the computer system. And somebody had started shooting at him and Sara.

And the guy was still in the building.

"Come on. Let's get out of here."

When he stepped back outside, Sara followed, turning to close the door behind them.

Out in the darkness, they both took a gulp of the fresh air.

"Almost home free," he whispered.

She nodded, waiting while he tied one end of the table-cloth to the railing and tested the line with a couple of stiff jerks before feeding it through two slats toward the ground. When he looked over, he saw that it didn't reach all the way, but at least they'd be a lot closer to the ground when they got to the end.

As more seconds ticked by, he debated what to do next. If he went first, he could turn around and catch Sara if she fell. But he didn't like the idea of leaving her on the balcony where she was so vulnerable.

"You go first," he said.

She gave him a panicked look.

"Go, before he catches us both up here."

She stopped arguing and slung one leg over the railing,

then lowered herself on the bars until she reached the makeshift rope. After testing her weight, she began letting herself down, using her hands and her legs.

He held his breath, watching her slow progress and praying that she would make it without falling—and before the gunman came back to his dad's office and started looking more thoroughly.

She had almost reached safety when he heard a sound behind him in the building.

Chapter Fourteen

The killer must have been coming back, doing a more thorough job of looking. And perhaps he'd remembered that there was a balcony outside Bill Morgan's office.

Leaning over the railing, Jack looked to see that Sara was almost to the ground. But not quite. Still, he had no choice but to swing his leg over and start lowering himself.

With both their weights on the makeshift rope, he could feel the knot he'd tied loosening. All he could do was keep going.

Below him Sara had landed in a bed of decorative rocks.

He followed as fast as he could, but the knot in the tablecloth finally slipped, and he fell the last six feet to the lumpy surface.

One thing he'd learned in his physical-therapy training was how to land without hurting himself. He rolled with the fall, righting himself quickly.

"Jack," Sara gasped. "Are you all right?"

"Yeah," he answered automatically, climbing to his feet and wavering dangerously as his bad leg protested the abuse.

Sara grabbed his hand to steady him, and they swayed together for a few seconds until he was steadier.

Above him, he heard the sliding glass door open. The guy was up there. Looking for them.

Stifling the impulse to run, he pulled Sara back into the shadows along the edge of the building under the balcony.

Maybe it was a good thing that the tablecloth had fallen, because it didn't mark the spot where they'd climbed down. But it was still lying on the ground.

Taking a chance that he had a few seconds left to act, he reached out and pulled it back under the balcony, then faded into the shadows with Sara.

Just in time, because he heard footsteps above them.

They both pressed back against the wall, keeping their breath shallow.

Long seconds passed before he heard the sliding glass door above them close again.

"Run for it," he whispered as he balled up the tablecloth.

Sara started to run, and he followed, carrying the wadded cloth and heading for the line of trees. He was about halfway there when his bad leg buckled, and he went down.

His cry of surprise made her turn and start back.

"Go," he shouted.

"No." She reached his side, bending to help him up. He staggered to his feet, cursing the damn leg.

"Get out of here," he muttered.

"Not without you."

She scooped up the tablecloth, and he leaned heavily on her as they made their way to the line of trees. He wanted to tell her to leave him, but he knew she wouldn't do it.

They had almost reached the shelter of the branches when he heard a bullet whiz past his head.

Reflexively, he pulled Sara down and lay with his leg throbbing. "Keep going."

"With you." She reached for his hand, linking her fingers with his, and he forced himself to ignore the pain in his leg as they crawled forward. The pain made him want to curl into a ball, but he kept going because he knew that if he didn't get away, neither would she.

Another shot hit the ground behind them, but they had made it to cover. The question was, would the shooter try to leap down from the balcony, or would he have to take the stairs to get out back?

It was too far to jump, Jack told himself. Unless the shooter was a trained athlete.

Although he kept expecting another bullet, the guy must not have been able to see them now, because he held his fire.

JACK'S NEMESIS CURSED. Following Jack and that nosy blonde tonight had seemed like a good idea. And their breaking into Morgan Enterprises had provided a golden opportunity.

If they'd gotten shot, it could all be explained as a terrible accident. And nobody would know who had done it. Nemesis had planned to be long gone when somebody discovered the bodies in the morning.

But once again, nothing had worked out quite right. Starting with the damn stupid robber. How hard was it to shoot somebody in a robbery attempt, then split?

It would have worked except for Sara's trick with the purse.

Now there was the present mess. It should have been easy to eliminate Jack and Sara.

Instead they'd hidden somewhere in the building, then escaped from the balcony. Could Jack have gotten away by himself?

Probably not with that mangled leg of his. But on his own, he probably wouldn't have thought of visiting Morgan Enterprises after hours. Sara must have suggested it. But why the hell was she sticking her nose into Jack's business? Did she know something, or did she just have a bad feeling about that robbery and the well?

Whatever the reason, she was becoming too big of a liability.

Maybe the thing to do was get her out of the picture first.

Yeah, that made sense. If she was dead, Jack would be distracted and vulnerable.

JACK AND SARA MADE IT to the parking lot on the other side of the trees.

He wanted to pull her into his arms and hold her. But he knew they weren't in the clear yet. The guy with the gun could still follow them.

When Jack started to open the driver's door, Sara stopped him.

"You're not in any shape to drive."

With anyone else, he might have gotten angry. He didn't like people suggesting that his physical disabilities were holding him back. But with Sara, he felt differently. He knew that she totally accepted him as he was. And that she knew he'd hurt himself falling to the rocks, as they tried to get away.

Without protesting, he let her lift the keys out of his hand. As soon as the doors were unlocked, he collapsed into the passenger seat and sat leaning heavily against the headrest.

"Get us out of here," he said.

She pulled out of the parking space, then headed for the access road, looking around for cars.

He did the same, spotting no vehicles in the darkened lots. Whoever had been in the Morgan Enterprises building didn't want to be seen.

When Sara drove to the rear of a convenience store, he shot her a questioning look.

"I don't think we should keep the tablecloth. And I think we should get rid of it somewhere that's not near your house, or mine."

"That's probably right."

She reached into the backseat, pulled it out and crossed to the store's Dumpster, where she pitched the wadded-up tablecloth inside.

The remainder of the drive to the warehouse was silent. But when Sara pulled up by the loading dock, he covered her hand with his.

"We'll go in, and you can pack a bag. You're spending the night at my house."

"What?"

"I'm not leaving you alone. It's too dangerous. He knows where you live. If he came after you at Morgan Enterprises, he can come after you here, too."

"He knows where you live, too."

"Yeah, but you never bought a gun, and I have one. Besides, in all honesty, I don't think he's going to make a direct attack on my house."

"Why?"

He heaved in a breath and let it out. "Because everything that's happened has been set up to look like an accident. I mean, even if we got shot at Morgan Enterprises headquarters, it could simply be a horrible mistake."

She kept her gaze fixed on him. "So you admit I'm not a paranoid nut."

"It's not paranoid when it's really happening."

"Jack!" She reached for him, pulling him into her arms, and they clung together awkwardly across the console.

He wanted to keep holding her, but he couldn't shake the feeling that they were sitting ducks in the car. "Bad idea to let our guard down out here."

She nodded against his shoulder and eased away.

"Let's get your stuff."

They both climbed out of the car, and he made an effort to walk normally when his leg was thrumming like a banjo out of tune.

As she started to step inside, he stopped her with a hand on her shoulder.

"Wait."

He went in first, looking around the darkened warehouse,

thinking that it was a good place for an ambush. Behind him, she flipped a row of switches, flooding the space with light, making it feel less threatening.

"I won't be long," she said. She hurried to the apartment in the back, where she pulled a carry-on from under the bed and started opening drawers. She packed some clothing, then went into the bathroom and came out a few minutes later with a little bag of makeup and toilet articles.

"You travel light."

She laughed. "I don't have a lot of stuff."

They were back outside in fifteen minutes.

"How's your leg?" she asked.

"Not fantastic," he said, as they climbed back into his car and left.

IN THE WOODS ACROSS FROM the parking lot, Nemesis uttered a low curse. Sara Carter wasn't staying home tonight. Smart move on her part. Because she'd just avoided getting killed.

Too bad, because she was getting to be a pain in the ass. Nemesis made an angry sound. This whole Jack Morgan episode needed to be brought to a conclusion, and quickly, before somebody else discovered what was going on.

But not tonight, apparently.

The watcher hurried back to the car parked on the other side of the wooded area and climbed in, thinking that all this following the happy couple around was getting to be a drag. But it was probably a good idea to make sure they were both going to Jack's house.

Then it would be time to go on to plan B.

SARA'S NERVES WERE JANGLING as she turned into the driveway that led to the modest ranch house where Jack was living. When she pulled up at the front door, she watched him scan the woods before climbing out.

"Come on. Let's not stay outside."

As she followed him to the front door, she was thinking that once again, she had something to worry about. For a whole new set of reasons. She'd been here many times. She knew where he kept the dishwasher detergent and which side of the bed he liked to sleep on. She knew that the water temperature in the shower was set very hot, and she shouldn't turn it all the way up. She knew where her clothes would be hanging in his closet when they decided to move in together.

Inside, he turned on a light, and she knew where the switch was, too.

When he pivoted back to her, he winced.

"Your leg is hurting."

"I guess I'm not hiding that too well."

"You don't have to."

"Habit."

And pride, she thought.

"I can massage it for you," she offered.

"Where did you pick up that skill?"

She hadn't been here more than two minutes, and she'd already slipped up.

Improvising, she answered, "I learned in a course I took."

"I didn't know you were interested in health sciences."

"It was one of several possibilities I explored in college. I mean, I knew I was going to have to make a living, and I wanted to do something that I'd enjoy."

"And you didn't want to be a medical assistant."

"I liked it, but the background was so dry. It was too technical for someone who likes decorating rooms."

He nodded. "I want to do something first."

"What?"

He brought his mouth close to her ear and spoke in a barely audible voice.

"Look for bugs."

Her eyes widened. "You mean listening devices?" she whispered back. "You think there are any here?"

He gave her a grim look, then went to the kitchen and pulled a pad of paper out of a drawer. On it he wrote, "Looks like somebody knows what I'm doing, almost as soon as I decide to do it."

"But you don't talk to yourself, do you?" she couldn't help writing.

"I talk on the phone."

"Where?"

"Most likely the exercise room. The bedroom. The kitchen."

She wrote, "You have an exercise room?"

He nodded, then said aloud, "It saves time to do my physical therapy at home."

"I'll help you look. For what exactly?" she whispered.

Again he used the pencil and paper to say, "Anything not right. Like a little hole in the wall that's not supposed to be there."

With a sick feeling, she watched him begin a careful examination of the living room, starting at the walls. When she saw him moving objects in the bookshelves, she did the same. Next he ran his hands over the walls, moving pictures as he went.

He found nothing in the living room. But when he got to the bedroom, he made an angry sound.

She hurried over to see him pointing to a small hole in the wall, just above the baseboard. Near the phone jack. He left the room and returned with a screwdriver. He used it to dig into the wall, and came out with a small black object.

His expression was a mixture of anger and triumph as he held it up.

As she started to speak, he pressed a finger to his lips, and she nodded.

When he took the thing into the bathroom to examine it under the light, she followed. He gave it to her, and she turned the device in her hand. It was dark metal, about the size of a pencil eraser, but with perforations in the top.

After she passed it back, he dropped it on the floor, then crushed it under the heel of his shoe.

"What was it, exactly?" she asked.

"A little wireless mike. Technology is wonderful."

"Oh, Lord. I never thought someone would go that far."

"Yeah. They must have broken into the house to install it."

"Do you think there are any more?"

"I don't know. But like I said, we should check the gym and the kitchen."

They didn't find anything in the kitchen. But there was another one of the little devices in the drop ceiling over Jack's exercise bike.

He gave it the same treatment as the first one.

She saw the anger reflected on his face.

"Won't they know the thing's not transmitting anymore?"

"I guess they will."

"They'll know you found them. Or—that you were looking for them."

His expression hardened. "Whoever it is also knows that we were at Morgan Enterprises tonight. And we have to assume it's the same person."

"That's logical."

"All of which means I'll have to bring this to a quick conclusion."

Below the anger on his face, she also saw pain, physical and mental. He'd accepted that someone he knew wanted him out of the picture. He'd pushed himself hard, and the extreme activity was taking its toll.

"Let me see what I can do for your leg," she offered.

He looked torn.

"Would you rather take some pain medication?" she asked, knowing he hated giving in to meds.

He shook his head. "Okay. I'll put on a pair of gym shorts."

He disappeared into the bathroom off the rec room and came out wearing a T-shirt and the shorts. At one corner of the room was a large padded table about the size of a double bed that he used for some of his physical-therapy routine.

He put a bolster near one end and lay down with his leg over it, but Sara saw the tension in his posture.

She went into the bathroom and got the bottle of lotion from the medicine cabinet.

When she came back, he eyed the bottle. "How do you know where I keep that?"

"An educated guess," she lied. Of course she knew where he kept it. She'd used it before, but she was so off-balance that she kept slipping up.

She struggled for calm as she scooped up some of the massage cream, but this whole night was setting her teeth on edge. It wasn't just that they'd gone to Morgan Enterprises and someone with a gun had chased them around the building. It was also the realization that none of this had happened before. She was off the charts, flying blind. Yet that was a good thing, she told herself. If so much had already changed, she had a chance to affect the big change. A chance to alter Jack's destiny.

He placed a pillow under his head and closed his eyes. She flexed her fingers. Even with him wearing the shorts, her touch on his thigh was going to feel intimate, and they both knew it.

She started by rubbing some of the massage cream on his skin, her fingers stroking over the scars that would always mar his flesh. They were too deep and too extensive to ever disappear. As she worked, she kept her gaze down in case he opened his eyes and saw the emotions on her face.

She would never get over the joy of touching him. And if she could ease the pain in his leg while she was doing it, so much the better.

She worked in the cream and began to massage his injured

muscles and ligaments, feeling the scar tissue and knots of tension below the skin.

He made a low sound.

"Am I hurting you?"

"A little, but I know that's part of what works."

"I hate that it hurts."

"You're doing the right thing."

The words held a wealth of meaning, and she wanted to know exactly what he was thinking, but she didn't ask.

Still, his husky voice told her that he was reacting to her touch in a way he wouldn't with his physical therapist.

Maybe talking about the suspects would distract them both from the intimacy of her fingers stroking and kneading his thigh. As she worked on a particularly tense place, she asked, "Who do you think was trying to kill us tonight?"

"I wish I knew."

"It could be someone in the company. Or hired help."

"Yeah."

"You think someone meant to lock you out of the computer? Or you just didn't get the memo about the password change?"

"I don't know. But that's one question I'm going to ask tomorrow."

"Ask who?" She kept working on his leg, her focus on the injuries.

"My father."

"Be careful." She dragged in a breath and let it out as she massaged a knot of tense muscles. "He's not making all the decisions anymore, is he?"

"No."

"Who is?"

"My brother. I came back to find out he's consolidating power in the company."

She nodded, glad that he was sharing information with her.

He cleared his throat. "I'm sorry I put you in danger tonight."

"I think it was my idea."

"I didn't expect anyone to come after us. Did you?"

She considered her answer. "I wouldn't have suggested going over there tonight if I thought we'd get hunted through the Morgan offices."

He shifted on the table. "There's something we shouldn't discount. Do you think they're after you, too? Or do you think it's because you were with me?"

"I don't know," she managed to say. "And I hate to think I've turned into a target."

"What do you want to think about?" he asked. The quality of his voice had changed.

Her gaze moved upward from the spot on his leg that she was massaging to his shorts, and she saw that he was aroused.

Chapter Fifteen

Sara raised her gaze farther, meeting Jack's eyes, an unspoken question hanging between them.

She grabbed the bolster and threw it onto the floor.

He reached up and pulled her down so that she was sprawled across him.

She clung to him, almost sobbing with relief. She'd thought he was trying to distance himself from her. Now he'd changed his mind.

She lifted her head so that her lips could meet his for a kiss that quickly turned frantic.

"Sara," he breathed.

Wanting to shut out the world, she closed her eyes so that she could focus on the man who held her in his arms.

She began to move her lips against his with a desperation that shocked her.

He gathered her close, and she clung to him, wanting him to be the only part of her reality that mattered. At least for now.

Threats still hung over them, but they had faded into the background.

She lay sprawled across him, burrowing into his warmth, loving the feel of his broad chest under her breasts.

All the while, he kept kissing her, his tongue playing with her lips, then her teeth and beyond, sending currents of sensation through her.

He was so familiar to her. So dear. So necessary to her existence. She had been forced to learn how to live without him once. It might kill her if she had to do it again.

With slow deliberation, she raised her hand, tracing a path along his cheek, loving the way the scratchy stubble contrasted with the softness of his lips moving over hers.

When her fingers trailed to the side of his neck, she could feel his pulse pounding there.

Her hands found the bottom of his shirt and tugged it upward.

He eased far enough up to help her remove the shirt, then reached for hers, pulling it over her head and unhooking her bra.

She tossed them both aside, crying out as she came back to him, moving her breasts against the roughened hair of his chest, sending shivers of heat like small lightning strikes against her flesh.

She wanted this to last because every intimate moment with him was a joy to her.

Her breath caught as he rolled her to her back, looking down at her before bending to take one of her nipples into his mouth, drawing on her as he used his thumb and finger on the other crest.

"Jack. Oh, Jack," she cried out.

They were both still half-dressed. By mutual agreement, they rolled away from each other long enough to shed the rest of their clothing, then came back into each other's arms, rocking together on the padded table.

He slid one hand down her body, into her hot, moist core. She had never needed a man more. This man. The love of her life.

What did he feel for her after knowing her only a few days?

She couldn't ask. She could only cling to him, touching him, kissing him, tasting him, trying to show him her feelings in every way she could.

Did he see the deep emotions on her face? Was that why his expression was so tender as he stroked her most intimate places?

"Jack, I need you now," she whispered, unable to hold back any longer.

He moved over her, then parted her legs with his knee.

His eyes locked with hers as he entered her, and she felt her inner muscles contract around him.

"Jack." She was too overcome with emotion to say more as he began to move inside her.

She matched his rhythm, grasping his shoulders as she climbed toward orgasm with him. She knew he was holding back, waiting for her to reach the peak of her pleasure. When her body started to contract around him, he let go, shouting in satisfaction as they spun out of control together.

As the storm passed, he looked down at her, his expression so sweet that she wanted to weep.

No, she wanted to tell him what she felt. "Jack, I love you."

When he looked shocked, she stroked his shoulder. "I'm not expecting you to say the same thing. That just slipped out."

"You haven't known me very long."

"I know, but long enough to feel like I know you very well."

He eased down beside her, cradling her in his arms, stroking her back and shoulders.

When she shivered, he raised his head. "We should get in bed."

"It's a long way away."

He laughed. "We can hold each other up."

They climbed off the table, arms wrapped around each other as they started upstairs. She knew where his bedroom was, but she let him lead the way.

"There's a bathroom in the hall that you can use." He gave

her a long look. "And I'll get out one of my T-shirts for you to sleep in."

"Appreciate it."

She used the bathroom, then washed. He'd hung the T-shirt on the doorknob, and she put it on before entering his bedroom. He was still in the bathroom, and she slipped under the covers, waiting for him. When he joined her, they reached for each other and began making love all over again. Much later, they both fell into an exhausted sleep.

Jack woke early, his eyes blinking open as he absorbed the unfamiliar sensation of finding a woman in his bed.

Not just any woman. Sara.

Everything from the day before came back to him. His talk with his parents. Her reaction to his telling her about it. Dinner. The trip to Morgan Enterprises, where they'd almost been killed. The bugs in his house.

And then making love with Sara with a kind of desperation he'd never felt before.

She'd said she loved him. Could that be true? He might have said that they barely knew each other, but maybe it didn't take months to fall in love when you met the right person.

What had his life meant before he'd met her? He'd been drifting along, and she'd anchored him to a part of himself that he'd thought he lost. His zest for life.

Yet at the same time, he couldn't completely trust her. Too many weird things had happened since they'd met—starting with the attack by the gunman on the street in Ellicott City.

He certainly couldn't blame that on her. Or the well. Or the people following them. Or the bugs in his house. Or the gunman at Morgan Enterprises. But they'd all started right after he'd met her. Well, maybe not the bugs. Or being followed. He couldn't be sure of that. But she was the one who'd made him aware of the tail.

He sensed that she'd been braced for trouble right from the start. Because a fortune-teller had warned her? Or because she knew something she couldn't admit? He hated to think the latter was the case, but he couldn't discount it.

Sara woke next to Jack but didn't immediately open her eyes. She wanted to stay here for a while longer and just enjoy being warm and close with him. But he spoke, and she knew he was awake.

"I need to go over to the office as soon as I can get ready, but I'll make some coffee first."

"In your fancy machine," she agreed.

"How do you know about my coffee machine?"

"I peeked into the kitchen and saw it," she answered. Another lie. She remembered his coffee obsession from last year. Quickly she said, "I'll take a shower."

"What kind of coffee would you like?"

"Surprise me."

She shivered in the cool air as she climbed out of bed and went into the living room to fetch the overnight bag she'd left there. Then she collected her clothing from the basement and went into the hall bathroom.

By the time she came out, the smell of coffee had permeated the house. Vermont Maple Pecan, she thought. One of Jack's favorites.

He was dressed in slacks and a blue dress shirt and standing at the counter with a mug in his hand.

"Any suggestions for how to play my return to the building?" he asked.

"Play dumb. You weren't there. We weren't there."

"Yeah. And I'll watch for reactions."

Despite what had happened, she knew he still wasn't comfortable thinking that someone in his family or in Morgan Enterprises wanted to kill him. Of course, she didn't blame him. Who would want to believe it?

"I'd feel better if you stay here," he said.

"Okay."

She walked toward him, holding out her arms, and he came

into them. She closed her eyes and hugged him tightly. Every time she held him, she couldn't stop herself from thinking it might be the last time.

"I wish I could go with you."

"It might look suspicious."

She wanted to protest that she could be inspecting the current offices to see how they were decorated, but that sounded like a pretty thin excuse. And probably her presence would get in the way of Jack's questions. Her being there would change the whole dynamic.

"Be careful," she said.

"Of course."

"I mean, don't let anyone know you're suspicious that something bigger might be going on."

He eased away and gave her a confident smile. Then he was gone, leaving her standing in the kitchen with her pulse pounding.

It started pounding harder when the phone rang. When she walked over and looked at the caller ID, she saw it was Ted Morgan. Maybe calling to tell Jack about the break-in. Well, he was already on his way to the office, and nobody was supposed to know she was there.

Instead of answering, Sara waited for the ringing to stop.

Jack had an answering system from the phone company, which meant she couldn't hear the message. If Ted left one.

JACK WAS ABOUT HALFWAY to Morgan Enterprises when his phone rang. He looked at the ID, saw it was his brother and directed the call through his radio speakers.

"Yeah?" he asked.

"I tried to call you at home, but nobody answered."

Good that Sara hadn't picked up.

"I'm on my way in now."

"There's been a development."

Jack waited for his brother to elaborate.

"Somebody broke in last night."

"You're kidding, right?" he asked, doing a decent job of sounding surprised.

"I wish I were. The cops are here now. I just wanted to give you a heads-up." Ted waited a beat before asking, "Do you have any thoughts about who did it?"

"No. Do you?"

"No."

"Did Dad make any enemies recently? Or could it be someone holding a grudge?"

"Maybe we'll find out."

Jack rang off, wondering why his brother had called. Did he really want to warn Jack? Or was he hoping for a reaction?

THE CALL FROM TED HAD SET Sara's nerves on edge. She had just convinced herself not to call Jack when her own cell phone rang. It was an unavailable number.

Who would that be?

She thought about not answering, then reconsidered, since it might be one of her clients trying to get in touch with her.

"Hello?" she said as she pressed the Answer button.

"Ms. Carter?"

"Yes?"

"This is Officer Robards."

She gripped the phone. Robards? The cop who had arrived after the attempted robbery in Ellicott City. What did he want now?

"I'm at your warehouse. Your car is here, but when I rang the bell, nobody answered."

"I'm not home."

"Where are you?"

"What is this about?"

"I'd like to speak to you in person."

"About what?"

"Can we speak in person?"

She swallowed hard. "I'm at Jack Morgan's house."

At least he was polite enough not to ask why she wasn't sleeping in her own bed.

"I'd like to meet you there."

Feeling that she had no choice, she answered, "Okay."

"I'll be right over."

Sara's heart was pounding as she hung up and looked around. Was there anything obvious that would point to what they'd been doing last night? Before they got back to Jack's, that is. Not as far as she could see.

The officer arrived so quickly that Sara thought he must have exceeded the speed limit.

Before he could ring the bell, she opened the door.

"I'm glad I caught you," he said.

"Come in."

"I'd like to take you over to Morgan Enterprises."

Probably he saw the shocked look on her face.

"What's this about?" she managed to ask.

"I'd prefer to wait until we get there."

Feeling numb, she nodded. Had the police figured out that she and Jack had been there last night? Obviously she couldn't ask.

"Let me get my purse." She retrieved her pocketbook, then hesitated.

"Is something wrong?" Robards asked.

"I don't have a key. I should lock the door, but I won't be able to get back in."

"Mr. Morgan is over at Morgan Enterprises. He can bring you back here when we're finished."

"Okay. Yes."

With her heart still pounding, she climbed into the passenger seat of the cop car and buckled her seat belt.

Robards headed out of the parking area.

"Ever been to Morgan Enterprises before?" he asked.

"I was at the new building. Not this one," she answered, not volunteering anything else.

They rode in silence for a few more minutes before he said, "How long have you known Mr. Morgan?"

"We met the day of the robbery. I thought you knew that."

"I guess that didn't register."

What was he thinking now? That she was spending the night with a man she'd known less than a week?

He didn't ask any more questions, and she was grateful for the silence—and anxious to talk to Jack.

What had he already said about last night? Were they going to have a situation where he said one thing and her story didn't match? They'd agreed to pretend that they hadn't been in the building last night. But that might not apply if they were being questioned by the police and not just his family.

WHEN JACK DROVE into the Morgan Enterprises lot, he found a couple of squad cars parked near the front entrance. After cutting the engine, he took a deep breath, then climbed out of his car and rushed into the building, acting like he was surprised and shocked.

Barbara was in the lobby, talking to his father.

"Ted said there was a break-in last night," he said in a breathless voice.

His father nodded. "Someone got in here and tried to access the computer system. And it looks like there was more than one person. Apparently there were some shots fired."

"Shots?" Jack asked. "And no one heard it?"

"The office park is vacant at night."

"Was anything stolen?" Jack asked.

"We're trying to determine that now," his father said. "Maybe a tablecloth, of all things."

"Who discovered that someone had been in here?"

"I did," Barbara answered. "I came into your father's office and noticed that the door to the balcony was open."

Jack pursed his lips. "Why would someone do that?"

"We presume they used it as an escape route."

A man and woman Jack didn't know walked past.

"Who are they?"

"Crime-scene technicians," his father explained. "They're collecting evidence."

The front door opened behind him, and he saw Dick Mac-Donald, the family financial adviser, stride in, looking unsettled. "I came as soon as I got your message," he said to Jack's father.

Jack took that in. The building had been burglarized, and Dad had called his broker? Was he here in some official capacity? Or had Dad summoned him for moral support because they were old friends?

"Can I talk to you for a moment?" Bill asked.

"Of course."

The two men walked a few yards away, and Jack saw them speaking in low voices.

When they returned, both of them were looking calmer.

A man in a rumpled sports jacket approached them. "I'd like to have a word with you," he said, addressing the group in general.

His father introduced the man. "Jack, Dick, this is Detective Montgomery. He's in charge of the investigation."

"Can we use the conference room?" Montgomery asked.

"Of course," Bill Morgan said.

Dick MacDonald spoke up quickly, looking like he wished he'd picked another time to come over. "I just stopped by to see if Bill was all right. Do you need me?"

Detective Montgomery turned to him. "Do you work here?"

"No."

"Then I guess we don't need you." The detective cleared his throat. "Let's get this over with."

"Of course," Bill Morgan answered.

As they walked toward the elevator, Jack drifted back so that he was beside his father.

"What were you and MacDonald talking about?"

His father gave him an annoyed look. "If I'd wanted you to know, we would have had the conversation in front of you."

"You don't feel that I'm entitled to know about your business dealings?"

"Entitled? I wouldn't put it that way."

"Am I part of Morgan Enterprises or not?"

"It was a private financial conversation," his father snapped. When he saw the detective looking at them, he said, "This isn't a good time."

Jack answered with a tight nod, wondering what his father wanted to keep from him.

They followed the rest of the group into the elevator and got off on the second floor.

"Can I see the balcony door?" Jack asked.

His father shot him an annoyed look. "Why?"

"Curiosity."

Without waiting for an answer, he strode down the hall to his dad's office.

The doorway was blocked by yellow crime-scene tape, but he could peer in from the doorway. He looked at the rug and saw footprints. Apparently there had been dust on the balcony, and he'd tracked some in. Also the killer had been out there, then come back into the office. And Sara had also briefly come back inside. But the footprints were smudged, making it difficult to figure out whose they were.

Jack involuntarily looked down at his shoes and was relieved to see that he wasn't wearing the same ones from last night. Instead, because he was going into the office, he'd put on his "dress" athletic shoes. A black pair.

"Any insights?" his father asked.

"Sorry, no."

"Then stop wasting our time."

When the elder Morgan turned and walked down the hall
to the second-floor conference room, Jack followed, thinking
that the old man was in a foul mood. But then he did have an
excuse. His building had been broken into and he was being
questioned by the police.

When Jack and his father arrived, Barbara Bateman was
already seated, and Ted was standing behind one of the chairs.

Jack and his brother nodded at each other before sitting
down.

Montgomery took the position at the head of the table.

"You have a surveillance system," the detective said, "but
it wasn't functioning last night."

"That appears to be the case," Bill Morgan said.

"When did it go down?" the detective asked.

"Eleven-fifty," Ted answered. "The same time as the security system was turned off."

"Which leads us to the conclusion that whoever broke in
had the door code and also the security-system code."

"That sounds logical," Ted said.

Jack wanted to object, but he couldn't think of a better
answer. And he was struck dumb when he saw Sara standing in the doorway.

WHEN SARA STEPPED into the conference room, she was surprised to see that the assembled group included Jack, Ted,
their father, Barbara and a man she didn't know.

"What's going on?" she asked.

"Come in and sit down. I'm Detective Jordan Montgomery of the Howard County Police Department."

"What's happened?" she asked again. Was this about last
night, or was there something else going on? From the detective's grim expression, she decided it was something she
didn't want to hear. But what?

"There was a break-in at this building early this morning," he said.

"But why is she here?" Bill Morgan asked, eyeing her suspiciously.

"We'll get to that."

She gave Jack a quick look, and he shrugged.

"Have a seat," the detective repeated.

She took an empty chair next to Jack. Although she wanted to reach for him, she kept her hands in her lap.

"We've already established that whoever broke in last night turned off the security system and the surveillance cameras."

She said nothing, waiting.

The detective kept his focus on her and Jack. "You were the victims of a robbery attempt a few nights ago."

"Yes."

"Then last night the Morgan Enterprises building was broken into by someone who knew the security system. Are the attempted robbery and the break-in a coincidence? Or are they somehow related?" Montgomery asked.

Sara shook her head. "I have no idea."

Montgomery resumed speaking. "You identified the man who attempted to rob you as a felon named Tucker Swinton."

"Yes," Sara answered.

The detective paused for dramatic effect, then said, "Tucker Swinton was found dead this morning."

Chapter Sixteen

Sara's heart thumped hard as she stared at the detective. "Tucker Swinton. The man who tried to hold us up?"

"Exactly."

"Where was he found?"

"At an old farm in the western end of the county. A real-estate agent was showing the property to a client and noticed an unpleasant smell."

Sara nodded. She might have asked another question except that she was pretty sure that the less she said, the better.

The detective was speaking again. "So how are these three events related?" he asked, as he looked at her, then around the room.

Sara had a pretty good idea. Someone had paid the man to rob Jack and shoot him. He'd failed in carrying out the assignment, so the man or woman who had hired him had punished him with death. And kept him quiet in the bargain. Then the same person had followed her and Jack into Morgan Enterprises and tried to kill them.

For a split second, she thought about trying to explain the whole thing to Montgomery. But it would probably sound like a paranoid delusion. Not to mention alerting everybody else in the room that she knew about the plot against Jack. Which was a very bad idea, considering that one of them might be the would-be killer.

They'd thought it was a man last night, but Barbara was a big woman. It could have been her.

Sara pressed her lips together and waited for whatever else the detective was planning to say.

He fixed his gaze on Jack. "Were you in the building last night?" he asked.

"Of course not," Jack answered.

After a beat he turned to Sara. "And were you in the building?"

"No."

"And you had no idea that Tucker Swinton's body was at a farm in the western district of the county?"

"Of course not."

"We'll keep investigating the break-in and the murder," Montgomery said.

"Are we dismissed?" Ted asked.

"I'd like to have a word with each of you," the detective answered.

Jack and Sara waited in the conference room with Ted and Barbara while Montgomery took the elder Morgan to one of the offices.

Sara sat with her hands clasped in her lap under the table, when she wanted to reach for Jack again.

He turned to his brother. "Is the security system back on?"

"Yes."

"A bit like locking the barn door after the horse has left."

"Unfortunately," Ted replied in a dry voice. He looked from Jack to Sara and back again. "Do you have any information you're not sharing about last night?"

"No," Jack snapped.

"Or about that dead guy?"

"No. Do you?" Jack retorted.

"No."

The two brothers stared at each other, until Ted turned his gaze on Sara. "What about you?"

"What *about* me?"

"Do you have any inside information?"

"Like what?"

"You tell me."

"I don't know any more than anybody else."

"Where were you last night?" Ted asked.

"She was with me," Jack said.

"All night?"

"That's none of your business," Jack snapped.

Ted looked from his brother to her and back to Jack again. "Maybe under ordinary circumstances."

"Drop it," Jack warned.

Sara's gaze flicked to Barbara, who was still in the room and was watching the action with a look of quiet satisfaction. What was she getting out of this, exactly?

"You brought her in on this," Ted said, obviously referring to Sara.

"What do you mean by *this?*"

"She's not part of the company. She shouldn't even be here."

"The cops brought her here, not me, but she's an innocent bystander who got sucked into something…unsavory." He was still addressing his brother, but Sara thought he was also talking to her, telling her to stick with their story. "She happened to be at the wrong place at the wrong time when that guy tried to rob me. She doesn't know anything about his murder. And she wasn't here last night."

Ted stood up and walked to the glass wall of the conference room, looking out at the guest reception area for the executive offices.

Sara watched the tension building between the two brothers. If it reached flash point, what exactly would happen?

When she put her hand on Jack's arm, he whirled toward her.

"Let's stay calm," she said in a low voice.

After a long moment, Jack nodded.

She wished she could send him a telepathic message. Or have a conversation with him where no one else would hear. But private communications would have to wait until they got out of here.

All she could say was, "We just have to tell Montgomery the truth, and we'll be okay. Like we already told him, we weren't here last night and we don't know about any murders."

"Yeah."

They stared at each other for a long moment. Before anybody else could speak, one of the uniformed officers came back and motioned to Sara. "Detective Montgomery is ready for you," he said.

With her pulse pounding, Sara stood and followed the cop to an empty office.

"Sit down," Montgomery said.

She sat, leaning back in one of the guest chairs and trying to look like she had nothing to hide.

"Let's go through last night in your own words."

"Jack Morgan came over for dinner. I cooked him chicken cacciatore. He helped me clean up and put the food away. Then we went back to his house for the rest of the evening."

"Why did you leave your place?"

She had been thinking about a good answer. "I have a warehouse where I store the furniture and props I use for my business. Which is staging houses for sale."

"Staging?"

"Making the interiors look attractive. To save money, I live in a small apartment at the back of the warehouse. It's not all that comfortable. We decided to go back to Jack's house."

"Whose idea was that?"

"I'm not sure."

"You don't remember who made the suggestion?"

"Is that relevant?"

"It could be." He kept his gaze on her. "And you spent the night with Mr. Morgan."

"That really isn't any of your business."

"You were there all night?"

"Yes."

"So you each provide the other with an alibi."

"If you want to put it that way."

"How would you put it?"

"That we were enjoying each other's company and we had no idea that...this situation was going to hit the fan in the morning."

"What situation?"

She swallowed. "The break-in here. The murder of that guy."

"And today is the first you heard about Tucker Swinton's murder?"

"Yes."

"And you have no idea how any of these events might be connected?"

"That's right."

"I must ask you to remain in the area."

"Why?"

"We might have further questions."

"Do I need a lawyer?"

"That's up to you."

When the interview was over, Sara stood, stiffened her legs to keep them steady and went back to the conference room, where she told Jack the detective was ready for him.

"How was it?" he asked.

She lifted one shoulder. "Okay."

"Wait for me. I'll come to get you when I'm finished."

She wanted to pull him into her arms and cling to him, but all she could do was give him a little smile.

Ted's cell phone rang, and he looked at the screen.

"I'll be right outside," he said, his expression carefully neutral as he headed for the door.

"You're sure that's all right?" Barbara Bateman asked.

"I'm not going far," he answered before leaving the room.

Through the glass wall, Sara could see him talking to someone.

She and Barbara stared at each other.

Last time around, Sara had been very polite to everyone. Now she was getting to the point where she felt like she had nothing to lose. Raising her chin, she said to Barbara, "Why do you dislike me?"

"I don't."

"Oh, come on. Do you really expect me to believe that?" When Barbara didn't answer, Sara continued, "Did I do something to threaten you?"

"No."

"Do you know anything about the break-in last night?"

"Of course not. How could you ask me anything like that? What are you—working with the police?"

"No. Should I be?"

Barbara scowled at her. "I'd prefer not to discuss anything with you."

"Clearly."

"You're the one who's acting hateful," Barbara said.

"Your interpretation. Just tell me what you think I did, and I'll try to correct the behavior. Or maybe you could tell me why you called Bill Morgan when Jack brought me to the other offices."

"I didn't."

"Of course you did."

Without answering, Barbara angled her chair away. Sara turned toward the glass wall. To her relief, she saw Jack coming back. He'd been gone less time than she. Because Montgomery suspected her of something—but not Jack? Or because he hadn't gotten anything different out of him?

She stood and met him in the hallway.

"Come on, let's go," he said.

They headed for the elevator.

Sara was bursting to speak to him, but it wasn't safe to talk here. Or in the parking lot, either.

Jack must have known that, too, because he didn't say anything when they left the building. Not until they got into the car and closed the door did he let out a sigh.

"What did you tell Montgomery?" Sara asked.

"The same thing you did, I hope."

"That we weren't here last night. And we had dinner at my place, then spent the night at your house?"

"Yeah."

"He asked whose idea it was to go to your house."

"What did you say?"

"That I didn't remember."

"Good. I said it was mine."

"And neither one of us knows anything about that guy turning up dead."

"Yeah," he answered again. His motions were jerky as he drove away from the Morgan Enterprises building.

"Where are we going?"

"To your place. So you can pick up your car."

"I guess you didn't get a chance to ask your father why you were locked out of the computers."

"Actually, I did. He said it must have been a mistake."

"You think that's true?"

He shrugged.

"And why did he call MacDonald?"

"He wouldn't tell me."

They were both silent for several moments.

"It's kind of strange that I can't get into the computers, but I could deactivate the security system," Jack finally said.

"It's lucky for us you could."

He pulled onto a side street.

"This isn't the way to the warehouse."

"I know." He eased to the shoulder, cut the engine and reached for Sara across the console. She came into his arms with a little sob, hugging him with all her strength.

"I'm sorry," she breathed.

"About what?"

"It was my idea to go over to Morgan Enterprises. I wasn't thinking about the consequences."

"I guess you didn't know the cops were going to find a dead body."

As she raised her head, he lowered his, and their lips met in a kiss that was equal parts relief and passion.

When he finally broke the kiss, she said, "I guess Montgomery thinks we were at the building last night."

"But he can't prove it. Good idea that you thought to bring gloves."

"Yes." She dragged in a breath and let it out. "And he's wondering if we killed that robber."

"Why would we?"

"What if we set up the robbery, then killed him to hide the truth—if he was caught."

He shook his head. "That's pretty devious."

"I'm trying to come up with explanations. Unfortunately, we don't know any more than we did." She stopped and gripped his arm. "One thing I'm wondering about. Does Barbara have some reason to hate me?"

"Like what?"

"I don't know. She's always cold with me."

He waited a beat before saying, "I guess she can turn that off and on. She was supernice to me when I came back from the Naval Medical Center. I think she was hoping that we could get something going, but I just wasn't attracted to her."

"That's a reason, all right. She wanted you, and you rejected her. But now I'm in the picture."

He hugged her more tightly.

"What are we going to do?"

"Act normal and try to figure out who was trying to shoot us last night."

She laughed. "That would be easier if I knew what normal was anymore."

He held her close for a few moments longer, then said, "We can't stay here."

He started the car again and drove to the warehouse. With everything that had happened, she was almost surprised that it was still standing when they pulled up at the loading dock.

"You should get some more clothes and come back to my house."

The conviction in his voice made her heart swell. He hadn't said he loved her, but he cared about her, and he wanted to protect her.

"Well, you said to act normal. I'd better check my voice mail and my email."

"You can do that from my house."

"Yes. But if anything needs attention, I have access to my stuff here."

She turned away, wishing she could figure out what was going on, but there was little chance of coming up with any easy answers. Things had gone so off the tracks that she had no idea what to expect next. She'd come back determined to save Jack. Now she didn't even know if she could save herself.

WITH THE INTERVIEWS FINISHED, Detective Montgomery gathered up his notes. He and Officer Robards left the Morgan Enterprises building.

Montgomery looked around the area. "Let's take a look at the back."

He and the officer circled the building, stopping under the balcony at Bill Morgan's office.

Montgomery pointed to some indentations in the grass beyond the decorative rocks. "Almost certainly someone came down this way, then took off across the grass."

"Who?"

"If I had to bet money on it, I'd say it was Carter and Jack Morgan. Something's going on with them that we don't know about. They're trying to act innocent, but it's not quite working."

"Jack Morgan broke into his own family's office building? Looking for what?"

Montgomery shrugged. "What I'm thinking now is that he and Sara Carter came here. Somebody else came in and started shooting at them." He paused for a minute and looked up toward the balcony. "Remember, the only thing taken was a tablecloth. Suppose they used it to climb down."

"With his bad leg?"

"If they were desperate to keep from being shot." He turned toward Robards. "What did you think about the interviews?"

"Like you said. That Carter and Jack Morgan are hiding something. Also Ted Morgan." He laughed. "Also their old man."

"Agreed. I'd say Carter and Jack Morgan are into something together. Ted's got some other agenda. And the father?" He shrugged. "Maybe he's just worried about something getting stolen in the break-in. I'd like to keep tabs on the first three. You think the robbery in Ellicott City was real?" Montgomery asked.

"Yeah. They were both pretty shaken up. After that, I don't know. Too bad we don't have the manpower to follow them, plus the other brother."

Montgomery nodded. "If you had to pick one of them, which one would it be?"

"Sara Carter."

"Why?"

"She seems like the one who knows more than she's telling."

"Agreed. I'd like to put a tail on her, but I have to get authorization."

SARA AND JACK CLIMBED OUT of the car, and she headed for the door.

"Let me go in first," he said, as he had the last time they'd been there.

She handed him the key, and he unlocked the door, then cautiously opened it and stepped inside.

Unwilling to let him take all the risk, she followed him in, sniffing the air.

"What are you doing?"

"It smells the way it should."

He laughed. "What's that supposed to mean?"

"One time, somebody broke in, and I smelled it right away."

"What was different?"

"I can't name it exactly. It was just wrong."

He made a dismissive sound as he flipped the switches by the door, turning on all the lights.

"Too bad there are so many places to hide," he said, as he began looking down the rows of shelves where she kept her props.

She helped him search. When he was satisfied, she tried to turn on her phone, but the battery had run down.

Switching to her computer, she checked her email and found a message from Pam Reynolds.

Quickly she scanned the text:

Sara, I'm showing that house where we met the Morgan brothers the other day. The one that I showed to Ted Morgan. But the elephant lamp in the front hall is broken. I need a replacement right away. I mean it doesn't have to be an elephant, but I need a lamp there. Soonest.

Jack had come to stand behind her.

"A problem?" he asked.

"At that house where I met you the other day—one of my lamps is broken. Pam Reynolds wants me to bring a new one over right away."

"I thought Ted was buying it."

"I guess he hasn't made an offer yet."

"I'll drive you over."

"It's only going to take a few minutes to drop off another lamp. Why don't you go back to Morgan Enterprises and see if you can talk to your father?"

"I don't like leaving you on your own."

"It's not for very long. I'll meet you back at your house." She stopped and gave him an exasperated look. "I locked the door when I left, and I can't get back in."

"There's a key under the flower pot at the side of the porch."

"Okay. And after I use it, we're taking it away. I mean, maybe that's how the guy got in to plant the bugs."

His expression darkened. "I didn't think of that."

"We'll meet there as soon as we're both finished."

"Yes. And since we're saying what we don't like, I don't like you going off without your phone charged."

"I've got a charger in my car. I can use it while it's plugged in there."

"Okay. Good."

"Let me get a substitute lamp." She searched through her stock and found one in the shape of a lion.

Jack walked to the car with her, and they hugged.

"Take care of yourself," she said.

"You, too."

She wanted to stay with him, but she forced herself to

leave. As she headed toward the house where they'd first met, she thought again about the past few days.

She'd assumed she had a handle on what was going to happen, but the more time passed, the less she knew. It had taken only a few hours for things to start deviating from her memories. And maybe that was partly her fault because she'd suggested a different restaurant for their first dinner. The only thing she was absolutely sure of was that someone was closing in on Jack. And if he was going to survive, she had to change his fate.

She was so deep in thought that she missed the turnoff to the house she'd called Tara in Howard County and had to make a U-turn.

With a shake of her head, she doubled back. When she pulled up in front of the large white mansion, she expected to see Pam's car, but it wasn't in the driveway or over at the parking pad in front of the three-car garage.

From the car, she tried to call Pam but only got voice mail that said, "Pam Reynolds is not available. Leave a message at the sound of the tone."

"Pam, this is Sara. I'm at the house. Are you on your way?" she asked.

She sat in the car for a few minutes, but she was anxious to get in, exchange the lamp and get back to Jack.

Deciding she might as well try the door, she retrieved the new lamp from the floor of the backseat and climbed the steps to the house. When she tried the doorknob, it turned easily.

"Anybody home?" she called out. "Pam, are you here?"

Nobody answered, and she had half a mind to back out. But that seemed stupid when she was already here. Taking a step inside, she saw the elephant lamp lying in the middle of the hall floor—smashed.

It could have fallen. But Pam wouldn't have left it there.

The hairs on the back of her neck prickled. At that instant, she knew that she should back out and leave while she could still get away. But when she turned, she saw a figure coming toward her around the side of the house. A man wearing a ski mask and carrying a gun.

If she tried to run, he'd shoot her. All she could do was dash into the house, slam the door and lock it.

Chapter Seventeen

Was the back door locked?

Probably, if the guy had been counting on herding her into the house.

With only a split second to decide what to do, she dashed toward the stairs and sprinted up, disappearing around a bend in the hall into the master bedroom.

Last night, she and Jack had gotten away by climbing down off the balcony. She could do something like that now. Climb out onto the top of the porch roof.

Below her, she heard the sound of breaking glass and knew that the man had smashed one of the sidelights beside the door. He'd be inside soon. And if he caught her on the porch roof, she'd be a sitting duck.

She was trapped.

And there was nowhere to go but up.

JACK WAS ON HIS WAY to Morgan Enterprises when his cell phone rang. When he looked at the caller's name, it said Pam Reynolds.

He clicked it on and said, "Pam?"

"Yes. I'm trying to get in touch with Sara. About a new job."

"Well, she got your email this morning about the house

you were showing to my brother. She's gone over there with the new lamp."

"I don't know what you're talking about," Pam answered. "I didn't send her an email."

His mind started spinning as he tried to process that information. Pam hadn't sent that email asking Sara to take a replacement lamp to the vacant house. The killer had done it.

She'd taken the bait, and Jack had let her go alone when he should have gone with her.

With a sick feeling, he pulled to the side of the road and waited for a car to pass so that he could make a U-turn.

"I'll tell her you're looking for her as soon as I find her," he managed to say before hanging up.

He found Sara's cell number in his contact list and clicked on it, but all he got was her voice mail.

As he drove toward the house where Sara had gone, he started praying, "Please, Lord, don't let me be too late. Please, Lord, let me get there in time."

SARA KNEW THE HOUSE WELL. The entrance to the attic was in this room. In the walk-in closet. Over by the storage shelves.

She used them as a ladder, climbing to ceiling height, then pulled on the cord at the front of the folding stairs. It came down with a creaking noise that made her cringe. If the gunman down there didn't hear it, he was deaf.

She scrambled off of the shelves and onto the ladder. She had just made it to the top when she heard someone running in the hallway.

Pulling the folding stairs up, she stood, panting, and looked around the attic. It was dark, with one small window at the far end giving her enough light to see what she was doing. The center of the large room had flooring. Under the eaves, there was only insulation between open joists.

Whoever had cleared out the house to put it on the market hadn't bothered to clean up the attic. The floored space was littered with old furniture and boxes. Maybe there was something up here that she could use as a weapon. And at least the clutter would provide a place to hide.

Seeing all the junk gave her an idea. She started piling boxes onto the trapdoor until she heard footsteps below her and darted toward the other end of the space.

She was on her way to the small window when the ladder creaked again. As she saw the trapdoor start to lower, she sprinted toward the window. She found a candlestick in a nearby box and bashed the glass, wrapping the tail of her shirt around her hand so that she could break off a good-sized piece from the ruined pane.

If she could lure him close to her, maybe she'd have a chance to cut him.

Clutching the glass, she ducked behind a chest of drawers.

From below, the guy pulled the trapdoor all the way down. As he did, the boxes she'd piled there came tumbling onto his head.

She had the satisfaction of hearing his loud curses as debris rained onto him.

"You little witch, you think you're so clever, but I'll get you for that," he growled.

JACK LEAPED OUT OF HIS CAR. He was trying to figure out where to find Sara when he heard the sound of breaking glass coming from above him. Looking up, he saw shards falling from the window at the gable end of the attic.

She must be up there trying to escape from the killer. He wanted to call out to her and tell her he was here, but he understood that announcing his presence could be a fatal mistake.

Quickly he tried to size up the situation.

Her car was parked in front of the house. It looked like nobody else was here, but the killer must have hidden his car somewhere nearby.

Whoever it was could still be downstairs in the house, looking for Sara. Or did he know she'd gone up to the second floor, then into the attic? Maybe he was already up there with her.

The possibilities raced through Jack's mind as he sprinted toward the house, then stopped short when he saw the broken window beside the door. The guy could be right in the hall, pointing a gun at Jack.

Jack waited a beat then peered inside. Nobody was there, but the broken lamp Sara had come to replace was lying in the middle of the floor.

As he stepped into the hall, he heard a loud voice curse, "You little witch, you think you're so clever, but I'll get you for that."

Definitely from upstairs. And Sara had done something to him.

Jack took the first few steps two at a time, but when his leg threatened to give out, he forced himself to a more normal pace.

When he reached the second floor, he stopped and listened for a clue to which way Sara and the killer had gone.

The killer's voice directed him again. It sounded like it was coming from the attic.

"I know you're up here. Come out and I'll make this quick."

SARA DIDN'T ANSWER, and she didn't move from her hiding place behind the chest of drawers as she scrabbled through the boxes around her, looking for something else that she could use to defend herself.

Probably she wasn't going to save her life with the Christmas ornaments she'd just found. Her best bet was still the piece of glass that she'd laid beside her as she pawed through another box.

She discovered it was full of old toys that would make

great props for a children's room, if she ever got to decorate another house.

Below old metal trucks and a rag doll was a bag of marbles. As the attacker crept toward her, she opened the bag and threw the contents across the floorboards, the round glass balls bouncing and rolling toward the killer.

In the dark he couldn't see what they were. As his foot collided with one, he slipped and fell, cursing as he went down.

But he was up in a minute, moving toward her again—and now she had given away her location.

IGNORING THE PAIN IN HIS LEG as he followed the sound of the killer's voice, Jack ran into the master bedroom. The closet was open. Junk that looked like it had tumbled down from above was strewn across the floor, and a fold-up ladder was hanging down from the ceiling.

The sound of cursing drifted down from above. Sara must have done something to keep the guy away from her.

"Stay away from me. I've got a gun," Sara called out.

"I doubt it."

Jack's heart leaped into his throat as he heard the exchange of words. Sara and the killer.

If he tried to climb the ladder, the guy could shoot him before he reached the attic level.

"Down here, you coward. I've got you trapped," Jack shouted, praying that he could divert the killer's attention from Sara.

He hadn't bargained for the killer's next move. The man hurled himself down the stairs in a rush of motion, leaping on Jack and throwing him to the closet floor.

The guy's face was covered with a ski mask, but Jack saw a gun raised in his direction. Like last night.

This time the attacker wasn't quite steady on his feet. Ducking low as the gun fired, Jack knocked the guy off his feet. He grabbed for the weapon, hoping to wrest it from the man's hand.

Sara came scrambling down the ladder, a candlestick in her hand. But the man must have seen her coming and didn't want to take a chance on fighting off two people. He gave Jack a mighty shove, dashing him to the floor as he wrenched away and leaped toward the closet door.

Jack made a grab for him, but the guy yanked himself away. Moments later, he pounded down the stairs and across the first floor. Jack tried to heave himself up, but his leg went out from under him.

Cursing, he fell back onto the closet floor.

Sara staggered to the window and looked out.

"He's cutting his losses," she choked out, coming back to Jack and reaching for him.

They held each other for long moments.

"Are you all right?" they both asked, then answered in unison, "Yes."

"He lured me here," Sara said, then raised questioning eyes to Jack. "How did you know?"

"I lucked out. I was on my way to Morgan Enterprises when Pam called, trying to get in touch with you. I told her about the email, and she said she didn't send it."

"It was the killer." Sara made a moaning sound. "As soon as I saw the lamp on the floor, I knew I had to get out of here. But it was already too late to run."

"But you got away."

"For a while. I never should have come here alone."

"You had no reason to be suspicious. You thought you were meeting Pam. Both of us did, or I never would have left you alone."

"Yes."

They clung together.

"Are we going to tell Montgomery?" Sara asked in a thin voice.

Jack considered the question. "Do you want to?"

"No. He'll just twist it around and make it look like this was our fault."

"You're probably right. Come on. We're getting out of here."

"Where?"

"Back to my house." He looked down and saw the gun, and she followed his gaze.

"Do we want to leave it?" she asked.

"It's evidence."

"We're taking a chance either way."

He sighed. "Windows are broken. Obviously something happened here. And the gun is part of it."

She nodded. "And neither one of us touched it. Unfortunately, I think he had on gloves." Her mind was still turning over the problem. "Even so, Montgomery or some other detective will be interested." She dragged in a breath and let it out. "What do we tell Pam?"

"That the window was broken, and you didn't go in."

"Right."

They both exited the house and walked toward the vehicles. Sara stood, swaying on her feet. Jack steadied her, then gave her a critical look.

"You shouldn't be driving."

"I can't leave my car here."

"Yeah. Let's split. I'll go first."

As Sara followed Jack down the long driveway, she scanned the woods on either side of the lane. But apparently the coward wasn't planning an ambush. He was still trying to make this look like it fit some other pattern.

What was his next move?

Maybe he was counting on their not calling the police, since they hadn't done that last night. Which meant that perhaps they should have a long chat with Detective Montgomery, after all.

She was torn when she thought about talking to the detective. He clearly assumed they were hiding something. Maybe the murder of the robber.

By the time they arrived at Jack's house, she was wiped out. She pulled into the parking area and sat in the car, leaning on the steering wheel.

Jack came over, opened the door and helped her out.

"You need to lie down."

"Probably."

"Certainly."

He unlocked the door, and she stepped into the living room. When she headed for the sofa, he gently guided her toward the bedroom.

They'd left without making the bed, and he straightened it now while she kicked off her shoes, then lay down on top of the spread.

She'd held herself together while the killer was after her and on the drive back here, but now she started to shake. Jack held her in his arms, rocking her. When she felt tears stinging her eyes, she struggled to hold them back.

"It's all right to let go," Jack murmured.

"We need to talk about what happened—while it's fresh in our minds."

"Okay."

"I guess the killer showed up earlier, opened the door and broke the lamp. But he was hanging around outside waiting for me to go in."

"Why wasn't he already inside?"

"I guess he was afraid I might leave. I was going to. Then it was too late."

Jack nodded. "What did I hear just before he started cursing at you?"

"I found a box of old toys and threw a bunch of marbles onto the floor and made him slip."

"Good going."

"It made him mad. He would have caught up with me if you hadn't arrived. But I had a piece of glass from the window. I wasn't going to make it easy for him to kill me." She turned her head toward Jack. "Do we have any idea who it was?"

He dragged in a breath and let it out. "It's not my father or my brother. I would have recognized them."

"Yes. But they could have hired the guy."

"I hope not."

She wanted to keep discussing what had happened, but maybe the mention of Jack's relatives had put him on edge. He kept backing away from that idea, and she couldn't blame him.

"You get some sleep," he said.

"I have to call Pam. I can't just let her find that mess."

"What are you going to say?"

"I guess what we already decided."

She pressed Redial for Pam's number. The real-estate agent answered on the first ring.

"Jack?"

"This is Sara. I'm using his phone." She swallowed before saying, "I went over to that house you showed to Ted Morgan. It's been vandalized."

"Jack said you thought I'd emailed you."

"Yes."

"Was it a prank, do you think?"

"I don't know. But you'll want to take care of it. There's a broken window by the front door."

"Good Lord. Did you call the police?"

"I just got out of there as fast as I could."

"I need to evaluate the damage. Do you want to meet me there?"

"I'm kind of wrung out. Can we talk about it later?"

"Of course. You take care of yourself."

Sara clicked off and lay back on the bed. "She's probably going to call the police. And then they'll find the gun. And

Montgomery will question us again. Maybe we can figure out what's going on before that."

Another thought struck her, and she gasped.

"What?"

"What if it's Pam?"

"Huh?"

"What if she has something to do with this? I mean, what if she deliberately got me over there?"

"Why?"

"Lord, I don't know. I like her, but I get the feeling she'd do…things…for money."

"Where does that leave us with her?"

"Cautious."

He shook his head. "We can't figure it out now. But you should get some rest."

She felt her chest tighten. "Are you going to stay with me?"

"I'll be right here."

He lay down beside her, pulling her close. She wanted to make love with him, but she thought she wasn't in good enough shape to make it good for either one of them.

Closing her eyes, she tried to relax. At some point she drifted off.

Her sleep was restless. She dreamed of being in the attic, only it was larger, an obstacle course where the killer chased her around boxes and pieces of furniture. Then Jack was there, fighting with the man, who ran away. But when she tried to reach for Jack, he kept moving away from her.

She screamed for him to stand still, but he kept fading into the background.

Jack's hand on her shoulder woke her. "Sara, wake up."

She looked at him, relief flooding through her. "I was having a nightmare."

"I gathered. I'm sorry."

"I'm fine," she answered, knowing it was a lie. The bad dream came from her subconscious fears that she was going to lose Jack again. She moved closer to him, closing her eyes, struggling for calm. "Did I wake you up?"

"Don't worry about it."

"Hold me."

He settled down beside her, taking her in his arms, and she clung to him. When they'd come in, she'd been too wrung out to make love, but now she was rested, and she wanted him.

She found the hem of his shirt and slipped her hand inside, stroking the hair on his chest.

When she slid a finger over his nipple, she felt it tighten.

"Um, nice," she whispered, then lifted her face to his. Every time with him was precious. A gift from fate.

She knew how lucky she was to have him again. And she knew she would do almost anything to keep him.

He brought his mouth to hers, responding with an urgency that thrilled her.

His fingers stroked over her arms, combed through her hair. "I was so scared for you."

"You got there in time."

"You slowed him down. Maybe you would have stopped him with that piece of glass."

"I would have tried."

He came back to her mouth for another devastating kiss. Rolling her to her back, he moved one of his legs between hers, pressing where she needed to feel him.

They clung together, both of them caught up in the need for each other.

He sat up and started unbuttoning his shirt.

She was about to do the same when his cell phone rang.

"Damn. Bad timing."

Fumbling in his pocket, he pulled out his cell.

"Yes?"

She could hear the man on the other end of the line. It was Ted Morgan.

"You have to come. Right away," he was saying.

"What's wrong?"

"I can't tell you over the phone."

"Where are you?"

Ted gave an address, but she didn't hear where it was.

"Sit tight. I'll be right over."

Chapter Eighteen

Sara sat up, staring at Jack as he put the phone back into his pocket, a sick feeling gathering in her throat. It was happening again. The endgame. When she'd come back here, she'd met Jack the same way she'd met him the first time. They'd gone out to dinner and a man had tried to rob Jack—only it was a cover for a murder attempt. After that, things had started changing. Events she remembered from the first hadn't happened again. And other things had taken their place. Things that she never would have anticipated.

The first time around, she hadn't really realized someone was trying to kill Jack, until too late. This time she'd been ready for it.

And this part she did remember.

Well, not exactly. Nothing was exactly the same. But Jack had gone off to meet someone at an isolated location. And he'd never come back. Last time she hadn't known who he was meeting. This time she'd been here when he got the phone call.

"That was your brother?" she asked.

"Yes. He says he has a problem, and he needs me to come right over."

"Is he at home?"

"No. He's at this property the firm bought on Willow Lane."

He had mentioned Willow Lane before. This time, she couldn't hold back a gasp. "Not there."

"What do you know about it?"

She closed her hand around his arm and pleaded, "Don't go."

"It's my brother. He sounded like he was in some kind of trouble."

"That's what he wants you to think. He wants you off alone because he's going to kill you."

He stared at her in disbelief.

"We've been trying to find out who wants you dead. Now we know. It's him."

"That's crazy."

"This call proves it. Jack, if you're going, take a gun. And take me."

"I'm not taking you, because he wants to meet in private. And I'm not taking a gun because he's my brother, and he wouldn't do anything to harm me."

Panic threatened to overwhelm her. She'd come back to save Jack, and she'd thought she was going to accomplish her mission. Now she saw she was going to fail because he was too trusting to listen to her.

She hung on to him. "I won't let you do this. I won't let you get killed again."

He stared at her. "What do you mean, again? I'm not dead."

"But you were."

"I lost a lot of blood in Afghanistan, but I was never technically dead."

Things she hadn't intended to say tumbled from her lips. "I'm not talking about the war. I mean here. In Howard County, Maryland."

"You're not making sense."

Desperation forced her to keep speaking. "Jack, it all happened before. You were murdered, and I came back from the future to save you."

That got his attention. He went very still, his gaze locked on her. "Of course not."

"Haven't you had the feeling that you've known me for longer than a week?"

When he said nothing, she leaped in to fill the silence.

"It's because we've done this all before. Well, not the exact same things. I came back, and it started off the same. Your meeting me at the house Pam was showing to your brother. And the robbery. That happened before. Well, at a different restaurant. But after that, it started changing. Like I didn't expect to see Tucker Swinton in the mug shots because I didn't see him last time. But there he was, and then Detective Montgomery said someone had killed him. And the part about the well, that's new, too."

"You're not making sense," Jack said.

"I know it's hard to believe. It was hard for me to believe when I came back, but it's true. Last time, you went off to a secret meeting. I didn't know who it was with, but you ended up dead." She gulped. "And you left me pregnant with your baby." She began talking faster as she saw the doubt in his eyes. "I had to move out of the warehouse because I couldn't raise a child there. I was living in a little rented house off 108. It was winter, and I was driving myself to the hospital in a snowstorm. I skidded down a hill and hit a truck. Just where the car almost hit us on the way to dinner that first night. The day of the snowstorm, I should have been dead. Only the angels who had come to take me to heaven decided that I could go back and have a second chance."

He stared at her with doubt in his eyes that made her stomach clench. "I thought there was something…off about you. I guess my instincts were right. You're delusional. I mean, do you seriously expect me to believe any of that?"

"It's true. I can prove it."

"Oh, yeah?"

"You asked how I knew where to find the massage lotion.

I knew where it was because I've used it before. And then there was the coffee machine. I didn't go into the kitchen. I've been here before. I can tell you what's in your kitchen cabinets. I can tell you—"

He cut her off. "Stop. I've heard enough of this nonsense. Are you really expecting me to believe that you came back from the future? We both know that's impossible."

"I thought it was impossible. It should be impossible, but it's true. The angels let me come back because I love you."

"You love me. But that story you told me about a fortune-teller in D.C. was a lie?"

She gulped. "Yes."

"Maybe you should get your story straight."

"I couldn't tell you the truth. Look how you're reacting now."

"Yeah, right. Your time-travel story is impossible." He sighed. "And I've had enough of this."

When he wrenched away from her and strode from the room, she followed.

"Jack, don't do this."

"I'm going to meet my brother," he clipped out. "And when I get back, I don't expect to find you here." He waited another beat before saying, "My family warned me about you. I guess I should have listened to them. What are you going to do, tell me you're pregnant and try to get money out of me?"

She gasped. "Of course not."

"Stupid of me not to use a condom with you."

The cruel words tore at her, even when she knew he was upset and being deliberately harsh.

Really, what had she expected? That he'd embrace her wild story? She hadn't dared tell him before because she knew he wouldn't believe her. And she'd picked the worst possible time to tell him. It had seemed like her only option. Instead it had made things worse.

He walked out the front door and closed it with a loud

bang. Through the front window, she saw him get into his car and drive away.

She might have collapsed on the floor weeping, if she had been a different kind of person. But she had too much determination for that. She'd been sent here for a purpose, and she wasn't going to give up, even if Jack Morgan thought she should be in a mental institution.

Back in the bedroom, she pulled on her shoes. Then she opened the dresser drawer. The gun was where he'd said it would be.

Her mother had kept a gun in the shop in case anyone tried to rob her, and Mom had insisted that Sara take shooting lessons.

She checked the clip, and it was loaded.

Jack had said he was going to Willow Lane. And he must think she didn't know where the house was located. But it was where his body had been found before. After the police were through with the place, she'd gone over there to see if she could figure anything out. And to mourn. She hadn't gotten any insights. And soon that tie to Jack was broken.

Not long after Jack had been killed, Morgan Enterprises had torn the house down. Maybe to make sure no evidence remained.

She exited the house and paused to scoop up the key Jack had told her about, then locked the door. It might be a stupid move, she thought, but she wasn't getting locked out this time.

JACK HEADED FOR WILLOW LANE, trying to focus on the meeting with his brother. Ted had sounded upset. What the hell was wrong with him?

It couldn't be what Sara had said. No way was his brother luring him to an isolated location to kill him.

When push came to shove, he simply couldn't believe that a member of his family wanted him dead. And certainly not

Ted. There was too much history between them. They'd been at odds plenty of times, but they loved each other. Yet Sara's warning rang in his mind.

She'd sounded panicked. And sure of herself. And terrified for him. Yet he couldn't let himself believe her wild story. It was simply too crazy.

On the other hand, he couldn't stop remembering the first time they'd kissed, and he'd thought it was almost like she knew what he wanted her to do. Like she knew him already.

Forget about kissing. What about the robbery attempt, and she'd come up with so many details he'd missed. Even before that, she'd been ready to assault the guy.

A smattering of conversation drifted back to him. After they'd made love for the first time, she'd said he was a man who didn't make calculations. He'd asked how she knew. And she'd said she knew him better than he thought.

He made a snorting sound. It was probably just an assumption she'd made—but what about the fear in her voice when he said he was going to meet Ted? She was sure that something was going to happen to him. What if she had some inside information that she was afraid to tell him? So she'd come up with the insane time-travel story to keep him from meeting with Ted.

He heaved in a breath and let it out. Yeah. Maybe she did know something. And maybe he shouldn't go charging into the meeting. He'd park down the road and walk up to the house. Get the lay of the land before he went inside.

He thought about the gun in the nightstand. He'd left it at home because he was sure his brother was no threat. But maybe somebody else was.

With a curse, he slowed. He could go back for the gun.

But there were a couple of good reasons not to go back. He'd already delayed too long. And Sara was at the house. He didn't want to get into another confrontation with her.

Because he didn't want to believe what she'd said? Or because she might convince him it was true?

He'd left the house absolutely certain of what he needed to do and why. As he drove toward Willow Lane, he was second-guessing everything.

His mind scrambled back over the conversation with Sara. He'd said some pretty nasty things to her. Things that would be hard to forgive. If he even wanted forgiveness.

SARA JUMPED IN HER CAR and headed down the access road from Jack's house. He had a ten-minute head start on her. It would be impossible to get to the Willow Lane property before he did, unless she drove like a bat out of hell. And she couldn't let herself get picked up for speeding. The way things were going, the cop would probably call Robards or Montgomery. Then she'd never be able to save Jack.

His name came out as a sob. She felt tears clouding her vision and dashed her hand across her face. She couldn't start bawling now. She had to be able to see, or she'd get into an accident.

Was that the terrible irony of this whole situation? She was charging off to save Jack, only she was going to get herself killed again?

She forced herself to slow down and pay attention to her driving. Yet fear for Jack was like a burning brand inside her.

She'd lost him once. Now it looked like she'd screwed up their relationship with her time-travel revelation. But she could still save his life.

Or die trying?

She banished that scenario from her mind. She had a chance to turn everything around. If she did it right this time.

But what was right? She couldn't rush in there. She had to be smart. And, much as she didn't want to admit it, maybe smart was calling the cops.

Or was she wrong about this whole situation? What

if it turned out this wasn't the day at all? Last time she'd known Jack for a month. This time it was only a little more than a week.

IT WAS LATE AFTERNOON by the time Jack turned onto Willow Lane and slowed as he surveyed his surroundings. Most of the houses here had probably been built about seventy-five years ago. But some of the older homes were being torn down and replaced by newer ones. He drove by the entrance to the property where Ted had called from. It had a long driveway, and he couldn't see much from the road, but he was pretty sure he spotted Ted's car in front of the old house.

Niggling doubts about what he'd find up there made him drive about a hundred yards along Willow, then pull into a place where the shoulder widened out into a little clearing in the woods.

Just to be on the safe side, he'd leave the car here and approach through the woods, then circle around to the back of the property.

As he started through the trees, his plan was hampered by the second-growth forest, which was thick with brambles and probably poison ivy, although the latter hadn't leafed out yet.

Still, the tangled underbrush slowed his progress, particularly since he was trying to make as little noise as possible. And when he stepped into a hidden hole, he almost lost his balance.

About halfway there, he cursed himself for taking this route, but going back would be as difficult as going forward.

Finally the house was only about twenty yards ahead across a stretch of weedy grass.

From the shadows under the trees, he surveyed the scene. The one-story dwelling was a type common in older areas of the county. A rectangular cinder-block structure covered with a stuccolike composition. The windows were small, and he could see no lights inside. What if Ted wasn't even there?

Taking out his cell phone, he dialed his brother's number. This time there was no answer, and his only option was to get to the house. Or leave.

And what? Call the police.

He recalled the scene with Sara. He'd been so sure that his brother meant him no harm, yet now that he was here, he didn't like the setup at all.

Moving as quickly as he could with his bad leg, he crossed the stretch of ground between the woods and the yard.

Through a grimy window, he could see into what must be the living room. In the far corner, he made out Ted sitting in a chair, his head down. He didn't move. Although Jack couldn't see him clearly, he thought his brother might be ill. Was he on drugs or something? Was that it?

Jack had thought he'd go in through the back, but now he was worried about Ted. Crossing to the door, he tried the knob. The door was open, and he stepped directly into the living room.

Ted looked up, panic in his eyes and a red splotch across his face. "Get out of here," he mouthed.

Jack was trying to process the words when he felt something cold and hard against his back and knew it was the barrel of a gun.

"Put your hands up. Slowly."

Chapter Nineteen

Sara slowed as she approached the Willow Lane property. Craning her neck, she looked up the driveway and saw Ted's car. When she spotted Jack's Lexus up the lane, she breathed out a small sigh. At least he hadn't charged in there without thinking. It looked like he was being cautious. Thank the Lord.

She pulled in behind him and started to climb out. When she'd come in to replace the lamp, she hadn't taken her phone, but it had been charging in the car.

Decision time.

She'd been so focused on saving Jack that she hadn't thought through any plan of action. All she'd thought was that she'd get here and make everything come out all right. But maybe that wasn't totally realistic.

She pulled a business card out of her pocket, looked at the number and dialed.

She had thought she might get an answering machine, but instead the man she'd called answered.

"Detective Montgomery."

"This is Sara Carter."

"Ms. Carter. What can I do for you?"

"We don't have much time to talk. I know you thought something weird was going on. You were right. Someone has lured Jack to an isolated location to kill him. I've just arrived.

The address is 463 Willow Lane. An old house the Morgans own. I'm going up there."

"Who lured Jack there?"

"His brother. And now I have to go save Jack."

The detective's voice turned hard. "Do not put yourself in danger."

"Sorry. No time to argue about it. I guess you'd better come and stop me," she said, as she clicked off.

She had no idea if Montgomery would get there in time, and she had no intention of waiting to find out.

Climbing out of the car, she peered into the woods. It would be dark soon, and nobody would see her if she approached through the trees. But the wood lot was a tangle of unruly underbrush.

Instead of taking that route, she opted for the gravel access road that led to the house, sticking close to the tree line as she headed for the dwelling. Ted's car was parked in front.

And another one in the woods.

Jack had said his brother wasn't the killer. But Ted could be working with someone, and they were both here to overpower Jack.

Her heart was pounding as she quickened her pace, stopping and studying the setup when she came to the open ground.

The house was typical of the older ones in the county. In fact, she was pretty sure it was just like the one she had rented after she'd found out she was pregnant.

Staring across the weedy lawn between the trees and the house, she estimated her chances of getting there without being detected.

If she dashed across the open space and the killer looked out the window, she was going to get caught. But crawling would take much longer, and she had to figure that Jack was already in there—and in trouble.

"Here goes nothing," she whispered, then darted across

the open space between the woods and the house. As she pressed against the wall, she struggled to control her breathing. When she was no longer gasping for air, she started moving toward a window.

Cautiously, she looked in and saw Jack standing with his hands in the air.

His back was to her, and another man was standing to the side, holding a gun. She took a quick survey of the room, watching Jack remove his cell phone and put it on a low table before crossing the room and sitting down in a chair beside his brother.

The other man followed Jack's progress with the gun, and she was afraid he'd see her if she stayed where she was. Ducking below the level of the windows, she made her way around the house, to the other side.

At the back of the house, Sara hurried to the door and turned the knob. Apparently the guy had been thinking about escape routes, because the door wasn't locked. Or maybe vandals had done it.

Sara opened the door and stepped into the kitchen.

Through the window, she'd seen that Jack and the other two men were in the living room, which was down a short hallway.

Cautiously she crept toward them, stopping just out of sight and waiting to find out what was happening.

HIS LIPS SET IN A GRIM LINE, Jack did as he was told. From where he sat in the chair beside Ted, he tried to rearrange his thinking as he stared up into the face of Dick MacDonald, the family broker.

"Dick?" he asked. "What's going on?"

MacDonald didn't answer.

Ted shifted in his seat. "He made me call you."

"Why?"

Ted licked his lips. "He's stolen money from the firm to

make investments he thought would pay off. Only the market slump wiped him out."

"Stole money? Or did you let him have it?"

Ted looked sicker. "Okay. I let him have some funds because he convinced me he'd pay it back with interest as soon as he sold the stock. But it went down instead of up."

Jack snorted. "Leaving both of you holding the bag."

"I told him he had to put it back before anyone found out. But he can't."

Jack looked from one man to the other. "What's that got to do with me?"

"Nothing. If you hadn't gotten shot and come home. But then you joined the firm. Dick knew your strict moral code. He knew you wouldn't go along with the deal—that you would expose him when you found out."

Jack looked at Ted. "What about Dad? Is he going along with this?"

"I've got a cover story for him. He'll believe me."

"Because he wants to believe you?"

"Yes," Ted answered.

"But not me."

"Sorry."

"So you locked me out of the company computer system?" Jack asked his brother.

Ted's face contorted. "Yes. Dick said he'd kill me if I didn't go along with him."

Jack's gaze swung to MacDonald. "You hired that guy to rob us in Ellicott City and kill me in the process. Did you take the cover off the well before the party?"

"What?" Ted asked.

MacDonald ignored him and addressed Jack. "Yes. And it was me last night at Morgan Enterprises and then today at that mansion out in the county. And I have Bill worried that you got your brains scrambled in Afghanistan and might be playing fast and loose with company funds."

"That's why he wouldn't tell me anything?"

"Yeah."

Ted was taking it in, probably hearing it for the first time, for all the good it did him. What the hell had he thought would happen when Jack arrived here? That Dick would threaten them both, then let them go? Sure.

Jack knew MacDonald was telling them about his recent activities because he knew the Morgan brothers weren't going to get a chance to tell anyone else.

But maybe there was some way to stall the guy. To stave off the inevitable, he asked, "Is that real-estate agent, Pam Reynolds, working with you?"

MacDonald laughed. "Not in the sense that you think. But I've been keeping tabs on the house through her."

"And now what's going to happen?" Jack asked.

"I've got to get rid of you both," MacDonald answered, confirming Jack's assumptions. Which meant Jack didn't have anything to lose by trying to take him down. Unfortunately, he'd have to be fast. And pray that his damn leg didn't trip him up.

Jack kept his gaze on the man who had been a trusted family adviser and had taken advantage of that status. "It's going to be hard to make it look like an accident."

SARA'S HEART POUNDED AS SHE crept closer, listening to the conversation. The man with the gun was Dick MacDonald, the family financial adviser. He must have been as crooked as a corkscrew. And a good talker, because he'd convinced Ted to let him use money from Morgan Enterprises.

Could she get the drop on him before he killed Jack and Ted?

She had to. But she needed a distraction.

Cautiously she peered around the corner, trying to size up the situation. The perfect solution came to her when she spotted Jack's phone lying on a low table.

Stepping back to remain unnoticed, she reached for her own phone.

The next words she heard stopped her in her tracks.

JACK WATCHED MACDONALD'S RUDDY FACE break into a parody of a smile.

"It's not going to be an accident. It's going to look like your girlfriend did it. She's the perfect suspect, don't you think?"

The words were like a blow to Jack's gut. "Sara? Leave her out of it."

"No way. She kept putting herself in the middle of it," MacDonald answered.

"No."

"Oh, yeah. How did she figure out something was going on?"

Jack shrugged, but he was pretty sure he knew.

"I guess she's smarter than you. Or maybe you're just too damn trusting."

Jack fought the sick feeling threatening to overwhelm him. Too trusting, yeah. He'd been sure nobody in his family was trying to kill him, and he'd been right. Too bad he hadn't trusted the right person—Sara.

If MacDonald killed the Morgan brothers and pinned it on Sara, it would all be Jack's fault because he had been sure she was lying—or crazy.

But he simply hadn't been able to believe her wild tale about coming back from the future to save him.

It was still hard for him to believe. Worse than the fortune-teller story. Yet despite all his doubts, he knew now that Sara had predicted this was going to happen. Well, not this specific scene. She hadn't said that Ted was going to be dead, too. But she'd also said that things hadn't happened exactly the way they had the first time around.

Jack was trying to decide what to do when the phone he'd set on the table rang.

And there was only one person who could be calling him now.

Sara.

Everybody whirled toward the phone, just as she stepped into the room, a gun in her hand.

But MacDonald must have seen her from the corner of his eye.

"What the hell?" When he pivoted toward her, she raised her gun and fired.

Too much was happening at once, and her aim was off. She hit MacDonald in the shoulder.

He made a grunting sound, then got off a shot in her direction, but she'd already ducked back into the hallway.

Heedless of the weapon in MacDonald's hand, Jack leaped out of his chair. MacDonald swung the gun back toward him, but Jack ducked low, plowing into the man's legs and knocking him to the floor.

They landed together in a heap, but MacDonald still had the weapon and was desperately struggling to get it into firing position. Jack pinned the man's arm to the floor as he fired again, the shot whizzing past Ted's legs.

His brother cursed. With his hands still tied, he stood and dodged to the side as Jack and MacDonald struggled on the floor.

SARA CHARGED BACK INTO the room, trying to get a bead on MacDonald. But she didn't dare shoot, not when he was rolling around on the floor, fighting with Jack.

Across from the struggling men, she saw Ted edging away along the wall.

How much of this was his fault? She didn't know, and she didn't have time to find out.

"Stay out of the way," she ordered. Shoving the gun into the waistband of her slacks, she dodged around the two men fighting for the gun on the floor, picked up the chair where

Jack had been sitting and slammed it down onto MacDonald's head.

The killer cried out and went still. Jack heaved him onto the floor, grabbed the gun and twisted it away, then sat up.

"Are you all right?" Sara asked.

"Yes."

He and Sara were both covering the killer when Detective Montgomery appeared in the doorway, his gun drawn.

"Police. Drop the weapons!"

Jack looked at Sara. "Do it," he said.

She reluctantly put down her gun. Jack did the same.

"This whole thing is about MacDonald stealing money from the firm," Jack said. "He thought that I would find out about it and turn him in. Which is why he was trying to kill me and Sara."

"That's true," Ted confirmed. "He forced me to lure Jack here. Sara must have followed him."

"We'll sort it out at police headquarters," Montgomery said, giving no hint if he believed their side of the story.

"Unfortunately, it looks like MacDonald's going to the hospital," Jack answered, pointing to the bloodstain spreading across the man's shoulder.

Montgomery called for an ambulance as well as a couple of patrol cars.

The ambulance took MacDonald to Howard County General, under guard, for treatment. Ted, Jack and Sara went to police headquarters in separate cars, where they were each questioned alone.

This time Sara and Jack had nothing to hide—well, except for her time-travel saga. They told Montgomery the full story, leaving out the part he wouldn't have believed anyway.

Two hours later, after they had all given statements and Ted had confirmed the money missing from Morgan Enterprises, Jack and Sara were free to leave the station.

"We need a ride to our cars," Jack said.

"I can do it," Robards offered.

He ushered Sara into the passenger seat of the squad car. Jack sat in the back, then leaned toward Sara and cleared his throat. "Sorry you went through all that."

"It came out all right," she answered, wondering whether she was telling the truth. She and Jack hadn't had a chance to talk since he'd ordered her out of his house. He'd said some pretty awful things to her, and she still didn't know if he thought she was crazy.

When they arrived at Willow Lane, the officer stopped beside her car, and she got out quickly.

Jack followed, and they stood awkwardly on the shoulder.

"This is no place for any kind of conversation," he said. "Come back to my house."

Not trusting herself to speak, she only nodded, wondering exactly what Jack was going to say to her.

She followed him back, waiting with her heart pounding while he unlocked the door and stepped inside.

Jack's face was grave, and she could barely breathe as he turned toward her.

When he spoke it was hard to focus on his words. Finally it registered that he was saying, "I said some awful things to you. Can you forgive me for being a jerk?"

"What?"

He reached for her and pulled her into his arms, folding her close. "Sara, I'm sorry for not believing you."

She began to shake as tears trickled down her cheeks. He tightened his hold on her, then lifted her and carried her to the sofa, where he sat down and cradled her on his lap, while she struggled to get control of herself.

"You weren't a jerk. My crazy story was hard to believe," she finally managed to say. "I know I couldn't tell you the truth. Then you insisted on charging off to meet Ted, and I was so afraid it was all going to happen again."

He stroked her back and shoulders. "I know that now."

"I couldn't let you do it."

"I know. I know." His voice turned gritty. "You could have gotten killed."

"Dead twice in a week?" She gulped. "What are the odds?"

"Dead twice?" he asked.

"I was trying to tell you what happened to me, but you didn't want to listen."

"I was too wound up in my own scenario. Tell it to me now."

"And you're going to believe the impossible?"

"Yes. Because I know it has to be true." He swallowed. "And because I love you. I couldn't admit that to myself before."

"Oh, Jack." She clung to him for long seconds, then slid off his lap so she could watch his face as she spoke. "Last time we met the same way. We got to know each other. We made love. We were together for a month. Then somebody killed you, and I was devastated. After that I found out I was pregnant."

"What did my parents say?"

"You're not going to like it."

"Give it to me straight up."

"They thought I was lying about being pregnant. Then when it turned out to be true, they thought I had done it to get your money. They tried to drive me out of the county, but I stayed here. For a few months, I couldn't get any jobs."

He reacted with a curse. "I can understand now why you didn't like them. It must have been hard for you to deal with them this time around."

"Yes."

"Finally Pam hired me again, and I started getting more business. I couldn't raise a baby in a warehouse, so I moved to a little house off 108. A house a lot like the one where MacDonald was holding you and Ted. That's how I knew the floor plan."

"Lucky for me."

"When I went into labor, I was driving myself to the hospital. But it was snowing and icy. The car went into a skid and plowed into a pickup truck. I think I was supposed to die, but two angels were hovering around me, arguing. They said I deserved a second chance. The next thing I knew, I woke up at that house Pam was showing to Ted. I was really disoriented, but I realized it was the day we'd met." She kept her gaze on him. "Saying all that out loud sounds really weird. Even to me."

"But it's the truth."

"Yes." She swallowed. "I thought I knew how things were going to happen. Then I saw Tucker Swinton's picture in the mug book. Last time he wasn't there. And I knew events were lining up differently."

"But you didn't give up."

"I couldn't."

"You must have felt so alone."

His words almost made her start crying again. "Yes. And I knew I was making you think I was weird because of some of my reactions. Like when I had to make up that crazy fortune-teller story."

"I'm so sorry."

"It wasn't your fault."

"But I should have been—"

She pressed her fingers to his lips. "You couldn't change who you are. You have too much integrity. That's why Mac-Donald knew he had to get you out of the way."

"Maybe you should call it inflexibility. And then there's the fear factor. At least with you. Something I never told you. I had been dating a woman I wasn't sure I loved. That was one of the reasons I joined the army. When I came back mangled up, it was clear she couldn't stand the sight of me."

"Oh, Jack. I didn't know. No wonder you had so much trouble letting me see your wounds."

"Yeah. Sorry. You're not her. But I couldn't wipe that out of my mind."

"I know I gave you reasons to think…" She shrugged. "To think I was strange."

"Yeah. But now I understand where you were coming from." He laughed. "The future. And thank God you did."

He pulled her close, kissing her tenderly, then with growing passion.

Caressing her lips with his, he said, "I think we're headed for the bedroom."

"Mmm-hmm."

"About that baby. Do you think you're already pregnant?"

"I don't know."

"Maybe we should be a little cautious, then. So we won't end up in a snowstorm on the way to the hospital. I mean, let's plan for a nice safe trip—next spring instead. But if we end up with a winter delivery, you're not going to be alone."

"'We.' I like that a lot better."

He helped her up, clasping her hand as they made their slow way to the bedroom, stopping to kiss and caress because it was impossible to keep their hands off each other.

"It's still sinking in, what you did for me."

"For us. I didn't want to go through losing you again. Not if I could help it."

They undressed each other, kissing as they went. And when they finally fell together onto the bed, they were both totally aroused.

But Jack did stop long enough to get a condom from the bedside table.

She helped him put it on, her hands shaking.

Lying back, she held out her arms, and he came to her.

She guided him inside her, and they moved in a rhythm that quickly became frantic.

She cried out as she climaxed. Seconds later, she felt him follow her.

In the aftermath, he murmured, "Oh, Sara, Sara."

"Jack."

He eased to his side, and she snuggled against him.

"Thanks to you, I have a future," he said.

"And I have the future I want. With you. Whatever you decide to do."

"Almost getting killed made me realize that I've been making a big mistake trying to fit into the company. One thing for sure, I'm not going to work with my brother at Morgan Enterprises."

"Are you going to press charges against him?"

"Probably not. Why make things worse? And now that he knows I'm watching him, he's going to have to stick to the straight and narrow."

"We hope. What about the missing money?"

He shrugged. "I guess it's gone. I hope there's enough left so that the company can buy me out. Then I'm going to start making plans for that children's center."

"Oh, Jack! I love that. It's the perfect thing for you. Not a business that you hate."

"Well, you've given me the push I needed to get out and do what I really want."

"You would have done it on your own."

"You think?"

"Yes. You wanted to make a difference in people's lives. You would have realized you weren't going to do it at Morgan Enterprises."

She reached for his hand and twined her fingers with his. "I know how lucky I am. My life shouldn't have turned out this way."

"Thank the Lord you had the courage to fight for what you wanted."

"I had to."

He kept his gaze on her. "I came close to dying today. Last time around, I did. And you're the only thing that saved me. I'll remember that every day of our lives."

Epilogue

A sharp, stabbing pain grabbed Sara Morgan's middle, and she gripped the edge of the seat.

"A bad one?" Jack asked from behind the wheel of the SUV.

"Yes."

The contractions were getting more intense and closer together. But nothing was the same as it had been last time. No backache. Just a gush of fluid between her legs and a call to the doctor reporting that her water had broken.

He'd asked her to come right in.

Now they were on the way to the hospital from their new house on Willow Lane, where Jack could easily supervise the construction of the children's center.

Sara smiled at her husband, and he smiled back.

She was still marveling at how different her life was from the way it had been the last time around.

She and Jack had eloped within a week of the confrontation at the old house. She'd dreaded going with him to tell his parents about the marriage. But they knew about the part Sara had played in saving the lives of both their sons. And they were likely also relieved that Jack was settling down and wasn't going to fight his brother for control of Morgan Enterprises. They'd accepted Sara as their daughter-in-law and been delighted when they'd found out she was going to have a baby. A boy again.

And Jack liked the name she'd chosen before. Daniel.

With her in-laws, she'd worked hard to put away the bad feelings from the first time around. In fact, she'd been able to see them in a better light once the tension of their previous dealings had faded.

This time they didn't think of her as a woman trying to get some of the Morgan money. Instead they saw her commitment to their son.

After a stern lecture to Ted for his reckless disregard for company funds, the elder Morgan had written off the missing money as a bad business investment.

Sara thought Ted had learned his lesson because he seemed to be running Morgan Enterprises without getting into any more trouble.

She was never going to be good friends with him, but at least they weren't enemies.

Another contraction brought her back to her own immediate situation.

She gritted her teeth until it passed.

"Hang on. We're almost there," Jack said, as the SUV approached the hospital.

They'd waited several months to get pregnant, and now it was late spring. A good time to have a baby, Sara thought, as Jack pulled up at the hospital entrance.

"Here we are. Safe and sound."

She squeezed his hand, more relieved than she wanted to admit. Even though the season was different, she'd still been worried about this trip.

Jack escorted her inside to the lobby, then parked the car and caught up with her in one of the birthing suites.

They'd attended childbirth classes together because he wanted to share every step of the experience. And she knew that he also wanted this time to be as different as possible from the last.

Now he helped her change into the oversize shirt she'd brought to wear instead of a hospital gown.

As she settled down in the bed, he pulled up his chair beside her, and she reached for his hand when another contraction grabbed her.

The doctor examined her and told her it would be a short labor.

Last time she'd wanted to use medication. This time she'd decided to see if natural childbirth would work for her, and she'd practiced breathing exercises. Jack coached her as the labor progressed. He rubbed her back, gave her ice chips, told her how much he loved her. And then when it was time, he was with the doctor at the foot of the bed, ready to welcome his son into the world.

"Push."

She gave a mighty heave, then another and another.

"I can see his head," the doctor told her. "One more good push."

She gathered her strength and bore down, hearing her son cry before he was all the way out of her.

"Perfect," Jack said.

"Do you want to cut the cord?" the doctor asked.

Jack did the honors, then the nurse washed Daniel, wrapped him in a blanket and handed him to Sara.

As she held her baby in her arms, Jack pulled his chair close, and tears filled her eyes.

"You did good," he said, emotion thickening his voice, and she knew he was tearing up, too.

"So did you."

"I think you had a little harder job."

"Having you here made it a whole lot easier," she whispered.

He kissed her brow. "I'll always be here, thanks to what you did."

She snuggled into his embrace, holding their baby, her happiness overflowing. She had come back to save the man she loved, and she had her reward.

* * * * *

"I heard a suspicious click right before the explosion. Someone wants you dead—with no evidence left behind."

"If you hadn't been here—"

She gripped his shirt and buried her head against him. He'd seen the reaction before. He held her tight.

"We'll find out who's doing this. I promise."

She wrapped her arms around his neck and hugged him tightly. He couldn't say no to her trembling frame. Each shudder evoked every protective instinct throbbing in his veins. He cradled her against him and stroked her hair softly, brushing a few stray snowflakes out of her hair. "You're okay. It'll be okay."

He was lying. Again. This assassin wanted a kill. Mitch could stop him only so long—unless he discovered who was behind the attempts on her life.

FINDING HER SON

BY
ROBIN PERINI

MILLS & BOON®

First published in Great Britain 2013
by Mills & Boon, an imprint of Harlequin (UK) Limited,
Eton House, 18-24 Paradise Road, Richmond, Surrey TW9 1SR

© Robin L. Perini 2012

ISBN: 978 0 263 90632 5
ebook ISBN: 978 1 472 01196 1

46-0613

Harlequin (UK) policy is to use papers that are natural, renewable and recyclable products and made from wood grown in sustainable forests. The logging and manufacturing processes conform to the legal environmental regulations of the country of origin.

Printed and bound in Spain
by Blackprint CPI, Barcelona

Award-winning author **Robin Perini**'s love of heart-stopping suspense and poignant romance, coupled with her adoration of high-tech weaponry and covert ops, encouraged her secret inner commando to take on the challenge of writing romantic suspense novels. Her mission's motto: "When danger and romance collide, no heart is safe."

Devoted to giving her readers fast-paced, high-stakes adventures with a love story sure to melt their hearts, Robin won the prestigious Romance Writers of America® Golden Heart® Award in 2011. By day, she works for an advanced technology corporation, and in her spare time, you might find her giving one of her many nationally acclaimed writing workshops or training in competitive small-bore rifle silhouette shooting. Robin loves to interact with readers. You can catch her on her website, www.robinperini.com, several major social-networking sites or write to her at PO Box 50472, Albuquerque, NM 87181-0472, USA.

For my mom—the most ferocious mama bear I know. Your love and unbending faith in me have given me the strength to persevere. I am truly blessed.
I love you, Mom. Always.

Acknowledgements

I'm living my dream. But no one gets to this wonderful place alone.

To my amazing editor, Allison Lyons, who saw something in my writing and took a chance.
You made my dreams come true.

To the most vicious critique group ever—
Tammy Baumann, Louise Bergin and Sherri Buerkle.
I love you all. You, my dear friends, sacrificed for this one more than anyone will know. I am humbled and grateful. Let's not do it again!

To Angi Platt and Jenn Stark for their keen insight and willingness to help. Thanks are not enough, and I expect payback.

To my best friend and the sister of my heart, Claire Cavanaugh, the wind beneath my wings.
This book wouldn't be here without you.
You know why.

Prologue

Icy wind howled through the SUV's shattered windshield, spraying glass and freezing sleet across Eric Wentworth's face. He struggled in and out of consciousness. Flashes of memory struck. Oncoming headlights on the wrong side of the road. Skidding tires on black ice. The baby's cries. Emily's screams.

Oh, God.

Why couldn't he focus? Above the wind, he heard only silence, then an ominous gurgling sound from his lungs. He shifted his head slightly to check on his wife, and a knife-like pain seared his neck. He stopped, staring in horror at the shaft of metal guardrail penetrating his chest. Blood pulsed from the wound, but he couldn't feel it. He couldn't feel anything.

Eric was dying. And it was no accident. He hadn't taken the threats seriously, hadn't told Emily what he'd done. Why they were all in danger.

"E-Eric?" Her voice was weak, barely audible over the storm gusts.

Thank the Lord she was still alive. In the darkness, he could just make out her small frame pinned by the dashboard. He had to warn her.

Emily. Escape. Before he comes back.

No sound came from his lips, and at the effort, his vision blurred.

"Eric, are you all right?"

Fear tinged her voice, but he could do nothing to comfort or reassure her.

A soft cry came from the backseat. The baby. Only a month old.

"Mommy's here." Emily pushed at the dash. "Eric, I'm stuck. I can't get to Joshua."

Headlights swept across the crumpled interior. A vehicle pulled up behind them.

"A car! Help!" Emily called out. "We're trapped! There's a baby in here!"

No! Emily. Get out. Now. Please. Take Joshua. Run.

A door slammed, but from the stealth of the approaching footsteps, Eric knew this was no rescue. Tears of impotent rage scalded his cheeks. *They're innocent. Don't kill them. They've done nothing.*

The back door ripped open, revealing a dark, hooded figure. The baby whimpered. After a moment's hesitation, the person unclicked the car seat and yanked it free.

The baby's cries filled the air.

A sob escaped Emily's throat. "Joshua? Is he all right?"

Without responding, the man shined the flashlight through the broken passenger window, scanned Emily, then focused the blinding light directly in Eric's face, illuminating his fatal wounds.

Emily gasped. "Eric! No! Please. Please, help my husband."

Struggling to remain conscious, Eric stared toward the beam of light, willing the man not to carry out the contract, silently begging for mercy for his family.

As if in answer, the man reached into the car, grabbed Emily and slammed her head on the door frame. With quick movements, he wrapped her hand around a jagged piece of windshield and forced it to slash across her neck.

No. Not Emily! Eric's silent scream echoed her agonized one. The man slammed her head again. She fell silent. Blood trickled down her throat.

With one last mocking salute, the bastard lifted the baby's car seat and turned away, smearing blood across the small, blue blanket. Utter grief overcame Eric as his son's cries disappeared into the night.

Spots danced in front of Eric's eyes. He stared at Emily's still body. His life flickered painfully within him.

Please, let her live. Give her strength. She has to find him.

Emily took a shallow breath as Eric Wentworth's world faded to black for the final time. *I'm sorry, my love. So sorry.*

Chapter One

One Year Later

Cursing under his breath, Mitch Bradford yanked his collar up against the bitter Colorado wind. Where was Emily Wentworth going? He stalked across Colfax, on a stretch of the street known as a candy store for illicit drugs and prostitution. He could've been home alone in front of the fireplace, his bum leg propped up, nursing a stiff drink and a double dose of ibuprofen. The irony didn't amuse him. He'd been tapped for the Wentworth case *because* of his injury. One more reason to kill the guy who'd shot up his leg during his last SWAT operation.

Mitch ducked his head and plunged forward into the night, ignoring the exchange of money on the corner. He would've busted the dealer any other time, but he refused to let his suspect out of sight. When she approached a group of gang-bangers, he tensed and reached for his weapon.

They circled her.

Two murders last night in the neighborhood. No time to be subtle.

He broke into a run, disregarding the twinge in his leg. He'd pay for it later, but they could shoot or stab her in seconds. Before he reached her, she tilted her head at the assailants like she was flirting and skirted through the wall of thugs. They let her go.

Mitch pulled back. Crazy woman. He tucked his Glock into the shoulder holster. He'd had enough of these cat-and-mouse games. He sped up and followed her across an alley. The scent of vomit and urine, and God knew what else, soured the night.

She stopped in front of a darkened building. After a furtive glance right, then left, she knocked. The door cracked open, then squeaked wider. Before he reached the entrance, she vanished behind the worn oak.

"Figures." Why would anything about this case be easy? Cold seeped through his jeans as he searched the front of the building for a sign. Nothing. No indication of what took place inside. That didn't bode well. His guess: drugs, sex, who knew what else.

A movement in the alley caught his attention. Carefully, he rounded the corner. A blond-haired kid tried to streak past. Mitch nabbed the boy's hoodie and lifted him off his feet. A familiar face glared at him. "Ricky?" Mitch released the young teen.

His on-again, off-again running back dusted his pants and groaned. "Coach. Man, why'd it have to be *you?* Gran'll have a fit if she has to come get me at juvie for breaking curfew."

"Then you better start talking. Is this why you haven't shown up for football practice the past two weeks? You hanging around the streets now?"

Ricky widened his stance and stared at Mitch, defiant. "I'm looking for Kayla."

"In an abandoned building?"

"Nah. Sister Kate runs a shelter out of here." Ricky bowed his head. "Kayla got herself pregnant by a real loser. But she was turning it around," he said in that earnest way that was half kid, half teenager. "At least that's what she told Gran last week. Kayla was gonna live with us again, but she didn't come back."

"You're hoping she landed here?"

Ricky nodded, and Mitch studied the street-smart kid. "You know how I can get in unnoticed?"

The boy's eyes grew large. "Something going down in there?" His gaze flickered to the front door. "Kayla might be in there."

Mitch rested his hand on Ricky's shoulder. "I don't—"

A loud, high-pitched scream pierced the night from inside. "Leave me alone. I won't go."

Ricky leaped toward the door, but Mitch held him back. He tossed the kid his cell phone. "A beat cop named Vance just rounded that corner not five minutes ago. Call 911, then get him."

"But Kayla…"

"I'll find your sister. Now go!"

Ricky took off down the street. Mitch pulled his Glock, braced, then barreled through the locked door, the rotted frame giving way much too easily. "Police," he shouted. "Nobody move."

A burly man spun around. "Do-gooders. You set me up. Well, I ain't letting 'em take me." He grabbed a pregnant girl, her face battered with yellow and green bruises, and held a knife against her throat.

"Please, Ghost. Don't do this." Emily Wentworth's husky voice shook as she stepped forward, her face pale. She clutched a bat in her hand.

She was a brave little thing, determined and fierce.

"I'm warning you," Ghost threatened.

With careful movements, she set the weapon aside. Her hand went to her throat. "Let Heather go. We'll work it out. I promise." She stepped closer.

"I said, don't move," Mitch snapped and glared at Emily. "That means everybody."

She met his gaze, the flash of fury in her eyes unmistakable, but with a curt nod backed away. Mitch took a quick survey of the room. Not a good setup. He could make the kill shot from where he stood, but he'd risk hitting the group of girls in various stages of pregnancy huddled around a nun. If Ghost had an automatic weapon under his coat, the situation could turn into a bloodbath.

Ghost pressed the knife closer, drawing blood at the girl's neck. "Back off. I'm leaving. With the girl. And you ain't stopping me."

After years on SWAT, Mitch recognized the wildness in the man's dilated eyes. "Come on, buddy. Put the knife down." Mitch lowered his weapon a bit. He could only hope the guy was high enough or stupid enough to relax his guard.

"She's coming with me. They won't pay me if I don't bring one of 'em back."

Mitch eased to his left for a better angle and met the frightened gaze of the girl. "You can't just *duck* out of here... Ghost." Mitch hunched his shoulders a bit and sagged, praying the terrified victim would understand his silent instruction.

"I don't want to go," Heather said, nodding. "I told him. Mrs. Wentworth said she'd help me." The girl went limp in the perp's arms.

Now.

Mitch spun on his good leg. One quick jab against Ghost's vulnerable back and the scumbag released his hold on the girl. Mitch shoved her toward Emily Wentworth and shifted his weight, but his injured leg spasmed and nearly buckled underneath him. He bit his cheek to block the pain as he covered the suspect with his Glock. No sirens and no telling if

Ricky had found help. Mitch needed backup before anyone realized his leg had locked up.

"On the ground. Face down. Arms spread. And you," he snapped at Emily, "call 911."

EMILY TAPPED THE PHONE to end the call. A cop. She should've known when the jerk burst through the door like some misguided superhero. He'd ruined everything. She and Sister Kate had almost guilted Ghost into talking. Now he was facedown on the floor, zip ties around his wrists, with no interest in spilling his guts to anyone. Great, just great. A month's worth of work down the drain.

Sister Kate knelt beside the man they'd hoped would be their informant. "You can tell us. It's the right thing to do."

Ghost glared at the nun. "Leave me alone."

"Sister," the cop said. "Step away from him. He's in custody."

An angry fire lit Sister Kate's eyes, one Emily had seen toast bigger brutes than this interfering officer. She waited for the blowtorch of words to fry him. In truth, she looked forward to it.

Sister Kate gave the cop a thorough once-over, then nodded her head before standing and walking away from Ghost. "You're one of the Bradford boys. Handsome as sin, the lot of you. The middle one, I'd wager. You've got the look of your daddy. I'll give you a pass. For now."

Emily almost smiled at the man's slack-jawed expression. "You know my father?"

"Oh, my, yes. Sergeant Bradford visited my halfway house to recruit for his football team. I hear you're following in his footsteps, Mitch." At his slight nod, she patted his arm. "I was sorry about what happened to him."

The man's jaw tightened, but Emily didn't miss the flash of pain across his face. She recognized the emotion all too well, but she couldn't let herself sympathize with him, even if Sister Kate was right, and his rugged good looks would make angels weep.

Emily had only one mission. Finding her son. And this cop—Mitch Bradford—had ruined her most promising lead. With nothing to lose, she bolted to Ghost and grabbed his collar. "Tell me the name," she said, her permanently husky voice still foreign to her ears, but an all-too-physical reminder of her entire purpose in life. "It's the only way you might talk your way out of this."

"Go to hell. You and your nun." Ghost flipped on his back and kicked out. A chair near his feet flew across the room. He lunged at Emily.

"Get away from him." Mitch grasped Emily's arm and yanked her to safety before subduing Ghost and pinning him with a knee to his back.

The brute on the floor grunted. "You should've stayed out of it."

"Shut up," Mitch said. He double-checked the zip-tie cuffs just as a cruiser pulled up, sirens blaring. A uniform raced inside.

"Get this guy out of here," Mitch said. "I'll file my report once I get back."

The cop nodded and escorted Ghost from the building. Officer Bradford walked toward the girls huddled in the corner, his gait slightly off when he put weight on his right leg. As he approached, they shrank away. Emily didn't blame them. It had taken her months to get past the fragmented flashes of memory when any man in a dark coat had come near her. For these teens—one girl's eye was swollen shut; another's face was mottled yellow and green from old bruises—all they'd see would be a tall, muscular brute who had shown he could incapacitate anyone who crossed him.

Then his expression softened. "You did great, Heather," he said softly. "Is everyone else okay? Anybody need a doctor?"

The girls shook their heads.

"Sister Kate takes care of us," one said, crossing her arms in defiance. "She's a nurse."

He nodded, not pushing just accepting. Emily couldn't get over the change in his demeanor. He'd transformed in seconds from a warrior—someone she was convinced could've killed Ghost if he'd wanted—to a man with a gentle gaze. Still, none of the girls would look him in the eye. His focus lowered to the discolored cheeks of one of the teens. His lips grew tight. Good. If nothing else, the evidence of abuse made him angry.

"Will you tell me about Ghost?" he said, still keeping his voice calm and low.

Amid the blare of more sirens, the girls looked as if they'd rather die than say anything.

"I got proof they're hooked up with drug dealers." Ghost's shouts rammed through the open doorway. "I can give you names, dates, places. I know their johns. I can help you put 'em away. Give their babies to people who deserve 'em."

Heather shivered and caressed her burgeoning belly. Her gaze rose to Mitch's. "He trolls for girls who get knocked up. Tries to sweet-talk the ones who haven't been around too long. He sells himself as someone who can help. We know better. They're buying a one-way ticket when they go with Ghost."

"You never see any of them again," Mitch said, the statement stark and certain, the ending unspoken.

A commotion sounded from the kicked-in doorway.

"I got something for Coach…Officer Bradford," a young kid shouted.

The cop stood and walked over to the boy, who handed over a cell phone. "I couldn't find Vance, Coach."

"That's okay, Ricky."

The boy received an affectionate ruffle to his hair, and Mitch guided the kid over to them. "Sister Kate, Mrs. Wentworth, this is Ricky Foster. He's looking for his sister, Kayla."

Over the next hour, Mitch questioned the girls and Ricky. Pregnant girls vanishing. Their babies gone. Not one of them reported missing. Until Kayla Foster.

"You'll find her?" Ricky asked, his voice laced with hope as Mitch led him to the back exit, past the front door he and Ricky had worked side-by-side to barricade to the back exit.

"Get me the picture, and I'll put the word out. We'll discover what happened."

Ricky walked out of the shelter with an expression that could only be described as cautiously optimistic.

"I wish we'd seen her." She spoke to the nun standing at her side.

"I have a feeling with Officer Bradford on the case, Ricky will be reunited with Kayla."

"It doesn't always end the way we'd want, Sister," Mitch said from behind them.

Emily hadn't realized he'd approached. She stiffened as his huge presence overwhelmed her, making her heart race. Not with fear, though. With something else—unfamiliar and enticing at the same time.

"Oh, I'm well aware of that, boy-o," Sister Kate said. "But we can't give up, can we? One soul at a time." The nun glanced at her watch. "Now, it's getting late. We're safe, and I need to do a bed check on my chickadees. Perhaps you'll walk Emily to her car? It's dark, and a pretty girl like her would do well to have a strong protector at this time of night."

The cop turned to Emily, his chocolate eyes studying her with an intensity that made her shiver. Heat rose into Emily's face, and she knew her cheeks must be crimson. When had Sister Kate turned into a matchmaker?

Her belly fluttered. He'd been so gentle and caring with the girls and Ricky, but she couldn't let herself feel anything. She just prayed a man like Mitch was watching over Joshua somewhere. And that someday she would find her son.

"You ready?" Mitch asked.

She clutched the satchel she always carried containing an age-progressed photo, fliers and the case details. Could this policeman help her? She'd never felt she could rely on the police department...or the cops in it. They'd never believed her. This man seemed different somehow, but she didn't know if she could trust him. With Ghost a lost cause, she needed another way to get information on these missing children and hopefully tie them to Joshua.

Mitch turned, and as his weight shifted to his right leg, he hesitated. She studied him for a few steps. His hip did most of the work on his right side. He tried hard not to let it show. If her job hadn't been to notice the signs of strain on the human body, he would've succeeded. He'd injured himself being a hero, trying to save them.

"You're hurt."

He stiffened, warning her to back off, but she wouldn't. Not when he was so obviously in pain. She dug into her purse for her keys and tugged out a card. "You injured yourself helping me, Officer. Come by. Let me take a look at your leg. Maybe I can do something for you." She thrust the card into his hand.

"Physical therapist, huh?"

"What've you got to lose?"

"I'm fine," he said. "Let's go."

He'd clearly shut her out. Emily remained silent, but she wouldn't forget what he'd done. He opened the back door for her, and she walked out of the haven that Sister Kate had created for her lost girls into a darkened alley filled with the sounds of angry shouts and crying babies.

When they reached the street, a tall woman in a spandex dress whistled at them. "You and your lady looking for some action?"

"No thanks. We're exclusive." Mitch tucked Emily's arm in his and shifted closer to her.

"Lucky lady," the woman said and turned her salesmanship toward a slow-moving BMW, so out of place on this street.

"You don't have to protect me," Emily said.

"After what I witnessed tonight, I'm not so sure." His gaze scanned the street before he guided her toward the crosswalk. "If you want to be a crusader, take some advice. Don't get too involved," he said. "It'll eat you up inside."

"You're a cop. You obviously think everyone's a bad guy."

Mitch's grip tightened on her arm, and he stopped. "See that kid on the corner? His name is Mario. He's twenty now. Was an amazing quarterback. Smart. Could've gone to any college he wanted. Gotten a degree. Maybe even turned pro. But he couldn't say no to his so-called friends. He was shot at seventeen. Severed the nerves in his throwing arm. No more scholarship. He gave up. He's dealing now. He'll be in prison within the year. Dead in five."

Emily doubted Mitch recognized how clearly his emotions for this young man showed on his face. "He was one of your team," Emily said. "Like Ricky."

Mitch nodded and guided her down the street. "I know the odds. I thought Mario would make it. I was wrong. I don't want to be wrong about Ricky. I'm going to fight for him. And his sister. But the odds are against them."

"You still try. And you still care."

A car screeched around the corner and barreled directly toward them. Before Emily could move, Mitch grabbed her and dove away from the oncoming vehicle. He slammed into the ground hard, wrapping her in his arms and turning so she landed on top of him. A heated gust from the car rocked them as the old Cadillac squealed past.

Mitch let out a sharp curse. "Okay, lady. Just what have you gotten yourself into?"

THE SUNSHINE-YELLOW curtains and serene green walls should've made Vanessa happy, but the colors mocked her. She'd been so very stupid. Why hadn't she left town when she'd first decided to keep her baby? The midwife had been furious. The doctor would—

A key jiggled in the lock. Vanessa huddled in the bed, cradling her newborn baby girl in her arms. Fine blond hair covered her sweet head, and Vanessa kissed the tiny cheek. "Mama will take care of you."

She prayed it would be so.

The door eased open, revealing the man who'd approach her in the mall just a few short months ago. "We had a deal." His voice was quiet and cold.

Vanessa shivered. She'd expected him to start yelling, and now wished he'd slammed open the door and screamed at her. This deadly anger made her insides quake. Bad things always happened when her daddy got like that.

"I'll pay you back. I promise." Vanessa swallowed around the lump in her throat. "I just can't give her up. I love her."

"You love her. Really? Well. That's just too bad. I have a family for her, and they aren't going to wait." He thrust a paper toward her. "Sign the form. Now."

"No."

"Marie," he called out the door. "Get in here."

The portly midwife rushed in. "But Doctor—"

"Do it."

She sighed and reached for Vanessa's baby. "I'm sorry, honey."

"You can't just take her!"

Vanessa kicked and screamed, holding on to her child, but it was no use. She was too weak from giving birth. "You can't do this," she cried as the midwife left the room with the baby. "I'll tell the police you forced me to sign. They'll give her back."

"No, my dear," the doctor said, his voice deadly soft. "You won't be telling anyone."

He moved fast, then grabbed her arm and secured one wrist with a restraint strap. She fought, rolling her body back and forth, scratching his cheek, anything to stop him.

He cursed and slapped her face. Her head snapped back, and by the time she regained her senses, he'd fastened her other hand to the rails of the hospital bed. She arched and twisted against the bindings, but he just smiled, his expression calm as he touched his hand to the cheek where she'd clawed him.

"This could've been so easy. You should've taken the money. You could've had a new life like your slutty friends," he said.

A sharp prick. She yelped at the sting as he tugged out the needle and untied her.

"What did you do to me?" She sat up, rubbed her freed hands and stared down at her arm where a small drop of blood formed.

"You'll know soon enough."

She looked at him, seeing for the first time that the eyes she'd once believed glowed with compassion were blank and hollow. "Let me have my baby. Please."

Begging him to listen, to do the right thing, suddenly she swayed. Her arms dropped, her head spun. She tried to breathe, but she couldn't. Something was choking her. She gasped. Oh, dear Lord. What was wrong? She tried to suck in air and clasped at her chest. It felt like someone was sitting on her, suffocating her. Desperately she tried to breathe, but she couldn't. The doctor's grin grew wide.

She reached out to him. "Help me. Something's…wrong."

"Sign this." He thrust the paper beneath her hand and placed a pen there. "And I'll save you."

She panted, listening to the short gasps as if she floated outside herself. She didn't have a choice. Somehow she'd get her baby girl back. But she had to stay alive.

Barely able to see the line on the page, she scrawled her name on the paper, then slumped back against the sheets. She reached out to him. "Help me. You promised."

"That I did. But then, so did you."

With the signed consent form in his hand, he walked out the door, closing it behind him.

Vanessa couldn't yell, she couldn't scream. She stared at the sunshine-yellow curtains, and they morphed into strange shapes and faces. The doctor's face. He laughed at her. Called her a fool.

And she had been. It was all her fault. What would happen to her baby?

She tried to breathe. She couldn't. Strange white spots danced in front of her eyes. There was nothing she could do. Nothing.

Please, God. Protect my baby.

Chapter Two

Chapter Two

Mitch grimaced as he limped into the police department. What a night. And it wasn't over. He'd called in the hit-and-run. Two reports of assault in less than an hour. He'd never live it down. Especially since the busy downtown street had suddenly gone ultrasilent right after the attack. No witnesses. No nothing.

Just a woman who'd seemed quite satisfied to have been attacked. She'd met his gaze and without blinking had said, "I've got them worried. That means I'm onto something."

Unbelievable.

Half of him admired her tenacity. She scared the spit out of his other half. Come to think of it, she'd acted a lot like his late mother when he or his siblings had been on the short end of trouble. Fearless. Mitch got that. Mama-bear syndrome. Do anything for your child. But with such an overt attempt on her life, Emily'd found more trouble than she realized. She'd made someone *very* nervous.

She'd even fought leaving. Had wanted to stay, canvas the neighborhood. Only the threat of spending the night in the police station had convinced her to leave. He'd tailed her to confirm she went home and hadn't doubled back. She was safe—for now. With an unmarked unit watching her, just in case.

He glanced at his watch. Midnight was around the corner.

He was on Emily duty first thing in the morning and still had reports to file. He straightened and struggled to hide his awkward stride. At this hour, maybe he could get past the desk sergeant and the SWAT Den without seeing anyone he knew.

His thigh was on fire; his muscles were seizing up. He had less than two months to pass the physical to get his real job back. If he didn't do something drastic, he'd lose his career.

With a sigh, he sank into the hard wood of his desk chair and massaged his leg. What if he couldn't go back to SWAT? He wasn't an investigator. He didn't like analyzing and waiting. He liked breaking down doors and grabbing the bad guy. No talk. Just action. It'd felt good bringing down Ghost tonight.

"What did you do, Bradford?" Detective Dane Tanner, his temporary supervisor, stalked into the room. "You're hobbling like an old woman."

Mitch stiffened at the truth in Tanner's words. "Nothing. Just a little twinge. What are you doing here this late? I thought high-powered detectives kept banker's hours."

"Ever hear of a police radio? I keep tabs on my guys, especially those wet behind the ears like you. I heard from dispatch about your adventures tonight—you bagged this guy, Ghost, for targeting young girls. Good job." Tanner's face twisted into a scowl. "Unfortunately, he broke out of holding. A couple of street thugs created a diversion and the perp fought his way out. Put two of our guys in the hospital."

Mitch shot to his feet. "He got away? You get his prints?"

"No such luck, but we have an APB out on him." Tanner shook his head. "He's a dangerous guy. You took a big risk going in alone."

"I tried to get backup."

"Yeah, you had a fourteen-year-old kid call 911 and then try to find Vance—who'd just gone off duty, by the way.

Better men than you haven't walked away from psychos like Ghost."

"Point taken," Mitch said. His father, Paul Bradford, had been paralyzed in a shootout five years ago. Being a cop and carrying a weapon hadn't protected him. And his dad hadn't been trying to fight on an injured leg.

"I hope so. I understand investigating's not your gig. But until you pass the SWAT physical, you're stuck with us. You follow our rules. One of which is not to go in without backup. The other is not to reveal your identity to a suspect. In your case, Emily Wentworth."

"Detective—"

"Don't even try to tap dance. Lives were on the line. I get it, but you better comprehend how lucky you were." Tanner crossed his arms, staring Mitch down with a warning the ex-special forces officer clearly expected to be heeded. "Did you at least salvage the Wentworth case?"

"She noticed my leg. She offered to help me with rehab, and I've got another angle I can work to stay near her."

Mitch ran down the Kayla Foster situation, and Tanner smiled. "It sounds like you're in. We might make a detective of you after all."

"Over my dead body," Mitch growled.

"I hope not. Your dad would kill me." Tanner bent closer, his expression deadly serious. "I want this collar. Someone orchestrated Eric Wentworth's death. His murder case was stone-cold until his mother discovered that bank account in Emily's name. It's a *lot* of money and puts a whole new spin on the investigation. I want to know how the wife's involved, and I'm not backing down this time."

"If Emily's guilty, why would she offer to help me?"

"To gain an ally in the office. To get intel on what's happening in the investigation. If she arranged the hit-and-run to take out her husband, then she's willing to do anything—

including slitting her own throat—to make herself look like a victim. You and I both know that's not as uncommon as it should be."

"You're reaching. Emily almost died. Her voice will never be the same. And my neighborhood contacts don't know squat about her being involved in *anything,* except she's a do-gooder." Mitch knew he'd been mistaken in the past, but he couldn't get past his feelings about Emily. If he could trust them. "What if we're wrong? What if she's just trying to find her son?"

"Could be." His boss's jaw tightened. "But she knows *something.* And someone tried to kill her tonight. And that someone wasn't Ghost. I want an explanation." His eyes were cold. "There's dirt there. I can smell it. Find the proof. Whatever it takes."

NO MORNING SUN PEEKED through the winter clouds closing in on the cemetery. The day *should* be dreary. Nothing good should happen on December fifth. Ever again. Emily ran her fingertips over the engraved inscription on the wall of stone. *Eric Wentworth. Beloved son and father.*

"Beloved husband," she whispered the words his family had denied her and wiped away a single tear.

She stood alone just inside the open archway of the Wentworth Family Mausoleum, the large marble temple as cold and unforgiving as Eric's family. They'd made their feelings perfectly clear with his marker. They had never accepted her. They blamed her for Eric's death and Joshua's kidnapping. If only she could remember that night. Something more than headlights, screams and a hooded man.

A gust of icy winter wind buffeted against her, and she stuffed her hands in her pockets. She should know what happened to her child. The diaper bag had been left in the car, but Joshua and his car seat were gone. "I still haven't found our baby, Eric," she said in the husky voice her husband wouldn't have recognized. "I'm sorry."

A lonely bell tolled from afar, and just as the tones died, a rustle of grass fluttered. She tensed. She'd had a sense all morning someone was watching her—again. For weeks she'd fought her instincts, but after last night's attack, she didn't doubt the feelings.

A looming shadow crossed the side of Emily's face. "You don't belong here."

Emily shivered at her mother-in-law's sharp words and turned slightly. Victoria Wentworth looked the perfect, elegant role of grieving mother, her black veil hiding her expression and eyes Emily knew were accusatory.

"You're not family."

"He's my husband," Emily countered softly.

"You killed him."

"Mother, you know that's not true." Victoria's son, William, stepped forward to pull her back. He shot Emily an apologetic look. "It was a tragic accident."

Victoria slapped William's hand away and faced Emily. "You set up the murder of my son and grandson. And someday I'll prove it."

Emily winced. She'd been eager to get along with Eric's family, but from the beginning the Wentworths had pushed her away until finally Eric had made a choice. He'd turned his back on them, their money and their corporation until Joshua was born and Emily had persuaded him to reconcile. Their baby deserved a family. The snowy drive to Cherry Hills Village last December had been *her* idea. In so many ways, his death in the hit-and-run truly was on her shoulders. "I loved Eric."

"You wanted a way at the Wentworth money," Victoria said as her husband, Thomas, entered the tomb and stood by her side. She reached out and clasped his hand. "Well, we won't allow it. Eric disinherited himself, and we told the insurance company his death was your fault. We even found your secret account. You'll get nothing. Nothing."

Account? "What are you talking about?"

"As if you didn't know." Victoria turned to her son. "William, get her out of here."

Victoria tilted her head into Thomas's shoulder and broke down in sobs. William whispered something to his mother and hurried to Emily.

"I think you'd better go now," he said. "I'll walk you to your car."

"I didn't *do* anything. You know that. He was my husband. I loved him." With one last look at Victoria and what might have been, Emily slid on her gloves, fighting tears of confusion, anger and hurt. William escorted her out of the cold building. Their footsteps crunched over frozen grass as they crossed toward the parking lot.

"I know you loved him," William said. "Mother can be a real witch when she wants to be. She can't let go of Eric. None of us really can."

"You think I've let go? I fight to find our son every day."

"And that's something else we have to talk about."

William's tentative voice, so similar to Eric's, sent a chill of foreboding through Emily.

"I don't quite know how to say this, so I'll just tell you. Mother and Father found my receipts for your private investigator and some of the airline tickets I bought. They came unglued when they learned I'd been helping you financially. I had to promise I'd quit."

Emily halted and faced William. "You can't stop now. I'm counting on your help." She clutched at his arm. "I'm so close."

"You've found Joshua?"

William gripped her arm, the eagerness in his voice gratifying, but she couldn't mislead him. "Not exactly. I'm collecting information on adoptions from last year because I discovered these missing babies downtown. Well, at least there are missing pregnant girls, and—"

"Oh, Emily. How many times have we traveled down this path?" He shook his head. "I'm sorry, but they're my family. In some ways they're right. It's been a year. We have to accept reality. We've tried to find him. Even my parents tried. But Joshua's gone."

"I'm not giving up. Not ever, but I need more time. With your parents painting me as a Black Widow in the gossip rags, my clinic is barely making it."

"I can't help anymore. I'm sorry." William opened the door of the decade-old compact Eric had complained about so often. When she slid onto the cracked vinyl seat, William knelt beside the car. "Take my advice. Move on with your life. Close this chapter."

"How can I do that when my son is out there somewhere? You may not believe I'll find him, but I refuse to accept that I won't."

William gripped her hands, his gaze regretful. "Then I'm sorry for you. Goodbye, Emily." He shut the door and, after a pitying look, walked back to the family crypt.

She shuddered and let out a slow breath, the cold filtering into her bones. This couldn't be happening. She started her car and cranked up the heater as high as it would go to ease her shivering, though that had little to do with the weather. She'd wondered why the life-insurance company kept stalling on the check. She had her answer. And what was that about the so-called secret account? She'd have to call the bank, but she'd never get at the money. The Wentworths would see to that.

She glanced at her watch. Officer Bradford had an appointment and would be waiting at her clinic. Could she trust him? Right now, she needed him as much as he needed her. The second phase of her plan made her stomach churn, but she had to take drastic action. She needed funds to ramp up her search for Joshua. Eric would've understood.

Snagging her purse, she dug into her pocket for the number she'd saved. With one last glance at the marble resting place of the man with whom she'd thought she'd spend the rest of her life, she placed the call. "Karen, it's Emily. Put the house up for sale. I'll take the first offer. I need the cash. Now."

THE PHYSICAL-THERAPY clinic looked too familiar. Mitch hated the fact he had a reason to enter the place, but after following Emily all morning, after zero leads on either the attempted hit-and-run, Ghost or Kayla's disappearance, the trail was subzero. He had to shake something loose.

Mitch groaned as he pushed open the door and surveyed the plethora of exercise equipment and tables. The scent of menthol wafted on the air—an odor far too familiar for his liking. Several rehab patients worked on recumbent bikes. A few more did stretching exercises with the help of staff.

When he'd discovered she had an opening this morning, he'd scrambled to get a copy of his records, threw on his sweats and headed out the door. Mitch could now infiltrate Emily's life, but he wasn't an undercover cop. He didn't like lying, he hated deceit and he was doing both. The bonus? He got the pleasure of being tortured in physical therapy for his trouble. A real win-win.

A young receptionist rounded her desk. "May I help you?"

With a quick, plastered-on grin, he scanned her name tag. "Hi, Cindy. Mitch Bradford. I have an appointment with Emily Wentworth."

The door behind them flew open, and a familiar dynamo dressed from head to foot in black raced into the room.

"Cindy, I know I'm late. Please tell me my new patient isn't—"

She skidded to a halt, clearly dismayed to see Mitch standing there. "Shoot."

Holy smokes. Emily Wentworth looked good. He didn't know how he could've missed the impact of her up close and personal last night. She was completely his type, with a petite, fit body and long, light brown hair swinging from a ponytail—obviously so silky it would be amazing spread across his pillow. Then he stared into her eyes, and his heart skipped a beat. Thick lashes framed the bluest, saddest eyes he'd ever seen. For a moment he felt lost. Her look was kind and sympathetic, with depth that could embrace his soul.

Where had that come from, waxing poetic? He had a job to do. But as he took in the plain black dress, with its high collar circling her neck, he recalled her complete aloneness at the cemetery. He'd been watching, forced to back away once the Wentworths arrived. It was the anniversary of her husband's death. Was she still in mourning, or was this all for show, all part of an elaborate plan to get at the Wentworth money?

Mitch's gut told him she was sincere. He didn't want to believe the pain on her face, the sorrow in her eyes, had been anything but real.

Then again, his gut hadn't been all that reliable lately. A few months ago, Mitch had learned his mentor had been a traitor to the badge. He wouldn't be fooled so easily now. Not anymore. He couldn't afford to give Emily the benefit of the doubt.

Mitch gave her a deliberately innocent smile. "Did I get the time wrong?"

She bit her lip, embarrassment tingeing her cheeks.

"No," she said. "I'm so sorry. Not a great way to make a first impression as a therapist. Let me change, and I'll be right with you."

"I'm not going anywhere." Not until he knew for sure whether he'd completely lost his ability to tell the good guys from the bad guys. If he was wrong about her, he'd get the evidence he needed. And if she *was* guilty, he might as well just turn in his badge.

With a smile of gratitude, she disappeared behind a staff door.

Cindy handed him a stack of paperwork. "Emily will be right back. If you'll fill out these forms…"

Mitch took the clipboard and sat in the chair closest to the receptionist before stretching his leg out. "So, I guess I was lucky to get in to see her so quickly. I heard she's really good. I thought I'd have to wait longer for an appointment."

"Oh, Emily's the best, but…" Cindy hesitated. "She's not that busy these days. Clients stopped coming because of her in-laws. They've said some things about her, and, well, some people gossip too much." Cindy bit her lip and took a furtive glance around. "I need to get back to work."

Obviously, Emily's business had taken a big hit. That money angle his boss had mentioned reared its head again, but Mitch didn't see the connection. *If* that secret account were hers, why not use it to save her business? Why work at all? Why not just disappear?

Mitch tried to get comfortable, but his leg had been giving him fits ever since that confrontation with Ghost. His body had revolted against a move he'd used a thousand times.

Once he finished the paperwork, he settled in for the long wait, but she returned in less than five minutes. Women usually took forever with clothes. Not Emily. Which shouldn't have been surprising really. Nothing had been usual when it came to this assignment. The turtleneck she wore under her scrubs was a subtle reminder of what he knew lay beneath. He'd reviewed the crime-scene photos, had seen the jagged cut across her throat that had permanently damaged her vocal cords.

"Officer, come on back." Her husky voice sent a shiver through him. He didn't know what her voice had sounded like before, but this one was downright sexy.

"Call me Mitch. If you're going to have your hands all over me, we should be on a first-name basis." He followed her into a private examining room, trying to avoid studying the sway of her hips under the scrubs she'd changed into. Down, boy. Do *not* let yourself get taken in by a pair of baby blues and luscious curves. If she were innocent and wore black on the anniversary of her husband's death, the implications made her so far off-limits, there wasn't a measurement long enough.

She shut the door and cleared her throat, nodding at the exam table. Mitch was just relieved she didn't offer to help him. His pride could only take so much. "Here's my chart, just like you requested."

He levered himself up on the table as she sat down and flipped through the pages. "You've been in therapy four months." She closed the chart. "I didn't really think you'd take me up on the offer."

"Normally I wouldn't have." The words slipped off his tongue easily—since they were the truth. "I've got two months to requalify for SWAT. I'll do anything to make that happen…Emily. Anything. And your reputation as a physical therapist… You're one of the best."

She nodded slowly. "The gunshot wound caused a lot of damage to your femoral artery and the surrounding nerves and muscles. What did your doctors say?"

"That I might never walk again. I didn't listen too hard."

A laugh escaped her, and the smile brightened her eyes. She sure was pretty.

"Good attitude. As long as you don't go too far too fast. You came a few centimeters away from losing your leg." She leaned back in her chair and set the chart aside. "Do you have the patience to follow orders? I won't work with someone who goes off on his own. Even though you saved my life. You'll need to do as I say. *Exactly* as I say."

He understood chain of command, but from this slip of a thing… He bristled and met her unyielding gaze. He couldn't afford not to play along. He'd seen the toughness in her before, the challenge. He'd give her a shot. It wasn't like he had a choice. She was his assignment. But could he get his leg strength back *and* investigate Emily at the same time? Without going crazy?

"I want my SWAT uniform back. You tell me to sweat bullets, run stadium steps, go to yoga, I'll do it. I'll even wear a Texas Longhorns jersey, and I'm an Oklahoma Sooner, born and bred. You come up with a program to help me pass that physical, and I'm with you one thousand percent."

"I'd have thought you a Colorado Buffaloes fan. But I believe you. So let's get a baseline. You wearing workout shorts under those?" She stood and indicated his sweats.

He nodded. "And just to be clear, my grandparents came from Oklahoma. Once a Sooner…"

"I get it." She smiled. "I like your loyalty to your roots, Mitch Bradford. I'll go get some equipment while you take your pants off."

A few months ago that order would have had him pulling her into his arms. Now Mitch simply slipped off his shoes, socks and sweats. He knew the drill. He'd never felt naked in a clinic before, but as he rubbed the gnarled scars on his thigh, he tensed. She'd know soon enough how damaged he really was.

After a slight knock, she entered the room. She glanced at his leg but didn't give anything away—not pity, not disgust. She moved in closer, and he caught a waft of sweet mixed with tartness. Vanilla and some kind of berry, perhaps? His heart thudded as she placed her hands on his thigh.

"Let's get started," she said.

A dozen measurements later, Mitch swiped at the sweat rolling down his face and bit his lip to stop himself from crying out. The white-hot shards of pain shooting across his thigh were much worse since his heroics of the night before. He tried to ignore them as he strained against the minuscule weight Emily had pressed against his leg. His muscles behaved like traitors. Weak as a baby.

She frowned at her notes as she compared them to his records. Then she glared at him. "What have you been doing to yourself? You've lost at least fifteen percent of your strength and flexibility gains in the past month. That didn't happen because of a single jujitsu turn. What aren't you telling me?"

Mitch grimaced, and she just shook her head. "Never mind. I know. You thought you'd be a cowboy and do a little extra on your own. More is better. Am I close?"

She shifted forward and placed her warm hands on his thigh, working the spasming muscles. Slowly, her touch eased the pain. As the agony became bearable, his focus shifted toward her fingertips on his skin, moved up her arms, to the concentration on her face. He wanted to lift her chin and lose himself in those blue eyes of hers. He wanted to forget everything that was happening around them and just escape in her caresses.

"Man, you're good," he groaned. "Can I take you home with me?" Emily on call 24/7. Part-time to massage his aching leg and part-time to take those magic hands and lips a little higher and to the left.

She worked the muscles up and down his thigh. "I know you want faster results, but if you keep working out on your own, you'll do permanent damage. You've really screwed up your leg, Mitch." She removed her hands. He missed her touch already, but her face had gone deadly serious. "I want a straight answer. Will you follow my rules?"

As he took in her no-nonsense expression, a shaft of fear sliced through him. Had he lost his chance to get back to SWAT? Follow her rules? He had no choice. For more reasons than she could comprehend. "You're the boss in the gym, Emily. I'll do whatever it takes to get the job done. I promise you that."

She paused and finally reached out her hand. "Okay. But you go off on your own, and I'm done. No second chances. Got it?"

He nodded.

The ringing cell punctuated her orders, and Emily's heart tripped at the sound. Every time she got a call, part of her leaped at the thought of good news while a small dark place trembled with fear of horrifying news. She shoved aside the terror and pulled her phone from her pocket. She glanced at the familiar number. Her pulse raced. Maybe this time... She tapped the phone and stepped away for privacy.

"Hello?" She struggled to keep her voice from being too eager, too hopeful, but she couldn't help herself.

"Mrs. Wentworth?" Her private investigator's voice crackled through the phone.

"Perry, any more on Ghost that I can use when I talk to him?"

"He lives up to his handle, ma'am. He really is a ghost, but I did get a lead. Sister Kate connected me with one of the girls. She saw a tattoo that he tried to hide. She won't go down to the police department, but she described portions of it. The art was complicated and colorful. I can fax you a picture of something similar, but I can't get into the police records, mug shots or tattoo database to verify his gang affiliation."

A tattoo. Pain shot through her temple, and she kneaded

the throbbing spot, the burn behind her eyes so familiar. A small whimper escaped her lips. It happened whenever she felt on the cusp of remembering the night of the accident. The threatening memories slipped away, and Emily pushed aside the pain.

"Another flash?" Perry asked, obviously hearing the familiar sound.

"Just images of pink, green and red."

"Like a tattoo?"

"Maybe." She let out a hiss of frustration. "I don't know. But the episodes are happening more frequently."

"You know something important, Mrs. Wentworth. You'll recall that night eventually."

She couldn't wait. She had to go to the police department. She didn't want to ask the detective in charge of her case for assistance, but wouldn't he have to listen this time? A car had tried to run her over. Ghost had threatened her. She was remembering something. "Keep digging. I'll talk to Detective Tanner." She tried to keep optimism in her voice, but even to her own ears she sounded frustrated. "Maybe he'll help this time."

Their connection ended, and she bit her lip as she studied her phone list on the small screen. A call wouldn't do any good. Tanner would only put her off again. She'd go over there and wait as long as it took to look at those tattoo records. He would give her access. She'd make sure of it.

She snagged Mitch's chart, grabbed her bag and turned to schedule the next session. He'd moved so quietly, she hadn't heard him, but there he stood, inches from her. She almost stepped on his foot and stumbled into his arms. He reached out to steady her, so close she could feel his warmth. She couldn't stop her body's reaction to his nearness.

"Whoa, there. Are you okay?" Mitch said.

Her cheeks burned hot, and she pushed back the hair that

had fallen in her face. She wanted to ask him for help but just wasn't sure enough of him. Not yet. "Sorry. I've got to run. Ten a.m. day after tomorrow okay with you?"

"I'll be here."

She bent her head to make a note, and her unruly locks fell forward again. With gentle fingers, Mitch pushed the hair back in place. His pupils went black as his gaze strayed to her lips.

She cleared her throat and stepped back, touching her fingertips to her mouth. "Um…I'd better go."

Mitch slowly nodded his head. "I think that's a good idea."

Emily filed away his record and raced out the door, her heart slamming into her chest. Her nerves tingled with awareness. Okay, so Mitch was strong and funny and determined. And hot. Despite his injury, he had a body that didn't stop.

Each step, each rub of her cotton turtleneck against her skin reminded her of what she wanted. What she hadn't experienced since before Joshua was born. Her breasts ached beneath her clothes. She couldn't deny her reaction to Mitch, but that didn't mean anything would ever happen between them. Besides, she didn't have time for a relationship. Not with anyone. Not until she found Joshua. Thinking of Mitch in any way other than a client or a potential resource was a big mistake. She was a widow. In some ways, she'd become one even before Eric had died, but her aching loneliness was *her* problem.

She looked back. He stood, watching her, his expression hooded and thoughtful. She might need him and his contacts. She'd promised to help him, otherwise she would've handed his case over to one of her colleagues. He and Carl would probably hit it off, but she couldn't risk letting go of even one potential collaborator.

She would find her son and just prayed Mitch would heal fast—before this unsettling temptation got the best of her.

THE ICY SHOWER HADN'T worked. Mitch secured the towel at his waist and padded across the cold tile of his bathroom. He'd almost kissed Emily. He'd wanted to, more so when he'd recognized the awareness that flashed in her eyes and echoed within him. He could think of a hundred reasons not to give in to the feelings, but that didn't make him want to touch her any less.

At least he'd bargained for a few hours not having to watch her. He was getting to know every curve of her body, every expression on her face. Bad news. Let another cop get tempted—until he had himself back under control.

The Oklahoma fight song sounded from his phone on the nightstand. His brother, Chase, and his best friend, Ian, gave him a hard time, but "Boomer Sooner" made Mitch grin. Who wanted Mozart or a simple ringtone? Just because his best friend and one of his siblings happened to be one pancake short of a stack and attended the University of Texas... well, sometimes you just had to live with your family's weaknesses.

"Bradford."

"It's Ian."

Mitch sank onto the bed. "Are you calling as the Coroner's Office Investigator or my goddaughter's father?"

"Sorry, bud. Haley's great, but you asked me to contact you if we received any pregnant guests. Jane Doe came in today. Not pregnant, but she gave birth just before she died. Blond hair, like the girl you asked me to watch out for."

"Is it Kayla Foster?" Mitch braced himself for the answer.

"She was in a shallow grave, so the animals—"

"Yeah. I get the picture. Was it Kayla?"

"I can't tell from the photo you sent. Her face is unrecognizable, but she has a gecko tat on her shoulder. I'm waiting on dental records."

Mitch kneaded his shoulder with his hand, working out the tension that had settled there. "How'd she die?"

"We can't tell from the external exam. Other than the birth, the body looks trauma free."

"I'd hate your job."

"At least my customers don't carry guns," Ian said.

"Funny."

"Seriously, how's the leg?"

"Almost good as new." The lie came easily...too easily. Denial or something more after misleading Emily? "I'm a half hour away."

"See you then."

Mitch ended the call and sighed for Ricky's sake. Mitch hoped this girl wasn't Kayla. But if she wasn't, then someone else's family had a daughter who was dead, a grandchild who was missing, and they didn't know anything had happened.

By the time he reached the coroner's office, Mitch had contacted Kayla's grandmother. He'd kept the questions low-key, but he couldn't fool her.

"You bring my girl home," she'd said. "Either way."

He entered the building housing the coroner and her staff and strode down the hall to the cracker box Ian laughingly called his office. The stench of formaldehyde and death rose to greet Mitch. He hated the odor in this place. Had since he'd been forced to visit as part of driver's ed.

He rapped on the door and pushed it open to find his friend and a woman swallowed up in a white coat comparing two photos taped to a cork board. Mitch didn't give Ian's visitor a second look. He couldn't stop looking at the pictures. One the high school photo of Kayla, the other—

"Is that Kayla?" His stomach churned at the sight of what was left of a blond-haired woman's face. Truth be told, he could only tell the features were a woman because she didn't have an Adam's apple. Her eyes were missing, her nose had been gnawed away by animals. She barely looked human. He couldn't show this body to Mrs. Foster. No way. No how.

One more reason to hate his temporary assignment and get back to SWAT.

Ian grimaced and stood, blocking Mitch's view. "This is Dr. Tara O'Meare. She specializes in facial reconstruction and identification. Without dental records, I thought she could give us her opinion."

The woman rose and shook Mitch's hand.

"Is it Kayla?" he asked.

Dr. O'Meare shook her head. "No. When comparing the two photos, the distance between the zygomatic arches—the cheekbones—is wrong, and so is the position of the eyes. The girl found in the shallow grave is still a Jane Doe."

"Her grandmother said Kayla didn't have a tattoo, but I couldn't be sure."

"Grandmothers don't always know everything," Ian finished.

"Yeah. Even if the body we found isn't Kayla, I still have a missing girl out there." Mitch rubbed his eyes. A missing girl, a missing baby and a Jane Doe. Not to mention Joshua Wentworth. With Emily in the middle of it all. Which pieces fit where? He had to pull it apart section by section. Somehow. "At least for the moment, Mrs. Foster gets good news. Don't take this the wrong way, but I hope you don't call anytime soon except for a game of touch foot…" His voice trailed off.

"I'll keep calling," Ian said. "You let me know when you're up for it."

Avoiding a last look at the photos, Mitch exited the room. He tried not to breathe too deeply until he left the building, then sucked in the crisp winter air. After he inhaled several times through his nose and mouth, he could finally smell and taste the snow tumbling around him.

Once in his car, he slipped on his hands-free device and dialed Kayla's grandmother's number.

"Mitchell?" Mrs. Foster's voice trembled as she said his name.

He hated hearing the uncertainty in the woman's voice, but he couldn't guarantee the next time he called, the news wouldn't be what she dreaded to hear. "It wasn't her."

"Thank the Lord." A small prayer slipped from the older woman's lips. "You'll keep looking?"

"Definitely. I have a deal with Ricky," Mitch promised. "He shows up for practice—"

"Oh, he'll be at practice, don't you worry."

"Mrs. Foster, you know I wouldn't stop looking for Kayla, even if Ricky never—"

"I know, dear. You'll find her."

He disconnected the phone and immediately "Boomer Sooner" filtered through the car.

"Bradford."

"Get your butt down here," Dane Tanner barked. "Now."

"What's going on?"

"Your assignment just walked in the front door of the police department. Without you."

Chapter Three

"Let me see Ghost," Emily pleaded. "Or at least look through the tattoo database. It might jog my memory."

Detective Dane Tanner clicked the door closed and sat behind the interview table sporting that same patient, dubious expression Emily had grown to hate over the past seven or eight months.

"What are you doing, Mrs. Wentworth?"

"Look, Detective, I know it seems far-fetched, but I'm on the verge of remembering."

"Why Ghost? And where did this brainstorm come from so suddenly?"

Here we go again. Emily took in a slow, deep breath. "He has a tattoo."

"Did you see it? Recognize it?"

"No, but my private investigator talked to—"

"Perry Young has a spotty reputation," Tanner said. "I've reiterated this every time you've brought one of his leads to me. All going nowhere, I have to remind you. He's a gambler and a drinker." The detective shuffled through some papers. "He's stringing you along for a steady paycheck."

Not so steady anymore. That's why she had to convince the detective to help her now.

"I got a flash of memory, Detective. If I could just see Ghost's tattoo, or at least look at the books, I might recognize something. Ghost's in custody, right? How tough would it be for me to talk to him?"

"I'm not breaking protocol because you had a *vision*. Go to a tattoo parlor."

"I know what you think of me, Detective Tanner, but do it for the missing girls. Maybe Joshua and their babies are connected."

"No infants have been reported missing or stolen. I'm sorry." Dane steepled his fingers and rested them against his lips.

"A pregnant girl is missing."

"And Kayla Foster's grandmother reported her. This MO's not a fit for Joshua's disappearance. It's none of your concern."

She launched out of her chair and leaned over the desk. "You can't turn your back on the vulnerable. Joshua is only thirteen months old. He's alone." She hated the idea of begging—especially to the detective who didn't trust her—but she'd do anything for her son. She knew the statistics, the chances of getting him back. Infants taken who weren't returned within a few weeks were almost never found. The numbers didn't matter. Joshua would be the exception. She grabbed the age-progressed photo from her satchel and shoved it at him. "Please. Ghost tried to force Heather to go with him. You have to help those girls. I can help, too, if you'll let me."

"I'll pass the information to the officer in charge of the assault case. That's the best I can do. You, however, couldn't have come in at a better time." The detective slid a document across the table. "Is that your signature?"

Emily stuffed the photo back into her bag, scanned the paper and lifted her chin. "You want to quiz me about money or bank forms, call my lawyer. My son is out there, and I need help to find him. If you won't do it, I'll find someone who will."

She slammed out of the interrogation room, the wooden door banging behind her, and sagged against the wall. Her heart pounded as reality set in. The Wentworths had closed nearly every door. She'd have to scrape together enough money for an attorney and for Perry. God help her if they blocked the sale of the house somehow.

"Emily?"

The deep voice that she shouldn't have recognized so easily sent a flood of hope through her. "Mitch." She turned, then rushed over to him. "What are you doing *here?* I thought you were SWAT."

"Temporary assignment while I'm rehabbing." He clasped her arm and guided her toward a chair next to a desk with his name. "What's going on?"

Mitch's concern wrapped around her like a warm blanket. She looked up as he escorted her, strong and able—almost a knight in shining armor. Last night, even though someone had almost killed her, she'd felt safe and protected in his arms after he'd snatched her out of harm's way. Could she trust him to do the same now?

She had no choice. She had to go with her instincts. She sat down and clutched her evidence satchel meeting his gaze. "Detective Tanner."

"My temporary boss," Mitch clarified gently as he hitched his hip on the edge of the desk.

"Oh." Maybe this hadn't been such a good idea, but she'd run out of options, and no matter what William had advised, she wasn't giving up. "I received a tip about Ghost's tattoo, and it reminded me of something from the night of the accident. I asked Tanner to let me see the mug shots or the tattoo database, but he won't. He wouldn't even let me see Ghost."

"Did you see his tat?"

"Well, no, but I heard one of the girls—"

"Tanner's a real by-the-book kind of guy," Mitch said. "He doesn't bend regs. If you didn't see the tat, he won't let you at the photos."

"Do *you* ever break the rules?"

Mitch quirked a small smile. "Let's just say in SWAT sometimes a little creative thinking is required. I wouldn't say I break regulations, but I might bend them a bit."

Hope flickered through Emily as she stared at the man who had taken down Ghost. She leaned forward in her chair and gripped Mitch's arm. "I need your help to find my son."

"I'm not a real investigator, Emily. Just on temporary assignment. You need—"

"I need someone who believes in getting at the truth…and in finding Joshua. No one here does. They never have." Bitterness crept into Emily's voice. "I know you've heard the rumors, but they're not true. I loved Eric. Please, help me find Joshua."

She saw the turmoil and indecision in his eyes, and something that almost looked like guilt. "It's not your fault this department has let me down, but you can change that."

"Bradford. In my office. Now."

Tanner's order made Emily jump, but Mitch had been expecting the interruption. He patted her arm. "I'll be right back. Don't worry."

He walked into his boss's office.

"Wentworth came to see me like you said she would. So… what does she want from you?" Tanner asked.

"Help to find her son. Because she doesn't trust the rest of your unit."

The detective sank back into his chair and smiled. "This couldn't be better if I'd planned it. Do it."

"Tanner—"

"This is your chance. She might let something slip. Maybe

her son's disappearance was part of a plan gone wrong. But even if she's not involved, she knows something. Tell her you talked me into letting you take over her investigation. Tell her you need to stick close because of Ghost's escape. Earn her trust."

"But—"

"Get out there before our chicken panics and runs away. Work Emily any way you can. Find out if she's into something that got her husband killed and her son taken. I'll work the money angle. I want to know who murdered Eric Wentworth."

His boss's jaw twitched as he passed over a single cardboard box. "Here are copies of the key forensic and evidence reports on the accident and kidnapping. No real leads. Most of that file's full of initial interviews and her PI's false tips. It's been vetted. Show it to Wentworth. Use it to gain her trust and get her reaction."

"I'll do my best." Mitch snagged the evidence and stared at his boss. "Why so rabid on this, Tanner?"

His boss let out a long sigh. "Eric Wentworth called me the day before he died. I'd taken time off. Turned off my cell. Wentworth said he had some vital information for me, but he needed to be discreet. No details on the message. He died before I could return the call. I never turn off my phone anymore."

"Damn, Dane."

"Find out who killed him."

Mitch gave a stiff nod to his boss and pasted a satisfied expression on his face as he returned to the bullpen. He lifted the box. "It took some convincing, but I got the case."

Emily's face broke into a relieved smile. Guilt burned through Mitch's gut. He liked straightforward and honest, not games.

He shifted the evidence in his arms. "Look, we *should*

talk in the conference room, but let's get out of here first. It may be bending the rules a bit, but there are things I need to tell you, and—" he peered around the room "—we have an audience."

Emily looked about then turned to Mitch. "I've been watched more than enough in this police station. Follow me to my place. Let me show you what I've done. Maybe you'll see something I haven't." She snagged a sticky note and pen from the top of his desk and scribbled her address. She handed him the yellow paper. "Just in case I lose you."

He took the slip but didn't need the information. He'd memorized her address.

Mitch didn't like the sour taste success left in his mouth. Emily trusted him, and every word he spoke had a lie hidden behind it. He'd have to live with the consequences.

As they passed the desk sergeant, one of his SWAT-mates, Reynolds, ran past. "Mitch. Wish you were back, man. We got a bad one at the Denver Federal Center."

Reynolds shoved through the doors to the SWAT Den, and Mitch could see the flurry of activity.

"Okay, children. Mount up," Lieutenant Decker, his SWAT commander, yelled.

The steel door closed out the noise. Mitch's knuckles whitened around the box handles. "I should be there." But until Ghost was caught, he couldn't let this case go…whether he was reinstated to SWAT or not. Emily was in danger, and he couldn't turn his back on his responsibility to her.

He felt the warmth of her hand on his arm.

"You'll get back to them," she said. "Soon."

Was her concern real or had she recognized his desperation to return to SWAT? Was Tanner right? Was she a black widow? A beautiful, tempting black widow, but a dangerous predator nonetheless?

God, he hoped not. They walked out together.

After shoving the box in his SUV, Mitch followed her around winding curves to an isolated neighborhood that backed up against the Rocky Mountains. She slowed to fifteen miles below the speed limit when they reached the curve where the accident had occurred. A single white cross with a red wreath of poinsettias decorated the side of the road. He'd watched as she placed them there. Would she stop as she sometimes did?

After slowly passing the spot, she sped up and took a few more turns to her house. A picket fence surrounded her ranch-style home. As she pulled into the driveway, Mitch frowned at the Priced to Sell sign in the front yard. That was new since this morning. So, money was as tight as Tanner believed.

He grabbed the evidence box from the backseat and met her at the front door. "How long has it been on the market?"

"Not long."

"You're in a nice neighborhood. That should help it sell faster."

"I hope so," Emily said. "Let's go into the dining room."

They passed a kitchen, and Mitch noted a single cereal bowl and coffee cup on a drying towel. Nothing out of place. He glanced past a living room with a layer of dust on most of the wood surfaces. He hadn't expected that. No magazines, no DVDs thrown about. The house didn't really look lived in. He opened his mouth to pry as she slid open a walnut door. The words stuck in his throat when he entered the dining room.

"Whoa." The walls had been converted to murder boards. Articles, photographs, dates had been attached, connected with arrows and lines, and adorned with notes.

Emily pointed to one side. "It's a timeline of every event from the month before the hit-and-run until one month after.

On the map, I've recorded every infant kidnapping in North America."

Mitch rounded the dining room table and stepped up to the dozens of photographs tacked across the country. "You have *found* written on all of them. None of these kids are still missing."

"Except Joshua."

"And the small *d* in the corner of the photo?"

"Deceased," she whispered.

Her words had gone so soft he could barely hear her. She probably hadn't been able to write the word. Either way, the letter became a stark reminder of the worst that could happen.

He studied the third side of the room. Tips and newspaper clippings of missing children papered from ceiling to floor. On the final wall, a photo of Sister Kate's refuge. She'd added two large questions. *How many babies? Adoption?*

No wonder what he'd seen of the rest of the house looked untouched. She spent all her time in this room, searching for clues to her son's whereabouts. He couldn't get over the detail. He disliked the tediousness of investigation, and this amazing woman had taught herself most of the techniques they'd covered in Mitch's training at the police academy. She impressed him more and more with each passing moment.

"You've done a lot of work."

"Not much else to do." She sat in one of the hard cherry chairs, the only one that wasn't perfectly aligned around the table.

"You have any help?"

"No one else seems inclined. Including your boss."

Mitch didn't blame her for the accusation in her tone. "What about your friends, family?"

"My brother's stationed overseas. And friends... It's been a while since I had any of those."

Mitch let his surprise show. "You seem like a person people would latch onto—for movies, hiking, dinner."

"I make most of my old friends...uncomfortable."

She brought a self-conscious hand to her throat. Mitch had become accustomed to her husky voice, in fact he liked it, but it was another reminder. "Because of your son."

"And this room. They said I was obsessed...the few who came over." She clasped a locket resting on the outside of her turtleneck. "I remind them that nightmares can happen. Do happen."

"You won't give up until you find him."

"Never. No matter what the Wentworths say or do."

Mitch eyed a high chair pushed into the corner, a bib draped over the back. A small teddy bear with one blue eye and one brown eye sat in the seat right next to an empty wooden cradle. Unused for the past year. She faced the memory every day. This woman didn't know where her child was. She didn't know who took him. If she'd had anything to do with her husband's death, she would know where to start.

If she were playing him, if this were an elaborate hoax, she deserved an Oscar. His job was to prove one theory or the other.

Placing the box with the few flimsy files on the floor, he sat beside her and stretched out his leg. "Let's ignore the records for now and start from the beginning. What do you remember about that day?"

Emily's expression fell, her vulnerability embedded in her eyes. Then she straightened her shoulders with an inner strength he recognized even after only a few conversations. While part of him wanted to take her into his arms and comfort her, he couldn't. He'd already crossed a line. He liked her. He believed her. He had to keep his distance. No matter how tempting he found her.

"I try to remember the details of that night a dozen times

a day," she said. "I don't know exactly what happened. Everything seemed fine. We'd barely left the house on the way to Eric's parents'. The road was slick, but nothing out of the ordinary. I remember the lights coming at us, and flashes, the sound of Joshua's cry—" her husky voice caught "—a hooded figure, but not much else."

She rubbed her eyes with one hand and clutched at her throat with the other. "By the time I regained consciousness, a week had passed. Eric was dead. His family had held the funeral, and they blamed me for his death and Joshua's disappearance. More than that, they thought I had something to do with the crash." She reached out a hand to Mitch. "I know they believe I cut myself with the glass, but I would never… You have to believe me."

"Think, Emily," he said. "We know from the paint scrapes that you and Eric were run off the road. The question is why. They took your baby. Was your son the target? Had you been threatened?"

She shook her head firmly. "Nothing like that. Look at the map. Infants aren't taken very often, not by strangers. And most of the time they're found within two weeks. There's not a slew of stolen babies in any one geographical area. Not anywhere in the country. And certainly not here."

Mitch rose and turned to the map. He ran his finger from pin to pin. "I know that. I don't necessarily think your son was taken as part of a baby ring. This was personal. About your family." He faced her. "You and your husband took out a life-insurance policy just before he died. Why?"

Emily stilled, her entire body tense with suspicion. "Wait a minute. How do you know about the insurance? And the paint? I just asked for your help today."

Oh, boy. His first big slip. Well, one thing SWAT had taught him was to think on his feet. "Tanner mentioned a few things, but I have to admit, after last night, I looked into your case. I didn't think the attempted hit-and-run was an accident. I still don't."

How long could he mix truth with lies and still remain credible? The question churned in Mitch's gut.

"Ghost could've called someone. He threatened me. Did you ask him?"

Mitch let out a long, slow breath. "I've got some bad news about Ghost. He's no longer in custody."

"You let him go?" She rose from her seat, her eyes sparking with fury. "How could he make bail? He'll disappear." She crossed to Mitch, hands planted on her hips, toe-to-toe with him.

He hated to admit the truth. "That's not quite what happened. He escaped. Before we could get prints or mug shots."

"I *have* to talk to him." Emily paced around the room. "He's all I've got."

"You can't, Emily. That's one reason Tanner gave me your case. I believe, and he agrees, that you're in danger. He knew, given your history with the police department, you wouldn't be receptive to protection."

"He was right about that." Emily glared at him. "Your boss should've told me the second I asked to see Ghost. He lied to me. And so did you."

"We didn't tell you everything," Mitch acknowledged.

"How am I supposed to trust you? I thought you were on my side. That you believed me."

"I do believe you. I don't think you know where your son is, but Ghost threatened you, and I'm sure he'll come after you. You need my help."

Emily let out a slow breath and met his gaze. "If we're going to work together, you can't lie to me, Mitch. Or keep secrets. I can't do that again." She bit her lip and turned away.

"Wait a minute." Mitch touched her shoulder. "What do you mean *again?*"

She whirled around and raised her chin in challenge. "It doesn't matter. You want to know about the money. Eric and I bought the policy because of the baby. Joshua was only a month old, but Eric planned for the future, especially since he and his family...weren't communicating."

Mitch didn't like the frozen expression on Emily's face. He'd really blown it. "Your husband didn't get along with his parents?"

"They'd been estranged for a while. Ever since, well, ever since we got engaged. I wasn't quite the daughter-in-law they had in mind. Not blue-blooded enough, if you get my meaning. They made no secret of it, so Eric left the family business. He gave up everything for me."

"Their loss," Mitch said before he could help himself.

Emily looked at him, her expression full of sadness. "It's easier to think I arranged this entire thing than acknowledge someone could have stolen Joshua and he's still out there."

"You believe he's alive."

"I have to." She lightly touched the photo of her son pinned to the wall, her eyes glistening. "Do you understand that?"

"More than some." He turned her to him and, with a gentle tug, pulled her closer. "I don't have kids, but I have a goddaughter. Her mother took Haley out of the country and wasn't planning on returning her to her father. I helped find her and bring her home."

"Is she...okay?"

"Oh, she's more than back to her old self." He couldn't help but smile at the thought of the shenanigans of his favorite and only goddaughter. "She'll turn six soon and has her daddy wrapped around her little finger."

"Maybe that will be me someday." A shuddering sigh escaped from Emily.

Haley's story had done more than sympathizing with Emily could ever do. The ice in her eyes had softened.

"I'll do my best to help you find your son," he said truthfully. "I promise that."

Emily reached out and laid her hand over his heart. "I believe you."

The utter faith in her words humbled him. Unable to resist, he cupped her cheek, and she tilted her head into his hand as if searching for warmth, for comfort, for something to hold on to. His heart slammed against his chest. His gaze lowered to her lips. Her tongue moistened them, and her eyes deepened to a rich cobalt. The awareness between them surged. Mitch knew it was wrong, but he wanted to comfort her. He wanted her to know she wasn't alone.

He leaned in and let his hand roam down her cheek to the edge of her turtleneck. Her pulse jumped beneath his fingertips. He stroked her palm with soft, tender caresses. She shivered, and her body moved in closer. The heat emanating from her made Mitch long to feel her softness pressed against his chest.

His fingertips drifted up her arms. Very gently he brought her to him. With a soft groan he lowered his head slightly. Her lips parted, her eyes drifted closed.

She sucked in a quick breath. "No. I can't."

He clasped her hands in his and studied their entwined fingers. If only he'd met Emily at another time, another place. When he could let himself get lost in her arms. She might've been the woman he could've trusted to fall asleep with and never worry about betrayal. "I understand." With regret— and relief—he eased away. "I'm sorry."

"Don't apologize. Everything's just confusing right now."

Mitch stood and turned away, willing his body to calm down. "Let's get back to work." He lifted the lid off the cardboard box of evidence. The photo on top was of a smiling blond-haired man and a radiant Emily on their wedding day. No sadness in her eyes, only joy.

He wanted Emily, but he shouldn't get involved. He couldn't let himself care too much. Not when everything he said was a lie. When she found out why he was really here, helping her, but spying on her at the same time, she'd never forgive him. God knew he'd never forgive himself.

"Let's go through the evidence box and compare it to your data," Mitch said to distract his traitorous body. He placed the box on the table. "Maybe something in these interviews will jog your memory."

Emily peered inside, and her hand paused over the wedding photo. "We were happy. Everything was perfect."

Or was it? Those last few weeks, Eric had pulled away. He'd said it was work and soon everything would be fine. He'd kept his secrets, and then she'd lost him.

His laughing eyes captured her. What would he think of her now? A year after his death, letting herself get taken in by the first cop who'd shown her any sympathy. She'd almost let Mitch kiss her, but he wasn't being her friend. Not really. How long would he help? Until Tanner pulled him into a more important case?

Her cell rang, and she answered.

"I need to see you," Perry said. The PI's voice was quiet. "I have a lead on your son. It's big, Mrs. Wentworth. *Really* big."

"The police department—"

"No. No cops. Can't trust anyone. Especially not the law. I don't know who's looking the other way there, but someone is."

"You're saying someone at the police department is involved?"

Mitch's head snapped up. She backed away, and he nearly dove for her. He pried the phone from her and, before she could protest, pressed the speakerphone button.

Emily shook her head vehemently and tried to grab the device.

"Do you trust me?" Mitch mouthed.

Did she trust him? His intense gaze made her insides quiver. His every action made her believe he wanted justice. The way things were going right now, she had to take a chance. She nodded, and he handed her the phone.

"You there, Mrs. Wentworth?"

"Sorry, Perry. Um…where do you want to meet?"

"I'm on my way back to Denver. Be at the main library when it opens in the morning."

Mitch scribbled a note on a piece of paper and passed it to her.

Must have proof.

"I'll be there, but I need something concrete, Perry."

"You'll have more than that, ma'am. I'm gonna find your kid."

With a shaking hand, Emily ended the call. "You've got a lot of nerve."

"My rules when it comes to the investigation."

"Perry's not the kidnapper. I don't like deceiving him."

"You need more than Perry. No offense, Emily, but he's not exactly top drawer. Word on the street is he has a drinking problem."

"Well, if I don't sell this house soon, I won't even have him. You're going to be my only resource." The stark truth made the long journey seem bleak, with only bright memories of Joshua lighting the way.

"Then let's get back to the evidence," Mitch muttered.

Darkness had long since cloaked the house when they came up for air. Emily's vision had gone bleary despite the pots of coffee and snacks they'd consumed. She glanced at her watch and blinked. "It's getting late."

"I'm not going anywhere," Mitch said, his voice flat and no-nonsense. "Not with Ghost at large."

"You're not thinking of staying here tonight." Or maybe he was. She studied the man who'd spread out at her dining-room table, surrounded by snacks, pens, stickies and a note-pad.

"Nonnegotiable," he said, pulling out another file. "I've got coffee, work, a laptop, the internet, my gun and a beauti-ful damsel in distress. What more could a guy ask for?"

Stunned, Emily sat back in her chair, studying the deter-mined face of the man who'd suddenly turned into her cham-pion. "Why are you doing this?"

Mitch walked over to the empty cradle and lifted the teddy bear with a gentle hand. "You've been doing this on your own long enough," he said. He centered the bear on the table. "And I don't like unanswered questions. Besides, sleep is over-rated."

"It's been a while since I've done an all-nighter," she said. "But I'm game." She took a sip of coffee and settled in for the duration.

Morning came too quickly. They'd barely moved. "What are we doing?" Emily said tossing another stack of notes to the table, her voice cracking. "There's nothing here. That's why I hooked up with Sister Kate. Desperation. Missing babies. Except they aren't missing. Detective Tanner was right. There's no connection."

"Not yet. Did you expect me to pull out a miracle in one day?"

"You're so determined, maybe I hoped you would."

She studied his alert expression and half smile. After a night together, she'd become ultra-aware of Mitch's sense of humor, his addiction to sugar in his coffee and his need to stretch his leg every few hours. He never complained, of course. She also appreciated his keen wit and how quickly he leaped from fact to fact, even though most led to dead ends. Sitting next to him, passing papers back and forth, touching casually a thousand different ways, made Emily feel more comfortable with him. It felt good. To have a real partner again.

She knocked shoulders with him, but when she should have pulled away, she lingered, giving in to a desire that had simmered the entire night. Their hands touched before she drew hers away, her face heating. "Sorry."

"Don't be." Their gazes caught, his lowering to linger on her lips.

He let out a long, slow breath. "Time to meet Perry. I'll follow you."

"He won't like it."

"I don't much care what he likes. If he has evidence against the department, I want to know about it."

Mitch packed up the evidence box and loaded in some of Eric's bank statements. Emily grabbed her purse and evidence satchel and, with a last glance at the murder boards, said a small prayer. Once outside, she slipped into her car and pulled out of the driveway with Mitch tailing her.

When she and Eric had moved into the house, she'd loved the view of the pine trees along the serpentine curve. Even the steep drops on either side of the road hadn't fazed her... not until that night a year ago.

She navigated the car along the narrow stretch of asphalt. A metal sign loomed toward her on the left. Her heart always jumped a bit as she approached the turn. Some days were worse than others, but she handled it. Once she found Joshua she'd conquer the road forever.

The gleaming white of the cross loomed at the horizon. She waited for the splash of poinsettias to come into view, but the flowers were gone.

Oh, God.

A small blue blanket splattered in red was draped over the top of the white cross.

Pain exploded behind her eye, throbbing in her head. Blood. Everywhere. Images, sounds. Joshua's cry. A flashlight. Eric's gray face. Blood pulsing from his chest. Red and green. Pain. Pink. Blood. Blue blanket.

Joshua. No! The blanket wasn't his. It couldn't be.

She had to stop. She had to know. Heart racing, she panted. She couldn't breathe. Her foot slammed into the floor. The car didn't slow down.

Her knuckles whitened on the steering wheel. A burning hit her throat. The copper taste of blood exploded in her mouth and lights flashed in her eyes.

She pumped the brake. Nothing.

The car sped faster on the downward incline. The metal guardrail raced past her. This couldn't be happening. She gripped the steering wheel so hard her hands cramped, and she kept pounding the pedal, but it was no use.

The slight slope became steeper. Fifty miles per hour. Fifty-five.

A hairpin curve waited ahead. She'd driven the road countless times, but not this fast. Never this fast.

Snow began to fall, small flakes.

Not again.

Behind her a loud honking sounded, but she couldn't afford to look in her rearview mirror. The phone in her pocket rang, but she couldn't pick up. She struggled to keep the car on the road. Much more snow and the road would become too slick. She'd never make the curve.

With all her strength, she wrenched up on the emergency brake.

Nothing.

Please, Mitch. Help me.

The road seemed to narrow; the cliffs on either side seemed to go on forever. Her life couldn't end here. Not in this place. Not before she found Joshua.

A car sped past her. Mitch.

"No brakes!" she screamed, as though he could hear her.

Mitch's SUV raced in front of her. He slowed down, and her car shoved into his rear bumper. They rounded the curve, but she was going too fast.

Emily struggled to steer. Her tires hit black ice. She skidded toward the cliff.

Joshua, I won't die. I promise.

Chapter Four

"No!"

Mitch watched in horror as Emily's compact car spun out of control. He had to save her. He wrenched his steering wheel and maneuvered his vehicle between her and the guardrail, pumping his brakes. Her vehicle shoved into his driver's side door.

With a curse, he turned into the spin, until finally his four-wheel drive caught traction. Tires squealed, and he gauged the distance to the edge. It was going to be close.

"Come on, baby. Stop." He yanked on the emergency brake, spun the steering wheel hard to the left and prayed. Brakes sparked and metal ground against metal as they skidded toward the drop-off.

The spin slowed the momentum, but the mountain's edge came barreling at them. Mitch's arms shook under the strain of turning the fused metal coffins, but it was working. They were slowing. Three feet away. Two feet away. Inches away, and finally, the front ends of both vehicles shuddered to a stop. A waterfall of rocks plunged hundreds of feet down.

He forced open his smashed door and headed toward Emily. Her driver's side had melded to his SUV; her head lay against the window. He rounded to the passenger side. He squeezed, then jiggled the handle, but it was jammed.

"Emily. Can you hear me?" He pounded on the glass, ignoring the icy wind that whistled up from the canyon and the sky threatening to turn into a storm.

She didn't move. No air bag on this ancient tin can.

She was so still. Too still. He had to get to her.

He ran his fingertips alongside the crumpled metal, searching for a seam. Yes, right there. He snagged a crowbar from his SUV. If he could get the leverage... He inserted the iron rod and, using his body weight, worked against the hinge. The metal finally gave way, and he forced open the door.

He dove into the car, careful not to jostle her too much. With a gentle touch, he moved some silky strands away from her face. No obvious wounds that he could see. He leaned closer.

"Emily?"

She groaned. At the sound, relief released terror's grip on his heart. "Can you move?"

Those ridiculously long lashes blinked, and her eyes focused on him. "What happened?"

"Brakes."

She nodded, and then her expression took a leap from confused to horrified. "The blanket!" She pulled at the door handle and looked at the crumpled side of his vehicle outside her window.

"It was the only way to stop you," he said, unclicking her seat belt. "Slide toward me, but let me know if anything hurts. Your car jammed into mine pretty hard."

She eased toward him, pausing as she tested one limb, then the next. "I'm okay. Just shaken."

As he clasped her hands, a distinctive odor slammed his senses. Gasoline.

No time to waste. He yanked her away from the car. "Move!" he yelled, grabbing her hand and hauling her toward a large boulder.

She stumbled after him, but her legs gave way. She sagged

to the ground. He swept her into his arms. Within seconds, he reached the large rock and settled her behind the massive boulder.

"What do you think you're doing?" She glared at him. "Your leg can't handle my weight."

"That'll be the day, when I can't carry a little thing like you. As to why—gas. Would you rather risk a spark setting your car on fire?"

"It doesn't sound like anything's happening." She tilted her head toward him. "Maybe we—"

His ears picked up a clicking sound over the wind. He held up his hand, and she went quiet. Mechanical. Definitely.

And familiar.

"Get down." Mitch shoved her to the dirt. A loud explosion shook the ground. Flaming debris flew toward them, hot metal and plastic shrapnel. Mitch covered her body with his, shielding her from the incoming.

Several hot projectiles nipped his back. He brushed them away. Soon the mini-explosions had stopped and only the roar of fire remained. He raised his head and scanned the wreckage. From their vantage, he could see fire leaping between the vehicles, taking out his SUV and charring what was left of Emily's. The remains might have been her grave.

The thought that she could've been pinned in the death trap froze his insides, but the fury at the psycho who'd planted the bomb boiled his temper. Emily could've died. On his watch.

He grabbed his phone and pressed a key. "This is Mitch Bradford. Get me the fire department and bomb squad. Now."

Mitch rattled off their location and ended the call.

"A bomb?" she said, her voice huskier than usual. "I thought the car exploded because of the accident."

"That's Hollywood. I heard suspicious clicking right before the explosion. There was at least one device, maybe more. Someone wants you dead—with no evidence left behind."

"If you hadn't been here…"

She gripped his shirt and buried her head against him. He'd seen the reaction before. Violence wasn't pretty, and the human spirit needed comfort.

He held her tight. "We'll find out who's doing this. I promise."

She wrapped her arms around his neck and hugged him tightly. He couldn't say no to her trembling frame. Each shudder evoked every protective instinct throbbing in his veins. He cradled her against him and stroked her head softly, brushing a few stray snowflakes out of her hair. "You're okay. It'll be okay."

He was lying. Again. This assassin wanted a kill. Mitch could only stop him so long—unless he discovered who was behind the attempts on her life.

Emily lifted her hand to his face, and her look of trust made his heart do a crazy flip-flop. "I'm only here because you saved me. I would have gone over the edge, and Joshua—" Emily's eyes widened. She gripped Mitch's arms hard, her nails biting into his flesh. "Joshua. The blanket! The blood. I have to check the blanket and see if it's Joshua's."

She rose, swaying as the heat from the fire buffeted them. Emily tugged at his hand in desperation. Mitch shifted his weight to his good leg and pulled her back. "Emily. Listen to me. We are *not* going out in the open. We're safe here."

"I have to see that blanket."

"No. The person who sabotaged your car could be waiting. You're not stepping into someone's crosshairs."

Mitch went to wrap his arms around her, but she shoved him back. Any vulnerability she'd let him see had vanished.

"I'm *already* a target." She pulled at her turtleneck and revealed the jagged scar on her throat. "The doctors said I held the glass. That I cut myself. Well, I didn't. And no one believes me, because my prints were on the shards." She met his gaze. "I put flowers on that cross just yesterday. I *have* to see that blanket. I have to know if there was...blood there. I need to know I'm not imagining things."

"I saw it, Emily. You're not crazy. Stay with me."

"I can't. I need to know." She jerked out of his arms and took off up the mountain. Mitch cursed, drew his weapon and started after her, his mind whirling. Emily's scar was vicious. She'd almost died. Had that been the perp's first mistake? If Emily had died from the wound, the whole hit-and-run could very well have been classified murder-suicide gone wrong.

The perfect crime. Her son would've been presumed dead.

She ran up the hill. She was in good shape. Normally Mitch would've caught her in a few steps, but his strides were uneven these days. He was gaining on her, but not fast enough. Mitch's eyes scanned the surrounding terrain. On one side of the road, the cliff was steep. Not impossible to hide there, but tough. The other side made them vulnerable.

Finally, he caught up with her. She'd stopped, bent over, trying to catch her breath. Her swaying made him curse again. "You're pushing too hard. You could be hurt and not know it."

"I'm not stopping until I get that blanket." She sucked in a lungful of air. "You wanted evidence. That's evidence."

"I should tie you up, but I can see it won't do any good." As frustrating as he found her determination, he admired it. "When we get there, don't touch anything. And stay on my right. Between me and the steep side."

Together they rounded the last curve. The cross poked out of the ground—a wreath of plastic poinsettias draped around it, a light dusting of snow completing a hideously wrong yet serene picture.

No blanket.

"What?" Mitch had seen the blanket and the red splatter pattern.

Emily collapsed on the side of the road. "They're trying to drive me crazy."

"You're not crazy." Mitch pulled her to her feet and lifted her chin. "Whoever's doing this is vicious. They used the blanket to make you hit your brakes. It was a setup. They tried to kill you and make it look like an accident, but they failed. You didn't go over the side of the road. You're here."

"But the blood?"

"It wasn't real. Too bright. Dried blood is dark in color."

She sagged against Mitch. "Joshua has to be alive. I can't go on if he isn't."

"We'll find Joshua. I promise." It was a vow he would probably regret making, but right now, at this moment in time, it was the right thing to do.

He scanned the area. Just to the side of a recently replaced guardrail, several tall pines and an outcropping of boulders would be good cover—at least until the units showed up. Mitch lifted her in his arms and walked to the shelter. Such a tiny thing. He set her down and unzipped his coat, tucking her against his chest, and held her.

He stood there, holding her, their body heat combining, the outside cold seeping away as he surveyed the landscape surrounding them, searching for a sign, a movement, of anyone watching them. A slight shiver fluttered through Emily.

"Why are they doing this to me?"

Her quiet voice twisted Mitch's heart. He'd seen enough depravity in his time at SWAT to realize human beings could do almost anything, but what they'd done to Emily took true desperation...and a special kind of callousness.

"I'm going to find out," he said.

She shifted away from him and pushed her hair out of her face. "I need to call Perry. He'll worry." She reached into the pocket of her jacket and pulled out the phone. Not much charge, but she pressed the button. "It still works."

Mitch stayed her fingers. "Perry knew when you were going to rendezvous. You realize that."

"I could've been anywhere when he called. He didn't know I was home."

"Not unless he's been following you," Mitch said. "You have to consider he's been paid off. His history—"

"I don't want to believe that. Except for William, he's the only one who ever helped me."

Mitch wanted to shout, "Until me," but he couldn't. The words were almost true. How could investigating her and deceiving her be considered helping her? No. Too many lies lay between them. He couldn't add one more. Trouble was, she was getting to him.

Screaming sirens tore up the mountain. Mitch's focus shifted from Emily to the decorated cross to her cell phone. He couldn't be sure who to trust, either. This case had just become very complicated.

EMILY SAT IN A PATROL car, out of the freezing wind, as law enforcement crawled all over the mountain like a swarm of ants. Quite the response when a SWAT officer's personal vehicle blew up. They'd blocked off the road and now searched for evidence.

The stench of burning rubber and plastic filled the air. The odor made her stomach roil, though not as much as the thought of what someone was willing to do to get her out of the way. All she wanted was to find Joshua. Why couldn't they let her have her son back?

Thank goodness Mitch had seen the blanket. Two attempts on her life in front of a cop had made Tanner take her more seriously. She couldn't let up, though. If she didn't push, no one would.

Emily shifted her gaze from the search to Mitch, who was focusing intently on his conversation with one of the bomb-squad techs. His ability to ignore the pain he had to be feeling left her in awe. If only he'd lean against the vehicle and ease the weight, but his dogged determination wouldn't let him show any vulnerability. She'd learned that about him in the short time she'd known him.

Her hand slipped into her pocket and pulled out her phone. It had gone dark. The battery must have died. She needed to try Perry again. They were ninety minutes late. Maybe the PI had attempted to call. She got out of the car and walked over to Mitch. "Can I borrow your cell to call Perry?"

His expression more grave than she'd ever seen, Mitch handed her the phone. He clasped her arm and walked her a few feet away from the tech, bending his lips to her ear. The warm breath bathed her neck, and she shivered at his closeness. "Don't tell him where you are. Just set up another meet. We can't be too careful."

Mitch backed away, his expression stonelike and chilled as he continued the conversation with the other officer.

She hated not being able to trust anyone. She stepped a few feet away. Her call went straight to Perry's message. Where was he?

The phone vibrated in her hand and started playing an unrecognizable tune.

"Turn that thing down, bud. You want to make everyone sick with that stupid fight song?"

Emily's gaze flew toward the voice. A striking-looking man walked toward Mitch, grinning and holding a cell in his hand.

"You never did have good taste, Ian."

Ian tapped his phone and Mitch's stopped ringing. His tension eased, and he smiled in a way she'd never seen. He looked at this man with complete trust and confidence. As the strong friendship between the two men became clear, Emily had never felt more alone. Mitch had connections.

She'd witnessed the trust when he'd spoken to a few of the cops. Without hearing a word, the camaraderie between them spoke volumes. How could Mitch ever be totally on her side? He'd saved her life, yes. But he was loyal to them. She should remember that.

"Did you find me a ride?" Mitch said.

Ian grinned with a mischievous glint deep in his eyes.

"Your brother Noah's SUV. He won't miss it."

"True. After that last big software deal, he went nuts and bought the Hummer. He's got five cars now."

Mitch tried to pluck the keys from his friend's hand, but Ian closed his fist. His face turned serious. "It's not every day my best friend's car gets blown to smithereens. What's up, bud?"

Emily's body tensed. How would Mitch respond? Had he believed her?

He looked around at the few cops who still stood near them. "Not now."

The vise around Emily's heart eased a bit. He might. He just might be on her side.

"Then I'm not leaving," Ian said, the keys still in his grip.

Emily recognized the tick in Mitch's jaw. She'd seen it when Ghost had cut the girl, and when he'd studied the pictures of the children on her wall. Friends were too precious. She couldn't be the cause of problems between them.

"It's my fault," Emily said quietly, stepping into their circle. She held out her hand. "Emily Wentworth."

At the mention of her name, Ian paused, the openness in his face evaporating. He reached out his hand to hers. "I've followed your case. Ian Archer. I'm the investigator for the coroner's office."

He'd probably studied the accident. She nodded, trying to gauge his judgment. Was she a black widow to him?

"No matter what you've heard, I didn't kill my husband,"

she said, deciding to meet his doubts head-on. "I just want to find my son. It's starting to look like someone doesn't want me to."

Ian studied her expression, and, as if he had made some decision, his face softened a bit. "I understand. I hope you find him."

She clutched at the small opening. "Did you look into the accident? Was there anything that stood out to you?"

Ian stiffened and slid a sidelong glance to Mitch.

"Emily's private investigator, Perry Young, indicated he had information that there might be some…irregularities in the police work. We were on our way to meet him when—"

"I see. Can I tag along?" Ian asked. "I'd be *very* interested in his theories."

She could use his expertise. "Sure."

"No," Mitch bit out at the same time.

She whirled on him. "Why? If he can help—"

"Ian has a daughter to take care of."

Mitch's face was uncompromising. The friends' gazes held, obviously communicating in a way she didn't understand. Ian finally nodded. "Fine. See you at your dad's for the tree trimming," he said. He turned to Emily. "It's nice to meet you. Good luck."

Ian tossed the set of keys to Mitch before walking away.

"Why did you do that?" she asked. "He might know something or have suspicions about who could be involved."

"He and my goddaughter have been through enough. Too many cops saw him here as it is, and if one of them is our mole, I don't want him associated with a case involving missing children. Understand?"

The fierce protectiveness in his words made her tremble with regret. What had she been thinking? She had no right to bring anyone else into her nightmare. "You're right. I'm sorry. There's no need to put anyone else in danger." She faced Mitch. "Detective Tanner is up that hill. Why not just give the assignment back? I don't really need you. I have Perry. I'll get by."

"I didn't mean it like that. I'll connect with Ian later. I just don't want to be obvious or make Haley a target."

Back stiff, she ignored his words and started toward the crowd of cops. Mitch yanked her arm. "I'm not letting you go," he said, tugging her against him. "You *do* need me. I saw the blanket. I believe you. Do you think these other men will?"

"Perry does. Keep your friends and family close, Mitch. I know what it's like to lose them."

"I'll look out for mine. That doesn't mean I'm going to abandon you. I'm in too deep." He gave her a small smile. "Now let's talk to Perry. He may suspect who wants you dead."

After a quick consultation with Tanner, Mitch led her to his brother's pristine SUV. The recently detailed smell assaulted Emily's memories. Her last fight with Eric had been about the compact. He'd wanted to get her something new. She hadn't wanted to risk it. He'd been furious with her, but she'd known they couldn't afford it. They'd struggled to meet the mortgage when he'd left his father's company. She didn't care, but Eric hadn't been used to budgeting or doing without. She ran her hand over the supple leather seats, and her eyes burned. This vehicle was just her husband's style. Top of the line. All the bells and whistles.

As Mitch steered the car down the mountain, she clutched at the armrests until her fingers hurt. Her breath hitched, and a small sound escaped. She rubbed her eyes. No. She didn't need to think about the past. She had to have faith that with Mitch and Perry she'd put what was left of her family back together.

"You okay?"

Emily cleared her throat. "I'm fine. Perry's office is just around the corner. I don't blame him for not waiting for us, but I wish he'd pick up."

Mitch pulled onto a rundown street. Iron bars decorated most windows. A few unsavory characters loitered on the corners. "He's not exactly in the garden district, is he?"

"He stayed on the case. I'm grateful.

"Just tell me you didn't come here alone."

"Sometimes."

"Emily, you've got to start being more cautious."

"I'll do what I have to do to find my son, Mitch."

One glance at her companion's strong jawline and determined expression reminded her things had changed. Mitch believed in her. She'd given him the out, and he hadn't taken it. He could have. Maybe, just maybe, she'd found an ally who would stick with her. And not because he received a check.

He parallel-parked and stopped the engine before twisting to face her. "I take the lead here."

"He trusts me."

"Precisely why I do the talking this time. I'll put some pressure on him, but I want to know if he's blowing smoke or not." Mitch's eyes grew cold, and his expression dangerous. "If we're really dealing with a breach in the department, I want to know now."

As charming as Mitch could be—and Emily had to admit, she liked him—he had that deadly look that she'd hate to be on the wrong side of.

They climbed up the stairs, and Emily kept a close eye on his gait. She could see a bit of strain, but he powered through the stiffness, not giving away anything. One more thing to appreciate about him—he had grit.

Mitch turned a corner. Perry's office door was cracked open. And quiet. Mitch paused. His entire body tensed; his stance screamed alert. He leaned forward. "You ever seen the door ajar?" His voice was so quiet she could barely hear him.

He pointed to the other doors down the hall. All of them were closed. She strained to remember.

"No," she whispered. "I've always knocked."

"Stay behind me."

He moved in front of her and pulled a gun from beneath his jacket. With caution, he eased toward the office. His back against the wall, he slowly pushed at the wood.

He stepped through the entrance and stilled.

Emily peeked around him.

Perry Young faced them, on his knees, his face bruised, his nose bleeding, his hands behind his head.

A masked figure stood behind the PI, a gun at his head.

Perry lifted resigned eyes and met Emily's gaze.

"Eighty-five!" he yelled.

The gun went off.

Chapter Five

Perry Young's face exploded. Blown off too fast for Mitch to pull the trigger at the killer. He shoved Emily into the hall and aimed his Glock. "Denver police. Put the gun down. Now."

The man leaped over Perry's rickety desk and crashed through the window. Mitch skidded across the old wood floor, hitching through the opening onto the fire escape. The perp bounded down to the first landing and then hurtled to the ground.

Mitch eyed the distance. Too far. He took the steps as quickly as possible, cursing every one. A few months ago, he would've had this guy the second the assassin hit the brown, winter grass. Mitch jumped the last few stairs and landed on the turf. His leg seized, but he ignored the pain. Some kids stood staring, a soccer ball rolling across the yard. Mitch couldn't risk a shot. He gripped his gun as the man raced past the group.

Mitch's legs pumped hard in pursuit as the kids scattered, but the man shot off like he was used to doing hundred-yard sprints. Within seconds the killer shoved through a fence. By the time Mitch slammed open the gate, his quarry had disappeared. A motorcycle revved and peeled away, but Mitch couldn't see anything through the thicket of trees guarding the street.

Cursing, Mitch slipped his gun back into the holster. What good was rehab if he couldn't run down a murder suspect?

And he'd left Emily alone.

Mitch raced back to Perry's office, using the stairs this time to preserve the scene. Expecting to see her trembling in the hallway, his gut fell when he reached the second floor. Empty. Silent.

Had the whole thing been a diversion? Had someone else been waiting to take her?

He redrew his weapon and entered the room. There she was, behind Perry's desk, rifling through the papers. Not just papers. Evidence.

"What are you doing? This is a crime scene."

"He's my last connection." Emily tore through another drawer, eyes wild with desperation, her movements frantic. "There has to be something here. Something about Joshua. The tattoo. The cops."

Mitch limped around the desk. He tugged at her hands, enclosing them in his fists, and pulled her away from the stack of papers. "Look at me, Emily." She raised her gaze to his, and he released one hand to let his finger run down her cheek. "Let's go into the hall and call for the crime-scene unit."

She tugged away from him. "Don't treat me like I'm a fragile doll. I'm not."

Her hand hovered over her throat as her husky voice cracked a bit—a stark reminder of just how much she'd endured.

"Perry can't just be gone." She stared at his body.

The killer had used a hollow point. The PI hadn't stood a chance. Her face lost all color, but she didn't look away.

"He told me to come alone. To tell no one." She rounded on Mitch. "You heard him. Did you reveal to *anyone* where we were going? Tanner, maybe?"

The unspoken accusation hung like poison between them, her suspicions palpable. Mitch stiffened, but as he stared at what was left of Perry's head, and the blood and brain splattered across the floor, his mind clicked through the possibilities of who might have known of their destination. Ian knew. Tanner knew. If his boss had told anyone…She had every right to be distrustful.

So did Mitch.

Until he was sure who had killed Perry and tried to kill Emily, he had to be extremely cautious. He couldn't trust the police department. The realization skewered his gut.

Mitch guided her into the hallway, pressed close against him. "A few months ago, I would've ignored the suggestion someone I know could be responsible for attacking you. Or for killing Perry. Since then, the man I trusted more than anyone on the force set me up for an ambush. He caused this." Mitch tapped his bad leg. "I'm not discounting anything anymore." He turned Emily in his arms. "That means we're on our own. Fewer resources to find your son until we're certain who our friends are. Can you live with that?"

"Perry paid with his life for helping me. It's my fault. I can't ask you to take that same risk."

Her voice had turned monotone. Shock had settled in.

"His death's not your fault. Blame the guy who pulled the trigger." He willed her to look at him until the cloudy, stunned look faded from her expression. "I will tell you one thing, though. This means Perry was onto something. He discovered a connection he shouldn't have, and they wanted him silenced."

Mitch pulled out his cell phone, and Emily stilled his hand.

"Who are you calling?"

"The police. I have to notify them of the shooting. No choice. If I don't, someone else will, and we can be placed here."

Mitch didn't like the churning in his gut. He studied Emily's jittery movements as he made the call. Her life was at stake. He couldn't let her down, so he'd have to accept the weight of his deception. Until he could uncover the truth.

"They'll be here in a few minutes. I need you to think back to every conversation you've had with Perry in the past month."

Emily bit down on the side of her lip, concentrating. "He got real excited about Sister Kate's shelter. Said things didn't smell right there. You heard the phone call. Oh, he really wanted me to get a good look at Ghost's tattoo."

Pain flashed in her eyes, and she massaged her temple. Mitch had seen that look before. When he'd pushed her to remember that night, she'd had the same expression.

"You're starting to remember," he said.

"A red and green tattoo. Some kind of figure, I think."

"What else did Perry tell you?" Mitch asked.

"I don't know. I took notes. They're at the house."

"How about the number he yelled right before—"

Emily's eyes cleared. "Eighty-five! His code. He talked about how when he got tidbits of information, he never wanted to be the only one who had them. He stashed them away."

"Good for Perry. Do you know where he kept the files?"

"He told me if anything ever happened to him, to remember that a sommelier would find the files before the bad guys."

"He hid his evidence in his wine rack?"

"I don't know." Panic laced her voice. "Oh, God. He never told me his hiding place."

"What about your contract? Paperwork he gave you?"

Her vision cleared. "Maybe. He wouldn't have just said that word without thinking I could find it, right?"

"Exactly. Let's search for a liquor stash in his office. The guy was an alcoholic from what I gather. We'll find it." He glanced at his watch and held her shoulders. Mitch whistled through his teeth. "Listen to me carefully. I can't touch the evidence in that room. Rules, you know." He slipped on a pair of gloves that hadn't been standard issue for him until he'd been benched from SWAT. "But your fingerprints are already on his desk. So…"

He watched her eyes widen with comprehension. She hurried back inside Perry's office, avoiding the body on the floor, but focused. His Emily was fearless.

He followed her into the room. They rifled through papers and opened drawers, but there was nothing helpful. No wine bottles, just a half-full flask of whisky. No address of a store. He shook his head at Perry's body. The man had a code word. That meant he had a plan. He had to have left a clue somewhere.

Sirens screamed in the distance.

"We're out of time." Mitch tugged Emily's hand and started toward the exit.

She tugged one last time on a last locked drawer before grabbing a letter opener and jimmying the lock. She snagged a small box containing files, notes and an unopened bottle of wine. She gave him a challenging look. He sighed, then nodded.

"What about his apartment?" she said. "Can we go there, too?"

"The investigators'll be all over his place. We'll stash the box in my SUV and wait for the cops downstairs. Then we go to your place and look at the evidence and your notes. Maybe we'll get lucky. I'll keep an eye on the investigation. If they find liquor bottles, I'll know about it."

"But you won't tell Tanner, right?"

Her voice made his skin prickle. He didn't like not trusting his colleagues. The men he'd put his life on the line for a hundred times.

"For now."

"I CAN'T GET PERRY out of my mind," Emily said quietly as Mitch maneuvered the SUV up the road toward her house. The image of his faceless body chilled her far more than the winter that had taken hold, or the clearing of leafless aspens poking through the surrounding pines.

They'd spent too long giving statements to the police. After a scathing lecture, Tanner had warned both of them not to leave town, informing them they were persons of interest in Perry's execution.

She pictured his endearing face, his ruddy cheeks, the deep crow's-feet at the corner of his eyes, the eagerness with which he came to her to give her one more bit of news. The excitement in his final phone call.

"His last words were to help me."

"And we won't let him down," Mitch said. "We'll find out what got him killed."

"And make them pay." She twisted in her seat. "I want them to pay for taking the life of an innocent man. He didn't have to die."

Mitch squeezed her hand. "We'll figure this out, Emily. I won't stop until we do."

She stared at his large, strong fingers engulfing hers. She believed him. He wouldn't give up. Not like William or even Eric had. The Wentworth brothers had both gone down the path of least resistance—Eric by avoiding his family, William by giving into them. Mitch would never have done either. He didn't walk away from a fight, he ran toward conflict and battled it out. He was a protector, a warrior. Perhaps that's why she felt safe when she was near him.

She gripped him hard as a familiar stretch of road loomed around the next corner. The police had removed the signs of the roadside investigation. Only the scarred pavement where the cars had burned remained. A few hundred feet farther, a white cross rose in the gravel.

A barren cross.

"They took the poinsettias," Emily whispered.

"Evidence. I'm sorry."

"I need to replace them," she said quietly as they passed the memorial. "Eric's favorite."

"I'll take you to a florist's," Mitch said as he turned onto her street. "Whose car is outside your house?" His voice had tensed; his hands gripped the steering wheel as if he were ready to spin the SUV around.

Emily turned. A familiar black Mercedes sat running at the front curb. She didn't need to see inside its tinted windows to know who waited for her. "Oh, no. Not today."

"Who is it?"

"Victoria. The woman who believes I'm the worst thing that ever happened to her family—especially Eric." Emily swiped at the errant hairs and the char and dirt on her clothes. Nothing like looking as if she'd just climbed out of a ditch to give her oh-so-perfect mother-in-law more ammunition.

Emily bit her lip and slid a glance to Mitch. "Do you mind staying in the car while I get rid of her?"

"Yes, actually I do. I'm interested in what Mrs. Wentworth has to say. Like how far she'd go to make you look suspicious. And why she happens by for a visit on the day you were almost killed."

The implication of his words sent waves of shock through Emily. No way. The Wentworths wouldn't risk anything that could cost them an ounce of respect.

Mitch pulled the SUV into the driveway. Just as he and Emily exited the vehicle, a driver opened the back door of the Mercedes. Victoria Wentworth stepped out and paused. Her simple black Chanel suit said much more in subtlety than her biting insults said with a smile. She waited, clearly expecting the peons to approach her. Emily sighed and started to her, but Mitch grabbed her hand and tugged her back.

"I don't want you out in the open. Go inside. She can come to you."

"You don't understand—"

Mitch's eyes twinkled a bit, and Emily recognized that hint of mischief behind the layers of steel. "Oh, I comprehend the situation quite well. Get in the house, Emily."

She turned to the front door before she realized she didn't have her keys. Quickly, she fished the spare from beneath a pot on the front porch. She chanced a glance back at Mitch, and he shook his head, clearly frustrated that she had stashed the item in such an obvious place. Well, at least she didn't have to break into the house.

She opened the door and slipped inside. Home. Finally. She so desperately needed to be here. Safe. Secure.

With more than a little curiosity at how Mitch would handle the formidable Mrs. Wentworth, Emily peered out the window at the driveway. Mitch's conversation with her mother-in-law would've been worth a front-row seat, especially since Victoria had actually let him escort her up the sidewalk.

How long had it been since the Wentworths had set foot in this house? Maybe only once in her and Eric's three-year marriage?

"I appreciate your understanding, Mrs. Wentworth. In reopening the investigation into Eric's death, we want nothing more than to find out what happened."

Mitch's smooth voice filtered through the open doorway. As he escorted Victoria into Emily's house, she bristled. What was he up to? Victoria had made it perfectly clear what she wanted: Emily to pay for Eric's death.

"Well, I'm not one to speak out of school, but I'm quite dismayed to see you accompanying Emily. She should be your prime suspect. Look at what she did today. Trying to sell Eric's home. It's disgraceful, and I'm going to put a stop to it."

"Now, ma'am. You know that I have to keep my options open." She'd never seen Mitch smile like that. It didn't reach his eyes. Each movement, each gesture was calculated and focused. Mitch led Victoria into the house's formal living room to the sofa that faced a photograph of Emily and Eric. He pulled up a chair as her mother-in-law settled into her seat but made sure she could see the happy picture. Emily recognized the ploy. He *wanted* a reaction from Eric's mother.

"I'd like to hear your thoughts," he said. "About your son."

Mitch's voice held just the right note of sympathy. He turned his face away from Victoria to Emily and gave her a small wink. "Could you fix your mother-in-law some hot tea, please? It's cold outside."

Amazing. He manipulated like a pro. Emily didn't know what he expected to gain, but she'd let him have his way. For now. "Certainly."

She pulled out a small, antique teapot she and Eric had found in a little shop on their honeymoon and set the water to boiling before edging back into the room where Mitch played Victoria like a Stradivarius. He charmed the woman. Emily placed her fingers to the lips he'd almost kissed. He'd done the same with her.

"I told Eric not to marry a girl like that, but he wouldn't listen. He was young, idealistic."

"Sounds like he was a good son."

"Perfect. The best son any mother could ever want. Until he met *her.* He stopped coming by to visit. We never saw him anymore."

Mitch laid his hand on Victoria's. "You miss him."

For the first time in a year, Emily really studied Victoria's features. Grief had etched lines in her formerly smooth face. Why couldn't they have clung to each other? That's all

Emily had ever wanted. Acceptance. Support. To be part of a family again.

"She was so intent on getting the insurance money." Victoria's face turned harsh. "That's when I was certain what I'd always suspected was true. She never loved Eric. She loved the Wentworth money. And now she's selling *his* house. She's throwing away his memory."

"That's not true."

Emily stalked into the room. She couldn't take the attacks anymore. "I *never* cared about the money for myself. I just want to find Joshua."

"Then why was *William* paying for plane tickets and bills for that private investigator?"

"To search for *your* grandson." Emily looked down at Victoria. "I want him back."

For a moment, she thought Victoria's expression softened a bit. Then that haughty look reappeared. "No. I'm not wrong. I know your kind. You care about nothing if you'll sell everything Eric ever gave to you." She faced Mitch. "You look into the $250,000 account I found. It's in *her* name. Not Eric's." Then she turned to Emily, her gaze as icy as her heart. "When you can explain that away, I *might* believe you weren't responsible for killing my son."

She rose and walked out the door, regal as ever.

Mitch whistled under his breath. "Wow. She doesn't mince words."

"I told you." The kettle shrieked from the kitchen. Emily hurried to remove the pot from the stove. He followed her. The room suddenly seemed much smaller, claustrophobic even. Maybe it was the low ceilings, but his muscular frame and larger-than-life presence sucked the air from her lungs.

"Want some?" she asked, her voice strangely breathless.

"The tea is for you. I figured you'd need it after your mother-in-law left, and I was pretty sure she'd leave before it was ready. I just wanted you out of the room. So, about the $250,000—"

Emily faced Mitch. "If I'd had access to that kind of money, do you think I'd be selling my house to pay for the investigation? The house Eric and I built together? I didn't even know about the money until today." She struggled to swallow back the sob that stuck in her throat. No. She couldn't let herself regret what had to happen. Without William's support, or Perry, she could at least count on the money from the house to help her find Joshua.

Mitch lifted his hand to her cheek. "I'm on your side," he said softly. "Remember that."

She nodded.

"Did anyone ask for your signature on anything unusual?"

The question harkened back to Dane Tanner's interrogation. Her entire body tensed, her neck muscles bunched in resistance.

"Remember," Mitch whispered.

His hands moved to her shoulders, kneaded the knots. She sighed at the comforting touch. She didn't know what good her answer would be.

"I've signed a million forms since Eric died. I signed papers to try to refinance the physical-therapy business. I don't remember opening a bank account." She lifted her gaze to his. "I saw the signature. It can't be mine. It looks like mine, but I didn't sign it."

"The account existed before the accident. This isn't something recent, Emily. I'll get the exact date from Tanner. Maybe that will jog your memory."

She couldn't stand so close to him any longer. She turned away and hugged her arms around herself. "Why is this happening?"

Mitch moved in closer, but she stiffened, trying to ignore the longing that had bubbled up inside of her, that still threatened to escape. She pulled a teabag out of the cupboard and poured hot water in a flowered cup.

Emily inhaled the floral scent of the herb drink, but it didn't comfort, soothe or distract her. She felt his warm presence again at her back. Her body tingled. He wouldn't give up. His persistence was one of his most irritating—and appealing—qualities. His heat warmed her from shoulders to hips. She wanted nothing more than to give in to her instincts, to sag against him, let him wrap her in a cocoon and make the world go away for just a few minutes, a few hours.

Gently, almost tentatively, he rested his hands on her shoulders again. "We'll get through this," he whispered, his warm breath at her ear.

His hands eased down her arms. She could've escaped at any moment. He would've let her go, but she wanted his touch. She needed his strength. She'd been alone for so long, battling the world for too long. For this moment, in this small room, she truly believed she'd found a champion. She and Mitch against a world gone crazy.

Effortlessly, he folded her against him, his hard body cradling the softness of her own. Her hands shook. His warm hands surrounded hers, and he took the cup in his hands and set it aside before turning her in his arms.

His chocolate-brown eyes had gone black with desire. His body fairly pulsed with need. He lifted her chin, and his finger toyed with a strand of hair near her face.

She understood passion. The electric longing had crackled between them before. But this was different. He could have swept her into his arms, tugged her to him and taken her lips. She would've given him what they both wanted, but he didn't. His hands worked slowly up and down her arms, then around her back to her shoulders, touching her with such a gentle persuasion that she melted deep in her belly.

Her heart pounded and she leaned into him, wanting his

heat to warm her from the inside out, needing to feel safe. He was the only one who could give her that. "Please," she said.

A small smile tilted his lips. "Please what?"

"Hold me."

With a groan, he secured her hard against him. She could feel every plane of his body, the muscles in his arms and chest. She hugged him close. He shivered, and a surge of female pride raced through her. She'd made *him* tremble.

What if she raised her head? Would he kiss her? Would he want her?

His hips arched against her. Yes, he wanted her, and he wasn't afraid of letting her know it. The loneliness of the past year crashed over her. Dare she risk letting herself care, or even feel something more than grief and emptiness?

The chimes of the grandfather clock shattered the moment.

He rested his forehead against hers. "It's too fast, isn't it, Emily?"

She bit her lip and nodded. He glanced at his phone. "I need to make a call. Drink your tea. And someday soon… maybe it won't be too fast."

He caressed her cheek and left the room, the phone at his ear. "This had better be good."

Emily sucked in a deep breath. Her nerve endings tingled. She paced the floor and noticed the message indicator on the phone she'd put in the charger. She couldn't believe she hadn't noticed. She dialed her voice mail.

"Mrs. Wentworth."

Perry's voice sounded through the speakerphone.

She staggered at the sound of the dead man's words.

"You didn't show up, and your cell went straight to voice mail. Call me as soon as you get the message. This thing is bigger than I thought, ma'am. Lots of money. Lots of influence. I confirmed the Denver PD is involved, but I don't know the cop's name yet."

A harsh curse sounded from across the room. Mitch had come back. A frown creased his face, and the muscle in his jaw throbbed.

Perry's voice continued. "Ghost shouldn't have escaped. Someone set it up." A bit of rustling shifted through the phone. "If something happens to me…you'll know what I know. I don't want to say more on the phone." Perry paused. "Be careful, Mrs. Wentworth. Don't trust anyone. Call me."

Emily sagged against the counter.

Mitch strode across the room to her. "Timing hasn't been on our side, has it?" He kissed her cheek, letting his lips linger there. "Remember where we were."

He lifted the cup and pushed it into her hands. "Now, take a sip and let's go through your notes so we can find Perry's evidence."

Emily clasped the tea and walked down the short hallway toward the dining room, Mitch at her heels. She slid open the door and the teacup fell from her fingertips, shattering on the hardwood floor. "No!"

The walls were barren. The boxes gone. Every piece of evidence, every notebook, every pushpin, everything she'd gathered over the past nine months, vanished.

Stolen.

Mitch dragged her toward the door. "We're getting out of here. Now!"

Chapter Six

Emily dug her heels into the floor and yanked out of Mitch's hold. "Wait a minute. We can't just leave—"

"Someone tried to blow your car up today," he snapped. "We're leaving until the bomb squad clears this place."

Her eyes widened. "Wait." She scooped up the teddy bear and two picture frames and threw them in a bag. "I'm not going without these," she said, her eyes fierce.

Mitch clutched Emily's hand and yanked her across the kitchen. No way was he retracing steps through the house. They'd have to make do without their coats.

She snagged her cell phone and charger. "But what about—"

"No time, Emily. We're not taking any more chances."

He dragged her to the back exit. After a quick inspection of the hinges and frame for a trip wire, he flung open the oak door. He couldn't believe he'd been so careless. They'd meandered around the house for a half hour. Making tea, for God's sake. A device set to the gas stove and it would have been all over. They'd both be dead, and no one would know someone had cleaned out all the evidence from her dining room.

She stumbled outside after him, their feet crunching on the leftover snow. He scanned the perimeter of the yard, searching for footprints or anything out of place.

No disturbances. The perp had probably come in through the front.

"I'm sorry," Mitch said. "I should've scoped out the house before you entered. I let you down. It won't happen again."

"The house was locked," she protested. "How did they—"

"When's the last time you used the key under the pot?"

She flushed.

"That's what I figured. You're a smart woman, Emily. You handled yourself well downtown, but you can't lower your guard, even on your home turf. Not ever. Now, we have to get out of here."

He picked his way around the side of the house. His body tensed with awareness, he tugged her near. "Stay close to me."

Emily's hand rested lightly against his back. He needed to feel her presence, to know she was safe. He'd rely on his SWAT instincts. Those he could trust. Clearly his detective intuition didn't make the grade. When he reached the corner, Mitch stilled, listening for any sign, searching for any movement.

She trembled against him. He gave her a comforting squeeze. "Let me check the SUV, and then we're out of here."

She nodded, and he did a quick sweep underneath the vehicle. Looked clean, but he gave it a second pass anyway. He couldn't be too careful. He motioned her toward the vehicle and opened the door. She jumped in, and he slid behind the steering wheel.

Clutching the bag with the photos to her as if they were a lifeline to her memories, she fastened her safety belt.

Within a minute, they were on the road, Mitch on high alert and determined that no one would catch him unaware again.

Emily peeked around. "What are we going to do?"

"First off, I'm hiding you someplace safe. Then we'll

figure out exactly what you've stumbled onto. Because it's big. And worth killing over."

Emily clutched the bear to her chest. "I should never have asked for your help. I didn't know it would get this dangerous for you. If you want out, I understand."

Mitch didn't like how her words cut him straight through to his heart. He shouldn't feel so much—except he couldn't believe that she'd said something so incredibly dense. His anger was about more than just her putting herself in danger. She had him. He was with her all the way. Until she was safe. Until she found out what happened to her son. But she didn't believe in him.

"I am not going anywhere. Get used to it."

"But—"

"Subject closed."

Mitch checked the rear- and side-view mirrors every couple of seconds. The neighborhood streets were abandoned. To his surprise, his Neanderthal declaration seemed to ease the tension in the car rather than ratchet it up. Maybe Emily wasn't as ready to go it alone as she wanted to appear.

"I wonder if I'll ever see my home again," she said, finally breaking the silence.

"I don't know." He wouldn't stop being honest. At least about some things. "If all the bad guys wanted was your research, they got that."

"The whole thing is so bizarre. Nothing was disturbed in the rest of the house. If we hadn't gone into the dining room, we wouldn't even have known."

"Since they took your research, you either found something or came close to exposing someone. Whoever did this thought you died in the explosion, or else emptied the house right after we left. If he'd succeeded in killing you, the cops wouldn't have known there was a home invasion or that anything was missing."

Emily sighed. "Very few people know about the room. If I died, there'd be no one to look for Joshua anymore."

She shivered, her eyes huge in her pale face.

Mitch's heart twisted as he thought of just how close she'd come to getting killed on his watch. Again. "I'll always look, Emily. No matter what."

She drew out the photo of an infant, gently touching the face. "Perry told me he would find Joshua. He had a lead, and he sounded very confident this time." She glanced at Mitch. "What was *your* phone call about?"

"Nothing helpful. Tanner letting me know that Ghost is still at large. There have been alleged sightings downtown and one near Sister Kate's, but nothing concrete."

"What if we can't find Ghost? All the evidence was back at my house."

"Not everything. We didn't take Perry's box inside." Mitch cocked his head. "Our luck could be changing."

Emily sank into the soft leather seats. "Where are we going? Your place?"

"Not secure enough, especially if there's a cop informant like Perry said. We'll head to my brother Noah's house. He *loaned* us the car. Might as well put us up, too. What he doesn't know when he's traveling to every corner of the world won't hurt him."

"What if they find us?" she said softly. "I don't want to cause trouble for you or your family."

Mitch exited toward Boulder. "Noah's place is like Fort Knox. Gated community, high-tech alarm system, video surveillance around the perimeter. No one can get in. Not without us being aware."

"Maybe I should find my own—"

"Do you have somewhere you can go that would be safe?" He said the words gently.

"Sister Kate," she said, her voice hesitating.

"Not with Ghost on the loose. Besides, the threats on your life started after you began working with Sister Kate's girls, right?"

Emily nodded.

"Enough said." Mitch pulled up at a booth to a gated community, and the guard waved him past.

"He let *you* in without showing an ID," she said.

"I watch Noah's place when he's gone. And play with some of his toys. He's got a killer man cave. Don't worry. No one else gets in."

Mitch pulled onto a long drive past a series of oaks and flicked open the SUV's console. He pressed a remote control and one of five garage doors rose. "I don't want any sign someone's home," he said as the door closed behind them.

He escorted her into the house, past a large interior courtyard with an Olympic-size pool. At her dropped jaw, he laughed. "Yeah, Noah went a little overboard on the decoration. You should see the hot tub. Looks like it's in the middle of Belize."

He placed the box they'd taken from Perry's house on a huge dining table, then started toward the kitchen. "You hungry?"

They could both use some food. And a distraction.

He turned, and Emily held the two photos and the teddy bear with its unique one blue eye and one brown eye tightly in her arms. She looked lost.

"You don't think we'll find Joshua, do you? Not really." She took in a shuddering breath. "I need the truth."

The vulnerability in her words shook him. He wanted to tell her yes, more than anything. Instead, he settled for the truth. "We have a chance." He walked to her, then gently tucked some errant strands of hair behind her ear. "And we will explore every lead we find, no matter who wants us to stop. That, I promise you, Emily, is the truth." He cupped her cheek and looked directly into her eyes, unblinking. "We can relax, have a good meal, do whatever we want. No one will bother us here."

She nodded as he tugged her toward an overstuffed sofa that looked like it might swallow her up. She settled on the edge, awkward and tense. He rested his hand on her back and circled in slow, deliberate movements. Her back stiffened, muscles tightening, but she didn't pull away.

"We're safe here? Really?" she asked.

Mitch nodded. "Yes."

"I could use a shower...." Her voice trailed off. "Except I don't have clothes or a nightgown or a toothbrush. Or anything." She looked at Mitch. "I feel like I'm drifting...rudderless," she said finally.

Mitch couldn't bear it. He reached for her hand and held it tight. "Look at what's happened in the past two days. Most people would've broken, but you've been astonishing. Strong. Tough."

She pulled away from him. "I don't feel tough. I feel as if I could shatter into a million pieces. That's not like me. I need to pull it together."

Mitch leaned toward her and twisted the soft strands of her hair, taking in the dark circles beneath her cobalt eyes, the strain around her mouth, the tension in her neck. "You need food and sleep."

He brushed his thumb against the soft skin of her temple, and she closed her eyes.

"Not yet," she whispered. "Can you just...be with me... quietly for a minute? 'Til I relax."

He shifted and lay down on the huge soft cushions with her tucked against him. "Like this?"

With a sigh, she sagged against him, her softness pressed close. "Yes."

They lay there silently for several minutes. He relished just holding her. Any other time, he would've been desperate to kiss her, to have her beneath him, passionately holding him, but he simply studied her features and enjoyed the feel of her against him.

How long had it been since he'd cuddled next to a woman and said absolutely nothing? How comfortable. How strange.

And yet, intense desire throbbed just beneath the craving he now had for her. One touch, one kiss, one seductive glance and his instincts would take over.

He shifted his hips away from her so she wouldn't feel the power of his desire. She didn't need anything but to feel safe.

She opened her eyes and stared at him.

"I've thought a few times that you might kiss me," she said softly.

"Have you wanted me to?"

"Sometimes," she said. "But my emotions are all over the place. I've been alone so long, I'm not sure I remember how to handle any of this. Or to know if you're even interested in me."

He shifted his body, and her eyes widened as he let her feel his need. "Don't ever doubt that I want you, Emily."

Nervous, she raised her hand to his cheek. "You need a shave. That will tickle."

"Let's check." Mitch nuzzled her neck, and she giggled. Within moments, her laughter gave way to sighs as he let his lips softly explore her jaw, her cheek, until his lips finally found hers. His body sang as she opened to him and he delved inside, exploring her sweet honey. It was as if he'd been waiting to taste her for his entire life.

She eased beneath him, and his hips settled into the cradle of her.

He raised his head and stared into her eyes. She wanted him, but something made him pull away.

He touched her hair and closed his eyes and the silky

strands slid through his fingertips. With a gentle kiss he rose from the couch and held out his hand.

"The shower's down the hall, second door on the right. Go."

"Did I do something wrong?"

"No, Emily, and I don't want to, either, so take a hot shower. I'll take a cold one."

Her gaze dropped down his body, and he knew he couldn't hide his reaction to her. Her cheeks blossomed, and she quickly headed for Noah's hallway.

"Mitch?" she said, turning back to him. "I still don't have anything to wear."

"I'll find some of my sister Sierra's clothes and leave them beside the door. Towels are in the bathroom." He nodded toward the guest room. "Go on. Afterward, help yourself to whatever is in the fridge. I'll probably soak in the hot tub for a while."

"Okay. Thanks." Emily's gaze slid southward again, triggering another response from Mitch, and she all but ran down the hall.

Cursing his suddenly chivalrous streak, Mitch turned away. He could've seduced her. Why hadn't he? She could be beneath him right now, writhing under his caress. He knew how to please a woman, make her want him, make her glad she'd spent the night with him as her lover. And he'd pushed her away. Why?

Because she's not ready.

And she's not a woman to make love to for fun. She was a forever kind of woman.

Off-limits. Unless he wanted more.

He clutched at his leg and massaged the sore thigh muscle. He couldn't want more. Not until he was whole again.

Not until he discovered who was after her. Not until he found her son.

Not until he could tell her the truth.

From the guest room, a shower turned on. Emily was in there, undressed, wet, waiting. And off-limits.

EMILY LET THE STEAMING water sluice over her, relaxing her neck, her back, her arms. Finally, she'd eliminated the smell of burning plastic from her nostrils. As she soaped her body, she remembered Mitch's hands on her, his gentle touch, his tenderness.

He was a good man. She'd seen the flare of desire in his eyes, but he'd let her take the lead. Part of her wished he hadn't. What if he'd simply stripped away her clothes and seduced her with all of the skill she knew he possessed.

She would have melted in his arms. She knew it.

And maybe regretted it. Something he'd been fully aware of. So, he'd hidden his passion with sensitivity, and doing so made her heart race for him all the more.

She stepped out of the shower and wrapped her body in a towel. When she entered the guest room, several sets of jeans, turtlenecks and sweaters had miraculously appeared on the satin-covered bed, along with a nightshirt. The idea that Mitch had been that close to her while she'd been naked in the shower did funny things to her stomach. What would she have done if he'd opened the bathroom door and come in? Would she have been brave enough to open the curtain? Ask him to join her?

Oh, my, what was she thinking?

She laid the extra clothes on a chair and slipped into the nightshirt. The feeling of the cloth on her sensitized skin let her know she'd better get herself under control before she did something stupid. She should be exhausted, but her mind whirled with crazy thoughts. She couldn't imagine even trying to sleep. She didn't want to be alone. And yet, she knew what would happen if she searched out Mitch. The very thing she wanted, and probably shouldn't have.

Taking a deep breath, she crossed to the door and slowly pulled it open. Silence and shadows greeted her. She could barely make out Perry's box on the dining-room table. She picked it up and carried it into the guest room.

Moving the satin comforter to the side, Emily tugged off the lid. She pulled out the wine bottle she'd seen earlier. Sealed. She grabbed a half-full flask and sighed with the knowledge that Perry's demons had clearly been with him constantly. She scanned several pages of barely decipherable handwritten notes that had to do with following some guy to Florida.

Several minutes later she picked up a receipt from a wine shop, and the memory of a story Perry had told her recently clicked. Yes! This could be the clue they needed to move on.

Unable to contain her excitement, she ran out of her room. Where was Mitch? She knocked softly on a bedroom door just down from her own. No answer. Then she heard music drifting from beyond the swimming pool.

She followed the sound until she reached the infamous hot tub. And Mitch. His dark head rested against the tile edge. The bubbling water was nestled among tropical plants, palms, orchids and other brightly colored flowers she'd never seen before. Mitch's brother had created a jungle paradise inside his house, but when she studied Mitch's face, expecting to see pure pleasure, she found tight lines of pain around his mouth, a furrow in his brow.

She'd known he was stoic, but he obviously had no intention of letting anyone know the true extent of his pain. After all the activity, his leg had to be hurting badly, because he looked like he was in agony. Well, he wasn't the only stubborn person around here.

She walked across the tile and slipped into the water, her nightgown clinging to her frame.

"The water feels good," she said quietly. "Is it helping your muscles?"

Mitch snapped upright, his hands dragging a towel into the water and covering his lap. "I thought you'd gone to bed."

"I couldn't sleep, so I looked through Perry's box. I found a receipt, Mitch. For a wine-storage facility." She couldn't stop the grin.

Mitch shifted in the water, maneuvering himself so he sat directly opposite her. "Another lead. That's good."

She slid around the edge of the water. "Your leg's giving you trouble?"

"Not really. Just trying to relax."

"I could help."

"Emily," Mitch warned, "I used up most of my self-restraint when I let you go the last time."

She moved closer and closer, until she was within arm's length. This time, he didn't back away. Cautiously, she placed her hands on his right thigh. The muscles rippled beneath her touch. "You've saved my life, you're helping me find my son."

"It's my job."

"Ouch. Okay, if that's the way we're going to play it, I'm your therapist. This is my job. Now shut up and let me do this."

She moved closer, and with small circular movements, Emily worked the muscles, nightgown floating around her. His skin was taut beneath her fingers, his thigh firm and strong, even as she felt the damaged fibers knot and tug in resistance to her ministrations. Gradually, the tensions began to ease a bit. Emily was very aware of every breath Mitch took. Of the way his strong dark hands gripped the edge of the hot tub as if he fought not to reach for her.

Her movements grew slower, then stopped. She took in a

deep breath, and Mitch moved, lightning fast, his own breathing shallow and more rapid than before.

Silently, Mitch grabbed the material of her nightgown and slid it back through the water until his hands rested on the wall on either side of her waist, the wet cloth of her gown pressed against her. She looked down and realized the thin material left no covering at all. She was practically nude.

Her heart pounded, and she lifted her gaze to his. His chocolate eyes had gone hooded and black. She could feel the desire pulsing through him. As her hands moved over his thigh, she brushed against the towel in his lap, and unintentionally the hardness beneath it. He sucked in a sharp breath.

"My leg is better, Emily. And if you don't plan on taking this all the way, you need to leave. Now. I'm not a slave to my anatomy, but even I have my limits, and you just reached them."

Emily bit her lip. He was giving her a choice. Was she ready? She so wanted to be. She wanted to feel alive again. Could she take a chance? She searched his passion-filled face, full of question, anticipation and desire. "I want—"

Mitch's phone vibrated on the alcove just left of his shoulder. He groaned. "You have got to be kidding," Mitch said crossly. He glanced at the screen, then back at her with regret. "This is work. Another case. I have to take it."

He turned his back and pulled himself out of the water. His back and arm muscles rippled. She averted her gaze, but not before she saw one very toned backside.

He quickly wrapped a towel around his waist, though it couldn't hide his body's response to her. "I'm sorry," he said softly. "You'll never know how much. I'll talk to you in the morning."

Mitch walked away from the hot tub and the temptation that was Emily. He watched as she got up and left, never once looking back. He'd very nearly succumbed to her seduction.

She'd wanted him. And yet, he'd resisted. Had he gone completely crazy?

Mitch tapped the mute off button. "If you're not calling with something important, you're a dead man, Ian."

His best friend was silent for a moment. "Guess there's no point in asking if I can come over and get in some game time while Noah's away." He cleared his throat. "I have the girl's identity. I thought you'd want to know."

Mitch's jaw clenched, and he prayed silently. "Who?"

"Vanessa Colby. She ran away from home about seven months ago."

Mitch let relief wash over him, followed immediately by guilt. "When she found out she was pregnant?"

"Bingo. She wasn't a street girl. At least not until recently."

Mitch breathed out a harsh curse. "That fits with what I learned at the shelter. Any idea what killed her?"

"No obvious injuries, though I found one injection site with some bruising. Could indicate a minor struggle. Toxicology's our last chance to determine cause of death."

Mitch would bet nothing would come of the testing, either. These people were smart. They tried to make murder look like accidents. But he still couldn't quite pinpoint the connection to Emily. She broke the pattern. "Still no sign of Vanessa's baby?"

"Not in the morgue. Unless something's turned up in your department."

Mitch paced the poolroom, his body still throbbing with unfilled desire.

"Hey, you okay?"

"Fine," he said, irritated. "Who do you trust in the police department?"

"Besides you?"

Ian didn't even seem surprised Mitch was alluding to corruption in the Denver PD. Not a good sign. His friend didn't speak for a moment. Mitch waited.

Finally, Ian sighed. "Honestly? If you're wondering about corruption, I'd call your dad."

"He's been out since the accident. Three years is too long."

"When's the last time you talked to him? He's not as out of the loop as you think. He came by just last week over my case about a cop's suicide that didn't feel right to him. Man, your dad can rip a new one when he gets going." A pager went off through the phone. "Gotta go. I hate December. Holiday idiots. I'll call when the tox screens come back, but it'll be several weeks."

"Great," Mitch muttered as the phone went silent. By then, Emily might be dead. He had to figure out what the hell was going on before they could get to her, and keep his pants zipped in the meantime.

Even if it killed him.

Chapter Seven

Mitch's ringing cell phone jerked him out of a sound sleep. Morning sun tinged with pink flooded through the bedroom shutters. He rubbed his eyes with a groan. No way. He couldn't remember the last time he'd slept all night.

"Bradford," his voice croaked into the phone, hoarse with sleep.

"What do you think you're doing, Mitchell?"

The barking question cleared the fog. "Dad?"

"Taking off with a person of interest, not checking in while undercover? You trying to get yourself drummed out?"

Mitch groaned and sat up.

"Are you listening to me?"

He forced his mind back to his father's berating. "Of course." But Mitch was in no mood to hear a lecture. He could turn the tables just as well as his old man. "Has Tanner been talking to you?"

Paul Bradford was silent for a moment. *Gotcha, Dad.*

"I have my sources." He eased the words out slowly.

That hesitation told Mitch more than his father's words. "Did your mole tell you I'm investigating not only a dead girl who just gave birth and the missing baby, but also a punk who escaped from custody? I brought him down for trying to kidnap a *pregnant* teenager. He broke out of holding. Can you remember the last time that happened? And more to the point, why wouldn't Tanner be surprised by it?"

The squeak of his father's wheelchair sounded through the phone. "Dad, you okay?"

Papers rustled. "Who was guarding him?" His father had gone into cop mode, snapping orders like the sergeant he would always be. Mitch had missed that part of their relationship.

"I don't have that information." His mind whirled with possibilities. "I can find out."

"You do that. Then feed me the name."

"Just how involved are you?" Mitch started to worry. His dad was a good cop, but he had to accept his physical limitations.

"Keeping my fingers in the pot. Just because my legs don't work anymore, doesn't mean my experience isn't valuable. Even to my son," Paul snapped.

"I never said—"

"You didn't ask, either." His dad's voice had softened slightly, with just a hint of accusation, and a bit of hurt.

"You're freelancing." Mitch realized the new computer equipment in his dad's office had more purpose than surfing the latest social-networking websites. "With Denver PD?"

"Sometimes."

"You've gone private. Be careful, Dad. The last PI I knew got his head blown off."

"Perry was a drunk. I'm careful."

"But you're not on this case."

His dad was quiet for a moment. "Not at the moment. Not unless you need my help."

Mitch didn't want any of his family anywhere near this case, but if his dad had inside information, he couldn't afford not to ask. "What do you think of Dane Tanner?"

"Ex-Special Forces. The latest hotshot detective." Mitch

could almost see his dad's fingers steepling below his chin, as they always did when he considered a question. "Driven. Wants to bring down the criminals. In a bad way."

"Is he an honest cop? Did his name ever come up in anything…unusual?"

"Not in the way you think."

"Spill it, Dad. Give me something. If I trust him, and something happens to Emily—"

"She might've killed her husband, Mitch. The evidence—"

Mitch slowly did the stretching exercises Emily had prescribed. Easy, slow, not too much pain. "I don't buy it. She was almost killed twice. Someone's out to get her, and I'm going to find out who."

"She's staying with you." The disapproval in Dad's voice came through the phone loud and clear. "Not at your place, I hope."

"I'm not a fool, but someone broke into her house on my watch. I'm being careful. She has nowhere else to go." Mitch paused. "She wants her son back."

"I know that hits you hard, especially after what happened to Ian's little girl, but—"

"I believe in her."

His dad sighed. "Okay. I taught you to trust your gut, but remember, we've both been screwed. My faith put me in this chair. Your trust of Adam got you shot. We should've seen the signs. You keep your eyes and ears open. I'll be madder than a starving tick if you get yourself killed."

"Should I go to Tanner?"

"Keep him in the loop. Not enough to put anyone in danger, but enough that if he's dirty he'll hang himself. Keep your enemy closer than your ally, Mitch."

"You talking about Emily or Tanner?"

"Both."

"That's what I thought. I'll contact Tanner."

Mitch ended the call with a quick tap to the touch screen.

"Why would you communicate with the man who might be trying to kill me?"

Emily's voice came out of nowhere. She'd cracked open his door and peeked through the opening, a towel around her head and another wrapping her body. She obviously didn't care she was one tug away from being naked in front of him. Her face was flushed, but he couldn't tell whether it was from the hot tub, a hot shower or pure anger.

She stalked over to his bed. Probably the latter.

"We had an agreement, but you're a cop at heart, aren't you? I thought I could trust you."

The accusation dug deep. He couldn't deny his deception or his assignment. That was one of the reasons he wanted to call Tanner, to convince the man to give him some room to investigate. He couldn't decide if his boss had called his dad for information or to warn him in a roundabout way. Either way, he must focus on who was trying to kill Emily. The tiptoeing around would have to wait.

"Things have changed."

"Yes. They're worse."

"Look. I won't reveal where we're staying, but I want to know what he knows."

"You're making a mistake. Perry said not to trust the Denver PD."

"I'm a cop, and you're here with me." Mitch rose from the bed and stood toe-to-toe with her, a fingertip away from snapping the towel from around her and finishing what he should never have started last night. "Why is that, Emily? Why haven't you just run?"

"Maybe I should have." She turned away from him.

"Don't. Either you're here with me, or you're not, but don't question my integrity. I've said I'll keep you safe, and I will.

If I have one inkling Tanner is involved, I'll push him out of the loop."

His stomach churned at the argument. Every word was true, except that their entire relationship was based on his lies, and he could see no way out of it. He'd long passed the point of admitting the truth to her.

"I'm your last chance," he argued. "Who else are you going to go to?"

She bit out a harsh expletive she had to have heard on the streets she'd so carelessly explored, then spun away from him and headed back toward her bedroom.

He raced after her wearing only his sweats and stuck his foot out as she tried to slam the door on him.

"Trust me." Mitch tugged her close to him and lifted her chin. "We're not done. I don't have this figured out yet, but I have resources. And we have new information. We'll find someone who knows something." He twirled a strand of hair around his finger. "People talk, Emily. This thing has too many players for someone not to crack."

She gripped his arm. "Don't talk to the police. Please. Not yet."

Could he answer her without one more lie? "As long as I believe it's not safe."

"I don't know if that's good enough." She blew out a frustrated breath.

"It'll have to be." He paused and let his finger toy with the tucked corner of the towel. "Get dressed. I have an errand to run, and I want to show you the safe room before I go."

"You're leaving me?"

Mitch crossed his arms. "I'm not taking you out in the open. It's not safe. I won't be gone long. Call in sick to work, because you're not going anywhere predictable until we solve this thing. Then go through Perry's box. See if you recognize anything else."

"I've been through every slip of paper and item in that box. The wine storage facility is on Kalamath. The number Perry yelled—eighty-five—could be a locker number."

"Or the year. You're not a bad partner," Mitch said, with a slightly bemused smile and a heavy heart.

A small rose blush traveled from her full breasts now barely hidden by the white terry cloth. Her lips parted slightly as she smiled at him, and the desire in her eyes flared. "Let me come with you."

"No. It's for your own protection. You can use the computer to track down the business owners while I'm gone."

Her jaw tightened. Just as quickly, the heat between them turned arctic again. "Fine." She pressed the door, trying to close it.

Mitch didn't budge. He didn't like the look in her eyes. It reminded him of her expression when the car almost ran her down that first night. Satisfaction. Secret knowledge. He couldn't let himself forget she was dangerous. "Emily?"

"I'm getting dressed. I'll run your check. I've become good at research."

"Which is why I asked for your help. You'll wait for me? You won't do anything on your own?"

"Contrary to your opinion, I don't want to die. I have to live. For Joshua." She tried to close the door again. He didn't move. "What?"

"Promise?"

"I won't follow the lead on my own." She glared at him. "Can I get dressed now?"

He nodded and let her slam the door closed.

Whew. She was sexy when she was angry. Mitch went back to his bedroom. He needed some space, a break in the case and a cold shower. And not in that order. Once he could tell Emily the truth, nothing would stop him from having what they both wanted.

He'd take her in his arms and wouldn't let her go until they were both trembling, exhausted and satisfied. Dropping his sweats, Mitch stepped beneath the chilly water, his aroused body fighting for control.

If she'd let him touch her when she learned about his lies.

EMILY STARED OUT THE front door as Mitch left in a huge pickup. Where, he wouldn't say. She'd expected him to hide the keys to his brother's other vehicles, but he hadn't.

He should have.

She'd promised not to follow the wine-store lead. She hadn't promised not to leave if she had a reason. Quickly, she headed to the basement, through the high-tech gym that Mitch's brother had stocked with more equipment than her own clinic. She weaved past the elliptical toward a nondescript door, more like the entrance to a hot water heater closet than a super secret panic room.

She turned the knob to reveal a concrete barrier with an embedded keypad. She knew that she'd be found out at some point, but it didn't matter. She couldn't trust anyone. Perry had told her that. She believed the man who had died for her.

She tapped in the code Mitch had shown her and walked into the safe room. Stocked with enough supplies to last weeks, it didn't look like a bomb shelter, but essentially that's what Mitch's brother had created. The elaborate décor and survival supplies weren't what attracted her attention, though. She wanted the fully operational security cameras, and the very high-tech computer system. She walked into a small secondary room. Sure, she could've used the office laptop upstairs, but there were more interesting toys in this communications center.

She'd watched Mitch carefully when he'd powered off the system. She sat down and turned on the switches. After a light-speed boot-up, she used the same identification and password Mitch had provided upstairs. She was in. She typed in the wine-storage company's address into the county's database and waited for the information to run.

While the government's computers churned slowly, she let her gaze wander to a small screen Mitch had surreptitiously turned dark. She flicked the switch. The system booted up. Just as she thought. GPS. She hadn't done all that research over the last nine months for nothing.

A green dot appeared on a screen, moving toward downtown Denver. The internal GPS provided the location of all the vehicles. Four dots were sitting a few hundred feet from her. The fifth headed closer and closer to the Denver Police Department.

"Please, don't go there," she said softly to the dot.

The car turned on the street, only blocks away, then slowed to a stop in front of the Denver PD building.

"You lied to me," she whispered.

The faith that had been growing ever so slowly since she'd met Mitch cracked. She didn't want to believe he'd lied.

The computer in front of her beeped. She had a name.

She glanced back at the green indicator. Still stationary.

With a muttered curse, she grabbed one of the portable GPS trackers from the table, scribbled names and addresses on a slip of paper and headed upstairs. She'd find out once and for all if she could trust Mitch Bradford.

She snagged a set of keys off the wall of the kitchen and headed to the garage. If he didn't have a heck of an explanation… She paused. She wouldn't do anything.

She'd be on her own. Again. Like always. But this time, her heart would be shattered beyond repair.

Mitch kept the engine running as he waited in front of the police department. He wouldn't go in. He rounded the block and came to a stop just as Dane Tanner walked across the street.

Mitch rolled down the tinted window. "You wanted to see me."

Tanner peered behind him. "Where you headed?"

"The vacant lot down the street. My kids have football practice, and I have some questions for one of the players."

"Is your charge safe?"

"She's holed up."

Tanner hopped into the truck. "I don't want to be seen with you. Drive."

"What's going on?" Mitch pulled onto the street.

"Ghost's breakout. It was too easy. Nobody saw anything. The cameras in holding mysteriously had a glitch during the hour it happened."

"Glad you finally acknowledged it was an inside job. I was beginning to wonder."

"Thanks a lot," Tanner said. "I hate cops on the take more than anything. Nice to know you thought I was one of them."

"I've been burned. You know that. Adam showed me the ropes. Saved my life more than once."

"And cost you SWAT," Tanner said. "Drug money will do it every time."

The words made Mitch's stomach seize. He shouldn't be surprised Tanner might think he was finished, but it still hurt like hell.

"I hate this." The disgust in Tanner's voice mirrored Mitch's thoughts. "I've asked your dad for some outside help."

Mitch couldn't hide his shock. "Why him?"

"He does a lot of work for…one of our top consultants." Tanner shrugged. "Maybe you should ask him. Sounds like an internal communication problem to me."

Mitch bristled at the thought of his family keeping secrets. Then again, had he let any of them in on the true state of his rehab? He rubbed his thigh. They might be guessing, but they didn't know. Just like he couldn't be certain about Tanner. This entire conversation could be a setup. "What can you tell me?"

"Not much, but don't call my office line, Bradford. Only my cell. And keep *her* with you until I clear this up. I want whoever's messing with the Denver PD as much as I want Eric Wentworth's killer."

Mitch pulled up across from a large dirt field. A group of teens hovered at one end of the vacant lot. "I'll keep her safe." Then he stroked his chin. He decided to plant a seed. "Tanner? You see a missing person's report go through on a pregnant girl in the last few days?"

Tanner shook his head. "This that case you asked the guys to run?"

"Morgue got an ID through dental records. She'd recently delivered a baby. It's missing."

"You think it's connected to your case?"

"Do you like the coincidence?"

"Hell, no." Tanner climbed out of the pickup and rounded the vehicle. His breath puffed in the cold Colorado air. "Missing babies. Car bombs. This is bigger than we thought. Keep your charge out of sight. I don't know who's talking, but the perp's in the know." He zipped up his jacket. "I'll be in touch."

Dane started jogging back to the station. Mitch let the reality sink in. He had no backup. At least officially. If he got in trouble, he had few people he could call. Including his father.

"Hey, Coach!"

Ricky ran across the abandoned field. "You find Kayla?"

Mitch shook his head at the boy. "I checked out your sister, Ricky. Why didn't you tell me her boyfriend was arrested for assault? You holding out on me?"

The boy looked down. "She wouldn't press charges. Stupid girls."

"You got any more little tidbits? If I'm going to help you—"

A black SUV pulled up behind Mitch's truck. A man stepped out of the car. "You owe me big, getting me out of a very comfortable situation in bed, if you get my drift," the man groused.

"Ricky, this is Ian. Ace football player. He's going to take my coaching duties on for a couple of days. Now, let's you and I talk." He turned to Ian. "You bring the equipment?"

Ian opened the back of his vehicle, revealing footballs, pads and more equipment than Mitch ever brought.

"You went overboard, but thanks, bud. I owe you."

"Yeah, you do. I swiped it from a local high school with the help of a very sweet English teacher who *was* going to make me breakfast."

"We'll return it, and I'll find a way to replace what got blown up yesterday."

Several boys shuffled over. Ian barked out a few orders and threw some balls to them. As they passed the ball around, Mitch rested his hand on Ricky's shoulder. "You know a girl named Vanessa Colby?"

"Sure." Ricky's face lightened. "Did you find her? She'll know where Kayla is. She's her best friend."

Chapter Eight

Nausea rose in Emily's throat as she approached the Denver PD building, but Mitch's truck wasn't there. She glanced at the portable GPS unit on the supple leather seat next to her. The blinking green dot indicated Mitch had parked his vehicle a few blocks away. She pressed down on the accelerator, her heart speeding up the closer she got.

She didn't know if she wanted to slap him or kick his injured leg. Okay, so she didn't want to really hurt him…or did she? Her heart felt empty, her entire being drained. She didn't want to believe he'd betrayed her. But the evidence… She didn't know how he could talk his way out of it. If he even cared enough to try.

Just ahead, she caught sight of his truck and an SUV parked behind it. She slowed a bit. The scene wasn't what she'd expected. Mitch stood with Ricky Foster, the teen whose sister had disappeared. Ian tossed a football around with some other boys in the vacant lot. She hesitated, but she'd seen the green dot parked in front of the Denver PD. She knew it. She deserved an explanation. She scooted in behind the second vehicle and stared out of the window. Mitch's narrowed gaze widened in recognition, then fury.

Before she'd even turned off the engine, he raced toward the SUV and yanked open the door, letting in a blast of cold. "What the hell are you doing here?"

Emily shoved him back and threw the portable GPS at him. "You lied to me. You went to the police. What are you, a spy? Undercover? Using me to prove I killed Eric?"

"I'm doing what I have to do." Mitch grabbed her arms. "They found a body. A blond-haired girl who'd recently given birth."

Emily gasped and shot a quick glance to Ricky, who caught a pass but then dropped the ball, clearly distracted.

"It wasn't Kayla," Mitch said. "It was her best friend. Seventeen years old."

Her anger flowed away. Guilt took over. "I thought—"

"Well, you should've waited until I got home. It's not safe—"

A shot rang out from the side of the street and pinged off the hood right next to Emily.

Mitch let out a shout at Ian and shoved Emily to the ground as the kids scattered. He draped his heavy body over her while she peered out from under him. Pounding footsteps slid to a stop next to them.

Ian crouched down.

"You see anyone?" Mitch asked.

"Shots coming from along the houses," Ian said in a clipped voice. "No visual on the shooter."

"What about the kids?" Emily panted as the rocks on the pavement bit into her back. She twisted just enough to see the once crowded lot now empty.

"Whoever it is, he's shooting at you, but the boys know what to do," Ian said grimly as he checked his .357. "A quick duck and disappear."

"Do all of your friends carry weapons?" Emily muttered, her knee digging into the pavement under her.

"Lucky for you," Ian said. "When you investigate dead bodies, you tend to question guys who carry knives and guns. A big gun keeps the lines of communication open."

"See if you can get a better view from behind my truck," Mitch ordered as he pulled out his cell phone and dialed for backup. After barking out the location, he pocketed his phone and shifted over Emily. She could barely breathe, and squirmed underneath him.

"Quit wiggling or you're going to get more than you bargained for."

She stared up at him as she felt his body harden. "How can you be thinking about—" her voice lowered to a whisper "—that when someone's trying to kill us."

"Stay behind the tire." He sent her a harsh glare. "I mean it."

Mitch rolled off of her, clearly keeping his body between her and the houses. Emily hunched over, trying to make herself as small a target as possible. Her lack of faith had put him in danger. This was all her fault. He peered around the front of the vehicle. Another shot rang out, and she heard the shattering of glass.

"Man, Noah is going to be livid," Mitch muttered. "The guy's a sucky shot unless he's just trying to pin us down."

"I can't see anything to pick him off," Ian called out.

Emily buried her head in her arms. She should've been more scared, but with Mitch here, she believed he'd get them out. She peeked up. Still placed between her and the shooter, he scanned the run-down houses across the street.

Another shot rang out, this time ricocheting off the front window.

"Ian," he called. "Get over here."

Within seconds, his friend was at his side. "He's behind a tree between those two houses," Mitch said. "I'm going in."

"You can't," Emily hissed. "Your leg."

He glared at her. "Do you want to get shot?"

"How about waiting for your SWAT buddies to get here?"

"I'm not waiting to be picked off like a carnival duck."

"Mitch…let me go," Ian said quietly.

"You haven't been trained for this. I have." Mitch gave a cocky grin. "Even with a gimpy leg, I've got one up on you, Ian. And you know it."

His friend paused for a moment, and Emily could tell he wanted to argue, but he finally nodded. She'd run into just enough of Mitch's stubborn streak to understand why.

"Protect her, Ian."

"I've got your back."

Emily shifted slightly, her heart pounding. Not for herself, but for Mitch. He serpentined from behind the truck. Two shots hit the ground behind him. She winced as his leg hitched about halfway across the yard, but he kept moving.

Four rapid shots fired. Then silence.

"Mitch! You there, bud? We clear?"

No sound. Emily's nails bit into her palm. Nothing but a siren coming toward them from the north. "Oh, God. He's hurt."

She tried to get up, but Ian shoved her down. "Don't. He wants you safe."

The intensity in Ian's gaze as he studied the houses made Emily shiver. He was afraid. "Mitch, you better shout out," he said, the sharp words the only thing that showed Ian's fear.

A sharp curse lit between the two houses. Mitch appeared in the yard.

Emily sagged against Ian's back. "Thank God."

"Perp took off," Mitch bit out when he reached them, dusting off his jeans. "He left his weapon. As he ran off, I noticed he wore gloves, so probably no prints. Hard to know if that was smarts or simply luck."

"Did you get a look?" Ian said.

"Dark hood, hidden face. Size and shape of Ghost, maybe, but it could've been anybody." He rubbed his leg and gave

Emily a solemn look. "I can't let you put yourself at risk like this again. You need someone who can really protect you."

She could see the intent clearly in his eyes. He was leaving her. He couldn't. Emily jumped to her feet and clutched his arm. "You can't do that. There's no one else I trust."

A black-and-white pulled up, followed by an SUV. Dane Tanner jumped out. He surveyed the scene. "Where'd the shots come from?"

"Long-barreled, scoped .22 semi-auto pistol over there." Mitch nodded toward the alley and then turned to Ian. "Get Emily into the truck," he said, pointing to the hulking, tinted-windowed vehicle. "I want as few people to see her as possible."

As Ian took her arm, Emily glanced at Mitch and Tanner. The detective looked back at her repeatedly. "Do you think he believes me?" she asked Ian.

"Mitch put his life on the line for you. How can you ask that?" Ian said.

"Not Mitch. Detective Tanner."

Ian opened the driver's side of the truck, and Emily slid in and over to the passenger's seat. "He's a tough one to read."

"Mitch hurt himself. I can tell by his gait," Emily said softly. "Because of me."

"You're a physical therapist. Help him."

"If he'll let me."

Ian let out a small laugh. "You already know Mitch well." He shot her a serious look. "Just don't let him down. He's one of the good guys." Ian closed the door and planted himself nearby, his stare alert.

Mitch shifted to his good leg. Maybe the best thing was for her to push him away, but how could she put Joshua's fate in the hands of anyone else in the Denver PD? Mitch Bradford was the only man who believed her, the only man she trusted.

Detective Tanner followed Mitch to the car and opened the door. "Are you okay, Mrs. Wentworth?"

"I'm fine. Mitch stopped him."

"I understand." Tanner faced Mitch. "I don't want to know where you're taking her, just keep her hidden." He turned his back. "Vance, keep those kids away from the crime scene," he ordered one of the flatfoots who'd responded.

Mitch eased into the vehicle.

"I saw that move as you ran across the street," Emily said. "Is your leg seizing up? I could—"

"Don't," Mitch said, turning toward her, his expression stone-faced. "You left the safe house. You followed me. You almost died. Again."

Emily couldn't deny the accusations. "If you'd only told me—"

"Don't put this on me, Emily. You're the one who left a fortress to wander around downtown Denver when you're a target." Mitch shoved the vehicle into gear and pulled away from the curb, studying the road behind him.

"You weren't honest," she muttered, knowing it was a lame excuse. She'd almost gotten them killed. She had gotten him hurt. Again.

The car jerked and his jaw clenched, but he said nothing. When he rounded two quick corners to confirm they weren't being followed, he sucked in a small breath.

He didn't know how long he could keep from rubbing his thigh, but he didn't want to give Emily the satisfaction or acknowledge how much that short, twenty-yard run across an uneven surface had brought the truth crashing down on him. He wasn't nearly where he needed to be to rejoin SWAT. He might never get there. And then where was he? A washed-up has-been, relegated to desk work.

"Why couldn't you tell me where you were going?"

Mitch slid her a sidelong glance. Her disappointment skewered him, and unfortunately he knew at some point she would feel the sting of his betrayal. "You have so much hope for the kids," he said. "Vanessa's story ended tragically. Kayla's probably will, as well. You didn't need that."

"I face a tragic reality every day, Mitch. Why would you still think I'm too weak to handle the truth?"

He shook his head. "You're one of the strongest people I've ever met. Don't doubt that. I just don't want to bring you any more hurt. Most of those kids will end up in places we don't want them to be."

"You still coach them. Following in your father's footsteps."

"Sometimes I don't know why. Dad's in a wheelchair because of that team. A punk my dad helped coach shot him while he was heading to practice. Severed his spinal cord. The boy got convicted but never admitted he did anything wrong. Never even said sorry." He turned to Emily. "It's why you have to be careful. You never know who'll turn on you."

"Were you coaching with him?"

"I was supposed to be there." Mitch stopped at a stoplight. Just the movement from gas to brake brought a wince of pain he tried to hide. Not as much pain as the truth, though. Still, he had to make Emily understand she had to guard her heart. Even against him. "He went alone, even though he knew the gangs had resurged into the neighborhood. Some of his kids were at risk. He just couldn't let it go."

"And now you're doing the same thing."

"That was *his* neighborhood growing up. He made his way out of it. He wanted other kids to have the same chance. He was betrayed, but I'm cautious." Mitch met Emily's gaze. "You can never be too careful."

Her blue eyes dripped with compassion. "He cared. So do you. That's not a weakness."

"You have to listen to me—"

"Yeah, not to care too much." She put her hand on his thigh, rubbing the ache there. "You care a lot." She eased her hand up his thigh just a bit. "I didn't believe in you today. I caused you to hurt. Let me help you now."

Mitch winced as sharp pains stabbed through him. She shifted her fingertips slightly, pressing hard against the knotting muscles. She released, kneaded again. One step at a time, one section after another she worked through the aching thigh muscle. The pain diminished into a dull ache as she pressed down in a particularly tender area just above his knee. Mitch let out a groan. That was the spot. "You have crazy-good hands."

"It's my job."

She worked through the trembling muscle fibers again. Mitch's hands eased on the steering wheel as the spasms and pain eased. She had magic fingers. Before the light turned green his leg felt almost normal.

"That's it," she whispered softly. "Ease up." She continued the massage. "You may not know it, but you are healing. If you relieve the strain and don't let it build, you'll mend even faster."

A car honked behind him.

Mitch pressed the gas. No pain.

"Better?"

"Thanks." Mitch hated he had to rely on her to get him through what should've been an easy chase, but this was his new reality. "I'm taking you straight back to Noah's. Then I'll call the owners of the wine-storage facility to let us in today."

"I tried already. No answer. It's Sunday."

"Try again," Mitch said, his voice harsh. Now that he no longer had the cramping and pain to focus on, he couldn't lose concentration on the slight vanilla of her lotion, the sexy sound of her husky voice or wishing those velvet hands would explore certain other parts of his body.

He adjusted in his seat to try to ease the pressure behind his zipper.

"Another cramp?" she asked as she pulled the slip of paper from her pocket.

"I'm good," he said. At her skeptical glance, he tried to smile without letting her see the want he knew flared in his eyes. "Promise. Just call."

Emily glanced down, and her cheeks flushed. She'd seen his arousal.

Squirming in her own seat, she dialed the number. "No answer. Again. Either home or business. They open at ten tomorrow morning, though."

"We get you to safety first," Mitch said. "Then regroup."

Emily was quiet for a moment. "I'm sorry I doubted you. I shouldn't have."

Yes, you should. Mitch wanted to scream the words, wanted to tell her the truth, but he knew better. Emily was just stubborn enough, just brave enough, to try to figure this out without help from him or anyone else in the police department.

He didn't speak, and she leaned toward him. "Can you forgive me?"

She whispered the words in his ear, her breath teasing his skin, making him shiver with awareness. Whether she intended the words to stroke him with sensuality or not, she'd awakened the fire burning just beneath the surface. He swallowed deeply as her unique scent wafted between them. He longed to touch her hair, turn her head to him for a kiss. His body tightened with arousal.

He sent her a sidelong glance. Her eyes widened, then flared in response to his need.

He could barely control himself before he waved at the

guard and accelerated toward Noah's drive. He pulled into the garage and switched off the key. The heat between them pulsed like an electrical storm. His pulse slammed against his throat. He should pull away from her, but he didn't want to. They were safe. They were alone.

Mitch unbuckled her seat belt and she scooted toward him, resting her hand on his chest. His heart thudded to meet her touch. He clasped her hand. "I won't stop this time," he said, his voice gruff. He looked at her, and she swallowed and licked her lips to wet them, begging for his kiss.

"I don't want you to."

"So be it." He opened his door and didn't say a word. He didn't have to. He pulled her out of the truck and slammed his mouth down onto hers.

Emily's head spun as he plundered her lips. Demanding, insistent, strong. He pressed against them, and she opened for him willingly, groaning as his tongue invaded her, tasted her.

His hands held her head steady as Emily snaked her arms around his waist. Her nipples tingled as her breasts pressed against his chest. She let her hands wander up and down his back, and he ground his hips against her.

"Give me what we've been wanting for the past two days," he said as he nipped her ear.

"Follow me." The husky words caught in her throat. She held out her hand, and he took it. She gave him her best come-hither look. "First one into the hot tub gets a massage."

Three steps and she stood in front of the door, waiting. Mitch pulled out the key, his smile more relaxed. "I've got the advantage."

"Perhaps." Emily eased toward him and let her fingertips toy with the waist of his jeans, releasing the button.

He sucked in his stomach and groaned. "You are a temptress."

Her lips pressed against the corner of his mouth. "No. I'm a woman who knows what I want."

She snagged the key from his hand and bolted through the front door, peeling off her clothes as she went. He followed, shucking his own. The muscles in his arms rippled as he tossed his shirt to the side. She wanted to memorize the lines and explore his hair-roughened chest all the way down to his narrow waist and beyond.

He obviously wanted her. He crossed the living room and grabbed her by the hips, pressing her against the wall. "I don't want the hot tub. I want you." His skin plastered against hers. She could feel every hard line of his body seeking hers out.

Mitch's lips lowered to her shoulder and he tasted her. "Mmm...you are so sweet, so sexy."

His leg pushed between hers, and Emily's body trembled. She'd never felt this kind of raw sensuality before. She wanted to shove him to the ground and take him, but she melted as he rocked against her, and an ache built deep inside her belly.

He pulled her closer, and her knees went to jelly. She clung to him. She wanted to be whole again, to be filled by a man who didn't keep secrets, who didn't hide from her.

She held him tight and rubbed her breasts against his chest. Her nipples beaded in response, begging for his caress. "Touch me." She leaned back, exposing her aching nipples to his gaze. "Kiss me."

He didn't deny them.

Still holding his body against hers, his hand traveled from her hip, past her waist and to cup her breast, kneading the soft flesh, teasing her.

Mitch grinned and kissed her cheek. "There?" His lips stroked her temple. "Or here?" Then he tested the corner of her mouth. "Or maybe here?"

Her mouth parted, and she tilted her lips to his, capturing him, her tongue tasting his, her hands holding his head to hers. A low rumble echoed in his chest. She couldn't get enough of him.

She grabbed his hands and took them to her breasts. "Here."

He lifted his head, and his smile vanished. He lowered his lips to her breast.

Her body soared as he wove his magic. She shivered and sighed against him. He lifted his head. "I want you."

She nodded, but she didn't stop touching him. She backed toward the bedrooms, and he followed, his arms still around her, his body pressing against her, then pulling away in rhythm with each step he took.

By the time the back of Emily's knees touched the bed, she could barely stand. She fell onto the mattress and tugged him to her.

Unwilling to wait, she opened her legs in greeting. Mitch looked down on her and groaned. "Protection?"

She flushed and shook her head, biting her lip in pure frustration. She wanted him. Now.

"This is my brother's house." He kissed her hard and rose from the bed and smiled at the view of her sprawled and waiting for him.

She knew her breathing was quick, her pulse pounding, her body ready for him.

"Stay right where you are. Don't move."

Her body hummed with anticipation, hungry for a touch, for release. What if he didn't find protection? There were ways to relieve the ache in their bodies, but she wanted him with her. She wanted him to be a part of her.

He walked through the door holding a large box.

"You expect we'll need all those?" she asked with a seductive smile.

"A man can dream." He stopped just inside the doorway

and stared at her. "*You* are my dream." Placing the box of condoms on the bedside table, he took a packet and stretched out beside her. "Help me," he said, his voice shaking slightly.

Her hands trembling, she touched him, and he surged in her hand before covering her with his body. He stared into her eyes as his hips flexed. She accepted him, and her body thrummed with joy as he filled her.

She let out a long sigh, and he smiled. He lowered his head to her throat and kissed her neck. Her scar.

She tensed under him as his mouth explored the ridge of skin at her throat that had so changed her life.

He raised his head. "You're beautiful."

"Don't kiss me there."

"You survived the attack." He moved his hips, and her world clouded over. "That makes you even more beautiful. I'll keep saying it until you believe it."

He drove into her again and again. The past melted away, and all she could feel was Mitch and his body as he worshipped her. He drove her higher and higher. His breathing grew ragged until finally she shuddered in completion.

When awareness returned, he was draped over her.

"Amazing," he whispered and kissed her throat once more.

Her hand reached to cover her scar, but he held it back. "Don't hide from me. You don't need to."

Tears burned behind her eyes at the intense satisfaction in his. She hadn't thought she'd ever feel this way again. Good. At peace. If only for a moment.

Her phone ringing stopped Mitch's caress from her throat toward her breasts.

"I don't want to move," she said.

"I'll get it." Mitch kissed the curve of her breast and rose, hurrying to find the phone tucked in her jacket pocket. "Blocked number," he said. "Sales call?"

Emily took the phone and pressed the screen. "Hello?"

"Mrs....Mrs. Wentworth?" The whispering voice was urgent...and scared.

Emily's hand gripped the phone tight while Mitch's hand squeezed her shoulder. "Who is this?"

"It doesn't matter. But I wanted you to know. Your son is alive."

Chapter Nine

Emily's face went milk-white. She dropped the phone, and fear slammed through Mitch. He picked up the instrument and wrapped his free arm around her waist. "Who is this? What do you want?"

Emily grabbed the phone from him, her fingers digging into his skin. "Please. Tell me where he is. I'll do anything."

The desperation in her voice twisted his heart. Only one person on earth would evoke that kind of response in Emily: Joshua.

Mitch pressed his cheek against hers so he could hear the call.

"Who was that? Who's with you?" The woman's voice trembled to a barely audible whisper.

"A...a friend," Emily said, her voice shaking.

A shuddering breath escaped through the phone; then the slamming of a door sounded. "They're back. I'll call later. You get your son if I get enough money to escape them."

"I'll pay you anything!"

The phone went quiet, and Emily stared at it.

"She's gone." Emily tilted her head and met Mitch's gaze. "She said Joshua is alive. He's alive."

Mitch wrapped her close as she shivered uncontrollably against him. "Emily—"

"I know what you're thinking." She clutched at him even

harder. "That it's probably a hoax. But no one's ever called before. With everything happening to us, I have to take the call seriously. We've got to find out who she is."

He kissed her forehead. "Do you still have the tracer the cops put on your phone?"

Emily moaned, sagged back into the bed and covered her eyes. "They stopped it after six months."

Mitch gently removed her arm from her eyes. He took her hands in his. "We can find the number."

"I don't want the cops to know," she said. "I don't trust any of them."

Mitch couldn't stop the tension from entering his jaw. "Except me. And I have an alternative."

He grabbed his phone off the nightstand and dialed his dad's number.

"Mitch? You okay?" Paul Bradford's voice was deep with worry.

"Until Noah gets a look at his SUV," Mitch said drily. "Dad, I need your help. A blocked number traced. No cops. Can you do it?"

"Of course, but it'll take a bit of time if I don't go through the usual channels."

"It's more important to stay under the radar," Mitch said then rattled off Emily's cell number. "When can I have it?"

"Tomorrow?"

"Try to make it sooner. We may have a lead on Emily's son. If not, I want to nail the person who called."

The color drained from Emily's face, and Mitch ended the call before hugging her to him. "I'm sorry, but she could be playing you."

Emily shook her head. "I don't think so. She asked for money, but she really sounded afraid. I believe her."

Mitch leaned back against the pillows and folded her in his arms, tucking her under his chin. "We'll assume she's trying to get out of a bad situation. For now. I'll let Dad do whatever electronic voodoo he's been perfecting. Until then, we wait."

As he cradled her in his arms, Emily rested her head against his chest. He listened to her breathing and lay still, amazed this woman had wrapped herself around his heart. He wanted to tell her the truth, longed to wash the lies from between them. But she was proud and strong. Those things he loved about her made him afraid for her.

"I'm so glad you're the real deal, Mitch Bradford," she said, snuggling closer.

No, he could never tell her.

EMILY FELT WARM AND safe and protected, and he held her tightly, her back pressed against a strong chest. She wriggled against him, a pleasant soreness shifting through her legs and obvious desire pressing against her backside. He wanted her, even after they'd turned to each other twice more during the night. She felt better than she had in…forever.

Then she remembered.

She stiffened, her mind whirling. How could she feel this way when her son waited for her out there somewhere?

"Easy does it." Mitch's husky voice rumbled in her ear. "You're okay."

With a sigh, she faced the one man she could count on. She laid her hand against his cheek, his rough stubble scratching her palm. His hair was mussed, but his eyes were clear and concerned.

He drew a knuckle down her jaw. "What are you thinking?"

"That today could be the day I find Joshua."

Mitch sighed. "It might not pan out. I don't want you disappointed if she doesn't call back."

"I need the hope today. Last night was amazing. I'm glad I found you, but I want my son." Emily rested her head against his chest, taking comfort in the solid beating of his heart. "I was close to giving up," she said softly. "I never admitted it, never let myself say it out loud, but I was tired. Bone weary from all the disappointments. Then you rescued me." She rested her chin on her hands and stared up at him. "You gave me back the possibility. I needed someone in my corner. Someone who won't ever give up. Not until we've found him. You're that man."

His discomfort made her smile, and she kissed his chest. "Don't be embarrassed. I love that you don't back down or hide or avoid. You face challenges head-on. You're the only person in my life who's ever *really* fought for me."

A loud buzzing sounded from the bedside table, and Mitch sat up and flipped the alarm off. His awkward posture told her more than he'd ever admit aloud.

"I said too much," she said with a smile.

He looked over his shoulder, his expression sober. "I don't want to disappoint you," he said. "And I will."

She hugged his waist, laying her cheek against his back. "I don't believe that."

"You will."

He rose from the bed and slipped on his jeans. She took in his powerful shoulders, recognizing that once again he wanted to protect her. From hope, from being disappointed.

He was a good man, but he couldn't stop her feelings. Not about him, not about the phone call. This was the first news she'd ever received. There hadn't been a reward posted. She hadn't been in the papers or on television recently. She'd considered raising public awareness with an anniversary push to search for Joshua, but the Wentworths' latest accusations had squashed that opportunity. If she became more of a media target, Joshua would get lost in rumor and innuendo.

Mitch turned to her, his expression grave. "I have to go to the wine-storage unit."

"Take me with you."

He shook his head, and she gripped his arm. "I know you want to keep me safe, but we're not going to be out in the open. Besides, I can help you. I spent time with Perry. Maybe I'll recognize something."

He hesitated, then lightly kissed her cheek. "Bring your phone. If that woman calls again, put it on speaker. I want to hear exactly what she says." He drew her into his arms and tapped her on the backside as he kissed her lips. "Now go get dressed."

They pulled out of Noah's driveway in the truck a half hour later.

"At least it's not too far off the highway," Mitch said. "We should be there right as it opens. Gotta give Perry credit. Who would think of looking in a wine-storage facility? He was a whisky guy."

Emily studied the phone and checked again for a signal. "Why hasn't she called again?"

Mitch patted her leg. "Even if she doesn't, Perry was onto something. He died for what's in that locker. It'll give us a lead."

She nodded and stared out the window as they drove along the highway. Mitch, silent, threaded his fingers through hers. She glanced down, and warmth flowed through her veins. He was there for her, and for the first time in such a very long time, she felt like Joshua had a real chance. Her desperation and depression had given way to determination. This time, she would find Joshua. With Mitch at her side, she could do anything.

The drive seemed endless. When Mitch pulled across the street from the parking lot five minutes before the business opened its doors, Emily's heart skipped a beat.

He twisted in the soft leather seats. "Keep the phone with

you. Stay here while I check things out. We weren't followed, but I want to be sure you're protected."

"No one else has this information," she said.

"If there's one receipt, there could be more. I just want to be careful."

Mitch exited the vehicle, scanned the area and walked across the street. She could see the tension in his back, the awareness in his body. Like a mountain lion on the prowl. Without pause, he chose a path near a stand of trees. Momentarily, he stood strangely still, as if feeling for danger.

He searched the area, leaving no corner unexplored, even going so far as to place his hands on the hood of the cars in the parking lot. His every move filled Emily with confidence. He was wonderful.

He disappeared behind the building and a few minutes later came around the other side. In no time he rounded the truck and opened the door for Emily.

"Looks secure. No movement inside, but the owners could be in the office. The engines were cold." He glanced at his watch. "It's ten."

She stuffed the phone in her pocket, and they walked to the front door. He tugged on the metal handle.

It didn't budge.

"Locked?"

He rang the bell and waited another thirty seconds.

Still no response. Mitch peered through the window.

"I don't see anyone," he said.

A shudder of apprehension skittered up Emily's neck. She clasped Mitch's hand. His jaw throbbed, his entire body tense.

"Should we try another door?" she asked quietly.

Mitch banged on the glass. "I'm not leaving without checking this place out." He drew his weapon. "Stay behind me."

When he rounded the back corner, the pristine lot looked safe enough. Mitch walked up to a steel door. He tugged. It didn't budge. He didn't like the feel. Every instinct in his body thrummed with anticipation. His training told him to call for backup, but who could he trust? If the evidence was inside, how could he be certain it wouldn't disappear, and, with it, Emily's chance to find Joshua? Mitch never thought he'd come to a point where he'd completely turn his back on procedure. He'd live with the consequences.

If he found Joshua, it would be easy.

Mitch lifted a roll-up delivery door and let out a curse. Boxes were strewn everywhere. Wine bottles were broken. A bloody boot lay between two crates.

Emily gasped and followed Mitch as he walked toward the foot. A man lay on the concrete, his eyes wide open, a bullet hole in his chest.

"Stay close," Mitch whispered and knelt down. "He's cool to the touch. Been here awhile."

He rose and methodically searched the loading room, keeping constant watch on the entrances. Once he'd secured the area, he paused in front of a closed door leading into the main building. He turned to Emily. "Stay barricaded in here until I call for you. If you hear anything, anything at all, don't wait. Run. Take the truck and call 911."

"What about you?"

"This is my job, Emily. I can take care of myself, but Joshua won't have anyone if something happens to you. Understand me?"

She hesitated. "Mitch…"

He took her by the shoulders and forced her to meet his gaze. "Just promise me."

Emily bit her lip and nodded. He gave her a quick wink, slowly opened the door, slipped through and pulled it softly shut. A purring filtered through the quiet from his right. He scanned the room, and a cat's eyes glowed from beneath a table. The tabby was curled up against a woman's body, her face, arms and throat cut, a broken wine bottle at her side.

He rested his fingers against her carotid, but she had no pulse. A search of the rest of the building came up empty, and he hurried back to Emily, who stood poised in the door with a broken wine bottle for a weapon.

He wrapped his hand around hers and took the jagged glass from her. "Always the fighter." He led her into the shop. "Come this way."

He escorted her past the woman's body, but she paused, her hand covering her mouth, her expression shocked and saddened. "That poor woman."

"These guys don't leave witnesses alive."

"How'd they know about this place?"

"Perry's face was pretty bruised when we got there. They may have beat it out of him."

"Did they take his evidence?"

"We're about to find out." Mitch stood in front of wine-storage locker eighty-five. The gate hung at an angle. The lock had been forced open. "They ransacked the place."

Every bottle in the wine cabinet had been broken. The shelving torn apart.

Emily dropped to her knees. "It's gone. They destroyed everything."

Mitch knelt beside her and hugged her close. "Yes, they did." He turned her to him. "Which may mean they didn't find what they were looking for."

"But—"

"The woman's throat was cut with a broken bottle," he said. "Maybe they wanted information."

Her hand clutched at her throat.

"Might be the same people who attacked you, though they weren't very tidy."

"If they didn't find the evidence, where is it?" Emily asked. "Another compartment?"

"They destroyed the cabinet." Mitch stood and looked around the facility. There were numerous lockers, all numbered. "Perry said, eighty-five."

"That could've been the year of the wine, not the locker number."

"Maybe," Mitch mused. "Eight. Five. Eight times five. Forty. Eight minus five. Three. Fifty-eight." He walked along the corridor, scanning those lockers. Some were full; some nearly empty. "If we have to, we'll search them all."

"Eight plus five," Emily said, her voice tentative. "Thirteen. Mitch! Perry's lucky number was thirteen. He made a point of telling me this long, involved story of how everyone else's unlucky number was his rabbit's foot."

Emily's enthusiasm warmed Mitch's heart, but more than that, he'd come to recognize Perry had, at least in the last month of his life, laid some groundwork for them. "Did he share a lot of information like that story with you?"

"Not really. That's why it stuck out."

"Probably just what he intended," Mitch said.

They hurried over to locker thirteen. Inside were only three bottles of wine. He slipped on his gloves and forced open the lock. One more act that would get him suspended. Or fired. Right now, he didn't care.

He pulled the bottles one by one from the cabinet. "An eighty-five Merlot," he said. He hefted the bottle in his hands. "The weight is wrong."

He turned it over, studying it from every angle, then smiled. "Well done, Perry." He twisted the bottom, and it screwed open. A tube fell out. He opened the lid, revealing several sheets of paper coiled inside.

"Clever guy," Mitch said.

Emily started to remove the papers, and Mitch shook his

head. "No. Not here. Not now." He pulled out his phone and tapped the speed dial.

"Our fingerprints are all over this place. We have to be here when they arrive."

Emily gripped the tube. "You're not going to show them Perry's files?"

"Not yet, but you have to understand what we've done here today could cost us a prosecution."

"I want these guys in jail, but I won't let one more of Perry's clues get lost in the police department, Mitch. I only trust us to find Joshua."

Her words solidified the dark cloud on Mitch's soul, but he pushed it aside. "Let's get outside and wait for the cruiser. Then we'll go back to Noah's."

EMILY SAT HUDDLED IN the truck. Heat blared at her, and she clutched the wine bottle in her arms.

Cops swarmed the wine shop. Ian had shown up alongside the coroner. Two bodies in black bags had been carted off, and Emily hadn't ever seen Detective Tanner as furious as he was right now—or Mitch's expression as cold and withdrawn.

Tanner, his face red, pulled Mitch aside and poked at his chest. Mitch's entire body went stiff, and he reached under his jacket. He pulled out his gun and badge and shoved them at the detective, then turned his back on his boss.

Oh, no. She'd watched enough television to know what that meant.

Had she cost Mitch his job?

She needed his help, but she knew enough about Mitch to know his career meant everything to him. Otherwise he wouldn't be fighting so hard to get his SWAT position back. His work defined him. She couldn't let him sacrifice himself.

The weight of the bottle they'd hidden from the police

turned heavy. Maybe Perry had given her enough that she could help herself and Mitch at the same time. Once they found Joshua, everything would be fine.

She twisted the bottom of the bottle open and slid out the documents. She rifled through them, but at the top of one paper was a phone number and a single word circled: *Adoption*.

The word screamed through her head. She looked up at Mitch, who still argued with Tanner. She bit her lip and with a deep breath took out her cell phone and dialed the number.

Every ring vibrated through her, rattling her already shot nerves. She held her finger over the end call button. Another ring. Then a woman's voice came on.

"Anderson and Wiley. We specialize in private adoptions. How can I help you?"

She couldn't move. Couldn't speak. Had Joshua been adopted? Could this woman lead her to her son?

"Hello?"

Emily forced herself out of the fog. "Umm, yes. I wondered…I mean—"

"You're interested in adoption?"

The kind voice seemed like a grandmother's, and even though she wanted to spill out her entire story and scream at this woman to tell her everything, Emily hung on to the calm and patience she'd learned over the last year of dead end after dead end. Her mind whirled through possibilities, and she finally settled on a strategy.

"Y-yes. I don't really know what to ask."

"You want a baby."

"Oh, yes." Emily could hardly keep the eagerness from her voice. "I've tried so hard…"

"I understand, my dear. You have to know it can be expensive, though. Our young mothers need their living and hospital expenses paid, postpartum visits seen to, that sort of thing. I hate to be indelicate, but if that's not something—"

"Money's not an issue," Emily said quickly. When it came to Joshua, she would hock or sell everything she owned.

"Fine. If you'd like, we could set up a meeting with you. Discuss your options."

"I'd like that. When's your soonest opening? I really want—"

She knew the woman could hear her desperation, but she couldn't help it.

"I understand. It's an emotional issue. Tell you what. You sound like a nice girl. I could fit you in—" rustling paper filtered through the phone "—Thursday afternoon, I think. At the end of the day."

"I was hoping we could talk today." Emily couldn't hide the real disappointment.

"I'm sorry, dear. We just don't have time. If you're not interested…"

"Of course I am. I'll be there. Thank you. Thank you."

Emily secured the appointment, gave the woman a false name and ended the call. She leaned back in the seat, clutching the phone.

"What have you done?"

Mitch's deep voice nearly shot Emily out of her seat. The phone flew out of her hand. Standing just inside the open door of the truck, Mitch snagged the cell out of mid-air right before he tucked his badge and gun under his coat.

"You scared me." She glared.

"And you terrify me." He pressed a couple of buttons on the phone. "Who were you talking with?"

He crossed his arms and stood there, silent, waiting.

"I thought Tanner fired you," she said in a lame effort to change the subject.

He shook his head at the obvious attempt but answered

anyway. "He threatened to. I quit. He walked away in disgust with a lecture about protocol, then returned my badge and gun. We'll see."

Many might not be able to tell if Mitch was happy or not. His face was expressionless as stone, but Emily knew better. His voice was clipped and short as he toyed with the electronics in his hand, but the tension in his neck and arms told her he was furious.

"I'm glad," she said gamely. "I know your job means a lot to you."

"Give it a rest, Emily. Who did you call?"

She toyed with her too-long jeans. "You looked like you were in trouble. I thought maybe if I could find Joshua on my own, you wouldn't have to be involved…"

Mitch's gaze snapped to the open bottle and papers on her lap. He plucked them and scanned them. "You used one of the numbers?"

His jaw went tight, and his eyes flared with fury with a dangerous look that made her shiver. She'd seen it focused on others. She didn't like being on the receiving end.

He slipped into the truck and closed the door before twisting to her. "The adoption number?"

She nodded, avoiding his glance.

"What did you tell them?"

The softness in his voice made her shiver. There was not a whisper of the desire she'd experienced last night and this morning. He was a man trying to hang on to control.

"I just called to see whose number it was."

"I can hear the *but* in your voice. You didn't hang up, did you?"

She shook her head.

He let out a violent curse that made her wince. "Tell me every word that was said, and don't leave anything out."

As Emily relayed the conversation, Mitch released a tired

sigh and rested his head on the back of the seat. The more she spoke, the more and more she realized she'd been a fool. She was so used to doing everything on her own, working around the cops, that she hadn't considered anything but her own needs.

"Didn't it occur to you that I have contacts? You called from your phone. What if they track the number?"

"Perry made me block it, so my name doesn't show up."

"Thank God for small favors. That may give us some time, but if they forwarded your call to an 800 number, call blocking doesn't work. If they have contacts at the police or phone company, it's only a matter of time before they have your name."

So much she didn't know. She pressed her fingers to the bridge of her nose to try to ward off the headache threatening to pound behind her eyes while he drummed his fingers on the dash.

"Okay, first we cancel your phone."

"We can't. The woman could call again."

"Damn." Mitch rubbed his temple. "Okay. I'll make a couple of calls."

"I'm sorry. I didn't want you hurt because of me."

Mitch twisted in the seat and tucked her hair behind her ear. "You *have* to trust me, Emily. Let me help you. That's why I'm here."

She nodded. "I do trust you."

Her clear expression made his heart ache. For now, he just had to keep her safe. He would deal with the consequences— and there would be huge repercussions—later.

"How much trouble did I get us in?" she asked.

"I don't know. We'll deal with the fallout when we have to. For now, we take Perry's papers back to Noah's house and go through them. Then we plan our next move. *Together*. No more on your own. You got me?"

142   *Finding Her Son*

"Together."

Mitch yanked the car into gear and pulled into the street.

"Mitch," Emily said, her voice quiet. "I wanted you to know that it won't happen—"

"Hold that thought."

Mitch's knuckles tightened on the steering wheel. She recognized the intensity on his face. He checked both mirrors, reached the next light and, after it turned red, made a quick right. He let out another curse.

"You buckled up?" he asked.

Emily snapped her seat belt. "What's wrong?"

"We have a tail."

Chapter Ten

Mitch stepped on the accelerator and maneuvered through several sharp turns as Emily twisted and looked at the nondescript vehicle behind them. The SUV jostled her, and she gripped the door handle.

Mitch let out a long breath. "False alarm. This time."

Her gorgeous baby blues met his, concern filling them. He didn't like making her worry over nothing. He'd overreacted, but without the security of his department or teammates behind him, he couldn't afford to make any assumptions. No one had his back. Except Emily.

"Don't worry," he said. "I know how to prevent a tail. I'm not taking a chance on our safe house being compromised."

Mitch took detour after detour until finally Emily leaned her head against the seat. "Can we stop soon? Even I don't know how to get to Noah's house from here."

"That's too bad, because it's right around the corner."

"Thank goodness."

Mitch parked and bit back a grin as Emily leaped out of the truck. Nothing serpentine about her sprint to the house. He followed her in after she'd unlocked the house and caught her coming out of the bathroom, a relieved look on her face. "Remind me never to go on a long trip with you," she said.

"Some of us hack it, some of us don't."

"Some of us have abnormally strong kidneys." She smiled and sat down at the large dining table.

Mitch tugged a chair to her side. He'd seen enough of Perry's notes to know there were likely some leads, and to know they'd probably need help. Emily opened the tube and spread out the few sheets of paper the PI had stuffed into the hiding place.

Mitch turned the bottle over. "Pretty clever."

"Have you changed your mind about him?"

"Maybe. I still think some of those leads of his were totally bogus."

"Me, too."

He leaned back in his chair and stared at her. "My God. Emily Wentworth admitting someone was less than who they appeared to be. I'm stunned."

"I wanted to believe him. I try to give people the benefit of the doubt." She glared at him. "But I can see now that a lot of his early leads weren't…"

"Valid?" Mitch said. "I saw them. Missing children who were clearly custody disputes. He wasted valuable time."

"So did the police department. They kept investigating Eric and me. We weren't responsible."

Mitch couldn't fix the mistakes, but he could make a difference now. Only if she let him. He turned Emily's chair to him and placed his hands on her thighs. "Do you trust me? Do you trust that I have your best interests at heart?"

"Of course."

Mitch let out a slow, steady breath. He met and held her gaze. "Did you know your husband contacted Dane Tanner the day before the accident?"

"That's impossible." A slow dawning settled in her eyes. She sagged back in the chair. "Why didn't someone tell me?"

"I probably shouldn't have now, but I want you to think

hard, Emily. Remember the weeks before the accident. Did Eric act strangely? Did he do or say anything odd?"

She gripped his hands in hers.

All he could do was be there for her. He couldn't tell her what to remember, he could only try to pick apart the clues and uncover the truth. "I know it's hard, but the more we know about what happened that night, the better chance we have of putting these pieces together. Right now, things don't fit. An organized attack on you. Someone trying to frame you. Missing evidence." He ticked through the list, the implications becoming clearer and clearer. "Then the murders of Vanessa, Perry and the wine-storage couple. It doesn't track."

Emily pulled her hand from his, and the loss of her touch tore at Mitch's heart, but not nearly as much as the heartbroken look on her face.

"I've been thinking about Eric a lot the past few days," she said. "He was a wonderful man, but he wasn't perfect. He pulled away from me the last couple of months of my pregnancy. He wouldn't talk to me. There were whispered conversations over the phone. At the time, I wondered if he was having an affair." Emily wrapped her arms about herself. "I've never said those words aloud. Not to anyone."

Mitch wouldn't let her fold back into herself. He clasped her hands lightly in his, stroking the pulse point at her wrist with his thumb. "What do you believe now?"

She stared at the floor and finally raised her head, her expression haunted. "I think he knew we were in danger. I don't know why or how, because money was tight, but I think he set up that account with money so we could run away if we had to. He just didn't tell me. He wasn't honest." She squeezed his hands so hard her fingers turned white with the effort. "Can I forgive him for that?"

The despair in her eyes made him hurt for her, and he shivered in apprehension for the future he'd recognized he wanted with Emily. Every hour that passed made him doubt it would ever happen.

"Did he say anything after the accident?"

"Not that I remember, but the whole thing is still bits and pieces. Flashes of a red and green tattoo, the bloody blue blanket, a hooded man. It's all mixed up in my head."

"That's why you wanted to see Ghost's tattoo." The request made sense now.

"I thought it might jog my memory. Perry agreed."

"It's all coming back to Perry," Mitch mused as he aligned the papers side by side.

"He was a good man," Emily said. "In spite of his mistakes."

Mitch smiled at her. "That's what I lo...like about you. No matter how much evidence you see, you still have faith."

Had he almost said *love?* Oh, God. He couldn't feel that way. Not with his deception still between them. He cleared his throat and leaned down to focus on the papers. "Besides the phone number, he has some notes. Too bad they're so random."

"I guess it was just too much to hope that we'd get an address for Joshua," Emily sighed.

"Well, well, well." Mitch looked at the circled words. *Tattoo—not Ghost. Florida.*

"Wait a minute," Emily muttered. She ran from the table into the bedroom and came back with Perry's box. She dug into it and pulled out a slip of paper. "Perry followed someone down to Florida."

Mitch turned one of the sheets over. "Here's something else. *Florida. Airline. December.* One year ago."

Emily's eyes widened. "Is Joshua in Florida? Did Perry know where Joshua was and not tell me?" She rose from the table and started pacing. "I know he wasn't perfect, but he knew what that information would mean to me."

"Maybe that's why he wanted to be sure."

Mitch couldn't believe he'd defended the less-than-stellar PI, but he understood the man's desire to protect Emily from any more disappointments. Mitch scanned the next spattering of notes. "*Cop. On the payroll.* Without more, that's no help." He flipped the paper over. "*Marie.*"

Emily peered at the notes. "What? A cop named Marie?"

"Marie is a midwife. And, according to Perry, a murder witness."

Emily pulled the phone from her pocket. "Do you think Marie is the woman who called?"

"There are no other names on this sheet of paper. And Perry's death made the news."

"She knew Perry."

"And she's probably helping deliver young girls' babies," Mitch said, his voice grim. "Perhaps she knows where Kayla is."

"But what about Joshua?"

"I still don't understand that connection. Joshua was taken well after he was born."

Mitch's pulse pounded, the adrenaline rush not much different than when he waited to bust through a door with a battering ram. Strange how a few pieces fitting into a puzzle could get him going. He nabbed his phone. "I'm calling Dad. He can probably use this information to speed up his search. Besides, I need more. I need to find a woman named Marie who's a midwife in Colorado *and* how many baby boys were adopted in Florida in the last year."

Emily tucked her legs underneath her as he made the call. He gripped her hand in his as he provided his father the latest information. Mitch already had a plan in mind. "I need a way to travel fast if something breaks," he said into the phone.

Once he'd hung up, he framed Emily's cheeks with his hands. "He'll find her."

Emily leaned into him and wrapped her arms around his waist. "Do you think we'll find Joshua?" she asked.

Mitch hugged her close. "We have a chance."

THE MORNING SUN FILTERED through the shutters. Emily watched the light dancing on the walls as she rested her head against Mitch's chest. She hadn't been able to sleep. He'd asked her to work his leg, but he'd just been trying to distract her. He'd done more than that. She let her hand wander over his bare chest, memorizing the feel of him, the light dusting of hair on his chest. He was so strong, so confident about everything. He'd even become more accepting of his leg's limitations.

Though a few well-placed caresses had helped that along.

She padded across the room and slipped into the clothes she'd borrowed. The phone was heavy in her hip pocket. No one had called either one of them since Mitch had spoken to his father.

Why didn't Marie call back?

After a quick stretch to work out the kinks, she made a cup of tea in the hardly used gourmet kitchen and settled into the corner of an overstuffed sofa in the living room. The dancing lights over the unusual view of Mitch's brother's interior jungle pool soothed her like a fine massage. She felt safe here. There were cameras, motion detectors, a sophisticated alarm system tied directly to the cops.

Emily just had to be careful not to activate it.

A slight clicking of the side door's lock made her tense. It opened slowly. Emily didn't hesitate. She opened her bag and pulled out the gun he'd given her from Noah's collection.

A bearded man in straggly clothes stumbled through the door.

Emily raised the weapon. "Don't move or you're dead."

The bum approached her, a duffel on his back. His head

tilted to one side as if he were trying to figure her out. *Great, just great.*

"Mitch!"

"You don't belong here," the deep voice muttered from behind the beard. He walked forward two paces.

Her finger tightened on the trigger. "Stop. Or I shoot."

He stilled.

Emily felt warm breath on her cheek.

"Mitch," she whispered.

"Nice girlfriend, little brother. Knows you just by feel. Since you're naked as a jaybird, I guess you two are together."

"Give me the gun, honey. I know you want to shoot him, but the flea-ridden carcass is Noah. Denver's most eligible bachelor, geek first-class, filthy rich and the world's most annoying older brother."

Mitch slipped his palm over the weapon, and she released the gun to him. He disappeared from behind her, hopefully to put some pants over that fabulous body of his, though she couldn't resist sneaking a peak at his very appealing backside as he walked away.

The man winked, and she felt the heat creep up her cheeks. Despite all his magazine covers as a tech whiz, she wouldn't have recognized him, though his eyes were definitely familiar. Noah Bradford had Mitch's eyes.

He crossed the room and held out his hand. "You *really* would've shot me?"

"No question."

"I like that in a woman."

Though his lips tilted up at the corner, the smile didn't reach his eyes. The dark pupils held shadows and a dangerous glint that Emily had only seen a few times in Mitch. Noah, however, had that expression even when he tried to grin. Mitch's family just grew more and more fascinating.

"But you hesitated too long," he said. "If I'd wanted to, I could've eliminated the threat."

"Why didn't you?"

"I like petite spitfires with gorgeous long, silky hair," he purred, sidling up to her.

"Watch yourself, bro," Mitch growled. "You have hundreds of women flocking to your bed. Bizarre, considering you make your living behind a computer monitor. Leave mine alone."

Noah threw up his hands and backed away. "Just seeing where you stand, little brother."

Emily shivered at the possessive statement. Normally she would've been irritated by such macho posturing, but she appreciated the brothers' dynamic. They were family. She missed that. So much.

"Thanks for coming so fast."

Mitch hugged his brother in one of those bear hugs that made Emily smile. There was caring there, and love and trust. Family.

"Seems like old times," Noah said. "Bailing you out of another mess, except you usually don't get my car shot up."

"Dad ratted me out, didn't he?"

"Actually, the cops called since it's *my* SUV."

"I'll pay to have it fixed," Mitch said. "Speaking of Dad, we're going to have a few words after this is all over about the high-tech investigation he's into these days."

"I was going to tell you—"

"You'll tell Chase and Sierra, too. Dad might be moving too fast. You ever think of that?"

The Bradford brothers clearly didn't mind a little conflict. So different from her family, and so very different from the Wentworths. William and Eric both avoided confrontation to the point where they turned inward. Strange how she noticed the flaw so much more now that Mitch had entered her life.

"Did the rest of you consider how you've discounted his abilities since he lost the use of his legs?" Noah challenged.

"He needs to take care of himself first."

"So, I guess that means your investigation should just be desk duty, bro. Let me fund someone who can take over. I know about your leg. It's seventy-five percent, and that's being generous."

Mitch didn't attack his brother. He simply stilled. "Touché, Noah."

Emily stepped between the brothers. She stood toe-to-toe with Noah and stared up at him. She couldn't care less that his six-foot-four-inch frame dwarfed her. "Are you a doctor? Because unless I see an M.D. after your name, you have no business judging his capability. I, on the other hand, as a physical therapist, know exactly the extent of his recovery. In any case, I've gotten closer to finding my son in a couple of days than the entire last year. And it's because of Mitch, so lay off."

Noah took a step back and raised his hands. "I surrender." He shot Mitch an amused glance, which made Emily's hackles rise even further. "Passionate little thing, isn't she?"

Mitch smiled. "You have no idea."

"I'm standing right here," Emily said. "Why don't you make yourself useful? Help us instead of attacking the man who's gotten me closer to locating my son than the entire Denver PD and FBI?"

A blush colored Noah's cheeks above his beard. "Sorry," he muttered. "Noah's taxi service at the ready. When do you want to leave, ma'am?"

Mitch snagged a notebook from the table. "Last night Dad narrowed the list to a few Florida families who took custody of baby boys the month following Joshua's disappearance. We'll start there."

"We're going to Florida? Now?" Emily said, her jaw dropping.

"As soon as you're ready. Noah's flying."

Noah picked up his duffel. "You calling the cops?"

"No!" Emily and Mitch yelled at the same time.

"Okay." His gaze narrowed. "Is that why you've got Dad running these crazy searches and keeping such a low profile?"

"There's an informant—maybe more than one—at the police department. I'm not taking chances. If they learn where we're going—"

"I could lose my only chance to find my son," Emily finished. "We can't trust them."

Noah's gaze had gone solemn. "Got it. We leave low-key." He rubbed his beard. "I was—out of pocket—but I think I'll keep this for now. Less chance of me being recognized. Give me fifteen minutes to shower and change. Can you be ready?"

"I've been prepared for this moment for a year," Emily said.

Noah disappeared down a hallway toward the master bedroom. Emily turned to Mitch. "When did you call him? You didn't tell me about it. Another secret, Mitch?"

"You were showering after last night's first round of… exercise. Luckily, he was in the country." Mitch cupped her face in his and lowered his lips to hover over hers. "This is a long shot. You know that."

She twisted under his arms and faced him. "Don't try to kiss your way out of this. I thought we had an agreement. You're keeping me out of the loop on the best chance we have."

"To stop you from doing anything crazy," he muttered under his breath.

She bristled, and he cleared his throat. "Look, we know Marie went to Perry. But we still aren't sure if she's credible.

She hasn't called back. If that was even Marie on the phone in the first place. I'm trying to protect you. I just don't want you disappointed."

She sucked in a deep breath. "It's the best chance I've ever had, Mitch. Don't leave me in the dark. I've been there for too long."

He hugged her close, resting his chin on the top of her head, and she settled against him, drawing strength. "I need you to believe in the possibility right now. Please. No pessimistic, cop attitude. Just be the man in my life who believes in me, who is honest with me, who is my partner."

He kissed the top of her head. "I'm in your corner, Emily. Always."

MITCH SLID HIS LONG shirtsleeves up. A drop of sweat trickled down his back as he hunkered in the rental car. "Eighty degrees in December is just plain wrong. Give me Colorado's snow and cold over Orlando, Florida, any day. I like winter."

Emily had tucked her knees up under her chin as she stared at the house across the street. Her face was tense, wary, her optimism fading after so many hours.

He slid his hand on top of hers. He wanted everything to work out, but there were so many missing pieces, too many unanswered questions. Even if they found Joshua, Emily would still be in danger. For now, he had to keep her spirits from sinking after the high hopes she'd had. "We still have a chance."

"I thought we'd come down here and just find him. It would finally be easy."

They'd peeked into the window of the first address. Recent photos had decorated the walls. The baby had been of African-American descent.

Noah hadn't had any better luck in Jacksonville. His quarry had had red hair and freckles. Even looking scruffy, the man had charmed the kid's mother in the park, getting her to show him the boy's baby photo. No resemblance to Joshua.

"We still have two more possibilities. Noah hasn't called yet about his second family."

"Maybe we're in the wrong place," she said. "Maybe Marie lied."

"Where's that faith you wanted me to give you?"

"I'm running on empty, Mitch. What if he's not in Florida at all? What if Marie is just some sick person who wanted to hurt me? Maybe one of Victoria's friends playing a cruel joke…"

"Then we've had a ride in Noah's Citation, and we regroup. We take advantage of the appointment you made at the adoption agency." Mitch kissed her. "We don't give up. You taught me that."

Mitch's phone rang, and he pressed the speakerphone. "Noah. What you got, man?"

"Sorry. It's not him. This little boy has dark hair, so I was doubtful, but these people are his aunt and uncle. His parents were killed in a car accident, and they adopted him."

"Thanks. You heading back this way?"

"I'll be ready to take everybody home when you're finished there."

Emily's fallen expression nearly broke Mitch's heart. She bowed her head and pressed her eyes against her tucked-up knees. His hand reached over and kneaded the back of her neck. "We still have this house. It's not over yet."

She sighed and tilted her head toward him. "This is the last chance."

"You're wrong. Perry gave us more than this lead. We have the phone number to the adoption agency. With Dad's help and Noah's taxi service, we have options."

Emily took a shuddering breath. "Right. Options."

Her eyes tracked to an SUV coming toward them. The vehicle pulled into the driveway and Mitch checked the license plate against his list.

"Jim and Judy Greenley."

Emily started to open the door.

"Not yet. No ambush. Let's take it slow. I don't want to scare them into calling the local cops. We still don't know who the mole at the Denver PD is."

Emily bit her lip. She nodded when Mitch's phone blared in the quiet car.

"That can't be Noah." He glanced at the caller ID. "Tanner. Damn." Mitch shoved the phone back into his pocket. "Not a distraction I need right now, since he doesn't know we left Colorado."

Emily's phone rang. She jumped, then scanned the screen. "Tanner must really want to talk to us."

"If it were news, Dad would've let me or Noah in on it. I'd rather return Tanner's call after we find Joshua and are back in Colorado."

Mitch studied the scene from where they'd parked. A man opened the front door and reached into the back, pulling a squirming baby out of a car seat. The flash of light brown hair looked promising; the blue shirt and denim overalls screamed *boy*.

Emily gripped the age-enhanced photo in her fingers. "He could be Joshua," she said. "His hair is the color of Eric's."

"And yours," Mitch said, letting the silky strands slip through his fingertips.

A woman exited the passenger side, and the small child reached for her. She laughed and took the boy, cuddling him to her.

"They look happy," Emily said, her voice solemn. "They look like a family."

"Yes, they do."

She gripped Mitch's hand. "What do I say?"

He stared into her eyes. "You tell them the truth."

"It's been so long. Joshua won't know me. What if he cries? I don't know if I can handle his tears."

"He might not know you at first." Emily's eyes glistened with tears, and Mitch kissed her. "But he'll recognize your love, Emily." Mitch held out his hand, and Emily placed her small one in his. "You can do this."

The walk across the street seemed like miles. Step after step. Emily hesitated. He didn't blame her. If the Greenleys didn't have Joshua, they were back to hoping Marie called again. The woman was another *ghost*.

They walked up the driveway toward the couple, who stopped, their faces curious.

Jim Greenley stepped forward, his stance curious but protective. "May I help you?"

Mitch pulled out his badge. "Mitch Bradford, Denver Police Department. Could we ask you a couple of questions, Mr. Greenley?"

Emily didn't move. She simply stared at the small boy toying with his mother's blond hair.

All Mitch could make out was the color of the boy's hair. He seemed healthy. He let out a joyful giggle as his mother tickled him. "Your son seems happy," Mitch said quietly.

The man preened with pride. "A chip off the old block. Now, Officer. What can I do for you."

At the sound of his father's voice, the boy turned and reached out his arms. "Da!"

His upper lip had a scar. A very identifiable scar. This child had had a cleft lip repaired.

He couldn't be Joshua.

Chapter Eleven

Emily sagged against Mitch as she stared at the baby's mouth.

"Do you have a problem?" Jim Greenley snapped. He folded his arms across his chest.

The man's combative stance made Emily realize she was staring at the boy. She forced herself to face the increasingly hostile parents. "I'm sorry. Your son is about the same age as mine."

Judy Greenley relaxed, then smiled. "Oh, is he with you?"

The words sliced through Emily as the truth took hold. She bit her lip to stop it from trembling. She couldn't get the words out.

Mitch stepped forward, tucking her closer. She needed him. So much.

"Emily's son was stolen when he was a month old. We have reason to believe that he was adopted here in Florida."

"You can't think…" Judy's hold on her son tightened.

Emily recognized the fear on her face.

"No, ma'am. Emily's son didn't have a cleft lip.

Judy let out a deep sigh.

Emily wanted nothing more than to get out of there. She stepped backward, but Mitch held her fast next to him.

"Your son is adopted, isn't he?"

Jim Greenley's expression grew suspicious.

"Please," Emily said. "We're just trying to find my son,

and we're not familiar with this area. It would save so much time."

The man's face softened. "He's ours. Everything above-board. We went through a well-known agency."

"I understand," Mitch said. "Would you mind giving us the name?"

"Sommerfield Adoption Agency. They're based here in Orlando." Jim Greenley pulled his wife into his protective embrace. "They have a good reputation," he reiterated, as if he were trying to convince himself.

"I'm sure they do," Mitch said. "Thank you for your help."

Sommerfield? That wasn't the name on Perry's notes. Was this all a wild-goose chase? Renewed fear shook her, but Mitch propped her up, standing strong next to her.

"I hope you find your son," Judy Greenley said softly, cradling her boy.

"Thank you. Enjoy your boy. He's a gift."

Emily's eyes burned with unshed tears. Their last lead was gone.

Mitch turned her away and whispered in her ear, "All we have to do is make it to the car."

She nodded and stumbled beside him to the street. She couldn't think, couldn't feel. Her entire body had gone numb with disbelief. No matter what she'd said as each disappointment had occurred over the last several hours, she'd never believed they'd fail.

She stared up at him, his face blurry through her tears. "I don't know where my son is. I don't even know where to look."

"Let's get you in the car," he said.

A black-and-white tore down the street at them. Mitch shoved her toward the SUV. "I shouldn't have used my credit card at the rental company. Get inside."

The police car skidded to a stop right next to him as the

stunned Greenleys looked on. Jim pushed his family inside their house just as a young cop slammed his door, his hand on his weapon. "Officer Bradford?"

Emily eased toward the SUV. "Please don't move, ma'am. Keep your hands visible."

"No sudden movements, Emily," Mitch said softly.

She stilled next to the rental, and he took a deep breath. "What's this all about?"

"Detective Dane Tanner asked me to find you. He needs to talk to you. Immediately."

"What the hell for? And how did you know where we were?"

"Rental car GPS. Um…the detective instructed me if you resisted, I should bring you in for questioning. In handcuffs." The young officer pulled out his notebook. "You're still conducting surveillance on a—Emily Wentworth?"

Oh, God. Surveillance. The word echoed around in Emily's head. Her knees shook. No. It couldn't be true. It just couldn't. She had to steady herself on the hot metal of the SUV. Not Mitch. Please, not Mitch.

His head whipped around toward her, and she could tell by the guilty expression on his face. It was true. He'd used her. He hadn't believed in her. Ever. He'd just been doing his job.

Everything that had happened between them…. She'd—oh, God. She'd given herself to him. She'd let him inside her heart. She'd thought she might even…love him.

What a fool. "You bastard," she said.

The cop wiped his brow. "I screwed up, didn't I?"

Mitch blew out a long hiss of air. "No, kid. I did." He pulled out his phone, walked away from them and placed the call.

Emily watched him, the man she'd thought she knew.

When he returned, she glared at him. "Are you planning to arrest me?"

"Of course not. I—"

"Save it, Mitch. Just get me out of here so I can catch a flight home."

"Noah can fly—"

"I don't need your help. Or your family's." She crossed her arms and planted herself solidly. "Don't try to talk your way out of this, *Officer* Bradford. You had plenty of time to tell me. In bed and out."

The young cop's jaw had dropped, but he listened unabashedly, and she didn't care.

"I know you're upset, Emily," Mitch said, his voice lowering to a whisper. "I don't blame you, but I did what I had to do—"

"To put me in jail."

Mitch thrust his hand through his hair. "Can you just listen for a minute? I did it all to protect you. It didn't take long to understand you were in trouble. I knew if you found out—"

"Oh, so it was inconvenient to tell me the truth. I told you what Eric did, and still you said nothing." She faced him, anger pouring from her, all the while disillusionment sucking the life from her soul. "You couldn't have hurt me more. How can I trust you again? With the truth? With my fears? With my heart? With my son?"

He paled, but she wasn't in the mood to sympathize. She hoped and prayed someday he would feel the pain that shot through her heart.

"I can only tell you that everything I did was for you. And for Joshua," he said quietly.

"How can I believe that? Your job was to prove I killed Eric, wasn't it? I've probably given you enough circumstantial evidence to tie a bow around a conviction. You can become the big hero. Get back your job with SWAT." Her entire being froze from the inside, despite the hot, muggy weather. "I want you out of my life. I don't want you or any other Denver police officer anywhere near me. Got it? I'll find Joshua on my own."

"You can't do this alone. You're still at risk. That's why Tanner called. They found a woman's body in the foothills of the Rockies. Not too far from your house."

Emily's heart skipped a beat. "Kayla?"

"No. An older woman."

The words shattered the last fragment of hope in Emily's chest. "Marie?"

He nodded. "Marie Dumond. She had a cell phone, and yours was the last number she dialed."

AFTER RECOGNIZING SHE couldn't afford to get back to Denver any other way, Emily succumbed to Noah's cajoling and agreed to fly home with the Bradford brothers. She couldn't think as Noah escorted her onto his CJ4 jet. She'd fully expected to have Joshua on the way up these steps. Now her arms were empty, and so was her heart. The one lead she'd counted on—Marie—was silenced forever. Her gullibility and stupidity were clear for everyone to see.

She'd believed Mitch had her back when they'd arrived in Florida even though she'd wondered about him in the beginning. Just like she'd suspected Eric. Why had she refused to listen to her instincts instead of believing what her mind wanted to be true?

She ducked into the cabin and sat near the rear, as far away from the cockpit as possible.

Mitch followed. He'd handled the steps well. Not that she cared, of course. Not her problem anymore.

He hesitated beside her seat, as if wanting to say something.

"This seat's taken." She placed her purse down and gave him the best glare she could.

"Fine. I'll sit up front with Noah."

Mitch snaked into the copilot's seat, and Emily let out a relieved sigh. Noah made the last checks around the plane and locked them in. He knelt beside Emily. "Mitch didn't want to lie to you."

"But he did. I can't trust him."

"And you won't stop until you find your son, will you?"

"No."

Noah patted her leg. "Let me have your cell."

"Why should I?"

"Because I'm one of the good guys." Noah gave her a cocky grin so like Mitch's it made her belly ache.

Hesitantly she dug into her pocket and handed him the device. He snagged a small tool from his back pocket and with a couple of twists opened the phone to reveal its guts. After a few deft movements, he closed the phone and returned it to her.

"I took out the GPS and put a handy little gadget in that will block your number, no matter who you call. Just to be safe."

"Who are you?"

"Just your standard, ordinary computer jockey," he said, flashing a charming smile.

"Right. Just like Mitch really cared about me."

Noah's smile vanished. "No, Emily. Mitch cares. A lot." Noah rubbed his beard. "You pulled a gun on me back at my house. You know how to use a .40 Glock?"

"My private investigator taught me how to shoot. He thought I might need the training." Poor Perry. He'd been right more often than Mitch or the police department had ever believed.

Noah opened up a small compartment over her head and handed her a large pistol and a clip. "It has a big kick, but it'll stop most anything or anyone. If you're going to try to investigate on your own, you're going to need it. Just don't use it to kill my brother. Even if he's an idiot, I'm fond of him. Dad would be disappointed if I provided the weapon that sent Mitch to the pearly gates."

Emily accepted the weapon. "Thank you."

Noah sighed and looked over his shoulder. "I think he loves you," he said and disappeared into the cockpit.

"No, I'm just a job," she whispered. She had to remember that.

"Buckle up." Noah's voice filtered through the intercom system.

Emily snapped on her seat belt and leaned back, gripping the weapon in her lap. Mitch's betrayal stung, but it didn't change her mission. With Mitch untrustworthy, Perry gone and Marie dead, she had one more option that she'd forgotten about until just now. She would keep the appointment with the adoption attorney. It was a long shot, but it was all she had.

For the next four hours, Emily went over every scenario she could think of. Mitch had tried to talk to her several times. She shut him down. She needed help, but not his. Not again. She thought about asking Ian, but she couldn't allow herself to use Mitch's best friend. He was a single parent with a young child. That meant going back to William. Trying to convince him to help her find another PI, and to pay for it until the house sold. Not an easy task in this market. Even more so considering her house wasn't safe with these people after her.

She didn't have a place to stay, either. Or a car.

Noah announced their approach to Denver, and Emily braced herself to see Mitch again. After the plane eased to a stop, she unclipped her seat belt and stuffed the gun into her bag.

Mitch left the cockpit and faced her once more. "Please. Don't go alone. Let me help."

Noah unlatched the door and extended the stairs. A blast of arctic air blew into the plane, no more chilled than her heart. "I'm fine," she said. "I know what to do."

Emily went down the stairs and walked toward the small, private-airport terminal. Noah put a hand on Mitch's shoulder, and he glanced up at his older brother.

"She's something else," Noah said quietly.

"Yeah. I screwed up big time. She doesn't trust that I really would do just about anything for her."

"Well, I helped you out." Noah handed him a small unit with a map on the computer screen. A dot slowly moved away from them.

"What is it?"

"I fixed Emily's phone for her. No GPS for the bad guys. No trapping her phone number. But you, little brother, can track her with this. Just don't lose it."

Mitch gave his brother a stunned stare. "You're a hell of a sneak, if I haven't told you that before."

"You let my other interests get out, little brother, and I'll change the code so you can't borrow my Harley."

Mitch sputtered.

"Yeah. I know about the Harley. But you found more than I'll *ever* have, bro. You found someone real in a world of cheats and liars."

"If she'll only give me a chance to prove I'm not one."

Noah slapped him on the back. "If she didn't care, you wouldn't have hurt her so much. Take heart in that. Heck, if you find her son, she'll have to take you back."

Noah took off, and Mitch let his brother's words stew in his mind. He didn't want Emily that way. Not out of some mistaken form of gratitude. He longed for her to want him in the same way he did her. Because he admired her, cared for her...loved her.

Oh, God. He'd fallen in love with her.

The recognition nearly made him sink to his knees. He'd blown it. He'd finally found someone whose loyalty and courage he could respect, whose passion lit a fire within him so hot it consumed his thoughts. And he'd driven her away.

He straightened his shoulders. His feelings didn't matter. All he could focus on was Emily. He made his way to the truck, keeping close watch on her location. The dot had sped up significantly. He turned on his phone, then played through six messages. All but one was from Tanner, ordering him back to the office, threatening him with a suspension and finally to fire him. The last one came from Ian with the news about Marie.

Emily's dot moved farther away. Where was she planning to go? He couldn't think of anywhere safe except Noah's home, and she wouldn't go there. The dot moved toward downtown, back to the first attempt on her life. Why should he be surprised? With Ghost still at large, she was much too vulnerable. He dialed a number.

"Teen Mother's Shelter."

"Sister Kate. It's Mitch Bradford."

"Officer. I was hoping to hear back from you. How are you and Emily doing?"

Mitch winced at the smile in the nun's voice. "Um...that's why I'm calling. Emily's in trouble, Sister. I think she might be heading your way."

"What kind of trouble?"

"Someone wants her dead."

"Ghost?"

"It's more involved than that. Can you hide her? Get her to stay put? I have something to take care of, but I'll be there soon."

"We can hide her, Officer. I'll tell her you're coming—"

"No. Don't do that. She…let's just say we've had a falling-out."

"But you'll be here?"

"She needs protection. It's my job."

Sister Kate laughed. "Oh, boy-o, it's way more than a job. I can hear the feelings in your voice. Don't you fret."

"I won't stop worrying until she's safe," Mitch said, leaving off the one phrase he wanted so badly to say aloud…*in my arms*. "Thank you, Sister."

He hung up the phone. He needed help, and there was only one man he could ask. He just wondered if he'd make it out of his dad's house in one piece.

MITCH PULLED INTO HIS father's driveway. The place hadn't changed much, except for the ramp leading to the front door. Before Mitch even rang the bell, the ex-sergeant opened the door.

"Cameras?" Mitch asked, scanning the perimeter and spying the small electronics in several strategic locations.

"Of course." He reversed his wheelchair to let Mitch enter. "I hadn't expected to see you here."

"Noah didn't call and spill my latest screwup?"

His dad shrugged. "He mentioned you might be by for some intel."

Mitch walked into the living room. The photo of his father and mother still held a place of honor on the fireplace mantel. Short of a few adjustments in the furniture to widen spaces, his dad's place hadn't changed much in the ten years since his mother's death from cancer.

"I need some advice. I'm out of my league, Dad."

"You're a good cop."

"I'm a good SWAT entry man. Emily needs protection, and clearly I can't do it. If I'd been one hundred percent, I would've caught the perp who blew Perry Young's head off. This would be over." He rubbed his leg and took a deep breath. "The problem is, I'm not a detective. And this case is complicated. She needs an investigator. She needs you, not me."

"How's the injury, Mitch?" His father nodded toward the leg. "Really?"

"Fine." Mitch quirked a smile. "Emily hates it when I use that word."

"Means you don't want to talk about it. I get that, son."

"I'm at seventy-five percent. Not good enough for SWAT, and if I can't be SWAT, what's the point?"

His dad pointed to the wheelchair "You're here asking for my help, despite this chair. What makes you think a slightly bum leg makes you less of a cop?"

"You were vice. You used your smarts. That was never me."

"You think on your feet. You strategize quickly. You're good at your job, Mitch. Investigation might be slower paced, but you have a gift for reading people. Better than your brothers or sister. Use your talents. What does your intuition say about the situation?"

"That Emily's going to die if I don't figure this out."

Mitch sank into the couch. He'd never said the words aloud, and he ached with the knowledge that if he couldn't figure out who wanted her gone, he could very well lose Emily, the only woman he'd ever loved. He had to push those emotions aside. He had to focus on the pieces that didn't fit.

"Follow your gut. About the investigation and the girl."

"It feels like there's more than one element, and I'm not seeing the connection. Perry knew a lot, but he's dead. His notes are like a few pieces of a five-thousand-word jigsaw puzzle. I know there's a mole in the Denver PD, but I don't know who."

"You asked me before about Tanner. Is he the mole?"

Mitch shook his head. "I trust him."

"Good enough for me." His dad rolled his wheelchair into an elaborate office. "Ever since you called, I've been doing a bit of *research*. Tanner's financials look good, but I've got the names of four cops who have some interesting data. Two were on duty the night Ghost escaped: Vance and Lincoln. I'm following up."

"Thanks, Dad. Call me if either one hits."

"You got it. And Mitch." His dad rolled over and slapped the back of Mitch's head. "Did you forget everything I ever taught you about women? If you care about them, what's the one thing you never, ever do?"

His father's ability to lecture hadn't changed at all.

"Lie to them. Yeah. Got that." He rounded on his father. "What was I supposed to do? If I'd told her the truth, she would've pushed me out of her life. No one believed her. She needed me. She still needs someone." He paused. "She still needs *me*."

"You took her to bed."

The accusation hit home. Mitch rubbed the bridge of his nose. "Yeah. I couldn't resist her."

"Not your smartest move, son." His dad looked up at the photo of his mother. "But I understand. Some women melt your brain when they smile."

"You think I got a prayer of salvaging this thing? I care about her. A lot."

"Groveling works well."

"I tried that. She blew me off with the force of an F5 tornado."

"Then prove she can trust you. That's what she wants, son. It's a precious gift."

"That I already threw away."

"Then convince her you've smartened up. That she's too precious to lose."

On the way out to his truck, Mitch took a long look back. Four years ago he'd never have thought to go to his dad for assistance on a case. Strangely, his father's injury had made him a stronger detective.

Mitch didn't dwell on the implications. He slid into the pickup just as an SUV pulled into the driveway.

His brother Chase and sister, Sierra, jumped out, their faces tense and furious.

Mitch met them on the lawn. "Did Noah call you?"

"Our brother is an idiot," Chase said, darkly.

"And you just learned this?" Mitch said.

Sierra shook her head. "I should've known something was up when his techy gadgets started getting cooler than mine. Is he okay? Really?"

"He's fine. We're the ones who need an adjustment." Mitch said. "Go talk to him. You may learn more than you bargain for. I've gotta run."

Sierra placed a hand on his arm. "You're not hurt again, are you?"

He kissed her cheek. "Not in the way you're thinking, little sister."

His brother gave him a speculative glance, but Mitch shook his head. They could talk later. Maybe. Chase had his own demons to battle.

As his brother and sister strode up the sidewalk, Mitch got back into the truck and stared at the tracking device. Emily had made it to Sister Kate's and she wasn't moving. He gunned the accelerator and headed toward the police station. This next hour wouldn't be pretty.

THE DENVER POLICE DEPARTMENT—a place Mitch had called home for a lot of years—didn't feel welcoming right now. He stood and faced his boss. Tanner's face had gone red.

"You might want to calm down, boss. You're going to pop a vein."

"What were you thinking?"

"That we have a mole in this office, and I didn't know who to trust. I couldn't risk Emily's life or losing her son's trail. Not for anyone or anything."

"I thought we had an understanding." Tanner paced up and down his office. "You made me believe you trusted me, Mitch. And you go off and put yourself and Emily at risk. On a hunch after I told you not to leave town, much less the state of Colorado. You should *know* better."

"We might've found her son. I couldn't risk the opportunity slipping away."

His boss thrust his fingers through his short, cropped hair. "Serves me right for giving such an important case to a damn short-timer."

"What do you mean by that?"

"I mean we all know you're going to quit when you can't make the physical for SWAT. I've seen your file, Bradford. You can't cut it. But nobody's brave enough to tell you to your face."

"You don't know that. With Emily's help, my leg's improving. I could make it back." Even to Mitch's ears the words sounded hollow.

"You sure that's the kind of help you're getting? She's your assignment, not your toy."

Mitch grabbed Tanner by the collar. "Shut up."

The detective gripped Mitch's wrists. "Back off. Or I will take you down. No matter how sympathetic I am to your reasons. I want you on desk duty until I decide if I have a use for you. Got it?"

"I'm not leaving Emily stranded. Perry Young may have been a drunk and a gambler, but he was right. This thing is big, and it's ugly."

"Fine," Dane said. "I'll put someone else on it. But you're benched. Starting now."

He'd expected the action and didn't know whether to feel anger or relief. "Then I'm taking sick leave." He spun around and opened the door.

"You don't have any left," his boss called after him.

"Then it's leave without pay. Either way, I'm off duty."

Chapter Twelve

Alone, Emily stretched out on the twin bed in the small room in Sister Kate's shelter, her bag at her side. She pulled out the photo of Joshua and traced the image with her finger. She'd been so close—in her own imagination. Never in reality. "Have I lost you?"

A soft knock sounded on her door. Emily's hand found the cold steel of the weapon in her bag. "Come in."

Heather peeked around the door. "I heard you were back."

Emily motioned the girl in and studied her face. "The bruises have faded a bit."

Heather touched her cheekbones. "I decided not to go back to him."

"I'm glad," Emily said, tucking Joshua's photo under her pillow. "You deserve better. We all deserve someone in our life who puts us before themselves."

"I'm finally starting to believe that," Heather said, tugging at her maternity top. "Sister Kate introduced me to the agency you told me about. They said they can find a good home for my baby."

"What do you think?"

"That I don't have a job, and my family can't help me. That I can't take care of my baby." Tears slid down Heather's cheeks. "I think I have to give her up. Does that make me a bad person?"

Emily stood and wrapped her arms around the girl. "I think it makes you a mother who loves her child more than herself. It makes you a hero."

"I want my baby to be with a family who will love her, but I need to be sure." Heather wiped her eyes. "Snake is going to be really mad."

"Snake?" Emily covered her mouth. "Your boyfriend is really named Snake?"

"Y-yes." Laughter filtered through the room. "Some guy was willing to pay twenty-five thousand dollars if our baby was born with blond hair. Can you believe that? Snake made a deal with the guy. Snake would do anything for that kind of money." Heather caressed her abdomen. "Even sell his daughter."

Emily's hand stilled on Heather's back. She met the girl's teary gaze. "I need to talk to your boyfriend. Would you be willing to call Snake for me? Lie to him?"

Heather paused, uncertain. "Would I have to see him?"

"No, but I need to know who's involved in taking these babies, Heather. Your boyfriend could be the key to finding my little boy."

"You've been so nice to me, Mrs. W. I'll call him."

"Get your phone while I write down what I want you to say."

Emily's pulse pounded, a flicker of hope reigniting. She could create an imaginary Scandinavian husband who wanted a blond-haired girl who looked like him. The adoption agency might very well contact Snake. It was worth a shot. Emily looked down at her clothes. No way would this sell her as a wealthy want-to-be mother. She'd have to go back to the house. Find something appropriate.

Within a half hour Emily had absconded with Sister Kate's keys. The nun had argued with her, but Emily had assured her she'd be right back. She struggled to find the gear on the ancient Impala and headed toward home.

As she reached the curve, she sucked in a deep breath. Eric's cross was still bare. "What did you know, Eric? What didn't you tell me?"

The memorial had no answers, and neither did she. Emily pulled down the street and studied the house she and Eric had bought together. Yellow crime-scene tape blocked the door, but that wouldn't stop her. Her key slipped easily into the lock, and she pushed into her home.

"I knew you'd come back eventually."

Emily froze. Ghost rose from the sofa. A line of opened wine bottles, crackers, cheese and trash littered the coffee table.

She clutched her bag closer, taking comfort in the heavy metal inside. "You've made yourself at home," she said, her words coming out slowly, feeling her way for the weapon. Just a few more seconds.

"Unfinished business," he said with an arrogant grin.

"We certainly have that." Emily pulled out the Glock and held it on the man who had come to symbolize her search for her son.

Ghost paused and then smiled, his glittering teeth giving her a glimpse of how he must've charmed all those young girls to give their babies away.

"Who's your contact?" she asked. "Where do you take those girls?"

"I have a lot of contacts, Mrs. Wentworth. A certain police officer you know very well, for example."

She shook her head. "Mitch would never—"

"Interesting." He continued to grin. "You assumed I meant your lover. I could've meant his boss, or a beat cop who roams around the neighborhood. You can never tell the good guys from the bad guys these days."

"I know which one you are," Emily said, disgust lacing her tone. "You take advantage of those teenagers."

"They're sluts. They get what they want. Money and no kid to take care of. I'm providing a valuable service." Ghost grabbed one of the wine bottles that Eric had taken so much pride in collecting and tipped it back. "You want your son?"

Emily nodded her head, her hand still steady on the weapon.

"You'd do anything, wouldn't you?" Ghost muttered with a smirk.

"Yes." She swallowed back the eagerness and tried to remain calm. She could do this. For Joshua's sake.

"Then come with me. Come with me, and I'll show you where your son is."

He could be lying, but she'd believed from the beginning that Ghost could lead her to Joshua.

"I keep my weapon."

Ghost took another step forward. "I don't think so." He smiled and kicked the coffee table aside. "You don't have the guts to shoot me."

With a howl, he launched his body at her, arms outstretched.

Emily squeezed the trigger.

MITCH STARED IN DISBELIEF at the tracking map. Sister Kate had promised to keep an eye on her. Why had Emily gone back to her house? He gunned the accelerator forward just as the radio he'd pilfered from the police department squawked to life.

"Report of shots fired…"

When the dispatcher quoted Emily's address, Mitch cursed and floored the gas pedal. She could be injured. Or worse. If anything happened to Emily…

He couldn't bear the thought. It would be his fault. He

should've locked her up to keep her safe even if she hated him for it. At least he'd know she was okay.

Sirens wailed behind him as he flew up the mountainside, but he didn't care. Let them arrest him…once he knew Emily was okay.

He focused on navigating the sharp turns, nearly running into an old, junky Impala trundling down the hill, until a loud beeping sounded at his side. He glanced at the tracking system. Emily was on the move again. And she'd just passed him.

His gaze hit his rearview mirror. He could barely make out the taillights of the Impala rounding a curve when his phone rang. Mitch punched the speakerphone as he searched for a place to make a U-turn on the mountain road.

"What the hell are you doing?" Tanner barked. "I've got officers in pursuit of Noah's car, with you at the wheel, I presume, and shots at Emily Wentworth's home address. You are so fired."

"Fine. Fire me. Emily was at the house. Now she's headed back down the mountain. Or at least her phone is."

"How do you know?"

"The cell has a tracking device planted in it," Mitch muttered.

"You keep after the signal. If Emily's in the car, we want to know. We'll check out the house. I'll get back to you. But, Bradford, we are having a *long* conversation before you're back in my unit."

"Dane." Mitch had to trust his instincts again. "Work with Lieutenant Decker to pick your team. I trust him. No one else."

"Will do, Mitch. I'll keep in touch."

Mitch dropped his phone on the seat. For ten minutes he tracked the Impala but couldn't quite catch up. Whoever drove it knew downtown Denver like the back of their hand.

Finally, the phone rang.

"Bradford."

"Emily's not here," Tanner said quietly.

The hesitation in the man's voice made Mitch's gut churn. "But…"

"The house is pretty trashed. There's blood spatter in the living room. Someone's hurt."

Mitch gripped the steering wheel and glanced at his side. "According to my tracker, the car's stopped."

"Where are you? I've got the lieutenant and his team on standby."

"Coming up on Fifth and Colfax." He caught sight of the car, and two figures disappearing into an abandoned apartment building, one slight, with a sway of hips he recognized all too well. Thank God. His heart started beating again for the first time since he'd heard the notification of shots. "I see her. With a big guy in a trench coat. Might be Ghost. They went into that old apartment building on Sixth."

"I know it. I'll get the team there. Wait for us, Mitch."

"As long as I can."

He stabbed the off button. Without any intel, he had no idea what he was walking into. All he knew was Emily was trapped inside.

He flipped his collar up and walked down the street, passing the Impala. Streaks of red smeared the front seat.

Blood.

GHOST SHOVED THE GUN into Emily's side and she staggered through the door of the decrepit apartment building. All but one of the windows were boarded shut. The place looked abandoned.

"Get me upstairs to the first room on the left," he rasped. "Don't talk to anyone or you and them are dead." They trudged up, and Emily studied the layout and each young girl's face she met as they climbed the stairs and entered the room.

A square-jawed man with a military haircut stomped into the room behind them. "What the hell happened to you? And what's *she* doing here? Are you crazy?"

"Sit down and shut up, Vance," Ghost said as he flopped back on the bed.

He pulled away the bloody hand from his side. "Witch shot me, but I got her here. Get me some disinfectant and some bandages, will you?"

"You need the doc?"

"Nah. She grazed my side. Some butterflies'll hold me for now." Ghost propped himself up against the back of the bed, still aiming the Glock he'd wrestled away from Emily. "Once we find out what she knows, we'll take care of her. I have to waste that kid, Ricky, too. He's still poking around." He glared at Vance. "You should've taken him out—"

"Shut up," Vance said.

As he handed Ghost the medical supplies, Emily caught sight of a badge hanging out of his pocket. He was the cop.

"I had a bigger target. That warning shot should've shut her up." He glared at Emily. "Doesn't matter now. Once our problem upstairs is taken care of, Ricky won't make trouble anymore. If he does, he and his grandmother will let a cop into the house. No one will care if an old lady and kid bite the dust. I'll plant drugs or something."

His calculated plan made Emily shiver. She'd thought maybe she could reason with one of them. This cop had gone all the way bad.

"We'll make it two for one, today," Vance added. "Keep our exposure to a minimum."

"Not a bad idea. How long 'til she pops?"

"A few hours. Maybe less. Boss doesn't want it done here, though. The last one pushed Marie over the edge. The idiot stole my data on my *guest*—" he nodded toward Emily "—and went to that drunk PI. Nearly blew everything. Doc doesn't want any more screwups. We kill them off site."

The man said the words as if taking someone's life was business as usual. A strange calmness came over Emily. She had the next few hours to find a way out. And, if nothing else, to come up with a way to get a message to Mitch. Despite everything, Emily recognized he would keep searching for Joshua, even if she were gone. She needed more information.

"You told me you'd tell me where my son is," she blurted.

"I lied," Ghost said. "We didn't take your damn kid, but you ask too many questions. You should've left it alone. Snake and Heather's baby was worth half a million bucks. Both blond-haired and blue-eyed. That's why we paid him to get her pregnant. Then you had to go and ruin the deal."

Emily's head spun. They didn't know where Joshua was. She didn't understand. "But Perry—"

"Young?" Vance laughed. "That fool stumbled onto the operation. That's why I had to take him out. He knew too much."

This couldn't be happening. She had to get away. To find Joshua and to warn Heather. Emily squirmed in her chair and wrapped her coat tighter around her, then shoved her hands in the pockets. Her fingers hit the metal of her cell phone. She clutched it, and her gaze flew to the men. If they would just leave her alone, she could call Mitch or 911. He'd find her. He'd save her.

She could count on him.

The truth filled Emily's heart with awe. She could count on Mitch Bradford. He'd lied, but he wouldn't let her down. She moved her fingers over the on button.

"Hey, there. What're you doing?" Vance grabbed Emily and yanked her to her feet. "You search her?" he asked Ghost.

"She shot me. I got the gun. Exactly when—"

"Idiot." Vance tugged her coat off and patted her down.

Emily shivered as his hands lingered over her breasts. He squeezed them and then pushed her down in the chair. Maybe he wouldn't look in the pocket.

He grabbed the coat and snagged the cell phone. "Fool." Vance pressed a couple of buttons. "No calls for the past half hour. You dodged a bullet, dude. The doc would've had me kill you, too, if she'd led the cops here."

Vance dropped her phone on the floor and rammed the heel of his boot into it, smashing the small device, then tossed it into a sink and ran water over it. "No cavalry."

His satisfied smile squeezed out most of Emily's hope. She'd put herself in this position, and now Joshua would never know that his mother had loved him very much.

Ghost finished applying several butterfly strips and pulled down his bloody sweater. "That'll do me. I'm changing, and then I gotta dump the car. Take care of her."

He pushed up his sleeves, and Emily saw the red-and-green devil tattoo. Her head ached, her mind whirled. It wasn't right. Something was missing.

Oh, God. Ghost wasn't the man from that night. Perry had been right.

"She'll be fine in here," Vance said. "One less room to wipe down for trace evidence."

They closed her in, and the sound of the door bolting sealed Emily's fate. Once the poor girl's baby was born, both of them were dead. Mitch didn't know about Ghost or Vance. Unless Emily found a way out.

MITCH HAD SEARCHED THE entire perimeter of the building and didn't see an opening. Odd. Usually an abandoned building like this wasn't so heavily fortified. All the windows appeared boarded. He needed intel. No way to know how many people were inside. Emily had disappeared five minutes ago. It felt like a lifetime.

How the hell was he supposed to get in? He had to be smart, or Emily was dead.

A familiar black van pulled down an alley nearby. Yes.

Lieutenant Decker jumped out, and his SWAT teammates followed. Mitch edged in the alleyway, out of the line of sight of the apartment building.

"Give us the sit rep," Lieutenant Decker ordered as the team surrounded Mitch.

Mitch spoke quickly and succinctly.

Decker nodded toward one of the other entry men, Reynolds. "Find us a way in."

"You got it, Lieutenant."

"Roof?" Mason, the sniper, asked, indicating a building across the street.

"That's your best bet," Decker said. "Keep a lookout for any activity."

"Our hostage. Can she help us?" Reynolds asked.

"She thinks she's alone in this," Mitch said. "With good reason. She doesn't trust the police department."

"Great," Decker muttered. "Does she trust you?"

"To save her life. Maybe. Otherwise, no."

Lieutenant Decker lifted his brow. "Man, Mitch. What trouble have you gotten yourself into? I heard Tanner was trying to palm you off to summons duty this morning."

"Long story."

"In position, Alpha Leader," Mason's voice came across the radio.

"Ten-four."

"What's the risk if we ram?" Greggson, the number-two entry man, sidled up to Decker and Mitch.

"Ghost, the guy I believe took her, lures pregnant girls off the streets. Then they disappear. I know of one girl, Kayla

Foster, who's missing. Another teenager ended up dead post-partum."

Greggson let out a violent curse. "A real winner."

"We could have a bunch of pregnant teens in that building," Mitch warned. "You gotta go in careful."

"Any way we can talk our way in?"

"Alpha One to Alpha Leader." Mason's voice crackled over the radio. "I've got movement. Second floor. Southeast corner. Someone just shifted a board."

Mitch grabbed the lieutenant's binoculars and peered at the window. Cobalt blue eyes stared out the small gap. He'd recognize them anywhere.

"Emily," he breathed. "She's amazing." Her fingers slipped around the second slab. "She's using metal to pry the wood away from the window."

Decker ripped back his binoculars. "Assuming she's locked in—and I doubt she'd try to break out of a second-story window if she weren't—putting someone in her room might give us an advantage."

"I can slip in and get her out," Mitch said.

"How's your leg?"

"Good enough for this."

Decker studied him. "All right." The lieutenant handed him an earpiece and a black tool bag. "Get in position. Reynolds and Greggson will pull you up."

Within minutes, Mitch had the harness around him and was walking up the side of the building. No alarm had sounded. Those inside had figured a few condemned signs would keep people away. That and a paid-off cop.

When he reached the window, he made a quick cutting motion with his hand. He dangled thirty feet above the ground. Emily's fingertips were clutched around the second board.

"Emily?"

The top of her head peered out, and her eyes widened when she saw him. Then they softened in relief. "I knew you'd come."

Then she smiled. Mitch's heart thudded against his chest.

"Stand back," he said. She nodded and moved away from the window. He quickly pried the boards from their hinges before sliding through the window.

Emily launched herself at him the second he touched down. He wrapped his arms around her and held her close. "Are you okay? You're not hurt?"

She shook her head, burying deeper against him, hugging him tight as if she would never let him go.

"There was blood at your house," he said, unable to keep the harshness from his voice.

"Ghost. I shot him."

He set her back from him and unfastened the harness. He couldn't stop grinning at her. "You are one spectacular woman."

He hugged her close again, relishing the feel of her small body against his, her breasts pressed hard against him. "They're going to kill me," she whispered. "And another girl. She's having a baby, and after she delivers they plan to get rid of both of us. We have to help her."

He took one last breath, inhaled the scent of her, one last second to hug her close, then stepped away. "How many girls? How many guarding them?"

"I don't know. I heard some teenagers laughing up and down the hall, so I don't think everyone's being held against their will. There's a police officer. Vance. He killed Perry. He's the one who shot at us, too. Just a warning," Emily said bitterly. "A doctor is here, too. And Ghost, but he said he was going to move Sister Kate's car. That's everyone I saw."

"You practically took a tour." Mitch smiled. "Good job." His dad had also been right about Vance. Mitch relayed the information to Lieutenant Decker. If Ghost exited the building, he could provide SWAT's access opportunity.

Mitch bent to Emily and kissed her. "We're going to get everyone out of here. I promise." Mitch knelt in front of the door, testing the lock. "I wanted to send you out the window, but the SWAT team is moving into position. No time."

"I heard the dead bolt shut."

"Not a problem," Mitch said as he pulled out a small tension wrench and eased it into the bottom of the lock and stabbed a pick above it. Two tries and the lock gave way. He pulled the pick out and slowly turned the wrench. "Voila."

"You learned that in SWAT?"

"Nah. Noah taught me how to sneak back into the house when I was about fourteen."

He communicated the new status to Lieutenant Decker.

"We'll stay put for a few minutes. The guys are set up outside to see if Ghost exits. That way they can go in quiet."

Emily studied Mitch's face. He looked energized and alive.

"This is the life you want. The excitement," she said quietly.

He turned his head. "I'm good at it. And yeah, I like catching the bad guys."

"You'll get back, Mitch. Your leg will improve enough to do the job. Then you can have what you want."

He laced his fingers through hers. "What if I want you, too?"

Before she could reply, a clanging alarm sounded in the hallway.

"Okay, girls, back into your rooms. Looks like we've got a new arrival almost here."

The jolly voice made Emily shudder in revulsion.

"The doctor," she said. "The baby's coming."

"We're out of time, but he's also made it easier. If everyone's in their rooms, we can make this thing happen safely."

Mitch tapped his earpiece.

With a quick relay of more intel, Mitch turned to Emily. "They have Ghost. They're coming in. Doing a room-to-room. You stay here. They'll come get you."

"Where are you going?"

"To find the room with the doctor."

He shoved a weapon into her hand. "Don't shoot the SWAT team. Officer Vance, on the other hand, feel free to take aim. There's nothing I hate more than a traitor."

He slipped out of the door, his stealth movements dangerous.

She gripped the gun in her hand and stood near the door, expecting screams or shuffling, but it was utterly silent.

A few minutes later, her hand had cramped around the gun. The lock turned. "It's SWAT, Mrs. Wentworth," a voice said softly.

An arm covered in black eased through a crack in the door. A split second later, a man had pivoted and stripped her of her weapon. "I'm Reynolds. Good to meet you. Now come with me."

Emily stepped out of the room, covered by the large SWAT team member. About four pregnant teens were being rushed down the stairs, a couple being carried with hands over their mouths.

Vance rounded the corner in a dead run. He headed toward Emily. Mitch plowed after him.

"Vance. Stop!"

Reynolds pushed her down, covering her body before taking aim at the errant cop.

"Bitch," Vance screamed and leaped at her.

Chapter Thirteen

Mitch caught Vance from the side and shoved him away from Emily. The man slammed into the floor, and with a quick move, Mitch pinned Vance to the ground and forced his hands behind his back. Mitch had to stop himself from taking a cheap shot at the guy who'd gone after her. "You're going down."

Reynolds stood and helped Emily to her feet. "Nice move. You back?"

"Almost." Although the ache in Mitch's leg indicated a SWAT assignment wouldn't happen anytime soon.

Reynolds knelt down and fastened zip ties around Vance's wrists. "Where's the doctor, traitor?"

"I wasn't doing anything wrong." Vance glared at them. "I just followed you guys in."

Emily stalked over to the man on the floor. Mitch could see the fury vibrating from within her.

"You were going to kill me," she said.

"Liar," Vance spat.

Mitch tugged the man to his feet and spun him around against the wall. He closed his fingers around the soon-to-be-ex-cop's neck.

Emily rushed behind Mitch, leaning over his back. The woman was fearless.

"You know something about my son. I know you do." Her husky voice had gone desperate.

"Idiot. Your son was never here. You were chasing the wrong devil from the beginning." Vance laughed.

Emily sagged against Mitch. "No. *Someone* here knows *something*. They just have to."

He shoved his arm harder against the guy's throat. "Unless you want me telling every inmate you're a cop, you give up the doctor's location. I find out you're lying, you won't last a week inside."

Vance went ghost-white and deflated like the coward he was. "Fourth floor. Insulated room so the other girls don't flip out when they hear them scream."

"What's the layout?" Mitch snapped. "And how do I get in without tipping him off?"

Their prisoner spilled the description of the room. "Doc's waiting for the midwife. She's not here yet, but he'll expect a knock on the door."

Mitch passed off Vance to another of his teammates, then turned to Emily. "Go with them. I want you outside."

She shook her head. "I can help. If he's really expecting a woman, I can get him to open the door for me. Otherwise, you place the girl in the room at risk if he panics."

"She's right," Reynolds said quietly.

Mitch wanted nothing more than to get Emily away from this place, but they were running out of time. "Get Vance out of here," he told Reynolds. "Emily, stay behind me," he ordered.

They ran up the stairs to the fourth floor, meeting Greggson at the top.

"All clear, except at the end," he said. "But check this out."

They followed him into a space with a wall full of monitors showing every room in the house.

Mitch cursed. "They knew we were here?"

"I don't think so," Greggson said. "This area was deserted when we arrived."

Mitch looked at the sea of empty rooms. Except one. Kayla lay on a bed, her legs bound in stirrups, but she was fighting against the bonds. "That's Kayla Foster. Does this thing have volume?"

Greggson flicked a few switches and turned a knob. The man in the white coat smiled, his face cold and terrifying. "Finally dilated enough, my little troublemaker. It won't be long now. After we deliver your brat, we're getting rid of you. Just like your friend."

"What did you do to Vanessa?" Her forehead damp with sweat and her face streaked with tears, Kayla cried out as another contraction began.

"She's not your concern anymore. Just push the brat out, or I'll cut it out," he said, nodding to the tray of instruments at his side.

"No. Don't hurt my baby." Kayla's plea echoed through the speaker.

"That's it. No more time. We're getting her out of there now." Mitch updated Decker and turned to Emily. "The room is soundproofed, so I'll knock loudly. You announce yourself, then move aside. That'll get the doctor away from her. Greggson, you go for the doctor. I'll get the girl."

They moved into position, and Mitch knocked on the door. He nodded at Emily.

"Doctor. I'm here," she shouted and flattened herself against the opposite wall.

The door slid open. "It's about time."

"Go!" Greggson's voice sounded in Mitch's ear.

They rushed through the door side by side. Mitch reached Kayla just as Greggson slammed the doctor against the wall and restrained his wrists.

Once Greggson had the doctor secure with zip ties, Emily

raced into the room and covered Kayla with a sheet, then knelt beside her, whispering words of comfort, holding her as the teen sobbed in her arms.

"How's she doing?" Mitch asked, his concern for the girl growing as she cried out in pain.

"Her contractions are coming fast. She needs a hospital."

Mitch barked out an order. Greggson communicated with Lieutenant Decker. Minutes later, paramedics were loading Kayla onto a gurney. She clutched Mitch's arm. "Coach? Can you call my grandma? I need her."

Mitch pushed back the blond hair from Kayla's damp forehead. "You got it, honey. I'll let Ricky know, too."

She shook her head against the pillow on the gurney. "I let him down."

"He loves you. He had faith in you. He knew something was wrong. That's why he searched for you."

A tear slipped down her cheek. "The doctor took Vanessa, and I haven't seen her since. Have you found her?"

Mitch met Emily's sorrowful gaze. "Let's get you to the hospital, Kayla. Then we can fill you in."

Kayla wiped the tears away. "Don't bother. He killed her, didn't he?" She looked at the doctor, now sitting in the corner of the room being questioned by Greggson. "It's all my fault."

Emily leaned in closer. "No, Kayla. You can't control what other people do."

"You don't understand. Vanessa and I changed our minds about giving up our babies, but we were stupid. We came back to tell the doctor. He was really mad and told us we had no choice." Kayla rubbed her eyes and raised a haunted gaze to them. "I told Vanessa we should pretend to change our minds and wait for an opportunity to sneak out. It was working. Until the night I wanted some milk from the kitchen. We were halfway down the stairs when we saw *him*."

Mitch instincts trilled in his mind. "Who? Vance? The cop?"

"Not him. A man. With a tattoo. He was yelling about needing a signature. He threatened the doctor. Scared him. Bad. Then Vanessa gasped. A contraction. The doctor saw us." Kayla wiped her eyes. "I never saw her again."

Mitch leaned over Kayla. "What kind of tattoo did this guy have?"

"The same gang tat as Ghost—a red and green devil on his wrist—but with a pink ribbon wrapped around it. Like those breast-cancer ribbons. Weird."

"Knife!" Greggson gave a shout as a loud crash reverberated through the room.

Mitch whirled toward the noise, shoving Emily behind him to protect her. The doctor knocked the surgical tray into them as he bolted from the corner and out the door.

"He stabbed me with a syringe." Greggson held the side of his neck. "Careful! He must've palmed a scalpel. He cut the zip ties."

Mitch cursed and bolted down the hall after the doctor, all the while relaying a message to Reynolds. How had a secure scene gone downhill so fast?

The doctor grabbed the banister and tried to rush down the stairs, but by the time he reached the second floor, he was panting and doubled over. Mitch took the stairs two at a time, each jolt slamming up his leg like a firebrand. He'd pay for it later, but right now he didn't care. He'd seen Vanessa's crime-scene photos. Mitch was taking this murderer down.

He was just feet behind the doctor when the man frantically looked around and veered into the same bedroom Mitch and Emily escaped from earlier. Mitch followed. The missing window slats allowed the sun to bathe the room in light.

"Don't come any closer." The doctor paced frantically, brandishing the scalpel and searching for an escape.

"Mitch, find out what was in that syringe," Reynolds said through the earpiece. "Fast."

Mitch closed him and the doctor into the room. Alone. "There's nowhere to go, and I'm not feeling friendly. So, Doc, what was in that syringe?"

"Nothing but air," the doctor snapped. "If done right, it's the perfect crime."

"You catch that?" Mitch said through his earpiece.

"Air embolus," the EMT said sharply. "Get Greggson to the hospital."

"He'll be fine," the doctor said bitterly. "It was a little bubble. I didn't even have time to hit a vein."

"Lucky for you."

"Oh, yeah, I really feel lucky now. Everything I've worked for is gone. Because of that nosy do-gooder."

Emily slammed into the room. "Who was the man with the tattoo? The one with the pink ribbon on it? The one you're afraid of?"

The doctor's eyes went wide; his face paled to a grayish-white. "No way I'm talking. They'll kill me."

"I knew it." Emily rushed forward. "Who are *they?*"

"Emily! Don't—"

The doctor grabbed her before Mitch could move.

"Stay back or I'll kill her. I got nothing left to lose." He held the scalpel to her throat and backed toward the window.

Mitch knew the man was telling the truth. He'd kill Emily. Mitch forced his pounding pulse to slow. He had to be smart. "Doc, we can work something out."

The guy wasn't listening. He clutched her tighter, shaking his head. "I shouldn't have let Ghost talk me into helping the guy. Easy money, Ghost said," the doctor muttered. "Just a birth certificate that looked legal. I didn't know who he really was. How could I know?"

"Please. Tell me," Emily begged. "Who has my son?"

Her eyes had taken on the desperate look Mitch had seen before. She struggled against the doctor, and he cursed. The blade nicked her neck, drawing blood. She gasped. Her eyes turned glassy. Mitch recognized the signs. Flashback. She pulled and jerked within her captor's arms, unseeing, screaming.

"Get away from me. No! I can't see your face. Don't kill me. Don't take my baby!" Tears streamed down Emily's face. Her agonized cries broke Mitch's heart.

"Are you crazy?" the doctor yelled. "Don't move or I'll slit your throat open." Suddenly Emily stilled, almost deadly serene. He took another step back, dragging her with him. Mitch couldn't tell if she was in shock or had come out of it. The situation could explode any second.

"I want immunity and witness protection."

"Doc, just let her go and we'll discuss it." Mitch lowered his voice to a calm, easy tone.

"I don't have time to talk. I can't let you take me in. I won't last a day in jail. They'll get to me. They can get to anyone."

"I believe you. But you have to show good faith. I need to let my bosses know you're a reasonable man. And that you're telling the truth. Give me something. A name. Proof."

"You're not listening." The doctor backed closer to the window, Emily plastered against him as a shield. "I'll jump. I'll take her with me."

"No!" Suddenly, Emily wrenched away, but to Mitch's horror, the doctor held on. Instead of falling into the center of the room, she stumbled closer to the window. The doctor shoved her hard at the opening.

Mitch dove toward her, slamming down on his bad knee but knocking her out of the way. The doctor tripped over their falling bodies, and his momentum carried him over the edge. Mitch twisted and grabbed the man's coat, ignoring the searing pains shooting through his leg with blinding intensity. He couldn't pass out. Hell, a full breath would be nice.

Emily gripped the material to help Mitch hang on to the doctor as he dangled from the window.

"Save me," he screamed. "Don't let me fall."

Mitch struggled to adjust his hold on the coat and, grimacing, got on his knees. "Give me a name," he said, reaching one hand down.

"Frankie," the doctor panted. "Please, help me up."

Mitch braced himself, and he and Emily tugged the man up by the coat until their hands almost touched the doctor's. Suddenly, with a loud tearing sound, the white garment gave way. The fabric split. Frantically, Mitch clutched for the man's hand, or another part of the coat, but it was no use. The doctor fell to the ground, screaming, until his head slammed against the hard cement below and there was silence.

Mitch leaned through the open window and stared at white, sightless eyes staring back at him.

Emily hugged Mitch from behind. "We did everything we could," she said softly.

"It wasn't enough." He turned into her arms and held her closer.

Shouts from below penetrated their momentary quiet.

"Mitch, you guys okay?" Decker called through the microphone.

"Fine. We're coming down," he said.

"Do you think Frankie is the man with the tattoo?" Emily asked.

"I don't know, but we're going to find out." Mitch turned, and his leg collapsed under him, spasms firing up his knee and leg. He clenched his jaw to keep from turning the air a colorful shade of blue, then pulled himself up into a seated position.

She knelt beside him. "What happened?"

He gave her a small smile. "Nothing. Knee popped. Just give me a minute. I'll be fine."

He was lying through his gritted teeth, and Emily could see right through him. He had a feeling that this injury might very well nail the coffin shut for returning to SWAT. Strangely, the prospect didn't devastate him as much as he'd thought it would. The injury was worth it, because Emily was safe.

He hugged her tight. She'd come too close to dying. "Don't worry about me, Emily. I'm okay. There's a lot of cleanup ahead. An adoption agency to bring down and a lot of babies to find, but right now, we need to locate Frankie and hope he's the man with the tattoo."

FRANK MANGINO ANSWERED the summons, his nerves close to breaking. He'd been on edge for a full year, but the past week had been hell. He stepped into his uncle's office, and his stomach clenched when he noticed the man to his uncle's right side. Great, just great.

"Uncle Sal. Mr. Wentworth."

His boss didn't smile in greeting. "I had an interesting call from a friend at the police department, Frank. There's an inquiry about a suspect with a rather unique tattoo on his wrist."

Frank's hand involuntarily covered the colorful devil inked there.

"Let me see it," his uncle snapped. "Now."

Frank walked forward and pushed up his sleeve. The red and green devil identified him with a gang he'd joined when he'd been a stupid kid.

"I told you to have it removed," his uncle said.

"It reminds me," Frank said, "of family."

"And why the pink ribbon?"

Frank looked at his uncle in disbelief. "For Francesca. Or don't you remember her?"

"Your sister's cancer and her inability to have children was a tragedy, but a mark like that identifies you. Especially after the stunt you pulled on Emily Wentworth. Blowing up her vehicle. I recognized the signature the second I saw it on the news."

Frank shifted his eyes away from his uncle. "She wouldn't give up. She was starting to remember the night of the accident."

"Another failure on your part. You were supposed to kill them all. That was our agreement with Mr. Wentworth. Now the cops are looking for that tattoo because you were fool enough to go to that doctor for a birth certificate. You let down the family. I can't allow it to go unpunished."

William Wentworth stalked up to him. "What did you do with my brother's son? The kid's not dead, either, is he?"

Frank backed away, his gaze darting to the exit. Could he make it?

William grabbed Frank by the throat. "Don't try it." William's grip tightened. "I know the answer to my question. I did a little research and found the truth too fast, Frankie. Your sister from Oklahoma adopted a baby boy last year. Amazing when she tried to go through legal channels for so long and failed. She was a bad risk. Cancer took her ability to have children, and her capacity to adopt."

William shoved Frank away and he eased toward the door. Just a few steps more.

"I don't think so, Frankie." His uncle lifted a gun.

Frank stared down the barrel. "Uncle Sal?"

"Sorry, kid. You made one too many mistakes. Loyalty only goes so far."

The gun went off, and a white-hot burn exploded in his

chest. Clutching his shirt, now wet with blood, he slid to the floor, reaching out to try to break his fall.

Sal turned to William. "I'll get the boys to clean this up."

"Fifteen years ago you made a deal with my father when he agreed to launder your money through the company. You were supposed to protect us. You failed."

"I know, but it can be fixed," Sal said. "I'll take care of everything."

"You and Frankie had your chance, you idiot." William Wentworth spat on Frank. "I'll have to stop Emily myself, or we're screwed."

Sal stood up, his gaze narrowed. "Don't go high-and-mighty on me, William. Your brother's the one who started this mess when he called that detective. No loyalty in your family, is there?"

"It was her fault," William muttered. "Goody Two-shoes. Eric turned his back on all of us. For her."

Frank felt blood gurgle up through his lips as William walked over to him. He slipped on gloves, reached down and removed Frank's weapon from his waistband.

"Sorry, Sal. I have loose ends to tie up." William turned and fired.

Sal slumped over his desk, then tried to raise his own gun. But William grabbed it from his hand. "You're both expendable."

The light left Sal's eyes as blood pooled around him.

William placed the gun he'd shot Sal with in Frank's hand and fired another round. Frank groaned.

"Still alive? Good." He took Sal's gun and pointed it at Frank's head. "No one lies to me and gets away with it. But in this case, Frankie, I'll end your life quick since I can use Joshua to salvage this mess. Thanks to you, when Emily Wentworth dies along with her son's kidnappers—Francesca and her husband—I'll become the hero who saved my nephew."

"No!" Frank hadn't meant for anything to happen to his sister.

A flash of smoke from the gun's barrel was the last thing he saw. *I'm sorry, Francesca. So sorry.*

EMILY DIDN'T KNOW HOW long it had taken Mitch to wrap up the scene. As she walked into the police department beside him, her entire body sore, her heart aching with loss, her mind rebelled against her mistake. She'd been certain that the doctor knew where Joshua was. Now she knew it had been a dead end. Except for one name.

"We're close," Mitch said. "I can feel it."

"I was wrong about the adoption ring."

"Not really. The man with the tattoo went there. We have a name. We'll find him."

Emily couldn't get over the determination in Mitch's voice. Her mind whirled. He'd lied to her from the moment they'd met, and yet he still fought for her. Could those actions erase his dishonesty? Was truth more than what Mitch had said? Was truth really in his every action? "You never give up, do you?"

"Not in my nature." Mitch gave her a slight shrug.

"So, how do we find Frankie?" she asked.

"Ghost's tat is a gang tattoo. We search the database for the gang members we've arrested. With any luck, we'll find him."

Mitch gave her a small smile and clasped her hand in his. He brought her palm to his lips. Emily shivered at the warmth of his touch, and her heart calmed. They would find Joshua. Together. There was still hope. Mitch had given that to her.

She stared at his strong jaw, and her heart swelled. She'd only known him a few days, but as she stared at their entwined fingers, she couldn't imagine her life without him next to her. Without one of his jokes, or looking into the mischievous glint in his eyes and wondering what he'd planned next. At times she'd wondered if it was just adrenaline that made her heart race whenever he came near, but it was so much more. She couldn't picture finding Joshua without Mitch at her side, without them as a family afterward. She could see a future with him.

Oh, my God. Emily stopped.

Did she love him?

He looked over at her. "What? Did you remember something?"

She turned and laid her hand on his cheek. "You're an amazing man."

He furrowed his brow. "We haven't found him yet, Emily."

"I know, but—"

"Mitch, Emily." Dane Tanner crossed the floor and greeted them. "I have someone I think you'll want to talk to. She's in the conference room."

Emily sighed. This wasn't the time.

They followed Detective Tanner. Mitch opened the door for Emily, and she stilled. Victoria Wentworth sat at the table, hands folded, trying to look calm, but Emily could see the redness in her eyes and the trembling in her fingertips. This was not a Victoria she knew.

The woman rose from her seat, unsteady, almost swaying, but proud as ever. She flashed a withering glance at Tanner. "I said I'd talk to Officer Bradford. I'm here because of Eric, but *she* has no business in this room. If she stays, I'm leaving."

With that, Victoria turned away. Tanner let out a slow breath.

Emily stared at Victoria's rigid posture. The possibilities she'd nurtured when Eric was alive had been foolish. "It could have been so different between us, Mrs. Wentworth, if you'd let it. We both lost Eric."

"You stole my son from me," Victoria said coldly.

"You shoved him away," Emily whispered. "He always loved you. Wanted you in our lives. Wanted you to come to know Joshua. That will be your loss." Without another glance, Emily pushed out of the conference room.

Mitch followed her, resting his hand on her back. "You okay?"

Emily gave him a regretful smile. "I expected too much. Why is that?"

He kissed her cheek. "Because you believe the best in everyone else, no matter what they do to you. It's one of the things I really admire about you."

Emily stared up at him. She gripped his hands in hers. "Go in there. Victoria's not here for me. If she deigned to come down to the police station, it's for a reason. I'll be waiting."

Mitch leaned into her. "See if you can find a place to hole up for a while." He kissed her forehead, then her eyes and finally gave her a soft, tender kiss on her lips. "You need to rest. With Vance arrested, the station should be safe now. I'll be as quick as I can. Then we'll identify Frankie."

He disappeared behind the conference-room door, leaving Emily alone in the foyer of the police station. She sighed and started toward the waiting area.

"Emily—" Her brother-in-law stepped just inside the building. "Thank God, I found you. I've been looking everywhere."

He seemed excited and flushed, appearing nothing like the calm businessman she was used to seeing.

"William, what's wrong? I know your mother—"

He shook his head. "No, it's Joshua. I think I've found Joshua!"

Emily's knees buckled. Her heart raced. "It can't be," she breathed.

William led her toward the exit. "You were right all along, Emily." He looked down at the floor, his embarrassment obvious. "I should have supported your search no matter what. I never should have listened to Mother and Father. There were things happening in the company that I didn't understand then. Things with my father…"

She grabbed his wool coat. "Where is my son, William? Where's Joshua?"

"We have to handle this carefully. I don't have proof yet. I'm checking into things, but there's a baby I need you to see who I think is Joshua. He looks just like Eric's pictures at the same age. Will you come with me?"

"Of course." She pushed through the door. "But what makes you think this is Joshua?"

William hurried toward his car, his cheeks flushed. "I found out a man who works for me is involved with some shady dealings—adoption rings, murder. I should've known when I saw the gang tattoo—"

"Wait a minute. He had a tattoo? Describe it."

William pursed his lips for a moment. "Ugly thing. A red and green devil, but with a pink ribbon around it. Not the sort of thing we should have at the office," he said distractedly.

Emily swayed. "That's the tattoo I remembered from the night of the accident. Of the man who took Joshua. His name is Frankie."

"Frank Mangino," William said, lips pursed. "I think Eric found out he was stealing from us and threatened to fire him. Frank retaliated by trying to kill all of you and stealing the baby for his sister who couldn't have kids. I didn't know Eric was trying to deal with this alone, Emily," William said earnestly. "I swear I didn't know."

Could that have been why Eric had become so distant?

He'd discovered a man embezzling from the company? She leaned against William as he escorted her to the car. The cold whipped her cheeks. She glanced back to the police station. Was this why Victoria hadn't wanted Emily in the room?

"May I borrow your phone? I need to text Mitch and let him know where I'm going," she said, her voice faint. "He can meet us."

"Sure," William said, his smile eager. "But I've got a ton of passwords. Can't be too careful these days. Give me his number and I'll program it." He opened the door of his BMW for her.

Emily slipped into William's vehicle and waited impatiently as William slid in beside her and set up Mitch's number. Her hands shook as she took the phone and tapped out the message.

She tried to hit Send. A password request popped up. She passed the phone to him, and he gave her a small smile. "Sorry." William typed in a few keys. "Okay, done."

Emily wriggled against the plush leather seats. She couldn't believe it. If what William said was true, she was going to see her son again. William seemed so convinced. She wished Mitch were here, but she couldn't wait to see his face when he saw her with Joshua in her arms. Everything would be okay. "William, thank you for what you've done."

"Father and the adoptive family should be arriving at the Wentworth corporate airport about the time we get there." William smiled gently and patted her hand. "Let's go find Joshua."

MITCH LEANED BACK AGAINST the wall and stared in exasperation at Victoria. "No more games. Who in the family business could authorize that type of money transfer, Mrs. Wentworth? Could you? Your name is listed on a lot of corporate accounts and checks. Why?"

Victoria rubbed her temple. "I received my MBA before I married Thomas. I was the Chief Financial Officer when we first started out." She looked up at Mitch. "When the company went through a rough patch about fifteen years ago, my husband pushed me out of my position, but I'm still a partner."

Mitch picked up the records Victoria had provided and poked at one of the highlighted numbers. "You do realize you've given us enough information to arrest your husband and son." Mitch studied the woman whose elegant persona had started to crumble. Shadows rimmed her eyes. Her makeup looked caked on, not the perfect mask he'd noticed the last time they'd met. "Why are you really here?"

The woman sitting in front of him lifted a devastated gaze. "Eric." She shook her head slowly. "I was certain Emily had killed him. She had the account. I was going to prove it, but I discovered Eric had money stashed away that no one knew about. He opened the account in her name, just before his death. He probably didn't have time to tell anyone before—" She dabbed her eyes. "Then I found the ledgers." She placed her finger next to one of the numbers. "Do you see that mark? That's Eric's mark. He knew about the money transfers."

"So Eric was involved?"

She shook her head vehemently. "My Eric would never do such a thing. But my husband and William, they would do anything to keep the business successful."

Mitch glanced at Tanner, who gave him a slight nod. They were thinking the same thing. Eric Wentworth had known or found out about the money laundering and wanted to stop it. His call to Tanner, as lead detective for white-collar crime, likely had gotten him killed.

What didn't make sense was the connection to Joshua's disappearance.

Mitch leaned forward. "Mrs. Wentworth? Do you know

anyone with a red and green tattoo, perhaps with a pink ribbon? It would stand out."

"Why, yes." Victoria's gaze widened. "The young man who works as my son William's right-hand man has a tattoo on his wrist. William makes him wear long sleeves to cover it, but sometimes it shows."

"What's the assistant's name?" Mitch snapped.

"I've only met him a few times," she said, pausing. "Frank. Frank Mangino."

"Frank," Mitch whispered. "Gotcha."

A knock sounded at the door, and a cop stuck his head in. "Sir," he said to Tanner. "You'll want to hear this."

Mitch and Dane exited the room.

"Two bodies just turned up downtown," the cop said quietly. "One had a wrist tattoo."

"Red and green devil tattoo with a pink ribbon," Mitch said, the frustration churning inside of him. Another lead. Dead.

The uniform nodded. "A gunshot wound in the chest and another through the head. The other body was found nearby. Different caliber."

Tanner turned toward him. "Frank Mangino. Bodies are piling up around here. Someone is not taking any chances of leaving witnesses behind."

Someone who believed he could get away with murder. Mitch slammed into the conference room. "Mrs. Wentworth. Where are your husband and son?"

Victoria started at his intrusion, then straightened her back. "Thomas decided at the last minute to take the plane on business today. I don't know where William is."

"How far would your husband and son go to protect themselves, Mrs. Wentworth?" Mitch asked.

Comprehension dawned on her face. "No, it can't be. They

wouldn't have." She sank back into the chair, stunned, her lip trembling. "Please tell me they didn't kill Eric."

Mitch nabbed his jacket and looked at her. "If they did, they'll pay."

Without pausing, Mitch returned to the bullpen. "I need everything we have on Frank Mangino, and I want any of Thomas or William Wentworth's flight plans for yesterday, today and tomorrow," he barked. "ASAP."

"You sound like a real detective, Mitch," Dane said. "What are you thinking?"

"That Emily will never quit until she finds her son. That makes her dangerous." Mitch had a bad feeling. He tore down the hall to the waiting room. Empty. He checked his phone. No messages. She could be searching the databases. He hurried down the hall and flung open another door. Empty. His gut twisted, and he doubled back to the police station's lobby. "Emily Wentworth? Did you see her?" he demanded of the desk sergeant.

"Sure. She left with some guy maybe ten minutes ago. Fancy suit."

Mitch's heart sank. He'd told her she was safe here. He'd been wrong.

Chapter Fourteen

The Wentworths' large, private hangar loomed tall in the distance. Emily could barely contain her excitement. Her entire body felt supercharged. She grinned at William. "We're almost there. I can't believe it. I'm going to see Joshua. Finally." She squirmed in her seat and leaned forward, staring at the horizon. "You're sure it's him, right, William? I don't know if I can take another disappointment."

"Almost one hundred percent positive," William said. "After a year, he's obviously changed, but this whole nightmare will be over soon."

"Does Joshua's adoptive family know he was stolen?" Emily let out a slow breath. "They'll be devastated." Her heart ached for the horror they'd all gone through because of the man who'd killed Eric and stole her son. The terrible thought hit her. "What if they were in on the kidnapping, William? Maybe we should wait for Mitch and the police."

"Don't worry." William patted her hand. "I've taken care of things."

He turned down a road, and the front of the thousand-square-foot hangar, with its huge sliding door, appeared in the distance. She could just make out the snow gathered around in dirty piles against the metal siding. Areas of black ice slicked the tarmac. William slowed as they made their approach.

Emily squinted. "What's that lying in front of the building?"

The hangar grew closer, and the black blob started to take on the recognizable shape of a man. The gray-haired figure struggled to rise, then waved at them.

Recognition ricocheted through her. Emily gasped. "I think it's your father."

Thomas Wentworth rolled to his side. His chest was bloody.

"William, he's hurt! Hurry!"

Her brother-in-law pressed down on the gas. The car lurched forward.

Emily clenched her fists, and her nails bit into her palms. Who could've hurt Thomas? Had the adoptive family been involved the whole time? Panic clutched her heart. "What about Joshua? Where is he? I don't see anyone else." Frantically, she searched for any other car or movement.

Then she noticed Thomas struggling. He held something in his hand and was pointing it at the speeding car. "Gun!" she yelled.

William wrenched the wheel to the left, just as the front windshield shattered. The car rammed into the side of the hangar and both airbags exploded, turning the world white. Seconds later, everything shuddered to a stop.

Emily shook her head to clear her vision, then released her safety belt and rammed her shoulder against the door until it opened. She had to find cover before Thomas opened fire again. She peeked over the edge of the window. Her father-in-law had fallen back, lying still as death. "He's not moving. Are you all right, William?"

Her brother-in-law groaned and pushed away from the steering wheel and the deflated airbag. His shoulder oozed blood. "No, dammit, I've been shot."

She reached into the car for his phone. "Give me your cell. I'll call for help."

"Leave it alone!" William slammed his fist into Emily's face. Her head snapped back, and her jaw exploded with pain.

"This is all your fault. You ruined everything. You just kept coming and coming, never giving up. You were supposed to be dead. You were all supposed to be dead."

William struggled out of the car, getting caught up in the mangled metal of the hangar door and the BMW. He let out a string of curses as Emily scrambled out the door. Only one place to hide. She bolted for the hangar, hoping there would be a phone inside. Her mind whirled in disbelief. William? She couldn't believe it. Was Joshua even here, or had he lied to get her here and kill her?

"Emily," a weak voice called out from at least ten feet away.

Thomas. She hesitated and crouched beside the car.

"Save Joshua, Emily. He's inside the hangar. Save—"

William stalked over to his father and aimed a Glock at Thomas's head. "Don't die easily, do you?"

"Why did you do this? Your own brother? Your nephew?" Thomas's voice was weak and disbelieving.

"Eric called the cops. Someone had to take the fall, Father. They still do, and it won't be me."

"No!" Emily screamed.

William pulled the trigger.

She scrambled to her feet and raced to the hangar. Was Joshua really in there?

"Don't bother running, Emily," William said. "I have a spot picked out for you. I know exactly where you have to die to make my story stick."

She wouldn't let him win. Not after coming this close. She yanked open the metal access door and fell inside next to the Wentworths' limo. She turned and locked the dead bolt just as William banged against the outside. Curses rained through the metal. Frenetically, she scanned the huge building for Joshua. He had to be here somewhere, but she could only see the plane and the limo and a lot of equipment. Where was her son?

She didn't have much time. She needed help. She needed Mitch. Surely he'd received her text by now.

Unless William had never sent it.

Oh, Lord, of course he hadn't. She had to find a way out, until somehow Mitch figured out what had happened. He wouldn't give up. He'd fight for Joshua. She'd never seen anyone as intuitive and smart as Mitch Bradford. Whatever story William told, Mitch would see through it. He would believe in her. He would uncover the truth.

She just wished she'd told him she loved him. She'd been reluctant and afraid. Now it was too late.

Unless she fought back.

She could do this. Heart pounding, she shoved a heavy metal tool bin against the door and pushed some barrels behind it.

Another shot rang out and pinged near the lock. How long would her barricade keep him out?

A baby howled from inside the limo.

Emily stilled, afraid to move, afraid to breathe. What if…? She raced to the limo, terrified the wonderful, heartbreaking sounds of the baby's cries would vanish like her morning dreams. She threw open the door. The smell of blood and death gagged her. A man and a woman sat motionless in the front seat, eyes sightless. Each had taken a bullet to the head.

Oh, no. Emily's knees quivered.

Another howl wailed.

She could breathe again.

Emily peeked into the back and saw a diaper bag, then a

car seat with an angry little boy in a snowsuit, waving his chubby arms and legs as he furiously tried to escape.

Beneath his stocking hat, he had brown hair. Like Eric's. And the same stubborn chin.

His deep blue eyes. Just like hers.

Her entire body shaking, Emily tugged on the back door. Her hands wouldn't work; her body could barely function. Finally the door opened, and she reached inside. "Joshua?"

The baby stopped crying and stared. Emily's heart paused with uncertainty as his wary gaze transformed into a smile. The dimples were all his own. They always had been.

"It's you." She couldn't stop the tears from rolling down her face.

Another shot rang out, this time at a side door she hadn't blocked.

The baby screamed in fear. "Don't worry, Joshua. Mommy will save you."

Her hands trembling, she shoved aside the heavy diaper bag, then tugged and pressed at the unfamiliar straps and latches of the car seat. "Come on, come on," she said, frantic now. Just one left. Joshua cried even louder. Why hadn't she waited for Mitch? He would've seen through William.

Another gunshot, and a metal crash sounded from directly behind her. She was out of time. The car seat's straps finally gave in under her hand. She grasped Joshua and turned around slowly.

"You're too late, Emily."

William Wentworth, gun and all, had found his way in.

MITCH FLOORED THE TRUCK and barreled toward the Wentworths' hangar. Thank goodness Sierra was a killer hacker. She'd pulled the data from the traffic cams and placed Wentworth's BMW moving toward their private hangar. The flight plans indicated the Wentworths had taken the plane to Oklahoma and back. Put that together with Frank Mangino's sister adopting a baby boy a year ago, and everything fit. Except Emily was still in danger. It didn't take ten minutes to kill someone; it took seconds. Emily couldn't be dead. He wouldn't let himself consider the possibility. She was strong; she was clever. She would stay alive. She'd know he would come for her. She had to know.

"You there, Dane?" Mitch said into his earpiece, praying his boss was close behind him.

"Still a few minutes away. SWAT is scrambling."

Mitch skidded to a stop and jumped out of the truck. He scanned the area, then ran over to what was left of Thomas Wentworth. "I can't hold off," he said softly. "I've got a BMW buried into the side of the hangar. Thomas Wentworth is dead. Shot twice." Mitch ran the twenty-five feet to the edge of the building. "The side door to the hangar has been shot open. I'm going in."

"Be smart," Dane said. "Come out alive."

"Get your butt here and make sure she gets out of this. You worry about Emily, Dane. Promise me. I don't matter," Mitch said.

"We're getting you both out," Dane snapped. "I'm almost there."

Mitch let out a quick breath. *Focus, man. She needs you. You love her.*

And he hadn't told her. He'd wanted everything perfect. He'd wanted to be whole. He'd wanted to find her son and have SWAT back. He should've just said the words. He loved her more than the job he'd thought he couldn't live without. If he got another chance—*when* he got a second chance—he wouldn't wait.

Mitch drew his weapon, eased toward the open hangar door and peeked in. His blood went cold.

Emily, standing in front of the open limo door, tears running down her face, rocked a screaming baby in her arms.

William, blood dripping down his arm, held a pistol aimed at Joshua's head. "Give me the kid or I'll shoot through him to get to you. You know I'll do it. I'd prefer him alive, Emily, but I can fabricate a reason why he didn't make it. Either way, I win. The choice is yours. Do you want your son to live or die?"

Mitch slipped inside the door and into position behind a metal bin and three huge barrels that blocked William's view. Moving silently, Mitch crouched down and leaned out farther. He focused on Emily, hoping she would glance his way.

As if she could sense him, she turned her head slightly. Their gazes locked, and he recognized the flash of understanding. She shifted her body slightly, drawing William's attention in the opposite direction. Man, he loved an incredibly brave woman.

Mitch's earpiece clicked once, and some of his tension eased. Dane had arrived. Emily hugged the baby tighter. "Why are you doing this, William? I don't understand. You helped me look for Joshua."

"I thought the boy was dead. What harm could it do to pay a washed-up drunk like Perry to search for clues and keep you busy? But the kid was alive, and that idiot Mangino's sister adopted him. Too many loose ends tying back to me."

"And a ton of dead bodies all over your property doesn't lead to you?" Emily asked incredulously.

"After today, I'll help the police wrap the entire case up in a nice bow. According to the paper trail and forensic evidence I planted, my father hired Mangino. He had Eric killed because my brother threatened to expose the company's money laundering. He murdered Joshua's parents because of the connection to Frank. All perfectly true. Except I've got more guts than my father ever did. I did what I had to do."

"You killed your own father," she said, still unable to fathom William's callousness.

"No, Emily. *You* discovered my father planned to kill the baby next, so you had to protect your son. You grabbed a gun and killed my father, but not before he fatally wounded you. And I, the poor grieving son, rescued my nephew. I'll end up on CNN. Business will thrive. And Joshua will save my reputation and follow in the family business."

"You're sick."

William's face went cold. He took a step forward. "And we're done. Goodbye, Emily."

She shoved the baby into the car. A bullet slammed into the metal beside her head. She whirled around to face William and swung the diaper bag at him, connecting with his gun arm. Most of the bag's contents scattered.

"Mitch, save Joshua!" She swung the bag again, aiming for William's head, hoping the heavy box of diaper wipes would stun him or at least slow him down.

William stumbled backward, roared in anger and aimed directly at her. His trigger finger squeezed just as Mitch dove in front of her.

A gun sounded. Another shot rang out from behind William. Emily closed her eyes, expecting to feel pain.

She didn't. The baby's howls mixed with shouts from inside the limo.

"Mitch!" A deep voice yelled.

Emily opened her eyes to the horrific sight of William slumped to the cement, the entire left side of his head gone. She scrambled to her feet, torn between running to the baby or Mitch. Then, as she watched, he stumbled to his knees in front of her, his chest soaked in crimson.

"No!" Emily fell to the ground and pressed her hand against Mitch's wound. Blood flowed through her fingers. "No, Mitch. Don't do this."

"Calm down, Emily," he rasped between clenched teeth, quirking a smile. "It's a flesh wound. No big deal."

"Don't scare me like that, Mitch Bradford," she said. "Ever again."

"I bet you say that to all the guys who stop a speeding bullet for you, you sweet-talker, you."

Footsteps pounded at them. She turned. "Dane, thank goodness. He's been shot."

Mitch's boss ripped off his shirt, revealing a side laced with scars. He knelt next to Mitch and pressed the fabric against the wound. "You're a magnet for trouble, aren't you, Bradford? You're never going to get back to SWAT at this rate."

"Being a detective must be growing on me, Tanner." Mitch coughed, then cursed viciously. He looked at Emily, his smile calm. "Why don't you go check on your son. I'm fine."

"You're sure you're okay?" She bit her lip, staring at the shirt soaked through with blood.

He smiled and nodded even though he was certain he wasn't. Emily didn't need to know that. Not right now. Breathing became more difficult with each passing second, and his leg... Well, Joshua had a better chance of getting up and walking out of here than Mitch did in the near future.

Emily hesitated, then staggered to her feet. Mitch watched, his emotions overflowing as she raced to the car, wiped the blood off her hands and picked up the squalling baby. Her entire body quaking, she carefully lifted her son into her arms, jostling him and squeezing him tight.

The baby looked at her, his expression curious. She smiled and touched the side of his face. Mitch could just catch her emotion-laden words. "Hello, Joshua. I'm your mommy."

She hugged her son close.

Mitch's eyes stung. He'd done it. With his help, Emily had found her son. She was safe. They both were.

An odd pressure bore down on his chest. He gasped for air, trying to fill his lungs. Spots danced in front of his eyes. He wanted to sleep. Needed to rest.

His eyes closed.

"Mitch." Dane pressed harder against the bloody wound at his chest. "Stay with me, man."

He couldn't move, could barely breathe. "Emily's alive. She has her son," Mitch gasped. "I'm fine."

"Liar," Dane whispered. "Luckily, the medevac is almost here."

Mitch barely heard him or the sound of Emily yelling out his name and a baby's cry. The world faded to black.

THE LIGHT HURT HIS EYES. Mitch opened them and stared at a too-familiar white ceiling. He looked down at his chest, at the tubes entering his body, at the wrap around his leg. Definitely not heaven. "I'm in the hospital again, aren't I? I hate this place."

His voice was hoarse; his entire body felt like it'd been run over by a truck. A fuzzy figure standing at the foot of his bed slowly came into focus. Her light brown hair fell in waves around her face, the light surrounding her like a halo. Emily.

But her arms were empty.

He struggled to sit up. "Joshua," he croaked. "Where—?"

"Shh," she said, hurrying around the bedside and pressing him back against the pillows. "He's fine." She poured him a glass of water. Gratefully, he took a sip. "He's cradled in your father's arms, holding a teddy bear." Emily blinked back tears. "Because of you."

Mitch didn't like the thankful tone in her voice. "I did what anyone would have done."

"You have no idea, do you? How good you really are?"

Mitch squirmed as he glanced away from her shining blue

eyes. He shook his head. "I made too many mistakes. I lied too many times."

Emily rose from the bed and walked to the door. She opened it and whispered. A few seconds later, she returned to his bedside, a small boy on her hip, a boy with eyes the color of Emily's.

He swallowed back the emotions that threatened to overwhelm him. This was a picture he'd longed to see for so very long. Emily with her son, at peace, happy. Mitch wanted to take them both into his arms and have them hug him, tight, as if they would never let him go. He wanted to feel her against him. He wanted her son to laugh up at him and smile. "I'm glad for you," Mitch said softly.

"You saved us both," she said. "I have him back because of you. Not because of the cop you are, but because of the man you are. You never gave up. You believed in me when no one else did. You stood by my side. That's more than I could've hoped for."

Mitch sucked in a shuddering breath. He didn't want gratitude. He wanted so much more. But how could he expect her to love him? "Please don't say you're grateful. I couldn't stand that, Emily."

"I'm grateful to Dane for being there for us in the end." Emily sat beside the bed and dangled a small stuffed animal dressed in a policeman's uniform in front of her son. The bear had one blue eye and one brown eye. "I'm grateful to Noah for tossing his money for a rush DNA test to prove to the world that Joshua is my son. I'm even grateful to Victoria for finally admitting the truth to the police and herself. She helped you save my life, and hopefully we can start over. Mostly, I'm grateful to your father for helping us and raising a son like you." She met his gaze. "But I don't feel for them what I feel for you." She cupped his cheek. "I love you, Mitch Bradford."

He closed his eyes, his heart exploding with joy. But at the same time, doubts washed through him. "How?" he muttered. "After everything—"

She pressed her fingers against his lips. "You did what you did to protect me. Just like I'd do anything to protect Joshua. Actions prove much more than words." She hugged her son to her. "Because I love him."

"I don't know if I deserve you, Emily, but I can tell you I won't lie to you again. I won't betray you." As Mitch spoke, Joshua turned to the deep voice. The baby's eyes blinked at Mitch. Joshua grinned, holding his arms out.

"He wants you," Emily said softly. "He trusts you." She bent down and kissed Mitch's lips, gently, sweetly. "Just as I do. I love you, Mitch. For your bravery, your determination, your loyalty. Because even if this had been another Florida—" she kissed her son's head "—I know you'll always be there for me. No matter what."

Mitch held out his hand to her son. Joshua grasped his finger and gave Mitch a toothy grin. His heart melted. "I'm not the man I used to be. I'll never be SWAT again," he warned. "I probably don't have a job after this."

"Do you think your injuries matter to me? Or to Joshua?" She laid her hand on his chest. "I fell in love with the man you are inside. I fell in love with your heart and soul and mind."

The dark cloud encasing Mitch's spirit broke free. He pulled Emily toward him and buried his face in her neck. "I love you," he whispered. "I've loved you forever."

She turned her lips to his, and he kissed her with every promise deep within him. His heart raced as she let out a small groan against him. She pulled away, her eyes sparkling with joy, her breathing fast. "I want you well soon, so you can fulfill the promise of that kiss, Officer Bradford."

A tentative knock sounded at the door.

"Is it safe to come in?" Dane Tanner pushed open the

door. He walked in, leading a parade of Ian, Noah, his other brother, Chase, and his sister, Sierra.

Lastly his father wheeled into the room. "So, Mitchell. You finally got the job done right," his father barked, the intensity belied by the relief in the older man's eyes.

"Hardly," Dane said, stepping forward. "He went against direct orders. More than once."

"He blew up his car," Chase and Ian chimed in together.

Noah crossed his arms and gave Mitch a half-frustrated grin. "He got my SUV shot to pieces."

Sierra ran across the room and kissed her brother on the cheek. "He almost got himself killed more than once." She scowled. "Don't ever do that again, big brother."

"If you'd just waited," Dane said, his expression unsmiling. "I could've made the shot before things got out of hand. Instead, you had to go all hero. Again."

"Are you saying I'm fired?" Mitch asked.

His boss looked him over. "Do I look like a fool? You did a slam-dunk job, Mitch. I don't know anyone else who could've followed those leads. You've got instincts. In fact, I think you're a better detective than you ever were at SWAT entry."

Mitch stared at his boss, stunned, and clutched Emily's hand. "I'm not fired?"

"You may want to quit, but if you want a job on my unit, it's yours for the taking." Dane gave him a small salute. "As long as you work on following procedure a little better in the future."

"That'll be the day," Noah said. "So, little brother? Did you fix things?" He nodded toward Emily.

"Did you grovel?" his father asked with a wink.

Mitch took Emily's hand in his and kissed her palm. "Dad, everyone. Meet Emily and Joshua Wentworth. We're going to be a family."

At the loud shout of approval, Joshua let out a squeal. Noah grabbed his soon-to-be nephew and threw him up in the air, then caught him in his arms. The boy giggled and wrapped his arms around Noah's neck.

Mitch laughed and tugged Emily close. "You'll marry me, right?" he said softly in her ear.

She turned her face, her lips hovering over his. She met his gaze, and Mitch's breath caught at the love in her every feature. She loved him. Truly loved him.

He knew. He believed. He had faith once more.

"I will," she whispered. "Together. Forever."

* * * * *

Have Your Say

You've just finished your book.
So what did you think?

We'd love to hear your thoughts on our
'Have your say' online panel
www.millsandboon.co.uk/haveyoursay

- 🌹 Easy to use
- 🌹 Short questionnaire
- 🌹 Chance to win Mills & Boon® goodies

Visit us Online | Tell us what you thought of this book now at **www.millsandboon.co.uk/haveyoursay**

The World of Mills & Boon®

There's a Mills & Boon® series that's perfect for you. We publish ten series and, with new titles every month, you never have to wait long for your favourite to come along.

Blaze®
Scorching hot, sexy reads
4 new stories every month

By Request
Relive the romance with the best of the best
9 new stories every month

Cherish™
Romance to melt the heart every time
12 new stories every month

Desire™
Passionate and dramatic love stories
8 new stories every month